D0111336

Kalimpura

Jay Lake

A Tom Doherty Associates Book
New York

This is a work of fiction. All of the characters, organizations, and events portrayed in this novel are either products of the author's imagination or are used fictitiously.

KALIMPURA

Copyright © 2013 by Joseph E. Lake, Jr.

All rights reserved.

A Tor Book
Published by Tom Doherty Associates, LLC
175 Fifth Avenue
New York, NY 10010

www.tor-forge.com

Tor® is a registered trademark of Tom Doherty Associates, LLC.

The Library of Congress has cataloged the hardcover edition as follows:

Lake, Jay.
    Kalimpura / Jay Lake. — 1st ed.
        p. cm.
    "A Tom Doherty Associates Book."
    Sequel: Green and Endurance.
    ISBN 978-0-7653-2677-5 (hardcover)
    ISBN 978-1-4299-4560-8 (e-book)
  1. Imaginary places—Fiction.   2. Murder—Fiction.   3. Hostages—Fiction.
4. Magic—Fiction.   I. Title.
    PS3612.A519K35 2012
    813'.6—dc23

                                                                2012024884

ISBN 978-0-7653-2716-1 (trade paperback)

Tor books may be purchased for educational, business, or promotional use. For information on bulk purchases, please contact Macmillan Corporate and Premium Sales Department at 1-800-221-7945, extension 5442, or write specialmarkets@macmillan.com.

First Edition: January 2013
First Trade Paperback Edition: September 2014

Printed in the United States of America

0 9 8 7 6 5 4 3 2 1

This book is also dedicated to my daughter.
Green's story is long since diverged from hers,
but the daughter of my heart still stands very close to this,
the daughter of my pen.

Kalimpura

Copper Downs, Postpartum

~

I HAVE RARELY recalled my dreams, not in those years of which I now tell, nor since. I do not know why this should be. Life has perhaps always been so vivid, so overwhelming, that the far countries of sleep pale by comparison. How can a dream offer more than the simple richness of a mug of kava whipped with cream, cinnamon, and red pepper? How can the illusions of the sleeping mind overwhelm the feel of the wind on one's face as dawn paints the eastern sky in the colors of flame and life, while the first birds of morning leap to the air in their chattering hordes?

Yet during that last month or so of my pregnancy, I had been dreaming as never before. Even now I recall my extraordinarily vivid awareness of life beyond the gates of horn at that time. I awakened time and again in the tent that my old friend and Selistani countryman, the pirate-turned-priest Chowdry, had made my own out of his concern for me. Swollen and awkward from the babies in my belly, I was barely able to waddle in order to break my fast amid the overgrown children who labored to build this new temple to this new god Endurance whom I helped create. Those last weeks of my pregnancy were certainly the dullest of my then-sixteen years of life.

Perhaps it was thus that the dreams came to prominence.

Not for me visions of the face of my long-lost father, ancient wisdoms dripping from his lips, as I have heard others tell. Nor the refighting of old battles. Little enough, judging from the books I've read that speak of such signs to be found in the night mind. Instead, my dreams had been of heaving oceans and sheets of flame leaping to the sky. Ships and burning palaces and always I ran, looking for those whom I have lost. Always I begged and swore and promised I would never again do wrong if only I could set right what had been over-turned in my careless haste.

Dreaming, in other words, of what was real. A girl and a young woman lost as hostages borne across the Storm Sea. The girl is Corin-thia Anastasia, child of Ilona whom I loved though she did not love me the same in return, stolen away by my enemies as a hostage to my fu-ture good behavior. Likewise the Lily Blade Samma, my first paramour from my days in the Temple of the Silver Lily. Those two, each dear to me in different ways, were being held to bind me to the will of Surali, a woman high in the councils of the Bittern Court back in Kalimpura.

In short, I awakened not from prophecy, but from memory.

And now my belly hung empty. Two tiny mouths gnawed at my breasts, which I swore belonged to some stranger. I was never pendu-lous, nor did my nipples weep before childbearing. There was little about pregnancy consistent with dignity. Motherhood had not begun much better.

If there had been a blessing of late, it was that the gods and mon-sters who haunted me stayed away from both my dreams and the waking moments between them. Somewhat to my surprise.

My children were my own. None of the prophetic threats made for them had come true.

Not then, in any case.

"Green?" Chowdry lifted the flap of my tent, though he did not peer within. "It is almost time."

"Thank you," I said. "When the children are done suckling."

"I will send Lucia."

Lucia? I thought. My favorite acolyte of late, and sometime bath-and-bed partner. *How odd that Ilona did not claim for herself the joyous task of dressing the babies this of all days.*

Chowdry withdrew, leaving me alone in my bed with my children. The little iron stove smoked a bit—spring had come to Copper Downs, but here in the chilly northern realms of the Stone Coast, that did not necessarily mean warmth. Bright-dyed hangings decorated the wool-lined canvas walls. Two chests, one lacquered orange in the Selistani fashion, the other a deep, rich mahogany, held my worldly goods along with what was needful for the babies.

Almost I could fit into my leathers again. That thought brought me immense cheer.

Lucia bustled in. She was a beautiful Petraean girl, her skin as pale as mine was dark, though we shared the same golden brown color of our eyes. It was something of a scandal around the Temple of Endurance that she had been an occasional lover of mine, before the last stages of pregnancy had forced me to give such up. I think she would have played nursemaid to my children every day, but Ilona was letting no one else near them for anything she could do first.

Her need for her lost daughter was so profound, and my responsibility in the matter so deep, that I could deny her nothing with respect to my children.

"Will you be ready soon?" Lucia smiled fondly. "Ilona is desperate to be in two places at once right now. Chowdry has convinced her to finish preparations in the wooden temple."

"And so she ceded her care of the babies to you." I found myself amused, though I realized that was unkind of me.

"All of them dressed and ready," Lucia said in a fair imitation of Ilona's voice. "And mind you don't forget the rags!"

I had to laugh at that. My girl shifted from my breast and mewled some small complaint. "Help her spit," I told Lucia. "I'll get the boy to finish."

It is the custom among the Selistani people of my birth not to name children until they reached their first birthday. The world was filled with demons, disease, and ill will that might be called to a weak, new child if their name were spoken aloud. Here in Copper Downs as all along the Stone Coast, I was given to understand that children were generally named at birth.

Having been born a Selistani but raised among the people of the Stone Coast, my compromise was to allow my babies to pass their first week in anonymity, then name them. Regardless of which practice I chose to follow, no child of mine would ever be safe. My list of enemies was longer and more complex than I could keep an accounting of. Some of the most dangerous among them even considered themselves my friends.

Besides, their father, my poor, lost lover Septio of Blackblood's temple, was Petraean. To name the babies was to honor him.

Lucia hummed and bustled with my girl, wrapping the little one in an embroidered silk dress that would serve for the Naming, even if the baby should do any of the things babies so often do to their clothing. I separated my reluctant boy from my aching right nipple and briefly hugged him close to my shoulder.

The love I felt for them was foolishly overwhelming. I knew it was some artifice of nature, or the gods who claimed to have made us in their image, for a mother to adore her child so. Otherwise no one sane would tolerate the squalling, puking, shitting little beasts. But I did love him and his sister with an intensity that surprised me then and continues to do so to this day.

It was akin to the sensation of being touched by a god—an occurrence that I had far more experience with than I'd had with the demands and requirements of motherhood thus far.

I sat up. The boy lay above my breast against my shoulder. My gut continued to feel empty, weak and strange. I would not care to be in a fight for my life right now. Soon enough I would be able to work my body as I was accustomed to doing. I scooped up a rag and gently dried my sore nipples. Lucia leaned to take the baby from me so I could clothe myself.

"Thank you," I told her.

Her eyes lingered on me. I had not dressed at all yet, still naked as birth or bath required. "You are welcome." Her smile was warm, welcome, and just a little bit wicked. "It is nice to see you more yourself again."

I took her meaning exactly and felt warmed for it. *Definitely time for me to dress.* Though it was very much not the fashion for women of status here in Copper Downs, I was still most comfortable in trousers— my midsection felt a bit better supported, somewhat more firmly held in. The pale blue silk robe would hide the pants well enough. Not that I cared so much what people thought, but that would reduce the potential for argument and satisfy the sense of propriety shared by various of those around me.

Somewhere in the recent months, getting along better with people had started to become important to me. Troubling myself with the opinions of others was still a new experience.

I strapped my long knife to my right thigh beneath the robe. My short knives I secured to my right and left forearms. I truly did not expect any sort of fight at this ceremony, and was not in much shape to join in if one were to take place, but they were part of me. Bare skin would feel less naked to me than going into public without my weapons. I had birthed my children with a knife at my hand, after all.

Lucia had both the babies ready. My girl was in a fall of flame orange and apple red silk that ended in a ruff of yellow lace. The needlework across her bodice was a vibrant, bleached white that stood out like the Morning Star. My boy's dress matched in cut and design, but was sea green and sky blue with a ruff of violet lace, embroidered in a blue so dark, it was very nearly nighttime black.

They were beautiful.

I stared into their strangely pale eyes, those unfocused infant gazes looking back at me. Though Lucia had one of my children balanced in each arm, they knew their mother.

My heart fluttered and my entire body felt warm. My breasts began to swell, which was not what I wanted. Not more milk, not right now.

I shrugged my careworn belled silk over my shoulders, then took my daughter's new silk in my hands to cradle her at my left. Her bells were so few and small that it hardly made any noise at all. Still, this custom was all I had of my grandmother and the family of my birth—the single memory of her funeral, the sound of her bells, and the constancy of my own bells.

Prepared now, I reached for my girl, then for my boy, who would have to find his way in the world without the protection of a cloak of belled silk. The four of us left the tent. As I stepped through the flap, I wondered anew how Chowdry had convinced Ilona to allow Lucia this duty. She had been by my side almost continuously since the birth.

The kidnapping of Ilona's child by my enemies hung over the two of us like a shadow. Or a blade, twisting by a fraying thread but yet to drop. That thought dimmed the glow in my heart a bit.

Outside was brisk. Spring might have been there, but the sun had not yet found her summer fires. Not in this place. Still, no one had told the trees and flowers. The brisk air was rich with scents of bloom and sap and leafy green.

The Temple of Endurance was blessed with high walls, thanks to an accident of location. This site was an old mine head, long since hidden away from view or casual trespass. Beyond those walls was the relatively clean, quiet wealth of the Velviere District. That meant here inside the compound we were spared the worst of the reeks that emanated from the sewers, slaughterhouses, fish markets, and middens of Copper Downs. In fairness, distant, tropical Kalimpura brought a whole new definition to a city's smells, but even the wrong district here on Stone Coast could put out a standing reek fit to stop a horse. I was glad of the air being washed with spring and nothing more for this Naming.

Beyond the line of tents, a scaffolding rose around the stone temple under construction. I'd helped a little with laying out the foundations before the last months of my pregnancy. Since then, Chowdry and his congregation had made great progress without my aid. Endurance was well on his way to having a permanent fane here in Copper Downs. Pillars rose, and wooden forms were being hammered together to support the laying of a grand vault.

So odd, such a distinctively Selistani god here so far from home. And entirely my doing. Even more odd, this was the first new temple built in over four hundred years, thanks to the late Duke's centuries-long interdiction of such activity. The lifting of his rule was also my doing, in point of fact.

We walked slowly toward a chattering crowd surrounding the wooden temple, the music of my silk ringing out our every step. This was the small, temporary place of worship, in effect a glorified stable built around the ox statue that was Endurance's physical presence here amid his worshippers. Both dear friends and total strangers awaited us. The acolytes and functionaries of Chowdry's growing sect were naturally in attendance. But also a few familiar faces from the Temple Quarter, and the women's lazaret on Bustle Street. Several tall, pale young men who were surely sorcerer-engineers on a rare venture into sunlight. Even some of the clerks from the Textile Bourse, home of one of this city's two competing governments struggling through a slow, apparently endless round of ineffective coup and countercoup.

Most important, Mother Vajpai and Mother Argai awaited me. Senior Blade Mothers from the Temple of the Silver Lily in Kalimpura, and Mother Vajpai one of my two greatest teachers, they had been stranded here by the betrayals of Surali of the Bittern Court when the Selistani embassy had come to Copper Downs the previous autumn. The Prince of the City had ostensibly arrived on these cold northern shores in pursuit of trade agreements, but he had really been brought across the Storm Sea to serve as the Bittern Court woman's puppet in a far more convoluted series of plots. These two lonely Blades so far from home were the closest I had to family anymore. In many ways, these women knew me best.

I smiled at them all, warmed even by the pallid sunshine of this northern place, and walked slowly toward the plain doors of the wooden temple. The crowd parted around me like a pond confronted by a prophet. The babies gurgled, enjoying the outing it seemed, and without fear of the people.

May they live a life free of fear, I prayed to no one in particular. I had too much experience of gifts from the gods to want any of them to hear me just now. Besides, twinned prophecies had hung over my children's birth. Both could go forever unfulfilled for all I cared.

At the door to the wooden temple, I paused and turned to the crowd. Dozens of faces stared back at me. Joyous. Friendly. Loving, even.

It was such a strange feeling, to witness this outpouring.

"My friends," I began. My son shifted in my arms, responding to my voice. He could not know this young that those simple words that were at once so inadequate and yet so true. "We are drawn together this day in celebration." I sounded foolish to my ears. Like a tired priest lecturing an even more weary congregation. I summoned my courage and my sense and continued. "My children are my life. My life is yours. Thank you."

With that, I rushed into the shadows behind me.

At that time, the temporary wooden temple was still little changed from the first occasion on which I had visited it. The beaded curtain on the doorway stroked me with the caress of a dozen dozen fingers. The walls held their same roughness, though prayers had been hung upon them. Brushwork in dark brown ink on raw linen, written in both Petraean and Seliu, they had the same beauty as those Hanchu poetry scrolls one sometimes sees decorating great houses.

Endurance was present in the form of a life-sized marble sculpture of an ox. His blank-eyed calm was soothing to me. Tiny prayer slips still dangled by red threads from his horns, but the usual array of incense, fruit, and flowers had been cleared away. Instead, I saw a line of offerings fresh from the bakeries and groceries of the city. Food still warm and crisp, the odors from the bread and nuts and, yes, more fruit, joined to form a lovely incense of their own. It was an offering for the eyes and nose and mouth all at once. I hoped Chowdry would allow the array of food to be eaten later.

The reluctant priest waited by the ox with Ilona. They were the only people in the wooden temple when I entered, though others pushed in behind me, led by Lucia carrying my girl. Chowdry wore a green silk salwar kameez that I'd never seen before. Ilona had found an orange silk dress that recalled the cotton dress of hers I'd loved so much back at the little cottage in the High Hills.

The two of them smiled, proud as any grandparents. I was pleased that Ilona did not feel the need to bestow her usual frown on Lucia. Not jealousy, precisely, but the two of them disagreed so much over me.

Holding both my children close, I advanced jingling toward Chowdry and Ilona. The jostling crowd behind me maintained a respectful silence.

"Who comes before Endurance?" Chowdry asked formally.

Resisting the urge to say, *Me, you idiot,* to this man upon whom I had bestowed both a god and the mantle of priesthood, I answered in kind. "Green, of Copper Downs and Kalimpura, to present my children to the god."

He swept his hands together and beamed as if delighted by some strange and wonderful surprise. "Be welcome, and come before the god."

Chowdry stepped to one side, Ilona to the other. Her face was troubled now. I knew why. My old would-be lover could hardly help thinking of her own daughter stolen away. With the heft of a baby in each of my arms, I was all too aware of how keenly Ilona missed Corinthia Anastasia, mourning her child's absence.

I have not forgotten my promises, I thought fiercely, willing her to hear the silent words from behind my eyes. Then I was before the god

I myself had instantiated from a flood of uncontrolled divine energy, naïve hope, and my own earliest memories.

Kneeling, I placed my children against his belly. Had the artist sculpted him standing, I would have laid them between Endurance's feet as I myself had once played and sheltered beneath my father's ox. This was the best I could do.

Then I touched one of the horns. A few of the prayers tied there stirred, so I brushed my fingers across them. Whatever power or influence I had with the divine I put to wishing the prayers might be heard.

"I am here," I told the ox.

Now all the prayers on his horns stirred. The air felt thick, even a bit curdled. *Something* was present.

"I know you will not answer me. That is not your way." Endurance was a wordless god, given to guidance through inspiration rather than immediate intervention in the lives of his followers. "But when I was a small child, you watched over me. Your body sheltered me. Your lowing voice called me back from danger. You followed where I wandered, and led me home again."

I paused for a shuddering breath, wishing in that moment that my father could have seen this time of my life. He would have been delighted at his grandchildren, I was certain of it. And amazed at what had become of his ox. That, too, was certain.

"Watch over these children of mine, so new to the world. They do not know its risks. Shelter them. Let them wander, and call them back from danger." In a rush, I added, "Also, please watch over Samma and most especially Corinthia Anastasia, for they are in grave peril, needing of shelter, and surely wish more than anything to be called back as well."

I touched my girl. She gurgled, bubbles forming on her lips, and stared up at the curving flank of the ox god with the myopic expression that all new babies seemed to share. "This girl-child I name Marya, to honor a goddess slain unfairly, and through her, to honor all women."

Behind me rose a muttering. People didn't like that name so much. Marya had been a woman's goddess, her name unlucky now after her demise, though I had avenged her deicide. These grumblers could fall on their own blessed knives. I was hardly going to name this child

Green after me, given that my own name was a product of my enslavement.

I touched my boy. He didn't bubble or coo, but rather turned his head toward me with a gummy, toothless smile. "This boy-child I name Federo, to honor a friend who died badly but bravely, his entire being possessed by godhood. And to honor the fact that nothing in my life would be as it is today without him. For good or for ill."

That name raised a greater hubbub behind me. Federo had very nearly been the death of so many of us. But he was who he had been to me—the man who had bought me from my father as the smallest of girls, fostered my secret training to slay the late, unlamented Duke, protected me, before turning on us all when he was corrupted by divine power. Everything and nothing, enslaver and redeemer both. But in the end, he was just another of my kills, and a city's-worth of trouble had come with that deed.

Careful of my balance and of their fragile little necks, I collected my children and turned to the crowd of well-wishers. "I give you Marya and Federo," I called loudly enough for my voice to ring within the confines of the wooden building. "May they live long and happily under the protection of Endurance."

That provoked a round of applause that was most pleasing to me. People pressed forward to touch the children, to touch me, to push gifts upon the three of us. I did not like this so much, but I understood it to be inescapable, at least not without deep gracelessness on my part.

So I smiled and let my children be welcomed into their lives.

Ilona had helped me back to the shadows of my tent. The brazier within was warm. I'd grown chill outside, and worried that the babies had as well. Their two little cradles were already drawn up before the potbellied brass heater on its curled-out chicken legs. Someone had placed chips of sandalwood on the fire. The scent was soothing.

My breasts ached again, and the children were fussing. I figured they would suckle a short while, then go down to nap. Both at the same time, if I were lucky. I was already learning what a trial twins could be.

"Let me hold Marya," Ilona said. "You care for Federo first."

I heard the pain in her voice. "If not for Federo, we would never have met," I reminded her. Fleeing from his army, wounded and exhausted as I'd stumbled through the unfamiliar High Hills leagues north and inland of Copper Downs, I had been taken in and sheltered by Ilona and her daughter.

From that, so much had grown between us. I wished then and sometimes wish still that more might have grown between us. How different my life would have been.

"If not for Federo . . ." She couldn't finish articulating her thought, though the words were clear enough to me.

"If not for Federo, Corinthia Anastasia would yet be with you. And your little house would still stand unclaimed by fire." I slid out of my belled silk and my fine dress, pulled on a quilted cotton jacket that I left open, and settled little Federo into my breast—one privilege his adult namesake had never tried to claim from me, to the man's credit. Looking up, I caught her eye and willed the haunting I saw in there to fade like darkness at dawn. "I know your pain, Ilona. And I *will* set it right."

"No, Green. May you never know my pain." She clutched little Marya so tightly that I briefly wondered if this was a threat. I was certain that Ilona had never trained to be a fighter, but a woman who'd lived alone in wild country as she had for years was dangerous enough in her own right.

"I have dreamed, over and over, of finding them. If I could run across the wave tops, I would already be gone." My own words captured my imagination a moment, boots from some magic cavern out of a child's tale that might take me from crest to crest in strides of a dozen rods per pace. I could feel how the wind would pluck at my hair, how the storms would dog my back without ever catching up to me.

"No one runs the waves except in a boat."

"Ship," I said absently, wincing as Federo sucked overhard. For a child with no teeth, he could chew far too well. "And I have crossed the Storm Sea three times already in my life."

Ilona looked down at Marya. "You cannot take the children with you."

There she touched on what had rubbed me hardest these past weeks. I had thought much about this exact question. "I cannot leave them behind," I said gently. "They would be . . . well . . . claimed. They would be claimed by others." Oh how true that would have been; I knew it then and still know it now all these years later.

"You stand too close to power." She laughed, though there was no mirth in her voice. The joy of the Naming had leached from me as well, I realized. "The gods will strip you naked and bloody, and all you will get in return is a demand for more."

The way she said that gave me a moment's pause. After considering why, I spoke. "I have never seen you pray. Or lay out an offering. And you came of age under the Duke, when the gods here were stilled."

"There are many voices in the High Hills." Ilona stepped toward me and helped me switch the babies. "Not all of them boom from the grave," she added as we completed our efforts.

She'd never spoken of her past, not between the time she'd left the Factor's house and when I'd met her living in the cottage tucked within the feral apple orchards. Who had fathered Corinthia Anastasia, for example? How had Ilona come upon the trick of listening to the ghosts?

I'd just been handed a hint. Huge and painful and difficult, and one I could not pursue now. Would not, for love of her.

"There are many voices in this world," I said gently. "As you said, not all of them boom from the grave. We will find your daughter, and we will bring her home. This I swear on the lives of my own children."

"Don't." Ilona's finger touched my lips. I shivered at the caress, though she meant nothing so intimate by it. "Do not make me promises you will not keep."

Stung, I replied, "I keep all my promises." But even in those days, I knew that was not true. Such a thing could be true of no one except she who was a miser of her spirit and never promised anything at all.

Ilona's eyes glittered with unshed tears as she walked away. Carefully I put the babies down in their cradles, then took up my knives and went out into the cold. My body might not be quite sufficiently healed for the work of readiness, but I could not deny it.

Besides, I needed to do something with my rage before someone else came along and stumbled upon the brunt of it.

I chopped again at the wooden man I had lashed together from beams and stakes. Chips arced away from me into the weeds. This was wrong of me—bad for my blades, bad for my own form, wasteful of the wood—but I needed to cut, and cut deep.

Everything ached, not just my breasts and loins. Muscles in my back and legs screamed their protest after long disuse. My arms burned with the exertion. My eyes burned with tears.

Trapped. So damned trapped. I had only one course open to me, and it was impossible for me to follow. *How* could I take the babies across the Storm Sea? *How* could I leave them behind?

Another flurry of blades and blows, and stinging pain to my wrists as metal bit wood. I imagined Surali's face before me, cheekbones crushed under my assault, eyes bleeding, lips spread wide by the slash of my knives. The architect of all my troubles, she was a human woman as confounding to me as any god had managed to be.

I drove my long knife into the target so hard the blade sang as if it would break. A rope snapped, bits of hemp flying off in the air as the wooden man collapsed. Embedded, my blade went with it. I would deserve the trouble it would cause me if I'd broken the weapon.

"Feel better?"

Whirling, I confronted Mother Argai. She'd spoken in Seliu. Even after months here in Copper Downs, her Petraean vocabulary was largely limited to coinage, drinks, and cursing.

"What?" I demanded, feeling as clumsy with my words as I had been with my weapons.

There was no watching crowd. My bursts of rage and energy were well known now. Even Lucia had not followed me out past the temple foundations to watch me scramble among the weeds and piled dirt. Only Mother Argai, her face quirked into a curious expression.

"What, indeed," she said softly. "What?"

"I don't know," I confessed. Now I was ashamed of my mood. Anger was not power. It was just anger. A disease of the soul, if one indulged the emotion overmuch.

Mother Argai sat on my broken pile of wood. "What don't you know? What it is you should be doing?"

"Oh, I know that. We return to Kalimpura."

"When?"

"As soon as . . ." As soon as what? When the babies were ready? When I was ready? My voice was small and shamed as I finished my thought. "As soon as I am able."

"Breaking weapons does not increase the likelihood of you being able." Her tone was mild, but I could hear the scorn as she tugged my long knife free of a shattered baulk of timber and flipped it toward me.

That was an old Blade teaching trick. Throw a weapon at a student and see what they did. Most people needed stitches only once or twice.

Not me. I'd never been cut that way. I snatched the spinning knife out of the air, whipped it against my forearm to sight down the edge, then sheathed it. "A dull blade."

"And you?"

A dulled Lily Blade, of course. I'd stepped right into that bit of rhetorical trickery. "We are going," I told her. "As soon as I can arrange passage. Will you inform Mother Vajpai?"

I had missed being so decisive. This was as if I'd woken up from a longer sleep than was reasonable.

"If you wish," Mother Argai said quietly. "She has gone back to rest." The amputation of Mother Vajpai's toes at Surali's orders was one of the many sins I held higher than the value of that wretched woman's life. "What of your friends and enemies here?"

"For the most part, they are the same people." I snorted. "Still, you have the right of it. I must make my farewells." And parting bargains, it would seem.

That appeared to satisfy Mother Argai. "I will pass the word. The women of the Bustle Street Lazaret will wish to know."

"I shall call there in the next day or so." My arms were flaccid and my body ached, but I felt like *me* for the first time in months.

"Farewell," she said in passable Petraean, and walked away.

Stumbling toward my own tent, I called for Lucia to help me bathe and rub liniment into my back and legs. And other things besides, no doubt, once we were snugged together and touching.

Of course, I had not reckoned on the babies crying and Federo learning a new trick of vomiting into his cradle while lying down. Neither bath nor gentle caress was mine that night.

The next day after having fed my children, I passed over breakfast and forced myself into my leathers for the first time since my pregnancy. They stank a bit of molder and old sweat. Sunlight and use would do them good. Not to mention the good such exposure would do for me.

It was time to go calling, remind Copper Downs who I was, and make my farewells to those who might care to hear them. I would start with the hardest parting of all—the god Blackblood, whose boy-priest had fathered my children, and who had prophesied to claim my son. Threatened to do so, speaking more accurately.

Ilona had goat's milk for the children and Lucia to argue with. I tucked spare rags into my sleeve to clean myself if my milk ran hard while I was away, and headed into the streets outside the temple walls.

At the time, I had not left Endurance's compound in almost two months, I realized. To simply feel cobbles beneath my feet was such a privilege. It was a delight to be passed in the street by total strangers. Horses! Wind! The rising scents of the slowly warming weather were welcome, as evidence of the wider world.

My children I already loved foolishly, in fact beyond reason, but these first few hours of escape since their birth were a blessing un-looked for. I thanked Endurance, which seemed safe enough, and proceeded happily upon my errands.

The Temple District was showing the first signs of spring. The trees that struggled in the great iron pots lining the Street of Horizons were putting out their first buds of leaf and flower. Vendors hawking food from carts and trays seemed to have improved their wares. People walking along the street smiled, or so I thought.

Life was better.

I paused in front of Blackblood's temple. I had done murder here twice, or near as made no difference. First back in the dark days at the end of Federo's reign as a god, I'd caused the then-priests of Black-blood to be locked within alongside Skinless, their patron's fearsome avatar. Vengeance was exacted for their Pater Primus' scheming treach-ery. The dents and warps in the great black iron doors were mute testi-mony to that day's sorry massacre.

Later, I'd fought the twins Iso and Osi, agents of the Saffron Tower, on Blackblood's front steps. They'd died a death of women. Whatever might have become of their souls afterwards, I could only hope and pray that they writhed in the unshriven torment foretold by their all too peculiar and misogynistic faith.

Staring at the steps, I wondered if their blood still stained the ancient, foot-polished marble. Though the steps were so worn and misused that any of a dozen shadows, stains, and discolorations could have marked the end of those wretched priests.

What was left of all my misadventures in this city besides the broken doors? I believed then that when I sailed away sometime in the few days hence that I would not be coming back. Too many complications here. Too many deaths.

And truthfully, Selistan was the home of my heart. My first memories were there. I harbored ambitions that my last would someday be as well.

I trudged up to the doors. They were tall, almost twice my height, and proportioned strangely to make the entrance seem narrow even to a large person approaching.

So much of religion was about architecture, I mused. Even the meanest godling has a shrine somewhere. The first impulse of followers seems to be to build.

Today I was not a follower, nor a supplicant of this peculiar god of men and their pain. I was Green, come to bid my farewells to one who had touched my life with long, strange fingers. My own fingers, short and narrow and oh-so-dark in this land of the pale-skinned, tugged at the doors to pull them open.

Within stank of old sacrifice and unwashed linens. A male smell. No woman's temple ever held such an odor. I looked around the familiar sanctuary. One time I'd descended from the clerestory, and nearly been killed for my trouble. On another visit, I'd entered this place through the tunnels from Below, and nearly been made pregnant for my trouble. Front doors were not so easy for me, it seemed.

Narrow, dark pillars lined the dusty shadowed space like a rank of starveling caryatids. Moth-worn banners depended from the upper reaches, faded bands as bars sinister upon them where the fugitive light of day touched briefly with each passage of the suns. A reservoir of mercury stretched ahead of me in the middle—the Pater Primus' scrying pool, where I had never seen anything but uneasy, muckled reflections.

Notable in their absence were the god's priests, who might pre-

sumably be found in this house of their holy. I had never seen worshippers here, and Blackblood did not have a flock as such. This temple
served other needs than the usual. He favored supplicants over congregants. Every wounded man or dying boy was his. That much was obvious from the lack of benches or kneeling bolsters or, really, anything at
all in this hall.

Once again, the architecture of the spirit predominated.

I did not bother to call out. Instead, I walked purposefully toward
the deeper shadows at the rear. Beyond was the fane itself, the altar
where sacrifices were taken up or turned back into the world. From
there the labyrinthine lower levels opened as well. Skinless, whom I
counted as a friend of sorts, could likely be found in those depths. And
the god himself, whom I had seen in two aspects thus far in my life.

The mercury pond rippled as I passed it. I glanced down only to
falter in my pace as I saw for the first time ever a vision there. Flames
heaved in a burning sea, and eyeless children cried out as their blank
faces beseeched me. My gut lurched in a momentary twist of terror
and I ran deeper into the darkness.

What the liquid mirror had shown was too close to my dreams of
late for my comfort. I growled a curse under my breath, damning this
god back to the titanics who had birthed us all.

Blackblood was mocking me.

Passing through the tripled doorway into the darkness beyond, I
came upon a familiar carved screen. It was barely visible, illuminated
by the flickering light of a single tallow candle. The throne above and
behind the screen stood vacant. The shackles at its arms and pediment
lay empty, useless, containing nothing but a slice of deeper shadow.
The languid young man I'd seen there before was absent. Who knew
what purposes a god was about? Whether being "here" was a concept
that held any significance in the face of divine ennui?

"I am arrived," I told the darkness in my best speaking-to-gods
voice. That, I had found, was rather like facing down a large and
irritated dog. The divine responded best to a firm intent and despised
any appearance of weakness. "I present myself to make my farewells."

Only the faint whisper of dust falling answered me. I listened for
the creak and pop of Skinless, or the footsteps of a languid god returned from whatever space they inhabited.

Nothing. The temple might as well have been a sepulcher.

"I honor what you have done in my life." Deep breath. "I honor your lost priest Septio." Another deep breath. "I honor you and what you do." One last shudder. "But I am leaving Copper Downs. I do not know when or if I shall return."

The necessary words spoken, I turned to find a man so close behind me that he could have encircled my shoulders with his arms. My short knives were in my hands and touching his abdomen between one moment and the next.

"It would be amusing to see you try," said Blackblood.

He did not breathe, of course, except when taking in air to speak. I had not heard him behind me, because he had not willed it. Still, one must keep up a good face. "There are worse temperings for my steel than the blood of a god."

When the god's smile dawned, I was sorry for my little joke. An acrid scent bit at my nose. I realized my hands were growing quite warm. I looked down to see both my knife blades glowing a dull orange. With a shriek, I dropped them.

"Temper, temper," said Blackblood. He bent and grasped each by the heated blade. The stench of burned flesh filled the air.

Despite myself, I gasped.

"What is pain to *me*?" With that, the god handed me my knives once more.

I held the weapons away from my body, wary of the fading heat even through the leather-wrapped handles. "Your purposes are ever mysterious."

"They should not be." He shrugged, so human a gesture, then in one step was upon his throne. I cannot describe how he covered the distance of a rod, or spun me about doing it. He just . . . did.

The manacles there stirred to fasten themselves around his wrists and ankles. With another sly, dangerous smile, Blackblood said, "It makes my priests feel better to see me bound."

Curiosity overcame my more difficult emotions. "What could men forge that would hold you?"

"Nothing. But even metalworkers have gods."

That I could well imagine. Smithing had to be one of the oldest magics of all. Metal drawn from deep within the earth carried the might of the deep darknesses and the secrecy of stone with it.

"I thank you for the lesson." My gut still churned, spinning like a child's toy. Apparently this day was meant for queasy, no matter what I did.

Blackblood's eyes flashed. The hair on my arms and neck rose like wires. "Where is my boy-child?" His voice had lost its human timbre and become something much more like what I'd heard from Desire, or the Lily Goddess. Weighty with the power of years and the might of the divine. A blunt instrument for persuasion and intimidation.

Holding in my bladder fiercely tight, I stared him down. "I do not recall you carrying a baby under your heart these past nine months."

The god leaned forward. Pale light flickered across his fingertips and along his chains. I realized he was nude, and his penis seemed enormous. Growing, even. A sword hardening in his irritation. "Neither do I recall you fathering a son on your own body, like some miraculous temple virgin." The dancing light reached his eyes and took up a place there like lightning from a distant storm at sea. "I have spoken for the child . . . Federo."

With that, he paused and laughed. Dust and small grains of rock rained down upon me from above. The floor quivered beneath my feet as my nose filled with the scent of ash and burnt flesh.

"You have named your boy so?" The god seemed torn between amusement and rage.

It finally dawned upon me that I was in real danger here. Would he let me go? I had captured Blackblood's attention in a more profound and frightening way than any of our previous encounters. His chains caught my eye again. *Blood and tempering indeed.*

I pushed past the screen to approach the throne upon its dais of black rock. His swelling cock dangled at my eye level, but I ignored it. The god's hands were out of reach, but his feet were before me. He was large, larger than human now, but still held that form.

"My child is mine to name and raise as I see fit," I announced. "You do not hold a prior claim. And he is not yours to take up."

"You cost me a worthy boy-priest." Blackblood's voice boomed loud enough to hurt my ears. "He would have been my Pater Primus someday. You owe me."

"No." I stood firm as I could. "I owe you nothing." I brought the knives up, still too warm for comfort, spreading my arms to drive them swiftly through a link in each chain upon his feet. From there I pushed the tips into the hollow spot of skin just before the great tendon at the back of each ankle.

The god was pinned to his own chains by blades tempered in his own heat and, perhaps, blood. There was very little else on the plate of the world that would possibly hold him back, but his remark about the gods of metalworkers had made me think that blades so treated might serve.

He gasped, not so much from pain as amazement, or so I thought. As he himself had said, what was pain to a pain god?

"Listen," I told him, my voice a hissing growl. I felt very large in that moment, as if I were greater than myself. "We made no bargain over this. And you cannot simply take my children from me. Your power does not cover me over. But I will make a bargain with you now."

"What would that bargain be?" Blackblood's voice was flat and sharp as a murderer's razor. I also noted he had not moved his feet from where I had pinned them.

"I will not leave my blades in your chains if you will release whatever claims you think to have over me."

"Do you believe it that simple?" Bemusement now.

"Never so simple," I answered honestly. "But I bargain with the chips in my hand. I will leave this city, I will take my children with me, and I would have honor between us at our parting."

Blackblood gave me a long, careful stare. The fires in his eyes died down, and he seemed to shrink a bit. He waved a hand. Some bit of his languor had returned. "Go," he said. "Your son will come to me in his own time someday. What are years to me? Like pain, they pass unnoticed."

"What are the years through which you slept?" I asked, challenging him. It was I, after all, who had slain the Duke and released the gods of this city from four centuries of enforced silence.

He did not like that so much. But still his hands twitched, and my knives fell away from his feet. "Take your audacity and go, Green. The tempered blades are my gift to you. May they protect your son until he has need of me."

"May my son never have need of you at all." I bowed and turned away. Skinless stood in deeper shadow, his glistening fat and slick muscle gleaming slightly. I nodded to the avatar before striding back out into the sanctuary.

Still no one was there, though I met the new Pater Primus hovering anxiously at the top of the steps outside the bent metal doors.

"What did you do to him?" he asked. His hands slipped across each other's wrists like birds fighting. This man knew whose deeds had brought him his accession to his current precarious position of power.

I took pity on him. "Nothing. We spoke awhile, and made a bargain."

"The ground shook beneath my feet."

Looking around, I saw no toppled walls or panicked horses. "These things happen. At least when you are very lucky." I tapped his chin with the tip of one blade, still warm and bloody from the god, and wondered what else this day could possibly bring.

I had other people to see, and passage to buy on a ship, but the morning was fine. A sense of freedom overcame me. Something in the air beckoned—the breeze, the temperature, the angle of the sun; I would not have been able to say precisely what. I could taste *potential*.

With a purposeful stride, I headed for the Dockmarket. I did not need to buy anything. For that matter, I had brought no money with me. A crowded place full of choices appealed nonetheless.

What I had been struggling against in those days was a sense of commitment. Choices made that neither could nor would be revoked. I was a mother now. My children needed me. That meant I could not take ship upon ship to sail until the seas were a different color and people spoke no language I had ever heard. Nor could I settle into a life as merchant or midwife or tavernkeeper. Not that I exactly wanted to do those things, but I found myself missing a sense of opportunity that I'd never really understood I had felt in the first place.

I knew I would always be a mother. I would always be too close to the gods. I would always be a woman who could kill with a casual hand and counted more ghosts behind her than most people counted friends in their life.

I would always be who I was.

My steps slowed at those thoughts. My heart grew heavier. Was this what it meant to be in the world? Was this how Ilona felt?

Looking about, I realized I was not heading for the Dockmarket, but for the lazaret on Bustle Street. Perhaps that was fair enough. Mother Vajpai had likely returned there after the Naming. Mother Argai would be back by now. Laris, former priestess of Marya and now priestess of Mother Iron, was often at the lazaret as well.

And women, a bit like I'd known in the Temple of the Silver Lily back in Kalimpura. Mother Vajpai was training up a cadre of Blades here. Given only a few short months thus far, they were laughable by the standards we held in Selistan, but this was a city where women never fought. Or more to the point, never fought *back*.

At least, women other than myself.

Small wonder the Interim Council had not known what to make of me. Despite my mood, my lips quirked into a smile I could not contain. Surely Jeschonek and his fellow councilors would be pleased to see the last of me. In my place, I would leave them an entire nest of women growing into their own power.

By the time I reached the lazaret, my deepening mood had lifted once more. The building itself was an old stronghouse or counting room set in a merchant quarter very much in decline. The architecture hailed from an era when handling money was a high-risk occupation with many pointed contenders. That is to say, the lazaret presented a strong, blank façade with slightly outsloped walls and narrow windows on the two upper floors for archers to shoot down into the street. Granite blocks formed the lower courses, with close-set brick above. The door was recessed to limit access, banded and armored against battering.

Nothing more valuable than the safety of women was stored there today, but that was temptation enough. From time to time, some angry father or husband with a handful of hired bravos would arrive, intent on forcing the door to drag home a bruised and weeping girl-child to her marriage bed. They were never admitted. Mothers anxious for the fate of potential grandchildren might be, if they came alone and soft-spoken.

Within, women looked to themselves and each other. Though I had not been there in almost three months, I knew that Mother Vajpai and Mother Argai had infected the inhabitants of the lazaret with ideas of strength and self-sufficiency. Not to mention more than a few techniques. From the acolytes at the Temple of Endurance I'd heard a rumor that two large girls had been apprenticed to an unusually co-operative swordsmith—*that* would be a first in the modern history of Copper Downs.

Like everyone else, I tugged the bellpull by the door. A minute or two later—quite a long time to stand in the street waiting—someone within flicked open one of the spyholes. I heard a squeal; then the door opened with a swift creak.

It was Laris, priestess of Mother Iron, who greeted me. She beamed her joy. I'd rescued her from the rubble of Marya's temple last winter, though I had been unable to save her sister Solis, already crushed to death in the attack on their goddess by the priests Iso and Osi, agents of the Saffron Tower.

"Green! Come in, come in. We're about to sit down to some roast pigeon, and Failla has brought us some fine white bread from one of the bakeries near the Ivory Quarter."

Indeed, the warm, rich smell of crisping fat greeted me from within. Potatoes, too, I thought, and someone had found a bit of wild marjoram with which to spice them. "You should have told me before," I said, laughing. "I'd have come to see to the cooking."

The most usual fare at the lazaret was the soup pot, which never truly emptied. A woman could always get a bowl and a sympathetic ear from old Neela, who tended it almost ceaselessly. Though the soup might taste strange, and sometimes went down poorly, it was ever warm and filling. If the women of the lazaret had made a dinner to sit down to, they were celebrating.

She replied with a smile, "In a house of women you may be sure there are more cooks than any broth needs."

"Of course there are." I doubted any of them had *my* training. If there was one thing I was good at besides killing people, it was cooking for them. And a cook generally received more compliments on her work than an assassin. "Still, let us go to the kitchen."

They had, thank the Lily Goddess, not put Neela at the pigeons. That woman could stretch a stone and three onions into supper for a score of diners, but I was unsure if she knew butter from batter in a proper kitchen. Instead, I found a pair of women who were unfamiliar to me basting a tray of birds with something oily and fragrant.

There was my wild marjoram. A great bowl of roasted potatoes steamed still in their jackets. Someone had left off chopping cabbage, so rather than interfere before the hot fire, I took up a knife and put my weapons skills to more peaceable uses.

Kitchens have a simple secret: It is a profound comfort to prepare food. Sharing a meal is a sacrament of human existence. In all my readings and travels, I have never heard of a place where people of goodwill would not sit down together over bread and salt, at the very least. Even so mundane a task as chopping cabbage, throwing away the wormy or moldering bits—this stuff seemed to have been salvaged from a feed bin—made me a part of the community of women. In my experience, few men cooked, and fewer men understood the magic inherent in a fire, a pot, and a spoon.

Too bad for them.

I spoke their language, too, when needed: hilt and blade.

Once I had the cabbage chopped down, I swept the mound into a great pottery bowl rather ineptly decorated with blue rabbits and looked to my seasonings. I combined a draggled onion swiftly diced, a quick whip of several egg whites and bit of precious olive oil, a sprinkle of salt, and regret that the lazaret could not afford peppercorns.

When I finally looked up again, the pigeons were gone, the potatoes were on their way out, and only Laris remained, still smiling. "You seemed so peaceful," she said. "And thank you for not interrupting Sion and Marchess at their work."

"I do not—," I began hotly, then stopped. Of course I did. I almost always knew better, and it was so hard to get people to listen. "Never mind," I added in a smaller voice.

Laris grabbed the slaw I'd made. "I'll carry the bowl."

I followed her into the courtyard. I'd been there only once before—the lazaret had never been a haunt of mine. Four tables had been set, and almost two dozen women were gathered, chatting noisily. Laris set the bowl down next to a metal tray of golden, steaming pigeon carcasses, then called for attention in a clear, penetrating voice much different from her usual soft tones.

"Sisters! Sisters."

Spotting Mother Vajpai's dark face among all the pale Petraean women, I sidled over to her. *Where is Mother Argai?*

Into the silence she had gathered around herself, Laris began to pray. Matter-of-factly, as if talking to us rather than leading us, but unmistakably prayer. One did not so much believe in gods, after all, as acknowledge them.

"We thank Mother Iron for this hour of peaceful assembly, and the food which graces our table. We thank her for protecting this lazaret, and providing us with our sisters from across the Storm Sea who have offered so much guidance and lavished such care upon our number. We ask her protection for those soon to depart from our shores, and offer our bodies, our minds, and our spirits to her for sacrifice as she sees fit." Laris brushed a finger from her groin, across her left breast, to end touching her forehead.

I had not seen this gesture before. Most of the women followed it smoothly, though Mother Vajpai did not. The meaning seemed clear enough to me. I was pleased that ritual was settling in around Mother Iron. The transition from the goddess Marya's death to Mother Iron's ascension in her place had not been kind to the women of Copper Downs.

Then we sat, while the two cooks passed the food into shallow bowls to share out. The fine bread sat piled on a silver platter that looked to have come from one of the great houses of the Velviere District or the Ivory Quarter, though I could not know whether that had been donation, salvage, or theft. A torn-off chunk came my way. I used it to sop at the pigeon gravy that kept my meat and potatoes warm and savory.

It was a moment of sisterhood and peace like I had not known since the better days at the Temple of the Silver Lily. A welcome gift in that difficult time. I was almost sorry to leave Copper Downs if this was what was growing here. Also, I felt quite pleased at my own role in helping foster these changes in the lazaret.

Beside me, Mother Vajpai touched my arm. "On what errand have you set Mother Argai?"

My heart seemed to seize cold and stiff. "None," I replied. "She left me some hours ago to return here."

Mother Vajpai glanced around. No one seemed to be paying us much attention among the smiles and the flying gossip and the pleased attention to the feast. "She has not come back."

I closed my eyes and sighed. My knives were heavy on my wrists, and my body was not yet fit for a hunt or a chase, let alone any sort of fight at the end. And neither was Mother Vajpai. She would never again be the fighter she was before the bitch Surali had her toes cut off.

"Do you have any notion where she might have stopped off?" I asked. The question was almost certainly hopeless, though perhaps Mother Argai had found a local woman with a taste for the rough and exotic. A bit of shopping was hardly her style.

"She was with you." I heard the almost-accusation in Mother Vajpai's voice.

"Not for some time." I worked at my pigeon, flicking the meat off the bone. There was small purpose in rushing back out into the street underfed.

As I finished it off, eating swiftly as I could with a modicum of decency, Laris rose again. "Green is among us," she announced, once more using her "praying to Mother Iron" voice. "Though she has not frequented the lazaret much, she brought me here in the worst hour of my need. She brought us Mother Vajpai and Mother Argai." At those words, Laris paused and looked around, her expression faintly puzzled. "She . . . she has been a friend to us. And it is she who will soon go, taking our Mothers with her."

A chorus of groans greeted that statement, along with several mock wails of grief.

Laris nodded to me. "Green, will you speak a moment?"

Rising, I searched for words. I could hardly just announce that Mother Argai was missing and I feared for her life. Suddenly tongue-tied, I reached for something more appropriate. What did I know of inspiring people? I was no leader and never then thought I would be.

"I am p-proud to be a friend to this house and everyone in it," I said, feeling very cold. "And I am sorry to be leaving without knowing you better. Eat well, and rest safely."

Stepping over to Laris, I whispered in her ear, "Mother Argai has not come back from the Temple of Endurance, though she left more than two hours ago. Send word swiftly should she come before I return, and especially of her condition."

Laris nodded, then glanced at Mother Vajpai. I followed her glance and caught my old teaching Mother's eye. In return I received a curt nod, before she buried her face in her hands.

I had never seen *that* before. Discomfited, I scuttled away, loosening my knives and praying I could sort this situation without hurting myself too badly.

Finding someone in a city is decidedly not simple. Finding some who has deliberately hidden—or been hidden—away is terrifically more complex. I could scarcely just roam about calling out Mother Argai's name.

What I *could* do was make the reasonable assumption that she'd headed from the Temple of Endurance to Bustle Street by the most direct route. Mother Argai was not fond of Below, and did not know her way about Copper Downs well enough to go casually wandering. I retraced the steps I thought she would have taken, looking for evidence of a struggle along the way.

It would have been useless to ask the Petraeans I met as I walked whether they had seen her. I did call out in Seliu the few times I saw a dark-skinned face, but none of my countrymen knew of a Lily Blade lost or taken on the street. Most of them did not even treat the question seriously.

I could hardly blame them for that. We Blades cultivated our reputation for invincibility with no little care. Still, anyone may be killed by a knife in the back or an arrow from a rooftop, no matter how mighty they are.

The sun was westering, dusk nearly upon the city. I moved as quickly as I could. By starlight, blood looks no different from dirty water, or even oil. A smear on a cobble might be my only clue.

I hunted, swift and careful, all the way up Durand Avenue back to the Temple of Endurance. Nothing. No sign of her, or a struggle. No dropped weapons, no freshly smashed wood, no blood smears. Nothing.

The ever-open gates of Endurance's home awaited me. They were as devoid of guards as always. Sometimes one or another acolyte might sit there in a chair, to welcome or direct visitors, but Chowdry claimed quite fiercely that Endurance forbade even self-defense. Twice I had met a tulpa at this gate, a ghost or wisp of divinity rising up from Below, but it was not here either on this increasingly chill evening.

Passing within, I realized that my breasts ached. My body knew I was going back to my children. It paid no attention to my intents or purposes. "Soon," I whispered, but first cast about the packed earth in front of the wooden temple where we'd held the Naming.

Odd bits of button and dropped cloth and incense stubs abounded, along with a few crushed fruits and someone's sandal now trampled into the dirt. Again, nothing to indicate more.

I stalked through the compound, looking for Chowdry. Ponce was cooking in the tent kitchen, and waved cheerfully to me from the open flap. A crowd of acolytes waited outside, smiling and talking. A few also waved at me.

No Chowdry, though.

The grounds were not such a large place. I soon found him by the rising columns of the stone temple, arguing with a rotund little man who sported a fringe of white hair surrounding an otherwise bald scalp. The stranger was dressed in a mason's smock, but that did not fool me—he was obviously used to being heard and obeyed. They both kept pointing at a sheaf of papers that could hardly be readable now that the light had almost failed.

As I approached, I realized they were becoming quite heated over the subject of stone. The stranger's hand strayed to his belt where a knife might have been found.

"When *are* you going to ordain more priests from that growing mob of children that follow you?" I snapped.

Chowdry turned, looking sad. The not-mason appeared surprised; then his eyes narrowed as he studied me. With my skin color, I knew I was little more than a shadow to him, but clearly he recognized me nonetheless.

"Green—," Chowdry began in Seliu, but the stranger cut him off.

"Not that foreign gabble, please. And you must be the girl-hero of Copper Downs."

My suspicion of this man cemented to an immediate and over-whelming dislike. Though I never saw him again before I left the city for Selistan, at the time I was concerned I was meeting a new and pow-erful enemy. If I weren't so tired and worried, I might have knifed him right there.

"Have you seen Mother Argai?" I asked Chowdry in our foreign gabble.

"Not since she came to see you about your weapons practice," he answered. Then, "No, I tell a lie. She came back to your tent later. With a man I did not know."

Panic seized me, stabbing my heart. "And you *let* them in?"

He was quite surprised. "With Mother Argai? What could happen? She is a Lily Blade."

"We are not immortal!" I shouted in Petraean, then gave the stranger a look that should have shriveled his tongue in his head before sprinting off for my tent.

Behind me, voices were raised, offense being both taken and given. I was already drawing my short knives, and wished I had taken the trouble to stick some sense into the fat fool.

As I approached my tent, I was out of breath. In no wise was my body ready for racing about and confronting either the good or the bad. Ponce was close behind me, having abandoned the kitchen when he saw me sprinting past. In turn he drew along with him a ragged line of acolytes. These children—though many of them were older than I—numbered both Petraean and Selistani among them.

A Blade handle's worth, I realized with bitter irony. A handle who were forbidden to raise their hands even in self-defense.

I drew three huge, whooping breaths, then stepped into my tent.

Inside was cold and dark. The brazier had gone out and none of the lamps were lit. Dim light had followed me in, a narrow triangle of it making a path before me across the rucked-up rugs. I could hear breathing. Federo's gurgling, I thought.

Where was Ilona? Where was Lucia? Mother Argai?

Blades forward, I scanned the room quietly. My effort was wasted when Ponce and several acolytes pushed in around me, one bearing a small lantern.

The stiletto glittered as it came out of the dark for my throat. A gloved hand held it, and the man behind it was wrapped in leather much as I was. Even his face was masked. I barely stepped aside from the thrust, and turned to trip him but lacked both strength and finesse, and staggered away. Ponce shrieked and jumped back, knocking the lantern from the acolyte's hand.

Flame arced, oil spilled, and I parried another stab from the long, slim weapon. It rang like a glass bell that had been struck. I spun, now careful of my balance and center of gravity. *I cannot afford this fight.* My body would not sustain the effort.

He came a third time as the wall of the tent caught fire. This time I stepped into the blade, allowing it to slip between my torso and my left arm. That brought both my short knives within reach of my attacker. I planted one in his gut and the other in his neck. They slipped into his body as if he had been made of butter.

What kind of leather was this man armored with?

My attacker staggered back two steps, then flopped onto his butt, so he was sitting on the floor with his legs straight out before him. Even with the covered face, I could see his puzzlement in his eyes. I spent a moment slashing the tendons in both his heels, so he would not surprise me, then turned to the growing orange light behind me.

The tent wall was fully in flames. The rug closest was smoldering.

I grabbed up one of my babies and turned to find Ponce edging back through the flap of the tent. Or had he even left? "Here!" I shouted, and passed him my child. Marya, I realized.

Federo next, into the hands of a familiar-faced acolyte. Now both children were shrieking.

Panic rose within me. *Where are Ilona and Lucia? Where is Mother Argai?*

I paced around the side of the tent not yet in flames. My bed was lumpier than normal, I realized. A swift sweep of my short knife pulled the blanket aside to reveal Ilona unconscious and twisted into an odd pose. Stepping over her, I slashed at the tent wall. The thick fabric parted easily at the touch of my knife. That, too, seemed peculiar, though in the moment I had no time to think why. I turned again to face the clot of people crowding the flap. Smoke obscured my view, and I was hot. I waved them in past the flames and pointed to the new slit. "Get her out!"

I looked behind the brazier, but no sign of Lucia. Water was already being splashed, but the tent was almost an oven. I grabbed one of the loosely flopping feet of my enemy and dragged him into the evening air.

Hands slapped at me. I realized my leathers had been smoldering. And everything ached. Muscles in my groin were strained, too. I was angry. Very angry.

"Find Lucia," I told Ponce, who was crowding close with a bowl of water as if I needed to be doused. "And Mother Argai. Find them now."

Turning to my attacker, I kicked him hard in the ribs. A wet, weak grunt escaped. He would not be much longer in this world without serious attention. Unfortunately for him, the kind of attention I was about to offer him was entirely the wrong sort.

I slit the leather mask, not troubling about how deep the tip of my knife sank. It fell away from his face in a stream of blood.

The man was Selistani. Not only that, his face seemed vaguely familiar. I stared at the beak nose, the dark brows, trying to recall why I knew him.

It dawned on me, to no surprise at all, that this was one of Surali's men. A Bittern Court agent, or possibly Street Guild.

Very gently I slit one of his nostrils for him. That woke him up with a muffled scream.

Chowdry touched my arm. "Green, no," he began, but stopped with an expression of abject terror when I met his eyes.

"No one threatens my children," I growled, then turned back to my victim.

He stared back at me, oddly serene as he mouthed in Seliu, "It does not matter."

"Not to you, it doesn't," I agreed. "Not for very much longer." I leaned close. "Where are Lucia and Mother Argai?"

He smiled. "That does not matter either."

"I know whom you serve." His other nostril opened at the touch of my blade. This time he winced, and that foolish smile was gone from his face. "I know what you want." I leaned very close. "You will never succeed."

"It does not matter."

Sick of his pride and certainty, I stood and dragged my assailant back toward the burning tent. His dead weight was a further strain on my already-abused muscles. But I wanted him to know some real fear before his imminent death claimed him. No one was placing this man on Blackblood's altar.

Propping the bastard up on his useless feet, I shoved him through the open flap into the roaring flames. Finally he screamed. I left him to his last moments of terror and stalked after my missing women. Later I would wish I had asked smarter questions of this man, but at the time, my anger was satisfied. That had seemed to be enough to me. The music of his anguished dying soothed my ears.

"We've found Mother Argai," gasped Ponce, running toward me.

"Where?"

"Hidden between the tent lining and the outer canvas."

I winced. "Alive?"

"Yes. A bad blow to the head, and she would have burned to death already if we hadn't pulled her free."

"What about Lucia?"

He shook his head, baffled and sad.

"Then bring me my children," I snapped.

I turned, looking one way then the other. Chowdry watched me from close by. His expression was closed and hard, lit in the dancing flames of the burning tent.

"There are no apologies," I told him.

Chowdry's face sagged into a species of regret. "You draw trouble like a mast draws lightning."

"I am leaving. I have business in Kalimpura." I nodded over my shoulder. "Which has become all the more urgent now." Surali's agent had waited until I was birthed and about because no one watched over me so closely now. Nor my tent.

Ponce came me to with one of my babies in each arm. I took them and clutched them close while I glared at Chowdry. Clearly I could not let my children out of my sight.

"I cannot bless your going," the priest said reluctantly in Petraean. "Nor can I be pressing you to stay." He seemed old and helpless now. Night's darkness hung around him like a shroud.

"You do not have a say," I told him not unkindly. "But neither do you deserve these assaults on your temple simply because of my presence." Not so long ago, two girls had died here at the hands of Surali's troublemakers hunting me. "I will be gone within a day or two. My children will go with me."

Chowdry gathered a long, deep breath. "I shall send Ponce with you."

Ponce? I had figured Ilona to accompany me, to assist me in tending the babies. I doubted I could keep her away in any case. Not from crossing the sea in pursuit of her own child. That she had waited this long without taking ship herself after Corinthia Anastasia was something of a miracle.

But Ilona was troubled. Nearly hysterical, grieving her daughter. Ponce could help mind Ilona while she helped mind my children. And perhaps a sea voyage would heal her heart enough for her to see me again, I reflected with a mix of anticipation and guilt.

"I shall take him," I said, then hastily added, "if he will go. But that is much to ask of a young man."

"This young man will not need to be asked." That was Ponce, close by again. He looked as if he meant to be brave. "I am going."

I turned to him, shifting my babies to my shoulders. It occurred to me I could *never* fight like this. Should the children have had small leathers of their own?

"Do you know where we are headed?"

"Kalimpura," he said promptly.

"A city full of women like me, and men like that fool who attacked us. Are you certain you wish to go there?"

"I will follow you anywhere." His eyes glittered.

"Then hold my children again, and guard them." I handed him back the babies. Unaccountably but still much in the fashion of babies, they had fallen asleep. "With your life," I added.

The fire was dying, defeated by water and the immolation of my tent that had served as its fuel. Ignoring the twisted and charred body of the man I'd killed, I stalked the perimeter of the ashes, marveling that the flames had not spread. Sister Gammage, the closest thing the Temple of Endurance had to a nurse, tended to Mother Argai and Ilona, both of whom were laid out nearby on a quilted blanket. With the tent in embers, lanterns had been brought out.

There was still no sign of Lucia. Ponce had acolytes out all over the tent camp, and looking in the two temple buildings. I stared at the collapsed ruin of the tent, smoldering, shredded canvas draped over the bed and the two chests.

The chests, I thought in horror.

I rushed to a nearby tent, pushed inside—it was vacant—and tore down one of the two poles propping up the central ring. The roof creaked and sagged as I ran out again. The ashes of my own were too hot to stand in, but I leaned as close as I could and shoved the pole through the ruins to the first of the chests. My impromptu probe dragged along the collapsed, burned cloth like a plow through a reluctant field. I did not have the leverage to lift and poke as if I had a giant finger, but I managed to force the pole to the front of the chest.

Despite the danger I quickly stepped into the ashes, working my way up the pole until I did have the leverage to lift the lid. I shoved, ignoring the heat seeping into my feet through my boots. The chest creaked open, burned tent sliding off it. Within were clothes and sacks, smoldering now, probably ruined.

No Lucia.

I sagged, relieved, then backed swiftly out of the circle of embers to dance from one foot to the other until they had cooled down.

By the time I was ready to brave the other chest, from the far side of the circle where the edge drew closest to it, a small crowd had formed around me. Someone brought me strips of wet canvas and tied them around my boots. Ponce sat on the blanket with Ilona and Mother Argai, still cradling both babies, but I had many other willing hands to help me prop the tent pole high and push it into the other chest.

That one opened with a wave of smell like roasted pork. Behind me, someone vomited into the ashes. I stepped close on my wrapped shoes and peered within. Her neck had been broken, either to kill her or to fit her into the chest. At least she had not died screaming in the flames. He must have slain her first and hidden the body more carefully to buy time.

"Lay her out as soon as it is safe to do so," I said roughly. "And the dead man. I will light the candles and pray for them both." Each of them was owed that respect from me, albeit for different reasons. I turned to walk away from the tents into the darkness around the stone temple's construction.

It was time to breathe some clean air.

I sat on a granite block and stared upward into the night. Only the stars looked down upon me—the moon had not yet arrived in the eastern sky.

Certain mystes aver that the world is a plate, wide as a man can walk in a lifetime and long as the cosmos itself. I had no reason to doubt this, nor any reason to believe this, but I had always wondered what role the stars played. Surely they were more than mere piercings in the curtain of night?

Right then I felt as cold and distant and small as any of the stars in this evening's sky. I had hurt a man, very badly, then made sure his death was as painful as possible. I would do so again between any one heartbeat and next to keep my children safe. But they never would be safe enough.

So long as I moved freely through this world, my enemies would follow.

Perhaps I would be better off behind walls and surrounded by guards. Had I so long ago taken the place originally intended for me as the Duke's consort, I would have been thusly secured. Like a pearl wedged inside an oyster, requiring a knife the size of an army to extract me.

Alone, any one man could pursue me. Anyone on a rooftop could kill me before I knew I was being attacked. I was a danger to everyone around me.

Most especially my children.

Anyone who sought their lives would be doing so to punish me. No inheritance of land or money or great title rode on the shoulders of little Federo and tiny Marya. The only treasure they carried was my own blood.

What was I to do?

In the darkness, I wept a little while. I had lost Lucia, my sly and willing bathing partner and sometime lover. Who yet knew how much hurt had been done to Ilona or Mother Argai?

My would-be assassin had kept them alive with an intent to torment me if he could. By now everyone knew the people of this temple would raise neither fist nor weapon against an invader. By what power did Endurance protect his own?

By my power, of course.

I began to laugh, mirthless and bitter. "When I go across the sea," I said into the darkness, "who will take care of these little problems for you?" Chowdry had once been a pirate, and had quite possibly in the course of his sailing days slit more throats than I ever would, but

he was settled in now as the priest. The man took the will of his paci-
fistic ox god seriously.

Someone else would have to be the god's knife. Not I. Not any
longer.

I sighed, stood, and walked back to the tents. I was long overdue to
feed my babies, for all that it was night. Then I would check on my
wounded. Then as promised, I would lay out the dead, painting them
both with the red and the white, and setting the candles around their
silent heads for both sin and virtue. Finally, I would sew that day's
bell onto my silk and think on the meaning of all this.

Then on the morrow I would go find a bedamned ship and arrange
to leave this terrible, cold city. But first in the morning I would find
whoever had been sheltering my attacker in the months since Surali's
departure. Whoever that was would be very, very sorry before I was
done with them.

When the day returned, I was so stiff, I could barely move. Last
night's troubles had vastly overtaxed me. We had sent Ilona and
Mother Argai both to the Bustle Street Lazaret late that evening, so
I had no one to help me with my children either. Their crying had
awoken me.

Groggy, I wondered whose tent I slept in. I pulled Federo to my
breast first and felt the strangely comforting bite of his gummy mouth
against my nipple. It was somewhere between joy and pain, but not in
the rough way that most of the Blades played at their sex. Something
more maternal, more primal.

Once he had suckled his fill, I lifted Marya to my other nipple. I
whispered apologies to her for making her wait. It was never too early
to explain the ways of men to a young woman, for her own protection. Brothers were men as well.

The children fed and burped, I dressed myself. Truly I wished for a
deep, hot bath, but the day awaited. Vengeance and transportation
were my agenda for the morning. With luck, I could handle both and
be back before dinner.

I looked outside the tent, ready to shout for Ponce, only to find him
dozing seated on the ground just by the flap. He awoke at my touch

on his shoulder. "Will you mind the babies while I run a few errands in preparing to depart?"

The smile I got in return was almost too devoted. "I am yours," he said.

"Be my children's." I handed both of them to him. "You run the kitchen, I don't need to tell you where to find the goat's milk. How are Ilona and Mother Argai?"

He frowned as he hefted the babies. "There has been no word from the lazaret this morning, which I suppose is a good thing."

"I shall see to them later," I said, resolving to visit the two while about the city today. Swaggering a little, I left him. I kept my proud step until I'd passed out of the gate, then nearly collapsed against the wall. I could not *do* this.

What choice did I have?

It was time to go see my countrymen. Someone among them would likely know where Surali's agents had been sheltering. Besides, then I could bid farewell to the Tavernkeep, in whose establishment so many of my fellow Selistani sheltered and drank away their meager laborer's wages.

Obols and taels never went as far as one needed them to.

The Tavernkeep's place was a nameless bar in the Brewery District, down an alley and through a door with no sign. When my old teacher the Dancing Mistress had first taken me there, it had been quiet, almost haunted, with few patrons besides the scattering of pardines who came down out of their distant hilltops and montane forests for whatever business called their kind among humans.

Long ago, that business had been slaughter. In time, wars had settled affairs between humans and pardines. Then the late Duke of Copper Downs had stolen one of the hearts of their magic in the form of the gems called the Eyes of the Hills. His power had been released by my killing of him only to settle into Federo in the form of the violent god Choybalsan. In turn, I had then killed Federo, and seated the power into the ox-god Endurance, before finally arranging the return of the stolen but now-quiescent gems to the pardines.

My relationship with these people was complicated.

Now their one retreat within Copper Downs had been taken over in large measure by Selistani immigrants and refugees. The Tavernkeep and his conspecifics had borne this with remarkably good grace, and surely for more than the sake of a busy till.

I slipped down the alley, too tired and worn to take to the roofs and not trusting myself besides on the high paths. Below would be no better in my current condition. Frankly, if some assassin with a crossbow were waiting for me high up, she could have me.

Though it was early for a bar, the Tavernkeep was behind his counter taking inventory of a rack of bottles on the back wall. Tall, rangy, furred with pointed ears and a long whisking tail, he looked like nothing so much as a great cat up on two legs. This was a dangerous confusion—pardines were far more powerful and capricious than any house pet. I'd had inklings of their might, and did not care to see more.

Otherwise the room was quiet—the perpetual dice games played by my countrymen waiting for work, word, or wages had not yet resumed for the day. Many of them were stretched by the faint remains of the fire, wrapped in cloaks or thin blankets. The large round tables with the pardines' traditional stone bowls were scattered across the room, interspersed with smaller, human-scale furniture that seemed to have multiplied every time I visited this place.

"Green!" The Tavernkeep seemed delighted to see me. "It has been some time. Have you littered successfully?"

That took me a moment to unravel. "Yes," I said. "I have borne twins, a boy Federo and a girl Marya."

"Fine human names, I am certain." He laid out a stoneware bowl and poured me some of the clear and deadly pardine bournewater. "Welcome."

"Thank you." I took a sip. As always, the drink was clear as morning air, deadly as last weekend's sin. "You are too kind."

"One honors what has come before."

"Indeed." I turned to look at my sleeping countrymen. Our voices were provoking a few of them to stir. Facing the Tavernkeep once more, I smiled. "Shortly I shall leave Copper Downs. I may not be back for some years. Or possibly ever." Some prophecies were simple enough to make.

"Across the sea again." He frowned at a twisted bottle of something clear and violently red. "The Dancing Mistress did not care for your foreign city."

"Kalimpura is not foreign to those who live there."

"*All* cities are foreign," he replied with the fervent conviction of the mountain-born.

I raised my bowl to him and carefully took another sip. One of my few regrets of the path of my life since those days has been that I shall quite possibly never taste bournewater again. "In any event, I have come to bid you farewell, and ask certain needed questions of my fellow southerners before I depart."

With a wide sweep of his arm, the Tavernkeep gave me freedom of the room. "They are yours."

"Sadly, yes." I smiled.

"Would you like some dhal when you are done?"

I cocked an eye at him. "You cook Selistani now?" His *kitchen* had cooked Selistani for a year or more, but always with human hirelings. Chowdry, specifically, at least until the business of the Temple of Endurance had grown to engulf his days.

"One learns," he said modestly, followed by a spitting word that had to be the pardine tongue, though I had quite rarely heard that language spoken.

"One does," I said, taking careful note of the sounds of his people. "As I am a brave woman, I shall try your dhal."

Leaving my bowl behind, and eschewing the din of pot and spoon this time, I went to wake those at their slumbers and ask them certain questions.

I spent an instructive time speaking quietly to sleepy men.

These were my people. Not just in the sense of sharing a birthplace or a skin color. Or even, to a degree, a language—I would never be quite as fluent in Seliu as I was in Petraean, though I had shaken the Stone Coast accent that was in my voice when I first relearned my native tongue. Rather, it was this group that had stood frightened in the snowy streets of the Velviere District to oppose Surali and her thugs not with fist or stave or sword, but simply by their presence.

These men—some of them, at any rate—had stared down crossbows and swords for me. And they'd done it under Mother Argai's leadership. In doing so, they had taught me that violence did not always have to be met with more violence.

This was a new idea for me in those days.

I explained that Mother Argai had been hurt and almost killed by an attacker intent on harming me and my children. That another young woman had been killed and my tent burned. They were solemn and sorrowful until I mentioned this was Surali's doing. The muttering that arose from that was more than satisfactory.

I knew that Surali's Bittern Court must have a few informers, and perhaps even an active agent or two, among these men. That was too easy an opportunity to pass up. *How* active was a different question. As well as how loyal.

"Even in defeat, retreated from this place, that woman seeks to strike me down. Others, innocents, have again died in my stead by her orders." I squatted low, bringing my face down closer to these men, most of whom were still lying in their blankets as we spoke. "You know that she does not stand for what you wish in life. If any of you were truly her creatures, you would not have troubled to cross the sea to this cold place."

It was the same argument I had used on them before. Selistan was not a society that encouraged people to rise above the station of their birth.

"Every one of you had the bravery to come here. Every one of you works hard now, or seeks to. Most of you will bring families over in time when you have saved enough taels and obols. Surali and her kind do not care for you. Do not care about you. She does not want choice. And so she attacks me, who shows all of you what you might be and who you might become."

Not exactly a true accounting of Surali's motives as I understood them, but not so far from the reality, either. And this casting of her intent would make sense to my countrymen.

Several of them glanced at one of their number. He was skinny, with a large mustache, and seemed to be preoccupied with scratching under his sleeping robe.

That would be my man, then. I continued to play to my audience.

"Someone in this city has hidden a dangerous agent of the Bittern

Court away. The man who tried to kill my babies was dressed in leather head to toe."

"So are you," observed a member of my still awakening audience.

"Well, yes, but that's different. I'm a Lily Blade. Besides, this would-be killer's face was covered, too. Except for the eyes." It had been a strange costume.

"Who is he?" asked the agent, paying closer attention now. "What did he tell you?"

"Mostly he screamed." I let an edged smile tug at my mouth. "People tend to do that when they are dying in pain."

A number of the men winced, including the agent. I stood and stepped over to him. "I know that people sometimes make mistakes," I said gently. "Mistakes can be forgiven." I bent down, my knees creaking and my abdominal muscles complaining as I did so. "But sheltering this killer? That will not be forgiven." With one finger I tapped his sweating forehead. "That will be *punished*."

All these men knew who I was. Every one of them knew my reputation. Just so this fellow, who shook a bit. I popped one of my short knives out of the right sleeve of my leathers and slapped the blade lightly against my left hand. "If you happen to know of someone who might have given this man shelter, I would be pleased to hear of it. I might even forget where I heard it, should what I find bear fruit. Because I will harvest a reckoning for the threat to my children."

"I am a poor man," he gasped.

"We are all poor." The circling point of my short knife had seized his vision.

"I-I am p-poor. Sometimes there is a bit of extra money."

"Sometimes there is." I let the point approach his nose, until he grew cross-eyed. "Sometimes there is forgiveness after confession, too." Speaking brightly, I added, "Which would you rather have just this moment? Forgiveness, or a bit of extra money?"

His gaze fixed on the tip of my blade. "F-forgiveness, Mother Green."

Leaning even closer, I growled in his ear, "Then give me a reason to forgive you, fool."

His words flowed now. "A-a man, one of these whitebellies, in-in-in a uniform. I always m-met him by the great red house on Montane Street. S-sometimes they are needing things written or read back to them in Seliu. I knew they kept one of us inside."

May all these pale bastards be broken on the Wheel! The great red house on Montane Street would have to be the seat of the Reformed Council. Originally a mansion, it had long served as a bank until Lampet and his little band of plotters had set up a second government to compete with the Interim Council that had ruled the city since the fall of the Duke.

Though I'd already abandoned the politics of Copper Downs, they had apparently not abandoned me.

It made sense. Especially given how Surali had worked through the Prince of the City's embassy to manipulate the local government here, when they had been in town.

I slapped my short knife against my palm again. Councilor Lampet and I were due to have a little chat quite soon. "You may keep your life," I said generously to the spy. "But I might suggest new employment."

"Th-thank you, Mother." He scuttled back on hands and knees, leaving a warm puddle behind.

I was pleased that I had not killed him. Perhaps I was growing more mature after all. With a nod to my fascinated countrymen watching in riveted silence, I went back to the bar for my dhal.

As I was preparing to leave, one of the men came up to the bar to speak quietly with me.

"Ghuji, is it?" I said, dredging a name from memory. I signaled the Tavernkeep for a second bowl of dhal. Likely a small enough payment for whatever he had to tell me.

Ghuji nodded, then stared at his feet. I glanced down just in case he was wearing interesting shoes. Horny, callused nails on grubby toes greeted me.

A peasant, as I would have been, had I been allowed to remain in the country of my birth. That was a bit surprising. Most of the Selistani in Copper Downs were either sailors who'd jumped ship or laborers who'd come looking for a different kind of work. Selistani with any decent amount of money had no reason to emigrate, while the peasants and urban beggars had no resources with which to attempt an exodus.

"Are you from the east?" I let a bit of a Bhopuri accent slip into my

Seliu. In Kalimpura, this would have marked me as a hick, but I'd picked up a sufficient handful of regional accents to make a pretense when needed. Sometimes being a hick was useful. People tended to ignore you, for example.

As, I suspected, people ignored Ghuji.

He looked up at me and smiled grimly. "A village in the Sister of Morning Mountains."

That would be the northeast coast of Bhopura. I'd never been there, though I'd glimpsed the peaks from aboard ship when passing Cape Purna.

"A long way from there to here," I said, though his part of Selistan was physically closest to the Stone Coast.

"Longer when there is no path home. My village was burned."

I waited to see if he would say more, or perhaps wanted me to ask, but Ghuji's gaunt smile faded. Now he held my eye.

"What can I do for you here and now?" I asked, taking care with my words. His reason for speaking to me was less clear.

"The man Paavati was telling you of?"

"Yes . . ." Well, at least we were on topic.

"When you saw him, his face was covered with leather."

A statement, not a question. Interesting. "Yes. I could see only his eyes."

"Men like him burned my village. Everyone was being slain. Even the chickens and goats." He paused for a deep, shuddering breath. "They spared me only because they did not realize I had been working down inside our well, repairing the brick courses. I was staying in shadow for hours until the screaming had long stopped and the crackle of flame had died. When I climbed out, I saw them rooting through the ashes of our little temple."

I was both fascinated and appalled. "For what?"

He shrugged. "Our small portion of silver? Our idols? I do not know." Then he leaned close and said something that would stay with me a very long time. "But these men, they are in Kalimpura as well. From there, I think. The beggars know them as the Quiet Men. When their faces are uncovered, they pass as do you and I. When their faces are covered, they kill."

Like Blades, but with far less discretion. I had never heard of this sect or order. Oh, would Mother Vajpai want to know of this.

Assuming she did not already.

I took a stab at the circumstances here in Copper Downs. "This Quiet Man sheltered in the Red House on Montane Street?" The Red House was what the Reformed Council's quarters were called around town, in a fit of particularly poverty-stricken imagination.

Another shrug. "I do not know. But he has not been among us here since the Prince of the City departed."

I pushed the steaming bowl of dhal in front of him. My purse was empty, I had no money to pay this Ghuji, but I could feed him. The Tavernkeep and I had our own understandings.

"My thanks," I said. "But please, a question: Why are you telling me of this now?"

A third and clearly final shrug. "No one will act against the Quiet Men. No one will admit they exist. But you slew one of them. Perhaps knowing what I could tell you will help you slay more."

"He died in a fire that he himself had set," I told Ghuji on impulse. "I made certain of it."

Something flickered in the man's eyes as his shoulders sagged. "Be careful," he said, then turned away, though not without taking his bowl of dhal with him.

I watched him thoughtfully a few moments before releasing my attention. There was a red house to visit on Montane Street. One last time I turned to the Tavernkeep. "It has been a pleasure to know you."

"May your soulpath be broad and rich."

"And yours."

With those words between us, I left, headed for the neighborhood of the old Ducal Palace.

Though it was still yet morning, I was already exhausted. I also buzzed with excitement. After spending months being pregnant, and even just a week tending to my babies, it was good to be out in the world. With a purpose, at that.

I did not propose to take on a building full of guards. The Reformed Council had Lampet's lads, the Conciliar Guard regiment raised by the councilor I trusted least out of any of that lot. The only reason Lampet was not running the city right now was that he had another plan. That, and I had forsworn politics in this place.

It did occur to me that setting fire to the building might be a solution to my problems. A bit messy, but it would smoke out any more Quiet Men or other agents of Surali's who might be lurking there.

Though I had to admit, the clerks and maids and guards who doubtless filled the place were not at fault. Somehow, it didn't seem right to kill them just to get at Lampet and one or two men he might still be sheltering.

I snorted. Motherhood was making me soft.

Lampet had sought harm to my children. I had no doubt it was he who had struck whatever deal with Surali. Anyone who worked to support the councilor was part of the problem. The clerks and maids could go hang if they couldn't see what it was they served.

Still, that did not mean they deserved to die.

By the time I reached Montane Street, I had talked myself out of killing everyone in the place by fire. The next most likely plan seemed to be to broach the front door. That had obvious drawbacks, starting with overenthusiastic or underinformed guards.

Finally I slipped into an alley to look over the back of the Red House. I didn't want to be seen approaching, so I started several blocks up, mugging an innocent clothesline inside someone's courtyard for a shapeless gray cloak to cover my leathers.

No point in announcing myself prematurely if I was not going straight into the visitors' entrance.

Back in my days of training within the Pomegranate Court, I'd spend quite a bit of time reviewing architecture with Mistress Celine. This was for several reasons, not the least of which was that I was expected to become a mistress of a great house, and a wise mistress knew exactly how everything in her domain worked. Chatelaines and majordomos were all to the good, but a family or household could be robbed into penury without proper oversight.

So I was quite familiar with kitchen deliveries, laundry entrances, gardening sheds, carriage houses, even smithies and carpentry shops, as ways in and out of stately homes whose owners thought only of the forecourt, or possibly the mudroom through which one visited one's dogs and horses.

A laundry never truly closed down, not in a large enough place, and certainly the kitchen did not either. Someone had to bake the breads overnight, and keep the stockpots bubbling and the spits turning.

I watched from inside a quiet set of horse stalls across the alley. A neighbor's back extents, unmonitored at the moment in the apparently long-term absence of horses. Having no great affection for those beasts myself, I could understand why even the wealthy might forgo them.

The Red House had active stables. Grooms raced about polishing a high-wheeled carriage to an especially wicked shade of black. I'd have bet a gold obol the interior was red velvet, and that the conveyance was for Councilor Lampet's particular use.

Likewise the kitchen, where in the space of thirty minutes, three different carters made deliveries, along with a dairyman with some particularly difficult wheels of cheese.

Other servants were about as well. These were not the temporary, loyalless hirelings such as Surali had populating her rented mansion during the recent unpleasantness. No, I knew this type. The senior staff would be very proud and jealous of their positions. The understaff would watch one another for any slight or error that might make the difference in advancement. I could kill, or possibly even bluff, my way in, but I could not walk among them as if I were another servant without the alarm being raised.

However, I could arrive on a cart. . . .

I retreated up the alley to await the next worthwhile delivery.

Less than an hour later, I returned to the back of the Red House clucking at a pair of mules who drew a cart loaded with cabbages and root vegetables.

"You ain't Marsby," said a redheaded boy in a clean but threadbare tunic who came out to meet me. He sounded cheerful about that.

"Marsby's been took sick." If by *sick* I meant "tied up in a wood box with his own stockings in his mouth," that was even a true statement.

I hadn't hurt him.

Not much.

"You're foreign," the boy announced. As if this were a notable discovery.

"I've noticed that, yes." I jumped down off the driver's bench and patted one mule on the flank. Like horses, but slower and meaner, I understood them to be. So far they had not argued and had played their part. But then, I figured the mules knew their way with or without me.

The boy fed each of them half an apple as I dropped the gate on the cart and tugged out a crate of rutabagas. "I don't know where to take this," I told him.

He grudgingly took hold of a crate of cabbages. "Marsby carries 'em two at a time."

"I ain't Marsby." I was beginning to wonder how often this lad received a good kicking, and if he knew how richly he deserved such treatment. Now that I was here, I wanted to be inside and about my business before someone of wit noticed me.

The idiot boy led me up three steps to a stone porch, and into the pantry beyond. I set my crate on a table, where an exasperated woman was counting out an inventory of herbs. She glared at me, then went back to her work.

Outside, my little friend had grabbed another crate of cabbage, but stopped to whisper to the mules. That was fine with me. I pushed around him with a crate of potatoes, walked right past the herb counter, and strode into the kitchen.

Such a place. In other circumstances, I would have liked to cook there. A central fire with a massive spit fit for a whole game carcass. Three bread ovens, each with their own firebox. An oil stove *and* a woodstove. A huge butchering counter. A cold room, judging by one overbuilt door. Copper pans hanging above like the rain falling from an explosion in an armory.

Cook's boys and assistants pushed everywhere, through steam and smoke and the smell of some fish meeting its end in a fry of olive oil, lemons, and capers. I closed my eyes, took a deep breath, then shoved my crate into the hands of a passing scullery maid. "Here, these are in the wrong place," I said in my best, and very genuine, quality-accented Petraean.

Contrasting with my dark skin, I knew it confused her, but that was the point. Confusion and continued motion: those were my weapons right now.

And being here, I was glad I had not simply blocked the doors and fired the house.

With that thought, I grabbed up a jelly pan and strode confidently toward the doors that led into the main house.

A hand grasped at me. Someone nearly had their wrist broken for their trouble, but I stifled the impulse and turned.

This was Cook. Not a cook, or even the cook. Just Cook. The tyrant of the kitchen, and in a great house, the only servant over whom the chatelaine or majordomo had no real power. She was red-faced with stringy hair and piercing gray eyes. Unlike most cooks, she was also quite thin. Her dress was dark blue in a cut a respectable grocer's wife might have worn. This in contrast to the simple striped smocks of the maids and undercooks. I noted the skin of her fingers was peeling. She shook slightly as she grasped me.

"You do not belong."

"No." I tried for honesty first. More persuasive methods were still readily available, and I was close to the door, in any case. "I am here on urgent purpose for the councilor, and preferred not to be announced through the front."

Her eyes narrowed, but she did not immediately reject my explanation. I was right in guessing that Lampet was the sort to have skulks and sneaks coming in at all hours. "Don't your sort usually present themselves to Master Roberti at the little gate?"

"I don't know any Master Roberti," I replied. "I report elsewhere."

Cook's glare did not change. "There is no Master Roberti. Good that you did not lie. Go on, then, but give me back my jelly pan."

I handed it to her, pulled up the hood on my stolen robe, and slipped into the hallway beyond. Just as well I had not fought in the kitchen. The world needed more cooks and fewer assassins.

Beyond was a reasonably conventional layout. The Red House was a turreted folly of the sort popular in the last century of the Duke's reign, and so did not have the sweeping, pillared front hall of so many older homes and buildings of its class. Rather, a long, full-height corridor joined the back to the front with staircases rising from each side to internal balconies on the second and third storey. There would be a ballroom nearby, a parlor, and a formal dining room. Bedrooms upstairs, with possibly another set of parlors and studios on the second floor.

All of it offices now, of course. Though this hall was empty of clerks and their files—nothing like the chaos at the Textile Bourse, where the Interim Council carried on the messy business of the city.

Realizing that I did not see bureaucrats at their work here, I understood that the Reformed Council wanted to rule, but were not so much interested in governing. While I could sympathize with that view as a matter of principle, as a practical matter, it seemed a terrible way to run a city.

Lampet would be up there, I was certain of it. He wasn't the sort to have an easily accessible office on the ground floor. One would have to walk a distance through halls to reach him. Then wait a while.

Lacking my misappropriated jelly pan, I swept a Hanchu vase of dried roses thin and crackling as paper off a delicate Siengurae period side table and trotted up the nearest stairs. One of the best ways to be invisible in a busy place was to carry something and look certain of yourself. The people upstairs would not be jealous of their positions, and so to them a servant was just mobile furniture. All the better for remaining unnoticed.

So long as I didn't run into any senior maids up there.

I walked at a servant's pace—swift without hurrying—past the stairs toward the far end of the hall on the second storey. It seemed wiser to scout all the doors before I started opening them and blundering into people. At the corresponding T-intersection on the east end of the house, I turned and saw two of Lampet's lads in their Conciliar Guard uniforms. Big lumps, as they all seemed to be.

He was the kind of leader who distrusted intelligence in his underlings. I could work with that.

"Fresh flowers for m'lord," I muttered as I approached the door with my chin tucked down. Fresh my ass—these were dry as Mother Iron's twat, but you work with what you have.

One of the guards huffed elaborately, then deigned to open the door.

I whispered a shy thank-you and stepped through.

Lampet's office had been a solarium once. Angled glass formed much of the ceiling and outer wall, while light flooded across the green and white tiled floor. Unlike the rest of the house, which was paneled in classically dark wood, this room had been finished in something blond and very fine-grained. A set of green leather wingback chairs was drawn up by a fireplace that had obviously seen much use in the recent winter. A large, very clean desk stood under the window, a bar nearby displaying a generous selection of wines and liquors.

Councilor Lampet sat behind it dressed as if for a court appearance and picking at his fingernails with a letter opener—no, I realized, a stiletto much like the one the Quiet Man had tried to use against me. A killer's weapon rather than the broad, honest blades of a fighter such as I carried. This man had always struck me as resembling a ferret. The stiletto was his fangs. Beyond that, Lampet's pale, perfectly oiled hair and pointed face did nothing to dispel that impression.

I shuffled toward the fireplace to put down my flowers on one of the side tables by the chairs there. As I leaned forward, Lampet spoke.

"I hardly expected you to come here, young lady."

His voice held all the vicious oiliness I'd come to associate with the man. He *knew;* he'd probably known since I'd arrived with Marsby's cart. No one in the house had tipped me. They all *did* serve this man, body and soul.

I should have set fire in the first place and the maids be damned. For Cook, I would reserve a special place on her own roasting spit as the flames raced through her kitchen.

There was nothing for it but to face him with whatever momentum I had left. That was my fighting style, after all—to just keep hitting until everyone was down.

So I turned, palming my short knives. He wouldn't be fooled for more than a second or two, but the long knife in its thigh scabbard was too much in this moment. "I come and go where I please," I told him, striding toward the desk.

To my right, the door clicked open. The two guards stepped in. When I glanced at them, they now seemed quite a bit more intelligent and alert than they had out in the hallway.

"You will stop where you are," Lampet said mildly.

I hadn't gotten this far in life by listening to scum like him, so I stepped right up to the edge of the desk. "Or wh—?"

My question was interrupted by a meaty hand on my shoulder. I twisted away from the grip only to run into a swinging fist with my left temple.

At least it didn't hold a blade, I thought as I staggered backwards. One of my short knives rattled on the floor until a booted foot stamped down on it. The guard with his hand now on my right arm twisted it back until my shoulder and elbow began to pop.

He was about to dislocate my joints. Then I would be under his control, nearly incapacitated by pain and dead at Lampet's next whim.

Short knife fully in my own fist, I turned *with* the twist, allowing my arm to be torn from its socket in return for putting a blade in the big man's neck from an unexpected direction. It slid in like he was made of butter. I didn't bother to swallow my scream of unnerving pain as blood sprayed in a fountaining jet from the slashed artery. He convulsed, releasing my arm, which hung useless now.

I was already moving, spinning rapidly into the other goon who was drawing a sword of his own. In that moment, I knew I would win, because only a fool brings a sword to a knife fight. We were too damned close for the reach of his blade.

He wasn't a total fool, however. The second guard ducked my erratic swing at his neck and got the sword between us as a shield of sorts. I slammed into his chest, tried to hug him as if we were lovers, and slipped my knife up under the back of his ring-mailed jerkin to find one of his kidneys.

I hoped.

The blade went in easily, but the bastard was tougher than I gave him credit for. He didn't drop screaming. Instead, he hugged me back with his free hand, putting pressure on my dislocated shoulder. I nearly blacked out from the pain, and my knees gave way. Only my opponent's grip kept me standing.

Lampet's stiletto appeared before my eyes, the tip waving in a tiny circle between my face and the chest of the panting guard. At least *he* was in agony, too. While focusing on the weapon in front of me, I stirred my short knife inside the guard's body.

"Sir . . . ," he grunted, then released me as we both collapsed. I found myself on the floor with my legs trapped beneath two hundred pounds of armored thug.

And I had lost my remaining short knife.

I concentrated on not losing consciousness as well.

The councilor stood over me now, still gripping his weapon. He looked excited—face flushed, panting, that narrow blade trembling in his hands. "You need some more scars, Mistress Green," he whispered. "I shall give you many before we are done with each other."

My free hand, the one not immobilized by the agonizing fire in my shoulder, slapped at the floor around me. The other short knife was here somewhere, the first one I'd dropped.

Lampet leaned down and slid the tip of the stiletto inside one of my nostrils. Oh, by the gods, I had done just this to his man. He flicked the blade up in a spray of blood and shot of exquisite agony.

My hand found something rigid. My blade? I tugged at it.

The damned sword. I did not have the leverage to lift the weapon. So I dragged it toward me, careless of the scrape upon the floor.

Lampet studied the blood on his knife. "You bleed just like everyone else." His thin smile was terrifying. "I don't know if you've heard this, but people in this city say you're a demon from the fiery hells of the south."

"Not all of them," I gasped. Keep him talking, keep myself awake and aware, pull that stupid, heavy, useless sword a little closer.

"All the ones that count."

"Do you even *know* any women?" I asked, then was promptly horrified at my own words. Why was I twitting this man who was working at killing me slowly? He might decide to kill me quickly.

And where are the rest of his guards? Lampet had an entire regiment at his disposal, at least in theory.

"Does it matter? You won't see them anymore."

He leaned close again, focusing on me. My mind raced. Was this man crazy? Cruel? Obsessed?

Not that it mattered. What he was, was standing over me with a weapon.

I noticed my grip on the sword was firm. That was good.

What was I planning to do with it? I'd had a purpose when I first grabbed it.

Something pained my nose again. A shape swam above me. Big. Threatening. Holding power over me. All I had was one arm and one sword and one chance.

He began to lean over a third time, and I shoved the overlong blade into his mouth before he came too close for me to use it.

What sort of idiot brings a sword to a knife fight, anyway?

I awoke, choking and sputtering. Blood filled my mouth. After a moment of panic, I realized it was not my blood. That created another moment of panic.

Amazingly, my head cleared, probably due to the agonizing pain from my left shoulder.

How long?

Seconds, seconds. Lampet lay next to me, heels drumming against the floor. His cheek was torn wide open. Blood poured out of his open mouth as if it were a wellspring of the stuff. A sword—no, *the* sword—was on the floor between us.

Time to get moving. Oh, by all the gods, I hurt.

I rolled sideways as far as I could, forcing my shoulder back where it belonged. *That* sensation caused my vision to fade into darkness, but I clung to consciousness. After a few deep, ragged breaths, I felt a bit more in possession of myself.

With the sword, I levered and cut my way out from under the fallen guard.

By the time I was on my feet, I looked as if I'd been through a slaughterhouse from the wrong end forward. I found one of my short knives, though bending to pick it up was a brutal experience. I slashed all three throats before me, just to make sure. I didn't want anyone jumping up and surprising me before I could recover a bit more.

None of them bled much, so I'd probably done it right the first time.

To get out of here was another project. I'd killed my best hostage, but, well, he was still here. I dropped to my knees and sawed awhile at Lampet's neck with the borrowed sword. This kind of work was the ruin of a good blade, no better than using it for cooking. After a while it occurred to me to use my short knife, which had kept such a wonderful edge just lately. I quickly had a piece of Lampet the size of a decent pork roast, and the oily bastard hadn't had a damned thing to say to me while I was doing it.

"Sorry about the hair," I whispered into one of his cold ears.

The liquor cabinet beckoned me. I did not so much want a drink as

I wanted to make a fire. The office would be so much more cheerful with a bit of warming. I propped Lampet up on top of a wine bottle, using the slender neck to support his head from within his own ragged throat.

"Thank you for stocking so much of the distilled drinks," I told him. "Unlike wine, some of that will burn."

He stared back at me, but still didn't have much to say.

Opening the blessed things one-handed was difficult but not impossible. Glass breaks, after all. I went through them as best I could, sniffing to see how high the proof was if I didn't recognize the contents by scent or the shape of the bottle.

What would burn, I poured out on Lampet's desk. Why the man didn't have the decency to keep drapes I could set alight, I did not know. No books, either. What kind of mind kept an office with no books in it?

Eventually I had a decent puddle dripping across the finished cherrywood and down into the drawers. "Stay here," I told Lampet, then staggered to the fireplace, where there were lucifer matches among the tools.

That set a nice pale flame going on the desk. It was the best I could do just then.

"Are you being ready to go?" I realized I was speaking Seliu, which Lampet didn't understand. So I apologized in Petraean. "I'm sorry, I don't meant to be rude."

With my good hand, I managed to wedge his hair into the fingers of my bad hand. His dead weight at the end of my arm was a screaming horror, but I very much needed to carry a weapon that I could have some hope of using. Threatening people with a dead councilor didn't seem very helpful.

"And we are off." Short knife in my grip, it was difficult to open the door, but I didn't want to put anything down for fear I would not be able to pick it up once more. The office was already filling with smoke, so I turned around and went to the glass wall of the solarium instead. Fewer guards that way, too.

I smashed the butt of my short knife into one of the big windows. The glass starred, then shattered outward. Some halfway decent kicks cleared the framing until the hole was big enough for me to step through. I looked down at a small garden about a rod below me.

"You think I can make the drop?" I asked the councilor.

A surprised yard boy looked up at me. So I jumped down upon him. Lampet's servants deserved no mercy, either.

A few blocks away, I turned to see a column of smoke rising behind me. It wasn't much, and they'd surely have the flames out soon, but I promised myself that if I had time before I sailed to Kalimpura, I'd go back and do a proper job of burning out the Red House and everyone in it. Even the accursed maids. And especially Cook.

For now, all I could do was keep walking. It did amaze me how many people found business elsewhere at my approach. I kept up a running chatter with Lampet, whose conversation seemed much improved over my previous experiences of him.

Under the old Duke, a bloody woman carrying a severed head would probably have been stopped in the street. These days, well, the world wasn't quite the same.

Which was fine with me.

By the time I reached the Textile Bourse on Lyme Street, I was singing both halves of a duet with Lampet and being followed by a crowd of small boys. No one was guarding the entrance there anymore, and they still hadn't fixed the place up properly from the last time I'd damaged it.

Well, the last two times.

I banged through the front door, shouting about the sorry state of affairs in Copper Downs, and swung Lampet around to give him a good look at the mob of clerks and their assistants who had all glanced up at my entrance. They did not make me feel welcome.

"Nast," I said, dredging names up from a memory that had grown unaccountably fuzzy. "Or Jeschonek. *Now.*"

Somehow my short knife was still in my good hand. I wondered where my other one had gotten to—I was sure to miss it soon. More than two dozen pairs of eyes watched the tip waver as I pointed toward the black and white marble stairs. My friend smelled funny, I realized, though it was far too soon for him to have begun to rot in earnest.

"In chambers, Lady Green," someone finally said in a choked voice.

"Brilliant." I lurched into motion, slipped briefly on some blood that had pooled on the floor. "And get someone to clean this place up. You people are pigs."

They were no happier to see me upstairs, but someone must have rung a bell or suchlike, because the upper hall with its senior clerks and Important People was mostly cleared when I reached the top landing. Mr. Nast, chief clerk of the Interim Council and a dreadfully thin man with a mind as narrow as a ruler and sharp as one of my knives, stood at the far end before the door decorated with stained glass images illustrating the wonders of felt.

"You have never placed your faith in appointments." His voice was freighted with disapproval as I staggered down the hall toward him.

Lampet was becoming heavy, but he was my passport into the meeting I planned to have next. "I brought my own councilor," I said brightly.

"So you did. Councilor Jeschonek and Councilor Staggs are meeting now over the disposition of the gate tax." He took a long glance at my little friend dangling in my hand, then: "I don't suppose you'd be prepared to wait."

By now I was nose to nose with the man. Nast was one of the few people in Copper Downs for whom I had any true respect, but at the moment he was just being ridiculous. "Do I *look* like I am prepared to wait?" I pulled my short knife away from his face with a muttered apology. "Besides, this city doesn't even have gates."

Nast sighed theatrically, opened the door, and announced me. "The Lady Green, to see Councilor Jeschonek."

"I thought—" Rising from his chair with a look of irritation on his face, Jeschonek interrupted himself on seeing me. He was as big and blond as ever, still looking the part of a man who'd worked the docks all his life before entering the rougher trade of politics.

Lampet's head landed on the table with a meaty thump. "I have once more resolved the governance of this city in your favor," I said. "Councilor Lampet was uncooperative." Carefully I tucked my short knife way, with a curious glace at Councilor Staggs, who'd risen to his feet along with Jeschonek. I'd never heard of him before. He had a mixed complexion and almond eyes, as if his grandmother had been Hanchu, and he was dressed like any prosperous merchant of this city might be—dark woolen pants, bloused pale silk shirt with a maroon-edged ruffle, and a cutaway clawhammer coat in a similar maroon. Somewhere nearby would be a tall furred hat; I was just certain of it.

"You look like a steward," I told him.

Staggs opened his mouth to reply, but Jeschonek urgently waved him to silence. Then: "You may have done us a great service here, Green." He eyed Lampet, who stared back blankly. "Though as usual, I must wonder at the cost."

"Oh, the Red House is not finished paying." My vision was beginning to cloud, darkness creeping in, and my left arm had transitioned from flaring pain to an alarming dullness. "I owe them another visit before I depart this city."

"I would take it as a great favor if you would refrain from setting fire to or otherwise destroying any more of our city's historic buildings."

Offhand, I couldn't recall the last time I'd destroyed a historic building, but I took his point. Oddly, my thinking was becoming more clear even as the pain and horror of the past hour were overtaking my consciousness.

"Now I must make my leave," I said shortly. "With luck, I shall never return to Copper Downs." Simply remaining standing seemed to be an increasingly great trial.

"Let us all hope for luck." Jeschonek stepped close, braced my arm, then to both our surprise, I am certain, drew me into a tight hug. "You are the bravest, strangest woman I ever knew," he whispered in my ear. "Now leave these shores before someone finally succeeds in killing you."

"You're lucky I already put my knife away," I whispered back as he released me.

I received the first genuine smile I'd seen on Jeschonek in the time since the whole Federo mess had started. He took my words for what I'd intended, and I realized there was another man here I respected as much as Mr. Nast.

Nodding at Councilor Staggs, I stumbled back into the hall. I left Councilor Lampet with his fellows. Though I would miss my little talks with the bastard. At the last, he had become a great listener. Much better than he had been in life, I was certain of it.

Nast had two decently sized young fellows set to prop me up.

"Chives and Innerny will escort you where you need to go, Lady Green." He showed me a thick folder tied with twine. "Your repatriation bonds, and papers for passage aboard the kettle ship *Prince Enero*. She sails tomorrow for Lost Port and then Kalimpura."

"How did you know to book me passage?" I asked through a deepening sense of haze.

"I have booked you passage on every departing ship these past four months. Please believe me that it has been very much worth the effort. Good-bye, young lady. I wish you well."

From him, I believed that.

We stumbled down the stars, my decently sized young fellows and I. "Bustle Street," I murmured. They seemed to take my meaning.

The lower floor clapped for me as I left. I was glad to note a boy with a mop cleaning the mess by the door.

When we reached the Bustle Street Lazaret, I was reciting ancient doggerel from the *Portfolio Indicus*. Summoning the last of my otherwise-vanished strength, I banged on the well-used armored door, shouting, "Drinks for me and my men, by the nether hells, or I'll have the place down around your ears."

I was standing only by virtue of Chives and Cream, or whatever their names were.

In retrospect, I might have chosen a calmer approach. Still, the small, barred viewing port opened and a crossbow pointed out, to be replaced almost immediately by a concerned face. "Green?"

"None other, and her brothers," I announced.

Cream, or maybe Chives, leaned close. "With the Interim Council's compliments, ma'am, and we're very much hoping you can take care of her. She's been hurt bad, and has gone out of her head."

The door swung open and I was snatched within. "You're all over blood," a voice exclaimed. "Is it hers?" another voice asked anxiously. Someone shouted for hot water and a filled bath.

I cried for strong drink until they gave it to me. In the bath my breasts leaked milk and I cried for my babies until someone fetched them, along with Ponce and a small knot of acolytes. Nursing my children, I cried for sleep until they left me alone in crisp sheets with my pains and my family.

Lastly, I cried for Lampet, though I could not even now say why, all these years later.

I awoke some hours later. My body was a giant bruise. Federo and Marya slept, blessedly. There was something that badly needed doing, but I had lost track of it. So I fell asleep again, instead.

Morning brought Euphronia, the scarred fat woman who minded the door and kept the business affairs of the lazaret. With her she had Ilona carrying a bowl of gruel, along with a plate featuring a slice of rough, dark bread and an old horse apple. Not that the babies wanted that, but she'd procured goat's milk as well for them, in a sugar tit.

Sitting up hurt like fire. My nose itched abominably. Still, I was so pleased to see Ilona. My heart skipped a bit, and I could not wait for her to offer me the food so I could breathe in her scent.

I allowed her to place a spoon in my mouth over and over. It would be a while before my left arm worked properly, and my right was busy holding Marya. Besides, it felt good to have her tending me closely.

"We stitched your nostrils last night," Ilona told me.

"They hurt," I complained. I was embarrassed at the petulance in my voice.

Euphronia gave me a strange look. "A lot more than that should hurt, judging by your bruises. And you had enough blood on you to make corpses of several others."

"Only one or two," I said, feeling sullen. No one ever believed in what I did. "Or maybe three," I added in a burst of honesty. Then, to make up for it: "I fell while visiting a friend."

Ilona snorted. "And the fire at the Red House was a coincidence."

Memory flashed into being in a flood of embarrassed triumph. She knew me too well, and besides, we'd shared the same hardheaded education in political and social realities back at the Factor's house. "Those bastards arranged the attack on you at the Temple of Endurance."

"Ah," she said. "What did you do about it, precisely?"

"I had an edgy conversation with Councilor Lampet of the Reformed Council." I giggled. "I suspect they do not have a quorum anymore. And I turned Lampet over to the Interim Council."

What had happened to my promise to stay out of the politics of the city?

Well, the politics of the city had not stayed out of me, for one thing.

Another memory stirred. "There is a folder. Where is it?"

Ilona pointed at a sheaf of documents on a small table beside my bed. "This?"

"Please," I said. "Read it. I believe that I have passage on a ship to Kalimpura. We will need more, for you and Ponce and the babies, as well as Mothers Vajpai and Argai." Guilty, I recalled Ilona's own circumstances. "How are the two of you?"

"My head aches," Ilona said simply. "And Mother Argai is still ill with whatever drug or poison was used on her."

"He was a Quiet Man." I knew only what Ghuji had told me, which was little enough, but if they used poisons, they were even more dangerous and despicable than I had realized.

"And you dealt with him." Her voice was soft, but her face pained. "I thank you for my life, Green."

It was clear enough what truly troubled her. "We are leaving soon to reclaim your daughter."

Ilona glanced down at the papers. "On this afternoon's tide!" she exclaimed. "Two cabins aboard *Prince Enero*."

I tried to sit up, but my left arm simply would not take my weight. Then the agony from even making that effort overcame me completely.

When my words came back to me, everyone was already in motion. I tried to give some instructions, but no one seemed to want them. Even my suggestion about securing a third cabin was already under discussion before I had managed to make it.

Finally I simply lay back and let them arrange these next steps. Clearly, I could not do everything today. For a while I worried about Marya's silk, and mine which I had not sewn last night either, but I realized Ilona would not forget those.

My only real regret was not paying another call on the Red House before my departure. I did not regret failing to give Councilor Lampet funerary rites, though I did find myself promising to pay my respects to the shades of his guards.

They took me down to the docks around midday in the back of an ice wagon that had been pressed into service. The bed was covered with a canvas top, and filled with damp straw, clumps of sawdust, and thick, wet blankets. Ilona and Mother Vajpai came along. My babies did not.

"Where are the children?" I asked, suppressing a flash of panic that Marya and Federo had not been brought down with me. They'd been taken away not half an hour before, "to be changed."

"Ponce took the babies," Ilona said with a glance at Mother Vajpai, who nodded. "With the training handle."

Interesting. "Are we in this much danger?"

Mother Vajpai snorted. "Someone killed a councilor of this city yesterday. There are groups of very angry armed men about searching for the culprit."

". . . and all three of our Lily Blades are disabled," I said, finishing the thought. Mother Vajpai would probably never be a fully effective fighter again, Mother Argai was reportedly quite ill, and I could not move my left arm, nor overcome a headache that made my skull feel far too large and far too soft.

"Even the Interim Council's thugs cannot do much once we are aboard," Ilona added. "Prince Enero is a Sunward kettle ship. They have much better weapons than anyone in Copper Downs."

Which was true. I was aware of the rumors of firearms and lightning jars and bombs-of-fire. Michael Curry carried such a weapon, small enough to be held in his hand, when I had slain him aboard Crow Wing. The Stone Coast had only the most primitive and useless guns, as much a danger to their wielder as anyone. Very few here found reason to trifle with purchasing a better quality from afar. Likewise Selistan, where even matters of violence tended to be resolved very personally, and ideally with considerable finesse.

Politics did not benefit from blowing up palaces. Well, except in the case of the Red House.

So I sat back and listened to our progress, trying to gain a sense of the route the drover took by gauging the surrounding noises and odors, and heeding the changing echoes of the cobbles, pavers, and bricks that had become so familiar beneath my feet.

At the docks, Prince Enero was moored alongside the Gramonde Wharf. That was a bit interesting in its own right, as Gramonde handled very little cargo, instead servicing the quiet ships of the wealthy, as well as courier packets and other vessels whose masters desired limited attention from those on shore. As a side benefit of that, Gramonde also enjoyed far less of the fish-guts-and-tide-wrack reek that characterized so much of any working waterfront.

Did the Harbormaster play a role in this? Paulus Jessup had been cagey about the politics of the city since the fall of the Duke some four years past. Or perhaps the ship's captain simply liked paying higher mooring fees and demurrage.

The ice wagon clattered slowly away from where we'd been dropped off. The women around me gathered baggage and checked papers while I took my last look at Copper Downs. It was nice to be free of my own responsibilities for once.

I found to my own surprise that I was sorry to be leaving. Even from there I could spot many familiar landmarks. The sense of direction in my head supplied more hidden from view by the folds of land or the sides of warehouses. The last remaining section of the ancient wall, now marking the boundary of the Ivory Quarter well within the city's current extents. To the east, the Dockmarket edging down to the water. A string of familiar taverns. The ridge to the north where the Duke's old palace stood, not to mention the Red House.

The Temple Quarter was far away, as was the Velviere District and the Temple of Endurance there. I had not bidden a proper farewell to the ox god, but I knew he would understand. Most of my good-byes had been rushed or omitted. This city did not want to let me go.

"We must board, Green," said Mother Vajpai gently in Seliu. Her hand lay upon my good right arm. My left arm we had bound up for this trip across town, judging the constraint less painful and dangerous than the possibility of me being jarred along the way, or catching myself against the gate of the wagon or a stray rope while boarding.

"Not yet." I had one more departure to observe. "I'll want a candle, some matches, and, well, some wine or flowers."

"There is no one to woo here."

Humor? Now? I shot Mother Vajpai a hard look. "If you will not help me in this, give me an obol or two and let me sort it for myself. I'll be perhaps thirty minutes."

Mother Vajpai appealed to Ilona, saying in her passable Petraean, "She wants a candle and a flower."

Ilona shrugged, casting me a rueful smile. "This is Green." She

called over Wencilla, one of our escorts from the Bustle Street Lazaret's developing handle—a promising girl of strong frame unlikely to
marry well, as she lacked both family and beauty. "Please fetch Mother
Green a candle and a flower."

"And lucifer matches," I said. "Wine if you cannot find a few blossoms."

Wencilla nodded and trotted off. A chandler would carry what I
needed, but only if I wished a box of candles or a cask of wine. She
might have better luck with a decently stocked tavern.

This was not my problem, either.

I sat down on a pitted iron bollard and watched Ponce pass my
children and *their* bags back and forth with another young woman
from the lazaret while they readied for the ship. I would need to feed
the babies soon, I knew from my own aches, but not out here on the
Gramonde Wharf.

Where the bags had come from, I did not know. All our belongings had burned with the tent. The mysterious, collaborative economy
of women had produced them, no doubt, through the lazaret and its
many friends both high and low in this city. I had never really been a
part of that connection, having not been raised with an open kitchen
door out of which to pass gossip or just the hours.

Still, I respected the connection. It was the same sisterhood, after
all, in its deepest form, that stood behind first Marya-the-late-goddess,
and then Mother Iron who followed her. It was my great hope that
Marya-my-infant-daughter would take her place among that world
someday.

For my children, I realized, I prized ordinariness above all things.
This city had been captor and prison and fighting pit for me. Kalimpura would with any luck at all simply be *home* for them.

My thoughts darkened in that vein until Wencilla returned with
two fat beeswax candles only a little burned down; a box of lucifer
matches; a pair of small, early roses; and a half-empty bottle of wine.
All of it was in a string bag a woman could carry one-handed.

"I judged speed more important than the finest quality," she said
by way of apology.

"You judged correctly," I replied in my kindest voice. Her basic
common sense cheered me somewhat. "I will return," I told her, as well
as Mother Vajpai, who hovered nearby.

A watergate opened from Below near the Gramonde Wharf, but I did not just then have the ability to make the climb down to it. Not with my left arm so thoroughly useless. I knew of a grating on Montrose Street, the road that ran a block inland parallel to these docks, but again, I did not think I could lift my way into it. I glanced at Wencilla. "Will you come with me part of the way?"

Prince Enero's kettle whistle shrieked a long blast, follow by two short. She would be sailing within the hour. There was not much time.

We walked swiftly as I could but in silence. I pretended at a peace I did not yet, or perhaps would never, feel. Montrose Street was lined with go-downs and the offices of small traders and freight brokers and the like, along with the sorts of businesses that catered in turn to them and their clients. There were far more horses tied up here than were in similar places in Kalimpura, where most people managed their affairs on foot. Quite a few carts, too, but I realized I saw the mounts of both couriers and men of substance.

The grating was in a little stretch of ragged grass, just behind a statue of Lord Shallot slaying the Great Worm. The statue itself was covered with bird droppings and painted scrawls, and not been attended to for far more years than I had been alive.

That was fine with me.

"Can you please open the grate?" I asked Wencilla.

She studied the metal. "There is a lock."

Surprised, I looked. Someone had indeed brazed a hasp to the metalwork and placed a new lock. A rush of frustrated anger reddened my vision. I did not know who might have done that or why, and in this moment I silently cursed them.

I set down my string bag and drew my remaining short knife to see if I could flick at either the hasp or the lock's loop. It was a dreadful thing to do to a good blade, but time was short and getting shorter.

To my shock, the hasp cut loose under a light pressure from my short knife. Pulling it back to study the shiny, fresh-sliced metal, I recalled that the god Blackblood's own blood had stained my pair of blades.

And they had cut all too well since then. Frighteningly so. If I had not been so hurried and distracted, I would have seen it already for myself.

Thoughtfully, I slid the point into a gap in the grate. With a bit of effort, I cut one of the cross bars in two.

This. I'd had two weapons like *this,* and in my stupor after the fight there had left one of them behind at the Red House. I hoped Councilor Lampet appreciated the mighty grave gift I never intended to send with him from this world.

With luck, someone had simply put it away, or dropped it in the smith's scrap bin. I hated to think of this knife's mate loose in Copper Downs. I hated even more to think of it not in my hands.

I sat back while Wencilla opened the grate. Fortunate, that she was strong and large enough to heft the dead weight of the rusted metal. One-handed and slow, I managed to descend the ladder. At my request, she came partway down with the string bag, then scuttled back up once I'd claimed my burden. The stinking darkness of Below required a certain familiarity before one could be remotely comfortable within it.

A few steps away from the dim light of the grate's shaft, I squatted down and began my ritual. At least this bit of tunnel was not a flowing sewer. Small blessings were where you found them.

I set out my candles, closed my eyes against the flare of the match, then lit the tapers. Fire Below was generally a very bad idea for several quite sensible reasons, but I needed to do this. I placed the flowers before the candles, scattered a few drops of wine, and put the bottle between them. Finally I pricked my finger—for I was afraid to slit my palm with this god-struck blade, lest it rip my hand all the way through unintended—and bled a few drops with the wine.

Libation, among the oldest ceremonies; candles for honor and prayer; and flowers for the women who were protected by Desire and Her daughters.

"Mother Iron," I said aloud. "You hear me, I am certain." Such prayers were never wrong, because an inattentive god would know no different, while one who was present would be pleased by the flattery. "I am leaving this place. Leaving you behind, along with all the others who have touched me, or whom I have touched." I squeezed a few more drops of blood. "Grant whatever protection is yours for the passage ahead, both to me and those who travel with me. Let Laris and the women of the lazaret serve you as best they can, and watch over them and all women here. And finally, I thank you."

I added a scattering of tears to the offering, then rose on creaking knees with my balance upset to walk back to the ladder.

Before I mounted the slimed metal rungs, I looked back. One of the candles had gone out already. The other guttered in a gust of hot, metal-scented air that reached me like an oven door had been slammed open.

She was close by, then, my tulpa-turned-goddess. I wished her well against the Saffron Tower should they send more agents after the defeated Iso and Osi, and began to climb. Beneath my feet, a great, muscled hand stripped of its flesh touched the lowest rung, visible in the light from above.

So Skinless had been watching over me as well. And through him, the god Blackblood.

I looked down and said, "Farewell, friend. May you find whatever it is you desire most from your god."

Once above, Wencilla replaced the grate and we hurried back to the ship before she cast off without us. My babies needed me, and I desperately wanted more time to rest, and a cabin to rest in. Kalimpura was two or three weeks' voyage distant, depending on weather and the seas. I had no illusions that I would be fully prepared for my return there, no matter how long the voyage took.

At Sea, Neither Lost Nor Forgotten

❧

DESPITE MY RESOLVE to rest, I found myself watching from the stern rail as *Prince Enero* sailed from Copper Downs. Kettle ships were not at the mercy of the winds, but wave and current nonetheless pushed her just like any sailing vessel. Still, she could leave the harbor without either the towing or the careful tacking that our own Stone Coast vessels would require. Or, indeed, Selistani. Neither the people of my birth nor my reluctantly adopted home had the trick of building the great steam kettles ourselves. The few such iron-hearted and iron-hulled ships that were flagged out of ports along the Storm Sea had been bought at great cost from the Sunward cities that held such knowledge close to hand. Even then, their masters still required engineers hired from those lands to operate and maintain the vessels.

Prince Enero was flagged from the place that built her, a city known as Bas Gronegrim. Though I would someday learn much more of the cities of the Sunward Sea, that meant nothing to me then. Besides which, my mind was at that time still much on Copper Downs receding before me.

As our distance increased beneath a trailing cloud of wheeling gulls, my vantage strengthened. The rising land of the city unfolded before me, until I could see the domes and spires of the Temple Quarter, the walls around the old mine shaft where Chowdry was building Endurance's temple, and even the site where the burnt shell of the Factor's house still stood, monument to the long imprisonment of my childhood. I was disappointed that the ruins themselves were too low for me to spot from this distance. My attention traced through the city, my mind following familiar streets and their corresponding—and sometimes conflicting—passages below.

The hills beyond were visible, albeit hazy from the smokes of commerce, industry, and cooking that tens of thousands of people living close together will make. Those slopes were in turn the foothills of the more distant mountains that the Petraeans called the High Hills. Through them I could trace a route to Ilona's abandoned cottage and the graves where Mistress Danae, my last surviving human teacher from the old days, still slept in her endless dreams of madness. Beyond even those High Hills, the Blue Mountains loomed on the purpling horizon. I had never visited that home of the pardines I was unsure I would ever meet again.

The wind took my tears as fast as my eyes could shed them. I was thankful no one stood close enough to mark my face just then. There was nothing for me to mourn there. Only memories to leave behind: lost years, many deaths, and the birth of my children. I returned to Kalimpura to rescue our missing hostages, but in my heart I intended to stay in Selistan's great city. The brawling, hot chaos of my own people was my place, even if I would never truly be one of them.

My fellow Selistani saw me as a northern slave, who never talked quite right and never quite understood everything. I knew this from my time in the Temple of the Silver Lily. I also knew that I was loved and respected there. Most important, the ghosts around the Duke and the echoes of his power that never ceased to devil me in Copper Downs could not so easily trouble me across the waters of the Storm Sea in distant Kalimpura. Or at least so I'd hoped at that time.

Eventually the city was a rough blur on the horizon. I could see another kettle ship making from the harbor for the open sea, its plume of smoke serving as a banner to mark its passage. My left arm was growing less numb and more painful, and my breasts ached. I went to see to my children, and rest awhile. The group of us could plot our arrival over the weeks to come. Corinthia Anastasia and Samma wanted rescuing, Surali awaited my vengeance, and surely affairs in the Temple of the Silver Lily cried to be set right.

All that beckoned from some point in the future. That day was for departing.

We called at Lost Port three days later. It was the easternmost of the Stone Coast cities, and marked with great, curious ruins both above and beneath the waves that I longed to explore. Instead, I kept to our cabin and waited out the short time at the wharf there. The captain swiftly put *Prince Enero* out to sea again, for this was a place with no profit in tarrying beyond the time required to discharge and take on cargo.

Once bound south by southwest on the open water, we soon found the Storm Sea living up to its name. We were far enough into the spring for the cold cyclones of winter to leave off, but still towering waves rolled across our course. *Prince Enero* was sufficiently powerful to turn into them, and large enough to ride them without much fear of foundering, but the experience was most unpleasant as a passenger. I could only imagine what would happen to a little vessel like Chowdry's lost *Chittachai* in such conditions.

I told Ilona and Ponce I wanted to go outside and watch the racing water.

"Are you insane?" he demanded, clutching Federo close. Ponce had struggled down the interior passage from his cabin to ours this morning, after it became clear the stewards would not be setting out a morning meal.

Looking at my leathers to wonder how they would fare in a vigorous saltwater wind, I replied absently, "No, just fascinated."

"The ocean trying to crawl through our little porthole every few minutes is not enough for you?" Ilona sat braced on her own bunk with Marya in her arms. Her complexion was much paler than normal, and she had to swallow several times before she could speak again. I wanted to comfort her. She continued: "You wish to go swimming in it, too."

"A rage greater than mine fascinates me. The sea rages like a god itself."

"Oceanus was a titanic." Ilona moaned, and I wondered if she needed a bucket instead of comforting. Then she added, "I should think you've had your fill of such."

Reluctantly, I put my leathers away. That mysterious economy of women had not provided sufficient rough weather gear for me to be out in this storm with any hope of protection. And they were right about the safety as well.

I was a mother now. I needed to think of such things. That thought in turn irritated me. "Well, at least I can go find something to eat," I snapped.

Ilona tried to nod, then stopped, still looking more than a bit green herself. "If you don't break your neck being tossed about in the hallway." Her tone sounded as if she might consider that option preferable.

"It's a passageway, not a hall," I snarled, ashamed of my frustration, and went out looking for ship's biscuits at least, or failing that, someone to argue with about their absence from our meager board.

Even after the storm had calmed the next day, the seas ran ragged and strange. I was permitted to go on deck without so much chaffer and watched the water foam purple and brown. These struck me as strange colors.

Twice the purser tried to chase me back to my cabin, but obduracy is a great skill of mine and I simply ignored him.

Finally one of the mates approached. He was tall, lithe, with skin a pleasant nut brown. One of the Sunwarders, I was sure from the lines of his face and the poise with which he carried himself, rather than some dockside hireling from the margins of the Storm Sea.

"Ma'am, passengers will be much safer out of this weather." His Petraean was curiously accented, and confirmed my estimate of his origins.

I glanced up at the uneasy sky filled with streaming clouds. "I see no rain," I said, though I knew that to a sailor, the weather meant the state of the sea as much as it signified anything about the air.

"*I* will be much safer if you are out of this weather." He grinned, and I liked the shine of his teeth. "Should we lose you, I will be buried in reports for a week. Then there will be a captain's mast to investigate the loss. Then there will be a funeral. Truly, I would be so much better spared all that unnecessary effort and expense."

"Have you looked to our stern?" I asked him, though we were at the starboard rail of the main deck right now.

"I believe the rudder is still there," the mate said politely. "Surely someone would have noticed by now had we lost it."

"We are being followed. A ship set out from Copper Downs an hour or so after we sailed. It called at Lost Port as well. I have seen it twice today."

The mate shrugged. "You cannot know this was the same vessel. Even if it was, what matter? Everyone who wishes to pass Cape Purna to the south coast of Bhopura or the islands beyond must set this same course we follow to Kalimpura. A following ship does not signify so much in a sea lane such as this."

"Hmm." I did not share his confidence, but then, I did not share his expertise, either. Instead, I gave him a slap on the shoulder with my good arm and returned to my cabin to sulk and sew the day's bell to my silk, and to Marya's.

Mother Vajpai and Mother Argai had come visiting. Mother Argai was still weak, but the confusion had left her mind to be replaced by a smoldering resentment at what the Quiet Man had done to her. We had not yet discussed her attacker's fate in any detail, but she knew I had dispatched him.

"The officers do not like me to be outside," I announced, shaking off the spume I'd accumulated there.

Mother Vajpai glanced pointedly at the deck, which in this moment was rolling through an angle that would make walking difficult. "I cannot imagine why. Or does the management of kettle ships also figure among your many talents?"

"Sadly, it does not." I lowered myself to my bunk and braced there with my good arm. Once reclining, I managed my position so my bad arm faced the cabin rather than risk being banged against the wall. Or bulkhead. "So if a sudden plague should take the crew, someone besides me shall have to see to our rescue."

"You *are* a sudden plague," Ilona said, almost giggling. That warmed my heart. She laughed so rarely that I ignored the lighthearted insult in favor of the obvious humor and smiled at her. And it was good to see her looking less bilious than the day before.

So we passed an hour, in easy banter and a certain amount of twitting, while fussing over the babies, who did not like the ship at all and seemed to be distracted from their misery only by constant attention.

No one really cared to broach the hard subjects yet. Decidedly including me. The voyage was long, and promised to continue rough. Bread, cheese, and meat had been handed out this morning in lieu of either short commons or a full breakfast from the kitchens.

We ate, we chattered, I fed my restive children again, then passed them around to be held and dandled. Finally, it seemed time to introduce more difficult topics. I slipped my remaining short knife from my right sleeve.

"There is something I need to show you," I told them, though my eyes went to Mother Vajpai.

I could almost hear the several sarcastic replies forming, but they all realized I was serious. "Watch," I said, reaching to slice a small notch in the oaken post of my bunk.

It was like slicing butter.

Ponce had no idea of the significance of what I'd done, and Ilona appeared puzzled, but both Mother Argai and Mother Vajpai were astonished. Neither bothered to hide their reaction.

I flipped knife across the cabin to Mother Vajpai, timing the toss to the roll of the ship. She was a Blade, and had no trouble catching it. I nodded. Mother Vajpai put my edge to the iron coaming around our cabin's hatch. A curl of bright metal shaved off.

She handed the weapon to Mother Argai, asking as she did, "What is this?"

"The blade was heated, then quenched in the blood of a god," I replied. "As was its mate, which I unfortunately left behind in the Red House."

"You left something like *this* behind?" Her tone was somewhere between appalled and astonished.

"At the time I was somewhat distracted," I answered snappishly. "And besides, I did not realize just then what I held in hand." Though by then I probably should have.

Mother Argai had declined to further vandalize the cabin in the name of proof, but instead was studying the blade carefully.

"Which god, if I may ask?" Mother Vajpai now looked very thoughtful. "Not your ox god, surely."

"Blackblood, who was giving me some trouble at the time." Now I wondered at his motives, and especially so in sending Skinless after me there at the end. Seeing me off? Or watching to make sure I left?

Was there a difference?

Mother Vajpai sighed. "Only you would stab a god who was giving you 'trouble.'"

"Only Green would think to try to stab a god at all," Mother Argai added.

"It was never so simple as—" I broke off. Small point in defending myself. Especially since they were essentially correct.

"At any rate," said Mother Vajpai, switching back to Petraean, "I implore you not to test this blade against anything important, such as the steam kettle or the plates of the hull."

She threw the knife back at me as both Ponce and Ilona winced. I snatched it out of the air, letting the hilt slap firmly into my hand and trying not to wonder what this oh-so-strange blade would have done to me if I somehow had caught the weapon on the wrong part of the spin.

"Show-off," muttered Ponce. Despite the better weather, he was looking as miserable as Ilona had the day before.

I still could not say if the blade was a blessing or a curse. None of my companions had any advice to offer, not even Mother Vajpai, from whom I'd hoped to find some wisdom.

Aboard ship, I began composing a letter to Chowdry. Or a series of letters. I wasn't sure which. Perhaps it did not matter. In many of the most important ways, my fellow Lily Blades knew me far better than he or almost anyone else. On the other hand, Chowdry was the only person who knew me well and also had a foot planted firmly on each side of the Storm Sea.

His experience and mine shared curious echoes that went beyond any obvious connection.

Besides which, writing to Chowdry was in a sense writing to Endurance. I wasn't sure any of the gods could read, for all that so many of them were fond of dictating scripture, but surely if any god could not do so, it would be the ox god. In Seliu, I wrote,

Weather continues rough here. Most everyone but me is miserable. So far they have not all needed to throw up at the same time. This is a great help with the children.

I am of the opinion that our vessel the "Prince Enero" is being pursued. If you have occasion to do so, I would take it as a great favor if you could direct someone to inquire of the Harbormaster's office which vessels weighed anchor the same afternoon of our own departure. As a practical matter, it will be weeks before this letter can reach you, and the reply just as long, but it would ease my mind to know.

I commend Ponce back to you. He is devoted to the children, and perhaps too devoted to me, but this will pass. I am a fit woman for no man at all, as you know of my history. At some point I may have to speak sharply to him.

He has also made a shrine to Endurance in his cabin. I do not know if the little ox statue carved of horn is a votive item of your devising or something he had found in the Dockmarket, but it seems to focus him well. I may yet pray before it myself, just to be sure, though I do not suppose the god will hear me so far from his home.

Do not stint the stone temple, and I hope your compound knows more peace in my absence than it ever did in my presence. Should you require aid of the sort represented by the Lily Blades, call at the Bustle Street Lazaret and ask for Salissa; or failing her presence, Laris. I do not believe Mother Iron and Endurance have much cause for jealousy between them, and each of your followings might profit from common cause with the other.

I wished I'd thought of that last *before* I'd departed. It might have been good advice to give out in my final days in Copper Downs, had I been able to fit such a conversation in between my busy schedule of murder, arson, and funerary rites. Once again, I wondered how ordinary people lived their lives, when no one was lurking about with an intent to kill them.

Later, I went back on deck to see that the sky and sea had calmed with the coming of night. We were far from any shore, so that every horizon but the north was that slightly wavering line the ocean makes for itself in the absence of rougher play. North was obscured by retreating clouds that threw lightning about, the last of the storm we'd been weathering almost since setting out.

Had I truly left the storms behind?

The next three mornings I learned that the answer to that question was emphatically no. *Prince Enero* ran against seas as high and rough as the first day's, maybe more so. Our fourth day at sea, I stared out the port awhile at the spray, with occasional breaks to see racing walls of water ranging again in color from cinnamon to violet.

It was as if the entire ocean had been made into some great stew.

The children were wailing, strapped into a pair of sleeping boxes because it was too dangerous to have them out. No amount of soothing had helped, so finally we'd just let them scream in hopes they'd tire themselves into sleep.

Ilona, bent over a bucket again, groaned.

"This is not natural!" I finally said, shouting over the wailing of my miserable babies. Ponce had been insisting on that point for the last two days, until he'd eventually locked himself in his own cabin, crying with fear.

"No," she gasped. "It is not. You've made this crossing three times?"

"Never like this." Ponce had been right. I wished I'd used kinder words with him.

Timing my movements with the roll of the deck so I could brace myself as it lifted and fell, I shrugged out of the woolen robe I'd been wearing and began to don my fighting leathers. My left arm was still a bruised mess, though the numbness and the pain had both given way to an unceasing tingling that was almost worse. Like hearing someone whistle tunelessly, without end, until you wanted to break their jaw and sew their lips together.

Ilona would be no help, however.

"Who are you going to fight?" She took several deep, whooping breaths and wiped a string of bile from her mouth as the cabin shifted from a steep angle to the port all the way to an equally steep starboard angle. An assortment of shoes, rattles, and other small objects flowed back and forth across the deck in a cacophony.

"The weather."

Not even my new, god-blooded blade could cut into the heart of a storm, though I did wonder what would happen if I tried to slash, say, the wind. Could I split a raindrop?

It mattered little in the moment. I wanted to speak to the captain, whose acquaintance I had not yet made. Even the mate I'd met had not given me his name.

"Watch over them," I told Ilona.

"Uhnnn . . ." was all the reply I received. It would have to do.

The inner passageway led to a compartment forward that in kinder seas served as the passengers' mess. Supposedly the captain kept a table there, but we had yet to see a formal meal service.

Wooden rails were bolted to the walls for exactly such times as this. I staggered with my right hand always braced, keeping my injured left arm close and protected, until I'd worked my way down the passage and through the forward compartment. A breezeway beyond included laddered steps leading up to the bridge.

Unfortunately, the breezeway was intermittently being filled with tons of seawater. When the ocean wasn't leaking in through the hatch and window frames, the wind was doing its best to make up the lack by forcing the rain against everything.

Again, I would have to time my progress to the swells and the ship's corresponding rolls. To have the hatch to the breezeway undogged when one of those waves broke over the deck would court disaster. At the least, I would leave a terrible mess behind me.

So I took my time and counted off how long between the floods. Even the weather has patterns. It is truly not so different from fighting an opponent who overmatches your strength and reach. You watch for her patterns of movement, and shift your own into the little valleys of opportunity that open between the peaks of her effort.

Likewise with the storm. My most significant impediment was my damaged left arm. I could not use both hands to quickly undog the hatch, exit, and clamp it shut once more.

I practiced instead. As soon as the next surge broke and began to drain away in a rush of dripping white foam, I undogged the hatch. Counting off the time I took to do so, I simply secured it once again without turning the bar and opening it.

About fifteen seconds by my reckoning.

We were seeing the big waves every minute and a half or so. Fifteen seconds to undog, perhaps fifteen more to move the lever one-handed. Open the door, step out. Another ten seconds. Close the door. Close the outside lever one-handed. Fifteen seconds. Dog the hatch from the other side. Another fifteen seconds. I was over a minute already before I could begin to scramble up the ladderway to the bridge, and that assumed I made no mistakes, or did not slip.

Why am I doing this?

Self-doubt in the moment of action was such a rare thing for me that I surprised myself in asking the question. I already knew the answer, of course. This storm was unnatural. God-raised or cursed or some such. I was the only person aboard who might even hope to call on any countervailing force. And we could not simply sail into this for weeks. Even the mighty kettle ship *Prince Enero* would founder.

The next wall of water broke outside. I began undogging the hatch while the wave still pounded on the wood, metal, and glass of the compartment's forward bulkhead. One of our own Stone Coast ships would already have broken beneath this assault, I realized.

I opened the hatch and stepped out. Foaming salt water was ankle-deep in the breezeway, and the wind shrieked like a demon out of the nether hells. I turned and one-handed pulled the hatch to. *Drop the lever, flip the dogs one by one. Move, move, move, don't bother to count, because the storm will do it for you.*

The deck rolled beneath me and I glanced up to see another wave rising. It was like staring at a wall. I wasted precious seconds watching the sea raise that giant hand against me, then began scrambling up the bridge ladder as the next great inrush of the ocean broke against *Prince Enero*'s port railing.

The raging water caught at my calves, my thighs, my waist. I kept climbing, praying to stay ahead of it. I felt as if I would be sucked down at any moment. Lost over the side without a trace. It boiled around me, stinging cold and angry as any jilted lover.

A jilted lover whose fists weighed as much as cities.

The water reluctantly pulled away without claiming me in its grip. Gasping, I climbed more, realizing from the agony in my left arm that I'd been clinging with both hands.

Oh, in that moment I would have given much to kill Councilor Lampet all over again.

I gained the landing at the top and pounded on the bridge hatch. A face loomed in the little glass port on the hatch—my friend the mate. He looked amazed.

A moment later it opened, and I was yanked within.

The bridge was warm, of a miracle. A little heater with white stones glowing red behind a grid kept them all from expiring of the damp. The air steamed. Three men stared at me in frank astonishment, the fourth gripping the wheel and studying the water ahead as if his life depended on it.

As if all our lives depended on it.

The mate exploded first, shouting in a language I did not understand until he registered my lack of comprehension. He switched to his accented Petraean. "*What* are you doing? They told me you were a madwoman, but I thought it was jealousy!"

That statement I marked down to explore later, because I very much wanted to know which *they* had told him that. "The storm! I have come about the storm." I was forced to shout back simply to be heard above the din of rain and wind and wave.

The man at the wheel glanced at me once, then turned his attention forward again, barking questions in that same language I did not understand. He and the mate argued briefly, before the mate turned to me once more. "I have explained to the captain that you are a madwoman let loose by your people as a sacrifice to calm the storm."

"Not that, you idiot. This is no natural weather, is it?"

By way of an answer, lightning danced across the bow of the ship, visible from the bridge's windows. Balls of it stayed there to spin and shoot sparks in half a dozen colors.

The mate looked forward, then back at me. His face was mottled by the swirling colors. "No," he finally said. "It would seem not." With that, he spat a curse in this crew's language that I did not speak. Some Sunward tongue that it might profit me to learn if we survived this, I thought.

"I am a kind of priestess." There was no way for me to speak at less than a shout and hope to be heard. "With the ear of several among the divine. Tell me what you can of this."

He shook his head. "We do not know. The weather should not be out of the south so much right now, and these seas seemed to be aimed at our ship. As if the ocean were fighting with purpose."

The captain barked another question without taking his eyes off the water.

I looked at them all. "Is there a walkway in front of the bridge?"

The mate nodded, his face uneasy.

"The seas are not breaking this high," I pointed out as reasonably as I could with such loudness. "I will manage myself out there."

He pointed to another hatch to the captain's right. I crabbed across the deck, sidling past the captain and the other two officers. There was small point in smiling at them. I'd be a hero or I'd be dead very soon. In either case, what happened in here would not matter so much.

Nodding at the outside hatch, I got the mate to take hold of it. We waited for the ship to roll such that it was uphill from me, so I wouldn't just pitch over the rail on exiting; then he threw it open.

I scrambled up and out into what felt like a solid wall of water. I knew this was only wind and rain, and not the wet fist of the sea rising up to claim me. Snatching hold of the rail, I clung through the top of the ship's roll with both hands though my left arm felt likely to tear loose from my shoulder.

When the starboard side of the ship dropped, I worked my way around the front of the bridge. Or wheelhouse. Whatever they called it, here was where the ship's fate was decided. Bracing my shoulders against the glass directly before the captain and my feet against the coaming that ran along the walkway, I once more grasped my short knife and pointed it at the lightning dancing below. I cut the wind that came toward me.

This I did not want to do. But even less did I want to die. Not here, not now, for so senseless a purpose as to satisfy the ocean's hunger.

"Desire!" I shouted. She was the greatest of the gods I knew, a titanic, which is to the gods as the gods are to men. And I had sworn never to call upon Her again. "Desire!" I shouted again. "I beseech You in the name of women everywhere. And most especially my daughter, Marya!"

Another wave broke across the port rail, drowning even the colored lights below. Though its body did not reach me, its fingers lifted and snatched at me with the strength of a dozen men. I turned my god-touched knife toward the water and imagined myself cutting through it like the keel of some racing yacht.

"Hear me!" I shouted again once the water had receded enough for the world to be anything other than pressure and wet. "I have so much to do yet, in your name and for the women of Copper Downs and Kalimpura. As I gave you a daughter in Copper Downs, save my daughter now, and me to care for her."

The wind whipped around my knife as if it were the prow of some granite eminence. The waves lifted again, then just . . . stopped.

The storm was not so much abated as halted. *Prince Enero* moved forward, laboring up a rising slope of water that roiled in place. The air was still, the rain hanging where it was like mist caught for a peaceful moment. Horizontal, daggered mist that cut my cheeks and pinged against the iron walls of *Prince Enero*'s superstructure like a fall of gravel, but still, not what it had been.

Something broke to the surface in the water ahead of the bow and slightly to the port. A great kalamar-fish, one of those fabled tentacled giants of the benthic depths. I could not see how long it was, for its very shape twisted and boiled with the water, but it seemed like I couldn't have paced it from tip to tentacle in less than forty steps.

We moved forward through an eerie, silent sea where the waves remained frozen in their cresting and the very rain in the air continued stilled.

A hatch clanged and the mate came to stand with me. "Vargas is throwing up with fear," he said quietly. Blood began to speck his face from the interrupted drops piercing him much as they already were piercing me, though he did not seem to notice.

I couldn't tell if he was amused or horrified.

"When this is over, I will do the same." I kept my knife pointing bow-ward, as if the shivering tip coated in god's blood were all that could pull us forward through this strangely quiet storm. My bones were cold, joints aching, and I could feel the chill settling into my lungs and heart.

It was not Desire who had answered my prayer, I realized, but Her brother Time. Time, fighting with or cooperating with Oceanus, I could not tell which. So much was frozen, and what moved—us— would be in peril of leaching away if we did not find the honest world again soon.

"The crew will all fear you after this," the mate observed a minute or two later.

I continued to tremble. There was nothing to do but point forward and pray. Hope. Trust. Something from that very short, desperate list of options. I would likely fear myself, but I no longer could spare the words. Each puff of warmth escaping my lips would be another wound.

He had the sense not to touch me, but he stood so close, I could feel the warmth of his body through the air. "I will not, though."

Who's mad now? I thought, and stifled a laugh that would surely slip out of control. What would I owe for this? I had raised Desire's debt to me, but a lifetime of my energies and attentions could not possibly offset the cost of an effort so massive as stilling this storm.

Prince Enero plunged over trough after trough. Frost formed on my blade, then on my leathers, then on the exposed skin of my hands and face. I held my place, a statue dedicated to fortunate travel, while everything leached away.

The still, tall waves grew shorter and smoother. The sky lightened from corpse dark to bruise green to something gray and faintly lemon yellow that recalled the memory of the sun. My face was no longer scored by daggers of rain.

Finally the mate very carefully touched my shoulder. "I believe you can let loose of this," he said softly.

I sagged and lowered the short knife. With a rush of air and noise like being inside a thunderclap, the storm resumed. This was just rain and the casual violence of open water, though not so far to the aft we could hear the wind shrieking and lightning crackling like fire in a granary.

Grasping the rail with my bad hand, knife still in my good hand, I forced out another prayer. "I do not know what sacrifices are now your due," I said quietly, certain that both Time and Oceanus had their hands on my fate just then. "My debt is as deep as your sister Desire will allow." Unsure what to do next—I could hardly light them candles here, and that seemed unfit for the titanic whose demesne was the very seas themselves—I ended as simply as I'd begun, my voice quiet on the wind. "My thanks to you, now and ever."

Without making any comment, the mate walked me back through the bridge, strong hands around my shoulder and gripping my good arm. The captain gave me another long glance, then shook his head silently. Vargas—I assume it was he—mopped a mess around a toppled bucket. The third man spoke urgently into a brass nozzle, giving orders to someone belowdecks.

I was escorted down the ladderway, through the passengers' mess, into the passageway beyond, and finally to my cabin. When that hatch was opened for me, I stumbled through and collapsed on my bunk twitching, weeping. The short knife I kept clasped between my breasts.

The officer shut the hatch and walked away with no word, only a sad smile. I lay there both steaming and freezing as Ilona and the twins slept.

Mother Vajpai and Mother Argai slipped in a few minutes later. After taking a close look at me, Mother Argai began wrapping me in blankets, while Mother Vajpai slipped out again. Shortly thereafter she reappeared with Ponce and some hot water. They poured it into me straight at first, until tea had brewed, then filled me with that as well. In time, Ilona spooned hot soup into my mouth. The galley must have uncovered their fires, though I did not recall seeing her wake up. It felt good to have her attention, simple and uncomplicated by loss.

In time I told them all what had happened, as best I understood it. They just stared, my friends, comprehending my words without understanding their import. Mother Vajpai looked sad more than anything.

"You will forget some of this," she said. "And that will be among your greatest blessings."

She was wrong, of course. I have never forgotten that day. And never again in my life was I to be such a mighty conduit for the divine. If I'd thought the uses the gods had put me to before then were cruel and debasing, well, I'd had only the blessings of ignorance.

Prayer is a dangerous business.

What will you do if one is answered?

I have saved the ship. No one is grateful.

That is not quite correct. I am not surrounded by fools. None of us were ready to surrender our lives and breathe out our last upon the ocean floor.

But what I did . . . Chowdry, my friend, I called upon the power of a titanic. And worse, my call was answered.

Even now, days later, my bones feel hollow as if they had been blown out. My joints are loose, though they tighten more every day. My body was borrowed like a suit, or a mummer's costume. When it was returned to me, the seams had been stretched.

So has my soul.

Sometimes, I think death might have been preferable. I know that sensation will fade with time, or at least I hope so. The crew is frightened of me. The other passengers avoid me completely. Even my own friends are cautious. They hide behind strained courtesy and counting their words like misers with copper half taels.

Do not teach your congregation to pray.

Someday they might succeed.

My sense of desperation receded with everyone else's caution. A week of smoother sailing, interrupted by several ordinary squalls, set everyone aboard *Prince Enero* to rest, or at least less on edge. Besides, what I had done was only rumor or secondhand testimony to all aboard except the captain and the three officers who had been on the bridge with him.

The mate, whose name had proven to be Lalo, messed with us almost every night of that week after the storm. Even when the captain kept his table, our party was not invited. Everyone understood. Lalo was both apology and ambassador, as well as a shield for the rest of the crew and passengers.

I noted that Ponce seemed jealous of his attentions to me, but Ilona managed to keep the boy sufficiently distracted to avoid trouble. That in turn made me feel a bit ill, for Ilona's interest in me had flagged so much. Not that I could blame her. She was ever half-sick over Corinthia Anastasia, and my children were a distraction to us all.

Only the babies remained unchanged by the events of the voyage. They suckled when hungry, squalled when they messed their rags, and generally slept, ate, and shat much as I had been told all babies everywhere did at this early an age. I divided my time between attending them and working out with Mother Argai on the poop deck aft. She was still slow from her poisoning, and I was recovering from both childbirth and my injuries since, so we were matched in our needs for careful sparring.

Our exercises together were slow and painful.

"I miss divine healing," I gasped after Mother Argai had delivered an openhanded roundhouse strike to my temple that I'd been a heartbeat too slow to duck away from.

"I have never experienced divine healing," she replied, her breath every bit as rough as mine.

We faced each other, my hands braced on my hips, Mother Argai's on her knees, both of us rolling with the motion of the ship.

"Always it comes to me slow and painful," she added with another whooping breath.

"Much like life itself." I dropped to a ready crouch. We worked without weapons yet—both of us felt too unsteady to safely spar without fear of unintentionally wounding the other.

It was an odd sort of sharing. Mother Argai had always been tougher than most women, myself included. I could be hardheaded beyond reason, even I saw that about myself, but she had a physical endurance that I could not match at my most driven.

This I admired.

We shuffled through another limited version of a Blade unarmed sparring match. Open palms, no handstrikes, no closed fists, and no leg drops or low kicks. It was as if we were both fourth- or fifth-petal Aspirants once more.

I staggered from a fierce smack to my shoulder. "We should train all the girls for a season aboard ship."

Mother Argai laughed, her voice rough with exertion. "You would have our temple with a navy now?"

Managing to land a flat touch to her chest, I danced back, or tried to. If she'd been willing to follow up, she could have knocked me down hard. "Why not? We could make runs among the fishes."

That brought another laugh, and with her laughter, I saw once more a light that had been absent in her eyes since the Quiet Man's attack. Not just a bit of joy for herself, but maybe a bit of restored regard for me.

This is what trust feels like, I thought, and renewed my attacks upon her.

It was the most loving thing I knew to do.

By the time we spied Cape Purna, the northeasternmost extent of Selistan, our councils had resumed, rising up out of the harried, fractured conversations between me and Mother Argai. So much had happened when I was still carrying the twins, and the ramifications of those events carried forward into question after question after question.

What to do when we reached the Temple of the Silver Lily? What if the Goddess Herself were in danger? Could we locate the rumored Red Man and his fey little assistant—Firesetter and Fantail, Laris had called the two of them—who were said to be god-killers from the Saffron Tower gone renegade? Would they aid us with their knowledge if not the strength of their arms and spells? What if Surali had seated herself as Primate of the Bittern Court? What of her Quiet Men, and who were they truly? What if the Prince of the City had fallen? What if we could not determine the fate of Corinthia Anastasia and Samma? What if we could, and they had met their end?

Those last sent Ilona sobbing, as it must wound any mother's heart, but still we worked through the possibilities. None of us knew enough to plan sensibly, so we did what we could, ate well, and accepted the prison of silence that had grown up around us amid the distrust of the others aboard ship. They feared me and avoided all of my party.

Still, I came to be quite fond of Lalo, and in other circumstances, might have sought to act on that. Later, even with all the pain of what happened during the storm and afterwards, that I did not try was my only true regret concerning that voyage.

Kalimpura: The Exile Is Returned

THE FAMILIAR JUNGLED coast eventually gave way to an equally familiar line of buildings and docks that even in those days I knew better than I knew the waterfront of Copper Downs. Kalimpura's broad, shallow harbor was crowded with the ships of a dozen nations and more. The place seemed so much like home to me that I might have stepped over the rail and walked across the choppy water.

Prince Enero loomed here over the low-sided traders accustomed to the calmer seas of the Selistani coast and the waters southward. She entered the harbor like one of those floating islands of ice said to be found where the oceans of the world approach the frigid walls that define the northern and southern extents of the plate of the earth. I watched from a place near the bow, wondering if my sentence of death or banishment still applied.

Not from what Samma had told me, but that was before Surali had suborned the new Temple Mother and turned the Lily Goddess' followers against Her interests.

We had much to repair here.

The water over the rail was filthy, litter and dead fish everywhere. That was familiar and strangely comforting as well. I spotted a few of the little skiffs that crawled the harbor trawling for useful flotsam. Anything in open water was fair game, though most things of value were too heavy to do anything but sink to the muddy bottom.

Like the Eyes of the Hills, those gems I'd stolen from the trader Michael Curry whom I had murdered aboard *Crow's Wing* so long ago. They were finally recovered and sent back to Copper Downs. Could I have averted much of what came later if I'd handled that differently at the time?

A fool's question, that was, except insofar as one might profit from learning by asking. *Could have done, should have done,* solved nothing in the present and did little to improve the future.

Mother Vajpai limped up next to me. "Are you ready to come home?"

"Is this home?" Of course, I had chosen it to be home, most specifically, in leaving Copper Downs as I had. Surali be damned, I was Selistani, and I would stay in Selistan awhile. Perhaps a very long while.

She sighed. "Once more I will counsel you not to go ashore. Let Mother Argai and me see to the streets and the temple before you."

"No." My voice was flat. We'd hashed over this argument a dozen times in the past ten days. I did wonder when I had stopped taking orders from Mother Vajpai, and what that might ultimately signify. "I must go ashore. If I arrive as a coward, I will live as a coward. Let my enemies see me coming."

"We do not even know who your enemies are."

"Oh, we surely do," I said, all hot breath and passion in the moment. "They are the people trying to kill me."

"You will never settle their complaints by killing them first."

A strange remark coming from a woman who had trained an entire generation of Lily Blades, and long commanded enforcement of the Death Right on behalf of Kalimpura as a whole. "My technique certainly does slow down the people who are sent after me."

"You must be skilled every single time. They require luck only once." It was an old saying among the Blades, and usually applied to the dangers of operating alone. We ran in handles for many reasons.

Prince Enero was closing on Agina's Pier at dead slow. We would be twenty or thirty minutes docking and tying up before anyone debarked. "Let us go see to the children," I said. Change of subject and peace offering all at once. And frankly, Mother Vajpai had taken surprisingly well to the babies.

Marya and Federo were two months old now. Already their personalities were emerging. At birth they had been tiny, squalling burdens
with unending hunger at one end and unending shit at the other.
Thank the gods for foolish mother-love.

Now, well, I loved them all the more. Federo was a little fussier,
more unhappy when he was not fed promptly, expecting to sleep
shortly after each feeding. Marya, on the other hand, already treated
the world as her personal plaything and fought to stay bright-eyed
and awake if anything was happening for her to watch or reach a
chubby little fist toward.

She reminded me of myself more than he did.

Both of them darkened as they grew. They had been born a sort of
wrinkled, graying pink, but their coloring seemed to be settling in to
a pleasing brown. It was the same hue my upper arms and belly grew
in winter when my skin was too long away from the sun. Here in
Kalimpura, they would be as strangely pale as I had been strangely
dark in Copper Downs. The twins would carry their dead father always on their hands and faces for the whole world to see.

I gathered Federo to my chest while Ilona swaddled Marya. Ponce
hovered about, packing our few belongings and annoying Ilona with
his attempts to help her. He made a hash of properly rolling my belled
silk, as well, which annoyed me. I felt a pang of regret at having spent
so much time arguing strategy with Mother Argai and Mother Vajpai
while my children had been cared for by the other two.

Yet . . . twins . . . On my own, I would scarcely have ever slept. The
babies certainly did not follow the same schedule. Three adults paying
close attention and two more hovering at the edges barely kept up
with them. How did ordinary mothers do this, while working in the
market or as maids, keeping a house, and doing all the things women
did? Me, for the most part I ran about raising holy hell and occasionally stopping to cook a fine meal, and still I felt overwhelmed.

Later on, I was to realize how much I missed out on, then and as
time passed. The world had never meant for me to be a mother tending her cradles throughout the watches of the day and night. That life
has gone as it has since those early days is enough of a blessing, I suppose. Who ever has enough time for their children? Who ever has
spent too much time with their children?

Buoyed by my foolish love, I gave both my children over to Ilona and Ponce. "Mother Argai will stay with you," I instructed them. "Do not leave the ship until someone she trusts comes bearing a message."

"What if the captain has the purser throw us off?" Ilona asked, ever practical.

"He will not," I said. "He is quite clear on what will happen if he does." Which was to say that I had spoken to the mate, Lalo, and said the only way *Prince Enero* would be gracefully rid of me was if ship and crew sheltered my children until I had made ready for them ashore.

"Three days," he'd promised me, "but no more," then gone off to argue awhile with the captain and the senior crew.

Sometimes I thought that my friends were every bit as strange, and possibly dangerous, as my enemies.

Though I'd been assured my banishment was lifted, those statements had come amid a much larger and more complex web of deceit. Mother Vajpai had since admitted she wasn't certain of the Temple Mother's position. In any case, Surali had been back in Kalimpura long enough to ensure any outcome she preferred.

It was quite possible that a Death Right claim had been filed against me. My best hope there was that the Blade monopoly on such judicial killings still held, as it had for decades on decades before I had arrived in Kalimpura. I doubted very many of my fellow Blades would be willing to carry such a mission out. Not with me as the target. I wasn't even too sure that the Lily Goddess might not find some way to object, though Her influence on Her followers was largely indirect. I'd learned that during my first stay in Kalimpura, when it had become apparent that very few besides me could see or hear Her manifestations.

In any case, there was little for it but to walk down to the docks and head for our temple. If someone approached me with murder in her eye, unless they made their intentions known by a crossbow bolt in my back, I would be able to talk or fight, or both. My left arm still ached, but it *worked*. The shipboard sparring with Mother Argai had worn off most of my pregnancy fat and restored me to something like fighting trim.

We descended the metal ladder to a dock surging as always with wharfingers, stevedores, couriers, news brokers, prostitutes, chandler's boys, draymen, food sellers, commodities factors, and the dozen other professions found along any working waterfront. Colored silk streamers waved aloft signified this specialty or that service, but Mother Vajpai and I were not buying.

And it was a *relief* to finally be back in a place where our leathers made a passage for us. No one trod on the foot of a Lily Blade, or landed a too-sharp elbow in one's ribs. No one who wanted to end the day with as many fingers as they began it with, at any rate.

The reality was that we were far more gentle and careful with our power than people seemed to believe. But a fearsome reputation had its uses. Besides, enough others in this city, notably including the Street Guild, plied such a rougher trade that anybody with sense avoided becoming entangled in the likes of us as well.

The most amazing thing, though, was not the shouting of Seliu from hundreds of mouths, nor the heat pounding down upon my head, nor the fitful sea wind that raised its own memories and the familiar line of buildings ahead of me. No, those were just a welcome for a long-vanished traveler. The most amazing thing was the smell.

I walked, caught up in the mix of rot from beneath the pier, the sharp freshness of a tide run in, cardamom and honey from a vendor selling fried locusts, the burnt smell of some recently passed festival or funeral procession, the scent of thousands of my countrymen sweating at their labors, the dung of horses and donkeys, the tang of sewage. . . . My nose found a riotous mélange that would have told me I was in Kalimpura even if I'd been swept blindfolded across the plate of the world by some kindly djinni to land here all unknowing.

My feet took me toward a cart with roasting pistachios in a clay vessel parked at the base of the wharf, where it met the seawall and the Street of Ships. The green nuts were unknown in Copper Downs. Though they were not a special, coveted favorite, they would taste of home to me. I turned to Mother Vajpai to ask if she had any coin upon here, but realized that three large men loomed behind her, raising staves.

She caught my glance and ducked even as the first wood whistled through the air where her head had just been.

The crowd danced aside like oil in a hot pan. These were Street Guild attacking us. When last I knew, they'd had the right to violence on the docks. Policing, some called it, but their role was little more than a monopoly for their own free use of force. Under the protection of the Bittern Court, of course.

I was already moving as those thoughts raced through my head. The pistachio seller's copper ladle served to scoop a handful of tiny, hot missiles for the first man's face. The ladle itself followed to bounce off the head of the second. I palmed my short knife but was unwilling to throw it, for fear of losing the second and last of the god-blooded blades.

When have I ever feared to throw a knife?

With that thought, I forced myself to hurl it overhand.

The short knife pierced the third man's chest like he'd been a paper manikin set out for some funerary pyre. He tumbled backwards as if he'd been kicked in the chest. Meanwhile, Mother Vajpai had reached up from below to tackle the first man—the one still flicking hot pistachios out of his beard. He would be dead in moments.

I charged the second man, who was obviously enraged about being batted with the ladle. Behind me, the pistachio seller yelled. I did not have time to draw my long knife, so I took my target with my good shoulder in his belly.

He refused to go down. Instead, he danced backwards, robbing me of my momentum and trying to box my ears. The corpse of his fellow was to my right, so I dropped away from the drubbing and scooped up my knife once more.

Ten seconds later, both his hands were lying on the pavement and he was screaming at the gushing stumps of his arms.

Mother Vajpai popped to her feet and quieted him with a punch to the throat.

I took a deep breath and scanned around us. This area of the dock had rapidly grown empty, almost unheard of during a Kalimpuri day. The people were drawn back to watch from a distance safe enough from thrown knives or shattered teeth. Their behavior might also have had something to do with the half dozen Street Guildsmen now approaching at a slow step. These had their own blades out, and looked as if they meant to fight as one man.

"Well?" I asked Mother Vajpai.

"A good student will always offer a solution," she gasped.

I neglected our attackers long enough to turn my head and just stare at her. "You jest," I said, incredulous.

"What would you do?"

"Well, I—" With that, I stopped, for she indeed jested, and I had caught the joke. God-blooded dagger or not, we were done for if they closed on us, for surely there were more of their fellows just behind.

I eyed the nearby edge of the wharf. "How well do you swim?"

She was spared the need to answer me by the arrival of a Blade handle, shouting in unison and swinging their long knives. The half dozen Street Guild who were approaching us fell back. Our ring of watchers, always ready for the violent theater of the Kalimpuri streets, suddenly swept into motion once more.

A minute later we were standing over three corpses, surrounded by eight women in leather with Mother Surekha in the lead. I recognized all the women, though none of them had been among my favorites. Nor the other way around.

"Welcome home," Surekha said to Mother Vajpai. Me she favored with a longer, slower glare. Much left unsaid.

She had never been an especial friend to me, but so far as I knew, we had not been enemies. The new order here in Kalimpura and especially among the Lily Blades was not promising.

"We should return to the temple quickly," Mother Vajpai said. "Before these Street Guild come for us in greater numbers."

Mother Surekha nodded. "Those are my orders, from the Temple Mother herself."

How many people had known we were coming? I wondered. This was not one but two welcoming committees here along the docks, all prepared for violence. It wasn't as if *Prince Enero* had signaled ahead.

Or perhaps the captain had done so. I certainly could not read the nautical flags they had used to negotiate their initial approach to the harbor.

"Let us go," I said, wishing briefly that I could light candles for these dead. It seemed important, if impossible.

As we began to run, I wondered if I might have been better off with my first group of attackers. At least their agenda had been clearcut. I had not made myself popular with the Street Guild during Surali's excursion to Copper Downs—they had left a number of men behind, all of them dead either directly or indirectly by my hand.

Really, the principle was simple enough, if I could just get people to listen: Don't attack me or my children, and I won't attack you.

We ran some more. Out of the corner of my eye, I watched Mother Vajpai limp. It was not for me to beg her some relief. She was Blade Mother, and would either assert her authority or step away. But her weaknesses belonged to her.

The Blood Fountain still flowed in the plaza before the Temple of the Silver Lily. I felt another wave of a sort of reversed nostalgia, pleased to be home and still very much a stranger. The Beast Market was in full swing and high odor both, while the temple's well-worn red marble steps were more crowded with beggars than ordinarily so. Many of them were unusually large and healthy—the Street Guild was assembling here in hopes of catching me out. The building itself rose with that distinctive almost-teardrop shape, the silver cladding nearer to the peak bright in the afternoon sun.

We trotted up the steps, barking out a marching chant, and cleared through the great doors at the top and into the foyer where once upon a time I had first arrived, lonely and scared and ill. The same tapestries greeted me, the same low benches. It was a peaceful place, and familiar.

Mother Surekha's handle stood down there, with some catching of breath and stretching of backs. I knew this drill—no one wanted to appear weak or tired, but bodies had their own notions. I was pleased enough that I wasn't aching or worse, and so stood breathing just a bit heavier than normal.

Yet none of them drifted off to eat or sleep or bathe or play amongst themselves, as we so often had after a run when I was here. All the women stayed near me, hard-faced with hands near knife hilts.

So I was a prisoner, though they had not yet bound me over. I glanced at Mother Vajpai. Her attention was unfocused. Banishing pain from her feet, I was certain. Seeking a bit of peace before the next act of this little morality play unfolded.

Betrayal was most certainly in the air. The only question was from whom, and of whom.

As Mother Vajpai and I entered, I noted the sanctuary had not changed since I was last here almost two years ago at my banishment.

This was a deep, galleried well that filled the central space of the temple's architecture. Seats rose in tiers so that the congregants could all see what their Temple Mother was about, and her words would be heard by all ears.

It was a curious arrangement, I'd come to realize. Most religious architecture places the goddess, and her chief servants, before and above the congregation. No one looked down upon a priest, in my experience. Not if that priest could help it.

Yet here the arrangement spoke of a different relationship between the worshippers and the worshipped, between the leaders and the led.

My life had once before depended on that relationship. I wondered today if it would so depend yet again. That seemed unfortunately likely.

The galleries were peopled but uncrowded. This was not an hour when services normally occurred. The whispering that had arisen at our entry died down quickly. I met many interested eyes, and even a few friendly ones, in the faces above me.

The Temple Mother stood composed but tense before the altar. That was, as always, a great silver lily almost six feet wide, sculpted as a flower yet half-opened. Mother Umaavani who had banished me was dead, I had been told by Mother Vajpai. She'd been succeeded by Mother Srirani. As so often in the recent history of the temple, we were once more governed by a Justiciary Mother.

In the quiet that preceded what was to come next, I reflected on the machinations within the Temple of the Silver Lily. Our two most powerful orders were the Justiciars and the Blades. Those were also the two best known outside the temple walls.

The Blades, of course, were my own order. Women trained to fight and kill who used their skills to keep the peace. We were as close as Kalimpura came to the Petraean idea of a municipal guard or city watch. Peace was something you purchased for yourself in this city, if you could afford it. The poor hid themselves away, and most often made their own justice, much as their betters did.

The Courts of this city were Guilds, or trading houses, though they often maintained the trappings of law. The Justiciary Mothers served as mediators among the wealthy and the poor alike. They sometimes sat as judges in a fashion that even a northerner would recognize, though their courts were convened for a single purpose, and disbanded again once the affair was concluded.

Law itself in Kalimpura was a matter of custom and persuasion. Justiciary Mothers tended to be legalistic in their thinking, careful and focused of mind. In a sense, they were the opposite of the Blades, who often solved problems swiftly and irrevocably.

Even then, I could see the balance this represented, action countervailed by consideration, thought bolstered by deed. In my years since, my appreciation for the arrangement has grown. At the time, I was mostly annoyed. Justiciary Mothers found Blades messy, and I was surely the messiest Blade since at least the youth of the late Mother Meiko, more than two generations ago.

The other orders of the temple grew naturally out of the internal functions of any religious house of women. The Domiciliary Mothers ran the kitchens and workshops, cared for the youngest children not yet taken into their training, and maintained the temple's physical and social structures. The Caring Mothers raised the older children, eased the lives of our most elderly Mothers, and served as the temple's healers. The Mothers Intercessory saw to the more basic and general education of the children, kept the libraries and scriptures, served as witnesses to what had been written before in prophecy and temple law, and tended the altar, relics, and other holy duties of our worship of the Lily Goddess.

I knew from my training here that the post of Temple Mother had once belonged almost exclusively to the Mothers Intercessory. About forty years ago it had passed between the Blades and the Justiciars several times before settling with the Justiciary Mothers. Fairness had been claimed at the time, and the supposed value of experience in negotiating with the city beyond our doors.

Many had their doubts, especially the Blades. Including me. Our temple seemed to have become ever more deeply enmeshed in the schemes of politics to the benefit of, well, no one.

I stared at Mother Srirani, knowing this show of open disrespect would irritate her. That concerned me in no wise at all. She stared back, scowling down her nose at me with lips pursed. The white and gray robes of her office did not hang well on her, and I wondered if she wore Mother Umaavani's old garments, or if she had lost weight of late. Mother Srirani was not so tall, only a bit more than I, and rounder of face and body than any Blade would ever be.

Just to trouble her further, I offered my sweetest smile. The look she returned me cleared any of my doubts. The Temple Mother seemed to take our silent exchange as her cue, for she straightened and addressed the congregation in a voice that was unfortunately reedy for a woman in her role.

"Mothers. Sisters. Women of the Temple of the Silver Lily, of Kalimpura, of Selistan." Well, that arguably left me out on all counts. Beside me, Mother Vajpai stirred a bit at the words. The Temple Mother continued: "We gather today to consider the errors of one who was once among us." At least it was only me who was on trial today, not Mother Vajpai. "Sent forth in exile carrying woes of our own beloved goddess with her, the miscreant Green has returned against holy writ and our goddess' will to once more trouble us here."

At that, I stirred, ready to leap up in answer, but Mother Vajpai laid a steely grip upon my right arm. I could have broken it—probably—but chose instead to heed her silent counsel.

"Across the seas in the barbarous place of her exile, Green to my certain knowledge has betrayed the interests of our temple. She has abrogated the writ and will of our beloved Lily Goddess. She has brought disgrace to us and upon our city with her behaviors public and private. Trusted persons of high station here in Kalimpura were subject to her depredations in a manner that could have called ruin down upon us all."

Mother Srirani turned from playing to the gallery to instead stare me down. That, at least, she would not best me at. I stared back at her, letting her see in my eyes what awaited her. I did not need to promise a bitter fate, I simply *knew*.

"You stand accused of misdeeds outside even my purview to adjudicate, Green. But it is within my purview to pass judgment upon your return from banishment without proper leave. It is within my purview to rule upon your fate as a Sister and Mother of this temple. It is within my purview to punish you for those infractions that are sadly ours to make amends for. For the rest of your crimes, well, you shall have to seek the mercy of those you have wronged, the powerful across Kalimpura."

The mercy of the powerful was a folk saying here in Selistan, implying something to be laughably unlikely. Much as a Petraean might have said *diamonds in the sewers*. I and everyone listening knew that what she meant by that was throwing me to our enemies without, and relieving the temple of responsibility for my fate. Death at the hands of the Street Guild—a very likely outcome given the display of an hour ago—would in this case go unanswered by the Lily Blades, who in general never let a slight or injury to their own go without strong response.

Mother Vajpai released my arm and rose painfully to her feet. She allowed a wince to cross her face, which I knew was her own playing to the gallery. "Hello, Rana," she said to the Temple Mother with a nod. Addressing someone in authority by a child's nickname was a supreme impoliteness only nominally disguised by her tone. Then she turned her attention to the gallery.

"How many of you here know me well?" Mother Vajpai pointed. "You, Mother Aasi, I shared a sleeping mat with when we were both too short to open the doors of the refectory. You, Mother Urgattai, argued the case of the Glassworks Poisoning that I uncovered during the Death Right action against that old bastard Mansajurat. You, Sister Feillig, I plucked from a wrecked cart on the Street of Silversmiths when you were a babe, and looked to the care of until you took your vows among the Intercessors."

The gallery was muttering again. Mother Srirani's face darkened with anger, and she opened her mouth to speak, but Mother Vajpai was just ahead of her, just forceful enough to stop her.

Even old Mother Umaavani would not have permitted this to go on, I thought with satisfaction. Embarrassment was the most potent weapon against a woman in the Temple Mother's position, because people lost respect.

"Every one of you knows I was sent forth with specific orders from Mother Srirani. The blessing of the Lily Goddess was *claimed.*" Oh, that bit of sarcasm was artful. "I was told to take Mother Argai with me and fetch the exile Green back from Copper Downs, for reasons that were said to be good and proper at the time.

"So how is it that such a mission, dispatched by the very woman who now accuses Green of violating her banishment and numerous other unspecified crimes, has become a gross violation of the will of our goddess? Could it be that the interests served never were those of this altar behind me? Could—?"

"Enough!" Mother Srirani's voice rang shrill. "You speak foolishness, and have been too long out of the councils of this temple to know what has been judged right. Mother Surekha will escort you to a quiet chamber where the Caring Mothers will see to your disturbances. There you may rediscover reason and dignity."

"I will not be silenced." Mother Vajpai's voice was ominous.

"It is not silence, Pai-pai." The Temple Mother lowered her own tones until only the closest could hear. "It is safety. Yours and mine."

Mother Surekha and two of her handle stepped up to Mother Vajpai. The women looked uneasy at effectively arresting their own Blade Mother. I wondered who had held Mother Vajpai's post in her absence, and if that one stood to gain it permanently should Mother Vajpai be deemed unfit to resume her duties.

Then my old instructor, the most dangerous human woman I'd ever known, nodded at me. A glint of satisfaction, of all things, rode in her eyes.

I could take that hint. Touching Mother Surekha's arm, I muttered, "Abide a moment," then strode from my bench at the base of the gallery straight toward the altar.

"Let the Lily Goddess to speak to us!" I shouted. This hand I had played before, that memorable day with old Mother Umaavani when the Dancing Mistress and I had been on trial here. This was a *temple*, after all. Ultimate authority rested with none of the women who served the Lily Goddess. Not when the goddess Herself could be summoned. "I have been back on these shores only an hour, and already I am tired of wordplay in place of simple, honest truth." I shot Mother Srirani an exaggerated glare that could surely be seen even from the highest gallery. "And I might have expected the lies to be slightly more clever. Or have we all lost our senses to fear, surrendered to politics, and given up who we are meant to be?"

"You will sit, or I will have you seated," snapped Mother Srirani.

"I am still a Mother of this temple, banishment or not." Not quite technically true, I'd never finished taking my vows, but that was how most of the women here viewed me. "I have the same right to appeal to the Goddess' intercession as any of my Sisters here." I turned my gaze from the Temple Mother back to the dozens watching. "If she can strip that right from me by whim, she can strip it from any of you. Are you all so eager to surrender your place before the altar to the coin of outsiders?"

That sparked an eruption of angry chatter from above. Several women jumped to their feet. A few hurried out.

Now Mother Srirani was trembling with furious passion. A bad tendency in one who would lead, I knew, ignorant then of the reflexive irony of my thought. "I will not have this fane be made a mockery!"

"Too late," I called, to a ripple of laughter from those who could still hear me. "Now, will you beseech the goddess or shall I?"

Silence spread from that statement. One of the questions long dogging the temple had been why the Lily Goddess was ever more difficult to address over the years. Even the Temple Mothers, who stood for Her in this world and spoke with Her words, we were all assured, had experienced much trouble with that. I had been able to call Her, more than once. I knew that had greatly troubled some of my elders, though I had largely ignored the discussion at the time.

From the flash of panic on Mother Srirani's face, I guessed that she had experienced little or no luck at the rite. The last thing she wanted was me interfering successfully.

In effect, I had challenged her authority. Oh, such games these women played. Why in the world had she even hauled me and Mother Vajpai here before an assemblage of the temple, instead of simply locking us up, or having our throats slit?

Because she is a Justiciar, and follows the process. The politics of the temple would allow her to do no less. Too many senior Mothers and Sisters would have questioned not just my disappearance on arrival, but the necessary vanishing likewise of Mother Vajpai and Mother Argai.

"Shall I pray?" I asked amid the quiet of dozens of watching women. Looking up at them, I added, "Or have the affairs of the temple reached such a state that urgent change is needed? Who among you thinks this whole business has been properly done? Rise if you would see another path."

The women already on their feet looked startled, but none of them sat down again. Several Blades stood, grim-faced with their hands loose as if for a fight. To my surprise, a few Justiciary Mothers stood. Then all seven of the Domiciliary Mothers in the gallery rose together—I had always been a favorite of the cooks, to put it plainly.

After that, slowly, with a rustle of robes and leather, every woman in the room stood. I turned back to Mother Srirani. "Where is your power now, Temple Mother? Let us speak to the Goddess ourselves."

"No," she said roughly, switching tacks in the face of such over-whelming opposition. "I was a fool to think you would respect our rules. You shall not profane this place with your foreign prayers and strange ideas. Mother Surekha will escort you from the temple. You and Mother Vajpai are expelled from your order, and from the service of the Lily Goddess. Her ears will be deaf to your prayers, Her eyes blind to your sacrifices. Our Blades will not help you. No hand will be raised to your aid. May you find what you seek in the justice of the streets of Kalimpura."

An urgent jerk of Mother Vajpai's chin caught my eye. In that moment of pause, I realized that she had the right of things. We were better off withdrawn from this place and shaping our own next moves than risking some new devilment from Mother Srirani, who had so clearly become Surali's puppet. Even if the Lily Goddess did choose to manifest, She would not play the politics this situation demanded. Her brushstrokes were much broader than that.

Looking up once more, I made my closing statement. "I go, not because I accept either Rani's authority or her edict, but because I wish peace upon this temple. I shall see all of you again."

Mother Vajpai and I walked out through the little door at the base of the gallery to the thunder of applause. Mother Surekha crowded close behind us, nervous and unhappy as any cat on ice.

Despite everything that was going wrong, I found myself smiling.

I ignored our escort and headed for the kitchens. Mother Vajpai kept pace with me, Mother Surekha trailing behind. There was no point in stepping out into the circular plaza of the Blood Fountain. The Street Guild awaited us there. And the Blades would not be of any aid. Not right now, not directly. I had my own doubts about the future effectiveness of Mother Srirani's ban, but they did not signify just then.

No one else followed us, not even the rest of Mother Surekha's handle. Mother Surekha herself seemed far more nervous now, judging from my frequent glances over my shoulder. She could be as nervous as she wished. I wanted to be sure she wasn't drawing a weapon.

Mother Vajpai seemed more concerned about Mother Surekha's state of mind. As we slipped down the Lesser Adamantine Stairs, she looked backwards as well. "Tell me, do *you* wish to see us on the street?"

Mother Surekha grunted. Then a confession: "I don't know what is right here."

Hot words rushed to my tongue, but I swallowed them. I had another purpose here. Argument with an angry Blade was not on my agenda. Besides, this was Mother Vajpai's question.

"It should not be so hard," she said gently as we banged into the kitchens.

Ah, the smell. Scent was the catapult of memory, and there was nothing like cooking to fire your thoughts into the past. Yeast, ash, spice, steam from the washbasins, the green and crumpled reek of vegetables. Such a familiar blend, all the way to the back of my mind.

I had been taught the many uses of a kitchen under the brutal hand of Mistress Tirelle, back at the Factor's house in Copper Downs. We'd always cooked with just the two of us. No one to serve the food to, no servants or undercooks to help. Though my taskmistress had spoken much about the varied practices of a more substantial kitchen— such as the one I'd snuck through in the Red House—that had been theory to me until I arrived in Kalimpura, some time after murdering my way out of both captivity and the city of Copper Downs.

Here, in the lower levels of the Temple of the Silver Lily, I'd had my first real experience of a great and busy kitchen. I'd never worked with large ovens and cooking for two hundred, recipes that were measured in catties and bowlsfuls rather than ounces and cups. I'd shown the cooks here recipes from the cold north, especially the baking that was so little of the tradition in Kalimpura. They'd taught me their crafts in turn, their spices and sauces and the use of the clay oven.

I'd spent a lot of time with these women, my arms dusted to the shoulders with flour and seasoning, or wrinkled from taking my turns at scrubbing pans. They'd spent a lot of time with me as well.

So there were not too many surprised faces when I entered the kitchen, trailed by Mother Vajpai and Mother Surekha. Some smiles, yes, and some frowns. Wings of rumor had flown here just as fast as anywhere. The kitchen knew most things before the rest of the temple.

Old Sister Shatta came hobbling toward me. She was the master baker in the kitchen, answering only to Mother Tonjaree, who was the kitchen's head steward. She was also one of the women who'd spent the most time with me in the years when I could be found down here.

"Hungry, girl?" she said with a gritty laugh. She nodded at Mother Vajpai and favored Mother Surekha with a fishy stare.

"Sister Shatta." I hugged her. "I have been gone too long." She looked so much older than I remembered, trembling as she walked but still refusing canes. Or at least refusing to show them to me. "I am sorry to be rude. I am in something of a hurry."

"Oh, we've heard, girl." She touched my face, fingers brushing down my chin. "And you've been talking to voices in the dark."

Everything seemed to still for a moment. Even the grumble of the fires and the pinging of the iron ovens quieted. In Sister Shatta's eyes I saw an unaccustomed depth shining past the wispy webs that would all too soon finish claiming her sight.

I dropped to one knee, clasped her hand, and said, "I have come home to You."

Briefly, I felt raindrops and smelled lilies. Then Shatta's old woman voice cackled at me. "Get up, girl. You shall never be outrunning those fools if you are bending a knee to every biddy who wants to give you a kiss."

Right then and there, I'd have told her of my children and my life, but this was not the time. And the less said in that place about potential hostages, the better. Rumor's wings flew in all directions.

The undercooks and kitchen girls drifted closer, casually forming a sort of wall around us. Mother Surekha looked even more uncomfortable, as if she'd never realized how much politics went on in the kitchens. And who would, if she'd never worked here? The interweaving of food and relationships was obvious to anyone who'd ever stood to serve, but not always to those who sat to eat.

"We must away and swiftly," I said. "You must know what has taken place in the fane. Street Guild gather outside in numbers too large to evade."

"I overheard Mother Maati saying she planned to send two girls marketing for herbs." Sister Shatta's voice was cackling and sly.

"We will need to cover our leathers."

"And these," said a girl I did not know, pushing two large cane baskets at me. I handed one to Mother Vajpai.

"Robes?" I asked.

Cloaks were thrust at us. Gray, patched, nondescript, still they re-minded me of my belled silk back aboard *Prince Enero,* and Marya's. These city folk thought that such a peasant affectation, but the habit of sewing a new bell every day was all I had of the region and people of my birth. Setting aside that thought, I shrugged into one and pulled it close around me. Mother Vajpai donned hers and picked up her basket once more.

There was nothing particularly convincing about us. Mother Vajpai especially would never pass a second glance as a scullion, but with luck we would not draw the first glance. So long as we didn't move like Blades.

"Go now," urged Sister Shatta. "We shall be dull-witted serving wenches should anyone come asking."

I turned to Mother Surekha. "And you?"

She glowered but held her harder words in check. "Once you leave, my duty has been discharged."

"Keep it discharged," I advised her. "There will be grief raining down aplenty soon enough. You will not want that."

"I saw you cut those men," she whispered.

My index finger tapped her chest as regret panged me. "You would have killed them, too."

"Not so easily. No one should die that easy." With those words, she turned abruptly and pushed through the crowd of onlookers.

Raising my voice, I said, "Thank you all. There are no promises I can make, but if I can manage, things will be different soon."

"Come back and cook awhile," someone said—I did not catch the voice.

"We will." With that, I headed for the pantry and the loading doors beyond where the draymen brought food from the various mar-kets around Kalimpura. Mother Vajpai ghosted close to my elbow. I could practically hear her being thoughtful.

For all the imposing glory of the frontage of the Temple of the Silver Lily, the rear facing was as anonymously crowded and busy as the back of any other substantial institution. Carters, beggars, small tradesmen—a steady traffic passed in the alley behind. We slipped into the stream, walking briskly with our heads turned down. Most of the servants in this city or any other walked briskly. A shuffling step would have cried out that we wished not to be recognized.

Swiftly we merged into the crowded streets beyond, losing ourselves away from the Blood Fountain with its swarm of angry Street Guildsmen. After about six blocks, I pulled the limping Mother Vajpai into someone's walled garden to rest a short while beneath the shade of a papaya tree. It was a shame about the latch on their gate, which I was forced to cut through with the god-blooded dagger.

"Those Street Guild bastards did not used to have so much power," I said, pacing before the bench whether Mother Vajpai unashamedly took her rest.

"Things have changed since you left."

We'd discussed this back in Copper Downs, we'd discussed this aboard *Prince Enero,* we would doubtless continue to discuss this, but still I was surprised. The Blades had always seemed to me to be so powerful, so constant, so . . . confident.

"Things have changed," I agreed. "That does not mean I must accept what they have become. But now I need to get back to my children." My breasts were not aching yet—we had left the ship scarcely two hours ago—but they would before the day grew much older. And besides, though I understood quite starkly why we had not taken the children with us on disembarking, still I feared for their safety. So long as the officers and crew of *Prince Enero* were more afraid of me than they were afraid of whoever challenged them from over the rail, things would remain stable.

But not any longer than that.

"We cannot return to the waterfront," Mother Vajpai pointed out. "Certainly not right now. The Street Guild will be there in numbers. And they are very stirred up."

"Without the help of other Blades, you and I would be ill advised to try that," I said, agreeing. Puffing air from my cheeks in a measured sigh, I tried to think what the next most likely course of action would be.

The problem with being a Blade is that you were a *Blade.* We formed no alliances to speak of, and neither gave nor asked the help of others. Our work was our own, and we alone suffered whatever consequences arose from that in turn.

So we had no allied Court or Guild to turn to. No other temple or god kept such a force to hand, for the Blades' long-held monopoly on the Death Right had always discouraged such adventurism. And our hoped-for allies in the Saffron Tower renegades Firesetter and Fantail were still far from our grasp.

"Who do you know that we could appeal to?" I finally asked.

"The same people you do." I heard a twist of amusement in Mother Vajpai's voice. She was playing the part of a teacher once more.

You know the answer, now think of it. At least the lessons here were not beaten into me as they had been back at the Pomegranate Court within the Factor's bluestone walls.

No, the lessons here carried their own life or death penalties.

"Everyone is armed, and no one is, in this city." We'd certainly done our part to discourage overtly competing forces, though obviously the temple and the Blades had failed quite badly in containing the growth of the Street Guild. "It is difficult to know where to turn."

"Some people are everywhere and nowhere," Mother Vajpai replied in a mild tone.

"Everywhere and nowhere . . ."

"You've been doing very well so far." She smiled at me, though her face was a bit drawn. "I am impressed."

"You were with me through much of Surali's mess in Copper Downs," I protested. Meaning, of course, *Weren't you impressed with me then?*

"That was Copper Downs. This is Kalimpura." She seemed to be stating a basic fact of existence, some immutable law of life. I was once again reminded of how much the foreigner I was here, for all my dark skin and command of the language.

"And in this city we have all manner of people everywhere. Vendors, children both free and enslaved, servants, bondsmen, beggars—" I broke off, thinking about that. Then: "You and Mother Meiko knew me before I arrived at the temple all those years ago."

Her smile broadened, bringing some relief to the pain on her face. "Of course we did."

"Because you'd paid the beggar boys to follow me." Another piece fell into place. "In fact, I rather imagine even Little Kareen had reported me to you." The beggar-chief had sheltered me awhile on my initial arrival in Kalimpura before deciding I was too violent for his gang of ruffians.

"We cannot learn everything from Blades and their runs. There is too much life in Kalimpura, too many walls behind which secrets dwell."

"Little Kareen . . ." I mused on the man. He'd seemed so fat and old to me when I met him, but I was a child then. Now, at sixteen years of age, my perspective had changed—or so I thought at the time, though memory of that moment's careless thought can still make me laugh at my younger self. I would have been so offended at that amusement.

He could not have been more than his early twenties, I realized. Not an old man, barely a young man. Just a bit older than a frightened, lost girl with the burden of killing close to her heart and mind. My dead bandit briefly loomed in memory before I dismissed his shade.

"Beggars move everywhere and are little noticed. We place too much confidence in caste in this city." She tapped her lips. "Though in fairness it is easier to move down than up, unless the people you want to fool are also down-caste. They are the hardest to deceive."

"We don't want to fool the beggars. We want to enlist them." I began to grow excited. Now I knew the path back to my children. "We need their help in fooling the Street Guild."

"Let us go find our beggar-king," Mother Vajpai said. "I am rested."

We harvested some fruits for our baskets from the garden of our unwitting hosts, then headed through the winding streets of Kalimpura for the Landward Gate, outside of which the bully-master kept his little kingdom, the better to harass the peasants and travelers come to the city from all over Selistan.

The crowd beyond the walls was not so great as I remembered it from my initial arrival here. But then the rice harvest was not yet in, so the farmers and their families knee-deep in the muddy fields of the surrounding countryside were a month from either selling to brokers or making the long trek themselves.

This subtracted only a portion of the traffic, though. Other fruits and vegetables were in season; there was a constant trade in animals, slaves, and children—my vision darkened at the sight of a coffle of five- and six-year olds, but this was not the fight I had today. *Later, later,* I promised myself, who had been seeking vengeance and an end to that custom since I was old enough to understand how I myself had been sold away.

That life did bring me a *later* for this is one of the profound blessings of the years that have passed since those days.

All those, and travelers of other sorts. Bandits come to pawn their thefts, pilgrims made destitute by vow or at sword's point. A few messengers on horseback or mule, though riding animals were not so common outside the city walls. Traveling mummers, fortune-seekers, confidence tricksters, all of them falling somewhere between the categories of predator and prey here beyond the walls where food sellers, guides, beggars, and the ubiquitous "agents" roamed indisputably in their own class.

I reckoned I still knew where Little Kareen's camp was, what he'd called his patch on a prime piece of land alongside a creek near enough the Landward Gate for convenience, but far enough from the road for at least a pretense of privacy.

Being out here brought forth another set of memories, different from that flood sparked by the kitchens. I turned to Mother Vajpai. "When I met Mother Meiko on the road, I took her for a pilgrim. Yet I have never since heard of our Goddess expecting pilgrimage. Where are the holy sites she had gone to visit? Why?"

Mother Vajpai's pace slowed, and she stared at me awhile. "You did not see it then, did you?"

"See what? I was just a girl, frightened and running."

"Her pilgrimage was to find you." A hand raised to forestall the dozen questions already springing to my lips. "Of course, we did not know your name. Barely suspected your appearance. But such, well, power . . . coming to Selistan from over the sea did not go unnoticed. What you had done, back in Copper Downs. It marked you."

Mother Vajpai was one of the few outside the original conspiracy who was privy to that whole tale, or as much of it as mattered. I'd never wanted to be known as the girl who slew the Duke. Somehow my name had never come into the matter, for all my infamy since in both cities.

Yet even then, not one person in a hundred on the street would have recognized my name, and far fewer known my face. Infamy was not so much as it might have seemed.

"Marked me, and you sought that mark?"

"That power. The Lily Goddess spoke through Mother Umaavani and warned us of a girl. If we found you and sheltered you, you might be an ally, or even one of us. If we'd missed your coming or just ignored you, you would have been even more dangerous to us than Surali herself has proven to be."

Something in my heart twinged, shriveling toward sadness at those words. I'd known I was watched once I'd entered the city. I did not realize the Mothers had laid a honeyed trap for me even out upon the rough trackway from Bhopura.

Yet how different was this from me concerning myself with the ghosts and tulpas of Below in Copper Downs? Power was dangerous if not identified, directed, and controlled.

"I suppose I'd thought you took me in because I was a girl lost and alone," I said stiffly.

"We did," Mother Vajpai replied. I hated the pity I heard in her voice. She went on: "We are women, and some of us have borne children of our own."

That remark screamed for a question, but I did not take the bait. Not then. Later, if chance and the turn of conversation permitted. After a brief pause—testing me?—she continued: "We would not have had you starve."

"You could just as well put me into the kitchen as a scullion. I might be washing pots to this day."

"I am finding that inconceivable, and so are you finding it as well. You'd already spent your years in that terrible Pomegranate Court, and you'd killed, what, three times? At least? You would no more have scrubbed pots than you would have taken up the mantle of the Prince of the City."

"The latter is being more likely," I muttered. Just then I was torn between a sense of flattery and a sense of betrayal, unsure which was the more applicable here.

I knew which was the more useful, though.

"Forget it," I said, not waiting for her next words. "I might better have not asked, but that knife is thrown and has found a target." Stopping, I set down my basket of fruit and took her hands. "You and Mother Meiko did well by me. And I do not despair of the Lily Goddess, whatever that foolish Mother Srirani says."

"You have never followed Her as we do," Mother Vajpai replied.

"Too much time spent too close to power has leached respect for the majesty and might of the divine from your character."

That made me laugh ruefully. "How much respect for any form of authority have you ever seen in me?"

"Indeed. You are as unseemly a supplicant as I have ever seen approach a god, yet still they listen to you and speak through you."

I thought about the theories thrown around by Iso and Osi, and from my own reading, of how a channel once opened became easier to use. "An oracle whose one size fits many. Right now my prophetic powers tell me we should get moving again before we draw unwanted attention. Little Kareen shall likely not want our company either, but at least it is ours to deliver."

"Understood," Mother Vajpai said. She released my hands. "Green, just so you know . . . I am proud of you. So very proud. I know Mother Meiko would have been, had she lived this long."

"Thank you."

We stalked through a stand of thornbushes, along a winding path, toward some grubby pavilions visible ahead. I tried not to think too much on what had just passed between me and Mother Vajpai, because I did not wish to cry just then.

A small boy scrambled away from us in a cloud of dust as we passed out of the thorn tree thicket. The sentry—and he had been napping, I was certain. Little Kareen would know, too, and make the child's life wretched for it.

Most of his boys were out working the crowds. Nighttime was the more natural element for such mountebanks in training, but daytime was when their likeliest victims were available. So the camp was largely deserted. Half a dozen pavilions rose on poles leaning to and fro. Some of their rips had been patched; others were allowed to flex in the desultory wind of the hot early afternoon.

That was more than I remembered. When I dwelled briefly among these lost boys, we'd largely slept on open ground with whatever pallets each boy's ingenuity could contrive through begging, borrowing, or stealing. Now there was a little iron stove under one roof, with a scattering of mismatched chairs and benches. They had not yet managed to appropriate a table, I saw.

The only true tent, in the sense of having fabric walls and a flapped entrance drawn open, was Little Kareen's. The child poked his head out as we approached. I figured on several unfriendly eyes watching us from within or nearby, but we were not the sort of armed threat that would provoke swift flight, nor peers enough to them to provoke an automatic fight.

Curiosity was a trait very hard to pound out of the human spirit, even for such as these who lived near the bottom of the great ladder of life in—and around—Kalimpura. They were more free than the peasants, and in some ways lived better than did the laborers within the walls.

Who was I to fault these boys?

I stepped into the tent, only slightly worried about a thrown spear or a crossbow bolt. Clinging to my earlier logic, I straightened in the shadows within. The fug was strong, a close, stale scent of unwashed bodies and dung fire. "Greetings." My tone was strong and clear, without a quaver. "An old friend comes to call."

"No one old is my friend," said a familiar voice out of the darkness. He had lit no lamp, and kept the walls of his tent rolled down tight.

When I had first encountered him, Little Kareen with his fingerless right hand and his ready left fist had been fat, almost to the point of gross, but still brutally efficient in his edicts. He kept two or three boys close to hand as lieutenants, and once or twice a year had the oldest one thrashed and expelled from the camp for the crime of growing up. Everyone understood the system, and in any event, no one really wanted to spend his life here. It worked, except, presumably, for the occasional ambitious lad who sought Little Kareen's own position on the top of this particularly stunted social ladder.

Them he had killed. I knew this because he was still here.

"I am Green, come with Mother Vajpai to treat with you."

"Ah . . ." The voice was thoughtful and slow. "Green. I had never expected to see you again." A rustle, as if he'd dipped his chin or shaken his head. All we could see was a shadowed bulk amid other shadows. "And Mother Vajpai. Your fame precedes you. Though you are thought to have left the city by ship. In pursuit of this one, in fact."

"We have been back in Kalimpura only a few hours," she said, speaking as if to an equal.

Has it only been a few hours? I was already as overwhelmed as if a month of madness were just passed.

"I would bid you welcome, but that would be a lie. We normally beat or kill strangers who blunder into here."

"We are not strangers," I pointed out. "Nor is any boy who grows out of his place here and moves on."

"Strange enough, Green. You are strange enough."

I let that ride, taking in the darkness with the other senses the Dancing Mistress had sharpened within me down Below. I knew the size of the place from the outside, and the fabric walls muffled echoes. The floors were covered in carpet or fur, and more must be piled around the edges or light would have glared through where the tent met the ground. The acrid odor of burnt dung signified a stove. Urine as well, and a chamber pot. Also wine, some of it fresh in the air. He was drinking now, or had been just before we came in.

Was Little Kareen such a tippler when I'd known him? I could not recall. As a younger girl, I'd not paid attention to matters of that sort.

More to the point, was he deep in his cups now? Or perhaps he was just drinking as the merchants did, lightly through the day to avoid the illnesses in the water and keep the palate sharp?

"What brings you to my domain?" he finally asked. "Surely it is not my legendary hospitality."

"No," I told him. "Not hospitality. Rather, your legendary capabilities."

"Legendary." He laughed, hollow and tired. "For what?"

"For being a clever, brutal bastard who runs a string of sharp and dangerous boys." There. If he knew Mother Vajpai, he knew we were Blades. Some flattery from our quarter might go a ways to improving his mood.

"We are shaking down peasants and harassing peddlers. Are you demoting yourself to small-time crime?"

"No, the biggest crime of all. I want to steal my way into Kalimpura, then steal the city from those who would claim it for their own."

Another long silence. Then: "You do not dream in small doses. But then you never did." He paused for one, two, three deep breaths. "Mother Vajpai, did you know I cast this one out for being too brutal? Too brutal, among my boys, is a mark of some distinction."

Her reply surprised me. "The Blades found her brutal as well, but biddable."

Now *there* was a lie, but I held my tongue. No one had ever styled me biddable. Not and kept their face straight in the process.

"And ambitious as well, it seems." Something creaked—the gilded bench he used for a throne, though the gilding was stage paint and mostly flaked away even when I had been here before. "I run a string of pickpockets and sneak thieves. You will not find the rulership of the city on the board of a cart here outside the walls."

"No. But we are pursued within." I saw no point in not being clear with him about my immediate goals, as I'd already blurted the outline of my larger plan. "We must get to the docks, specifically Agina's Pier, without being slain out of hand by the Street Guild, let alone captured. I have . . . small cargo to be removed from a ship there. And soon."

"The docks are far from my patch." Kareen wheezed. "There is nothing I can do. If the Street Guild is out for you, well . . . That I understand. Much against my judgment, you may remain here tonight for shelter as you need. It will be instructive for my boys to meet you. Some of the oldest still recall your last stay here."

My fingers brushed Mother Vajpai's elbow. Overnight was not what I wanted. I needed to feed my babies soon, or at least relieve the tension in my breasts. *That* would be ill-done here in a camp of boys, where I might find myself pushed to the ground by too many to fight off. And I needed to be back with my children.

Mother Vajpai grasped my wrist, squeezed lightly. "We thank you for your hospitality," she said. "We will accept for this day. Perhaps tonight our discussions will bear greater fruit."

"Perhaps," said Little Kareen. "For now, go. Panjit will show you where to rest, and provide such as we have fit for august visitors like yourselves."

I bowed, though I doubted he could see me do so in these shadows. We felt our way back to the flap. I glanced back as the light speared inward, but saw only a narrowing triangle of filthy rugs and one edge of his metal stove.

Evening brought boys large and small filtering into the camp. They appeared as the blackflies do, out of nowhere and suddenly all around in a flock. Panjit had provided us with sour milk and dried dates, and a shaded place to sit. Once the boys began returning, other provisions had come in with them.

There was a very careful buzzing and circling of us as they approached. Not fear, exactly, but wariness. Two women sitting at ease in this camp was unprecedented, I knew. Little Kareen had no use for the foolish and stupid, so I was not worried about being rushed or called out by these ones. At least, not unless he ordered it done.

After a while a delegation led by a boy surely too tall to remain here much longer approached. He spoke cautiously, but with confidence rather than trembling fear. "Ravit says we know you."

"You might. I was here once." In truth, I did not recognize him at all, but that was how children grew, I supposed.

"You are Green."

"I am. And you?"

He seemed disappointed that I could not name him. "Penagut."

That meant nothing to me, but it would not cost me to give him a boost. "It is good to see you again."

He smiled shyly.

I realized then that I was seeing these boys as a mother would. Children, lost and lonely, enslaved to crime and near-starvation as surely as any child chained to a basin behind a tavern kitchen was enslaved to water and the filth of the men within. These youngsters were dangerous, would doubtless kill me in my sleep if they saw profit and believed that they would go unpunished. But they were also boys. They had suckled at a mother's breast for a time, as Federo still suckled at mine. Someone had once held pride and hope and fear for them.

I found those emotions peopling my heart a little while, and for my own part wished with a bitter intensity not to ever have to fight here. Them I could not wound or slay. The tracks of innocence still haunted their young faces, whatever crimes had been committed this day.

A meal was called, a thick stew consisting mostly of lentils and millet. A few globs of fat floated for flavor, though I did not see the meat they might have come from. It certainly could have used some spice, but I had eaten worse. One could garner a full belly and night's sleep from such fare.

Little Kareen did not come out and join us, but Penagut did. He proved to be one of the ever-changing crew of lieutenants.

"You make the boss nervous," he said, chewing on a bit of flatbread. I saw no more of it, and had been offered none, so assumed that was one of the fruits of Penagut's own labors.

"Nervous is how he survives."

"Well, yes, but ain't what I mean." Penagut glanced around, apparently satisfied himself that all the boys nearby were among those he trusted, and continued. "He is more still now. No ambition anymore. You have stirred him."

"The docks excite him?" asked Mother Vajpai. She'd kept her own counsel through much of the afternoon, though she seemed amused now.

Penagut's voice sped up as he grew more animated. "The pickings there would be so much richer than anything out here."

Those *pickings* were someone else's livelihood, but I was hardly one to moralize. I would have been far more comfortable with potential allies who stole from those already burdened with too much wealth, rather than boosting a poor man's last copper paisas, but these were who I had to work with.

"That is true," I said carefully. "A beggar's run against the docks would bring me to where I need to be, and provide you with opportunity." The mother within me forced the next words out of my mouth against my better judgment. "But it will be dangerous. There are many men there, real fighters with serious weapons. Street Guild and others."

"We can handle them," he said boastfully. I knew a boy's bravado when I heard it.

"You will learn much," Mother Vajpai intoned.

After some inconsequential chatter, the boys drifted off. Mother Vajpai leaned close and whispered in my ear, "They will lose much, too."

That struck at the heart of my own incipient guilt. It was one thing to set adults against one another. Life was risk, and if you played blade games, you accepted their consequences.

But this . . .

Still, they would get me to Marya and Federo. That thought made my breasts leak, and I muttered under my breath.

Just then Ravit trotted up. "Little Kareen will see you now," he announced, as if offering some magnificent gift.

"We come," Mother Vajpai replied. She grasped my hand and urged me to my feet. In a funk, I followed her through the night-dark camp to Little Kareen's tent.

This time lamps were lit inside. The same rolled rugs that had kept daylight out also contained these night-lights within. A curtain shrouded the door, so by entering we would not shout our presence to any watchers in the dark.

The tent was much as I had expected from before. Little Kareen, however, was not. He had grown enormously large, simply the most enormous man I had ever seen. His face was pocked with sores. The red bugge, or some disease much like it, ravaged him. Something else was wrong, because no one could eat themselves to that size, even on purpose, if their body was behaving only somewhat normally.

Huge, he overflowed his bench-throne. I saw that it had been reinforced by bricks. That explained the urine smell. I doubted he could rise and walk far enough to pee in a trench outside.

A handful of older boys stood as witness. Or possibly the threat of force, though I was not too concerned about whether we could defend ourselves. I could not attack them, though. Would not do so.

"What is in this for me?" he asked without preamble, as if we had not left the tent for so many hours.

Following Penagut's lead, and feeling only somewhat ashamed of myself, I answered, "Richer pickings than you would see in a year of work out here. All in the space of an hour or two."

"And the toll?"

I shrugged, more ashamed of myself now. Mother Vajpai spoke. "Some tuitions come at a cost. Those who return will be much the wiser."

Little Kareen snorted. "And when the Bittern Court comes for me, will you shield me from those charges?"

"The Temple of the Silver Lily will stand for you." *If we win*, I thought. I knew he heard the unspoken words clearly.

"Assault. Theft. Destruction of property. Public disorder. Even if no one dies, certain people will be very excited about such an excursion."

"Certain people are going to be very excited no matter what I do," I pointed out. "You can profit by it, or you can stand aside."

One of the boys stirred at that, objecting perhaps to my lack of respect for his master. Little Kareen raised his fingerless hand to his lieutenant before addressing me again. "Protect me and mine from the law. We will handle the thugs in our own way."

Again, I found this optimistic, but held my tongue.

"If we do this right," said Mother Vajpai, "so many people will join in to the riot that your place at the heart of it will likely not be noticed."

"Then make your plans, and I shall make mine."

Soon, I thought. *Soon*. The ship would not await me overlong. As well the nightmare of Ilona, Ponce, and the babies being put over the side before I could return to them.

Well, we had two or three days, and I had not yet used even one. If only my enemies were even more lax in their diligence, I might yet prevail.

Later that night, Mother Vajpai and I sat on the ground next to a rather clever little stove consisting of an iron box filled with coals from the much larger stove inside Little Kareen's tent. We were each wrapped in borrowed blankets, and had eaten a few more offerings of sometimes dubious food from the boys who continued to eye us. My breasts ached, and I discreetly expressed milk into a rag under the cover provided.

The night around us was noisy. I was not so sure why Little Kareen bothered to hide his camp, given how many men and animals seemed to be blundering about in the darkness. Kalimpura-the-city was surrounded by Kalimpura-the-town, a restless and churning community without doors or walls that was nonetheless very real. Also, it seemed odd to feel so crowded out here among the thornbushes and plane trees, when the streets beyond the Landward Gate were a dozen times more thronged at every step. Even at this time of night.

"I want to go into the city and scout our path for tomorrow," I told Mother Vajpai. "We should strike at morning."

"Green . . ." She sighed, as if gathering her wits. The Blade Mother had not been the same since Surali caused her toes to be chopped off. The amputation had stolen something of her spirit as well. "This is your mission. I have been cautious about advising you, and have not tried to order you at all."

"I . . ." Words failed me, briefly. A denial had leapt to my lips, a swift vow of obedience, but we would have both known the lie. I was here to mount a rescue of Corinthia Anastasia and Samma, and to extract vengeance from Surali as well as her Bittern Court. Those deeds were not the will of the Temple of the Silver Lily. No point in making promises I would never keep. "We are cut loose from the temple," I finally said, knowing the words to be weak and purposeless.

"From the temple, perhaps, but not from the Lily Goddess." I heard more than saw the gentle smile in her lips. "Blades rarely act so, but we are priestesses. Consecrated to Her service. Our work is Hers. Our practices are Her rites. Mother Srirani can cast you out and mark your name anathema, but who is she?"

I waited a moment, then realizing that question was not rhetorical, stepped carefully into the answer. "She is a woman, as we are. She is sworn to the Lily Goddess, as we are." Old lessons, some at this woman's hard hand, came back to me. "But it is not for each of us to follow our own dictates. The temple functions as it does so that any can draw power from all."

"The practice of hierarchy is much debated in every generation, believe me. Some decades we are rigid; some decades we are loose. But this, well, *business*, with the Bittern Court has deformed the politics of the temple. We are pulled from our natural arc."

Ruefully I smiled, though I knew I was just a shadow to her eyes. "All of which is a long-winded way of saying that while I am not obliged to obey you, I would be wise to heed your words."

Mother Vajpai snorted. "Indeed, Green. And here are the words I hope you will heed. Forget the docks. Rest, and dream on your children. This is not enemy territory or unknown land. All the older boys have been there before, and likely most of the younger. All we need do is direct them toward Agina's Pier and be about our business aboard *Prince Enero* while the Street Guild is distracted. Beyond that . . . Well, let it be Surali's problem. This is one fight we do not need to finish."

My feet were twitching to be off. Quite literally so. "I am being discomfited to lie here in the dark while need awaits."

"So sleep it off. How much more discomfited will you be if the Street Guild catches or kills you alone in the city? You know what sort of watch they must have on that ship by now."

I paused to remove my milk-soaked rag and press another into its place. This being in milk was a tedious and painful affair that sometimes made me feel like a kept goat. And my breasts ached much of the time. "Afterwards? After we fetch my children?"

"There are safe places, even in Kalimpura. Before we left, Mother Argai and I each made some arrangements."

That caught me short, but on swift reflection, I realized it should not have done so. "You knew what you might come back to."

"The elevation of Mother Srirani was . . . contentious." Her voice seemed more distant now. "Some of the senior Blades have sought other paths for a while."

"Away from the Lily Goddess?"

"No! Away from the Justiciary Mothers, perhaps."

She was talking about that pendulum of governance again, and how the path of the Temple of the Silver Lily had been bent aside by outside influence. I was tired of governance but in resolving my own problems, if I could resolve this, so much the better. "I will not overthrow another city," I told her.

"Better to overthrow the evening in favor of sleep," she said.

And so in a short while, each in our own fashion, we did that thing.

I was up before the dawn, brushing away tears. This was not a day to weep for my children. Who, at that moment, were far safer than I.

Ponce, Ilona, and Mother Argai did not have a backup plan. If Mother Vajpai and I were taken or slain, their best safety might well be in sailing on with *Prince Enero*. I tried to imagine my children fostered in one of the Sunward cities. At such a distance, Selistan would be barely a rumor except to a few far-ranging sailors.

That would not happen, I told myself, and went for a walk among the thornbushes to avoid waking Mother Vajpai with my fidgeting worries.

The faintest predawn light lent a shadowless cast to the mists that clung to the bushes. These rose a good deal taller than my own height, their branches a crazed reach like dozens of bony arms scrabbling toward the sky. It was easy to see monsters or demons in the odd-shaped gaps, but I'd witnessed sufficient true strangeness Below in Copper Downs to render such phantoms of the senses laughable.

The ground was lush in some places, bare or trampled in others.

I did not know enough of the lives of plants to say why, but I did treasure the pale flowers that peeked from among the clumps of wiry grass.

In the near distance, Kalimpura glowed above the predawn mists. There were always torches, lanterns, the business of the streets that never slept. On first arriving, I had marveled at the slow carts that circled the city streets, not stopping except to change teams of mules or oxen, wherein one could rent a bunk for a half paisa and sleep awhile. So many people so close together that one person must rise up so another might rest.

The Temple of the Silver Lily was truly a refuge. Much as the houses of the wealthy could be. Even the meager poor of Copper Downs had more space to themselves than most people here. That city had buildings standing *empty*. In Kalimpura, if you left a crate standing empty on a street corner, an hour later, it would be occupied by a family raising chickens for the market.

In this early morning stillness, I could hear the city as well, in a way that was not possible in daylight. The sound was a murmur, like the distant sea. Hooves and voices and squawks and shouting and barking and clattering all combined into that susurrus. Even the scent came over the walls in darkness, though from this distance it was largely woodsmoke and a generic gutter reek.

Someone approached through the darkness. I drew my god-blooded short knife and faded close to a tree, but then I realized by his footfalls that it was Penagut.

"Green? . . ." Anyone could have pegged him from twenty paces by the noise alone.

"Why are you here?" I asked quietly from almost behind his ear.

I heard the hiss and thump as he caught his breath, startled by me. "Looking for you," he said after a short, shocked interval.

In point of fact, I'd meant the question more generally, but that was a fair answer. I slid my knife back into my sleeve. "You have found me. Are the boys awakening?"

"Little Kareen decreed we would begin to pass through the Landward Gate starting at dawn. A few at a time, to avoid attention."

Kalimpura did not have a city watch or any such formal policing. Nonetheless, the walls and gates were guarded by the Prince of the City's men. Not those foolish peacock warriors who served him as bodyguards, but real guards who might have been watchmen in a city that wanted its streets overseen, as Kalimpura did not. Once you were past the walls, you were on your own here. But they had the right to inspect at the gate. Not just that, but also the right to turn people back.

It was Kalimpura's way of setting itself apart from the rest of Selistan. Other cities of substance rose to the west and south, but Kalimpura stood alone in this northeast corner of the continent, and served as a port of entry for those coming from beyond the Storm Sea. As well as those arriving from the interior villages. *We are different,* the gates proclaimed. *We are proud.*

"So you send them out already?"

"Yes. We think it best if you go early as well."

Not that the Street Guild kept working hours, but he had a point. They were unlikely to be out in force during the first part of the day. Especially not those who had been drinking last night. Men were men, after all.

"I am coming back," I said. "We will go robed as servants."

My plan of storming the docks with the dawn had melted into the middle hours of the morning by the time I shuffled through the Landward Gate with my basket in my arm and my eyes upon my feet. The guards did not even give me a first glance, let alone a second. That was fine with me. Not that I could not have taken them down handily, but that would have started the fighting too soon.

Penagut and the other senior boys had each escorted a drawn-out string of excited youngsters through the gate, then gone recruiting. Little Kareen knew of the other child-gang bosses, and they certainly knew of him. I'd learned more in the past few hours than I'd ever known there was to learn about their secrets.

Rollers, I now understood, were the younger children who moved in groups and swarmed drunks, the ill, and the unlucky. A man could have his purse taken, his pockets picked, and the sandals off his feet in less than a quick five-count, and be left shouting and swinging his fist at nothing but shadows.

Slitters worked alone or in pairs, walking through the crowds to cut open purses and money pouches from behind and below. In pairs, the second slitter would make a deliberately clumsy pass at the victim while the first finished the job.

Likewise the dodgers, runners, dog-boys, crust-eaters, pickers, flickers, and more. Every one of these boys had a specialty, and some of them were quite good at it. So did the bosses—different gangs tended to concentrate on different aspects of the trade, with a rough division of activities and territories.

It was rarely in any of their interests for the child-gangs to fight openly. In that way, their structure mirrored the Courts and Guilds into which the wealthy and powerful of Kalimpura were organized.

Much like the hierarchy of the gods: as above, so below.

Through his lieutenants, Little Kareen had put out the word that there would be a beggars' run today. All the rollers and slitters and dodgers and the rest of them, from all over town, were easing toward the docks. Not in a great, armed stream—that would have been obvious. Rather, a general movement of boys and girls aged from three to thirteen or so, edging all in one direction for a change.

If one knew what to look for, it was like watching the turn of the tide.

And as I'd promised Little Kareen, in their numbers, any of them would be anonymous. Even the Street Guild could hardly hunt down and kill every child in the city. No matter how put out they or their masters were.

Mother Vajpai was not with me. She'd entered Kalimpura with another group perhaps half an hour ahead of me. Our plan was to meet at the foot of Agina's Pier, waiting until the last moment to find each other. We walked apart because the Street Guild were surely looking for a pair of Blades.

I moved along with the mounting flood of children until Penagut had us stop near the Ragisthuri Ice and Fuel bunker. We sidled into an alley, me the tallest of them except for Penagut himself, and took up dicing for a bit. None of them had much notion of the time—a close watch of the hours was more of a Petraean fixation—but even the smallest child could tell when noon arrived.

And so my dawn raid on the docks became a midday riot. When Penagut judged the time to be right, he signaled Little Kareen's boys with a series of low whistles. Chaos moved out among the merchants and sailors and half a hundred other trades working the waterfront.

In moments, the uproar had transcended deafening. I pushed through the swirl of outraged adults and racing children and rank opportunists of various sorts, intent on finding Mother Vajpai before any of this riot happened to me personally.

She was right where we'd agreed to meet, close to the spot where we'd fought off our welcoming committee just the day before. *So little time for so much to happen,* I marveled briefly.

I signaled for us to move up the pier. Some of the stevedores were rapidly setting a makeshift barrier of cargo and timber baulks, but they let two serving women through. If we'd been walking openly as Lily Blades, I wondered if they would have done the same.

Clear of them, we pushed through the crowds toward *Prince Enero.* Something cracked loudly ahead. A weapon, perhaps, though it sounded more like a small, intense firework. Or possibly thunder of a sort. Wisps of blue smoke eddied from the kettle ship's deck.

Fire?

Or guns?

That second thought was sickening.

I redoubled my efforts, shedding my robe for the advantage the leathers beneath would give me in clearing my way. Even that did not avail me much, because by now the people on the pier were in full panic. Most of the ships tied up had already pulled in their planks, and I saw more than one crew cutting their lines so as to stand off from the riot.

More thunder echoed ahead. Someone fell screaming from *Prince Enero's* rail.

Mother Vajpai was close behind me. She simply could not run as I, not on her poor, mutilated feet. I no longer cared. My long knife I drew into my left hand, the god-blooded short knife in my right.

Now people cleared the way. Some jumped right into the stinking harbor to give me passage.

Moments later, I pushed two armed men into the water between hull and pier to rush up *Prince Enero's* ladder. A Street Guildsman climbed ahead of me. I glanced down to confirm the first pair were the same.

By all the Smagadine hells and the broken Wheel besides, they are.

I stabbed up through the nail-studded sole of his boot. The god-blooded blade slid in. He shrieked and looked down at me.

All I had to do was grin, and the man kicked away from the hull to drop toward the water, rather than face me. Unfortunately, he pushed too hard, and smacked his head and shoulders into the stone edge of the pier with a sickening thump.

My grin broadened as I cleared the rail and laid into the two of his Street Guild fellows before me. They'd been fighting several of Lalo's men, so I had a clear swing at both their backs, and was not afraid to use it.

Honor was for people who could afford to lose. Winning was for the rest of us.

One of the sailors lowered his cutlass, looked at me in amazement, then pointed aft toward our cabin. He tried to tell me something. Even though we shared no language between us, I already knew what he meant.

I charged past the bridge tower, into the breezeway I'd struggled through during the storm, and from there through the hatch that opened on the passengers' mess. Sounds of fighting echoed from beyond, and a short, sharp scream.

"No!" I could not run fast enough. The Street Guild were closing in on my children and their protectors.

Perhaps a dozen men clogged the passageway before me. From the far side I saw several more of *Prince Enero*'s crew with a dismounted iron hatch for a shield. About half the Street Guild present were engaging them, forcing the shield back. The rest shouted into a door, blades stabbing within.

I was close enough to hear Ilona shrieking, and a rhythmic grunting that could only be Mother Argai laying to.

My babies were in there.

The next minute or so passed in a spattering blur and the echo of more guns firing. My long knife snagged on the mailed collar of one Street Guildsman, so I left it there and gutted him like perch with the short knife. From the back I severed spines, slashed through ribs, punctured kidneys, and opened necks the hard way. The first ones died before they could turn to face me. They fell so fast that their fellows did not realize what was come behind them.

The last two by the door I killed to their faces. Screaming, I was screaming, though even then I did not know what words I uttered, and years of memory have not unlocked that since. Whatever I said, they perished with terror bleeding from their eyes.

Mother Argai looked at me, her face stark and pale, then shouted something. It was enough to keep me moving. By now, the five Street Guild farther down the passageway had realized their peril and turned to face me, ignoring the ship's defending crew.

That was fine. I could kill from the front quite as well as from behind. I kicked off a blood-soaked step to rush them. At my second step, one's chest exploded from within. Then another's head. More of that thunder echoed, and the stink of burning and sulfur filled the passageway as if magic were going wrong. The survivors turned one way and the other, knowing they were fatally trapped.

I obliged, breaking two necks and slashing a third. My next strike nearly landed on Lalo, but I pulled my blow to bury the short knife in his ship's iron bulkhead.

"Enough," the mate breathed in his Seliu, his voice barely audible over the frightened wailing of my children. I could read terror in his face as well, but also strength. "The deck is ours," he added.

"I am taking my children and departing." The snarl hung in my voice as I worried my long knife free.

He nodded. His men, two of them holding long wooden batons with metal rods, just looked terrified as well. No, not batons. Guns, just as I'd thought. But big like crossbows rather than Malice Curry's little pistol. Only firearms made the stinking, magical thunder.

Spinning once more, I stepped back to the cabin as Mother Vajpai entered the corridor from the far end. "We go now," I called at Ilona and Ponce and Mother Argai.

All three of them were struck to openmouthed silence as well. *"Now!"* I repeated.

They moved.

Not two minutes later, we were back on the deck looking down at Agina's Pier. The riot had stopped, frozen. Everyone on the pier and along the docks ahead was staring at *Prince Enero.*

In effect, at me.

How very strange, I thought.

Ponce tugged at my arm. "Green," he whispered over little Federo's burbling breath. His voice was still, almost strangled.

I turned and looked abaft.

The harbor had risen up behind our ship. It stood quivering in a mountainous slope taller than *Prince Enero*'s bridge deck, a fist ready to slap down the vessel and everyone foolish enough to still be aboard her. Shivering and still, just like one of those swells from the mid-ocean storm we'd escaped through my prayers. As if the ghost of that weather had come to haunt us now.

Foam raced down the slope, boiling lace straight from the deep waters of the ocean. Dark shapes moved within. Sharks. Monsters. Souls. I could not tell, and did not want to know.

My knees jellied and my bones chilled. This was about me. The sea did not come calling like this for any normal person in any normal moment of life.

Desire, or one of Her brothers Time and Oceanus, or some sending of the Saffron Tower—I could not say. But this thing was focused on me.

"We go," I said roughly, breaking the spell that held everyone on the deck still as rabbits beneath the circling eagle.

The ladder was clear. I ignored the rushing noise that was now horribly audible. Like a waterfall over my shoulder. People below stared up—this riot had swept up everyone from gutter urchins to grandmothers to shopkeepers. Though we had meant only to create enough of a ruckus to mask our movements, the hatred of the smallfolk for Street Guild who enforced their own brand of false justice along the docks had brought people out in great numbers. All those folk were stilled with the same awe that had just captured me as well.

Little Marya in one arm, my short knife clenched in that same fist, I one-handed slowly down the ladder, dropping the last body length to land on the pier.

The others crept down behind me. It was as if we were afraid of awakening that foaming mountain of water to its duties with respect to gravity. I was sickeningly desperate to be away before that eldritch wave broke.

With any luck, we would be swiftly lost in the crowd. They were riveted by the standing wave, not by us. I slipped my short knife up my sleeve and turned to take one last look up at *Prince Enero*. As I'd hoped and feared, Lalo stood at the rail, staring back at me.

His face twitched, and he offered me a slow salute, then shooed us on our way. I sketched a bow, then turned and led my little handle into the silent mess we'd made of the waterfront. For the first few steps, it was like weaving through a garden of warm statuary. At least this time, no one stood in my way.

The water remained poised over *Prince Enero*'s stern as we reached the Street of Ships. At the foot of the waterfront's seawall the bottom muck was exposed as if at low tide. Which made sense, a logical part of me declared amid the incipient panic of such bizarre magic behind me. The wave had to be made of water.

Those stilled mountains of stormy rage had been one thing on a ship at sea, alone in the middle of the ocean. They'd had place and purpose and context, for all that it had been a bizarre experience. Here in Kalimpura's harbor, one of their fellows seemed like a cosmic blunder. Or cosmic threat.

As we turned away from the Street of Ships onto Prince Suravati Street, I heard the water collapse with a thunderous rush. That was immediately followed by screaming. The slop from the wave was loud. It must have swamped Agina's Pier badly, not to mention the waterfront around there.

I muttered a prayer to Desire and Her brother titanics—whether thanks or supplication, even I could not have said. I hoped that *Prince Enero* was not much damaged. The ship and its crew had served us better than we deserved.

Mother Argai led through the streets now as dirty seawater lapped at our heels. This was not by discussion, but simply because she pushed ahead. Three blocks inland, there was no sign of the riot or the ocean's misplaced might. Such was Kalimpura, where the gods could stage the ending of the world on one street and the people thronging the next street over would never notice.

For my part, I felt wrung out. Decisions were beyond me right now. I clutched my child close, kept my head down, and hurried after her. We moved in a huddle. No eye contact, no rough play, just sliding through the crowds.

Eventually our way eased. I looked up—briefly confused, for I had not been attending to our route—and realized we were on Shalavana Avenue. One of the streets where the houses of the wealthy lay cheek by jowl, separated by mere rods of formal garden and modest but high walls.

Traffic was much sparser here, too, and I felt deeply conspicuous. My shoulders itched as if expecting a shot.

Quite soon, Mother Argai led us to a small servants' gate at one corner of a walled property. She even had a key for the brass lock, to my considerable surprise. She must have been carrying that all the way to Copper Downs and back. The gate was jammed, but a moment with her shoulder and it creaked open. That in turn popped the lead and wax temple and Guild seals that showed this place enjoyed strong protection. We filed through into an overgrown garden where insects hummed and frogs peeped and no one had seemingly walked for years.

> *We are lying quiet in an empty house. I had not known there was such a thing here in Kalimpura, where every corner belongs to some beggar and her family. At least there is paper here, and ink stones with fine metal nibs for writing.*
>
> *Though I am consecrated, and therefore a priestess in my own right, I have never been much for ritual. My relationship with the gods has been far more prosaic than hieratic.*
>
> *Yet today a miracle happened. It was not the little magic of a heeded prayer or a quiet sacrifice. Some power, and I suspect several, made a show in front of half the city. Or at least all of the waterfront.*
>
> *I do not understand it, and I am frightened. Has the ocean decided to follow me like a dog?*
>
> *You do not have these answers, I know. But you are one of the few who might understand the questions.*

I lay awake in the late afternoon light, naked, exhausted, and wondering that something as simple as a gun could make a man's chest explode. To kill so carelessly from more than striking distance and at the speed of thought was a frightening power to hand anyone.

Yet I had seen it for myself.

We occupied a silent mansion. Much of the furniture was draped in coarse muslin, though that was grimy and in some places water-stained. Our footprints on the floor were the first in months or possibly even years, judging from the thickness of the dust there. Mother

Argai had said very little once we'd gained entry to the house—which took some doing, given the little golden monkeys in the garden who'd pelted us with sticks and dung. Exhausted, she had lain down on a settee, not even bothering to remove the cover. She was still sleeping when I'd finally retreated with my children to an inner room with a strange, high bed of teak ornately carved in some style I did not recognize, the ceiling painted with frescoes out of Selistani myth and legend.

Marya and Federo were fed, and slept now as well. I had nibbled on fruit gathered by Ponce from the garden despite the threat of monkeys, but rest eluded me. Too much to do, too many questions to resolve. We were no closer to rescuing our missing than we had been on sailing into the harbor. All we'd gained thus far was the apparent safety of this refuge.

Those "arrangements" Mother Vajpai had mentioned must have included this house. I was suitably grateful for a quiet place that was not filled with knives other than my own.

I startled awake in the deepening shadows of evening. Federo nuzzled me, though Marya still slept until I began to move. Before I did anything else, I took my time feeding them. Once both my babies were sated, I wrapped myself in a section of furniture cover, bundled my bloodied, soiled leathers in another section, then gathered babies and gear to go searching for my companions.

They were all sitting in the dark of the kitchen. Not even a tiny fire was lit in the great cooking hearth. Such light as there was came from the moon's rays slanting in through the slatted east-facing windows, and a bit of the city's glow. Pans dangled overhead like threats. Long trestle tables loomed beneath more of the ubiquitous furniture covers. A series of huge wooden and copper tubs lined the far wall—laundry as well here in the kitchen? Unusual, but not unheard of, especially if there was only one boiler on the grounds.

"Well," I said quietly.

Ilona raised her hands for one of the babies. I handed her Federo, and Marya to Ponce. My bundle I tossed on the floor. At least it wasn't dripping blood.

I went and found a stool and carried it to a point between Mother

Argai and Mother Vajpai, both of whom were seated in low wooden chairs scavenged from outside, by their look.

Looking around, I tasted the heavy silence among them all. Everyone was exhausted. Fair enough. So was I. Still, there was no need to sulk in the dark. We had much to do. "No fire, no light. We are not at home to the neighbors, I presume."

"No," said Mother Vajpai shortly. "Nor to the Street Guild."

Mother Argai nodded. "I repaired the gate seals."

They were all staring at me now. Four pairs of adult eyes glittered in the dimness of the kitchen.

Finally I asked the question implied by their careful expressions. "What troubles you?"

To my surprise, it was Ponce who finally spoke. "That . . . thing . . . in the harbor. What was it?"

"I do not know," I said honestly. "Whatever force saved us at sea has followed us here."

"Followed *you*, Green." Ilona sounded as if she'd been crying. That twisted my gut. I wanted more for her, from her.

With her.

I felt cold, my heart sinking. These were my friends, the people I trusted most. The people I trusted with my *children*. Everyone around me seemed to be receding.

"Followed me, yes." I picked my words with care. "I cannot say what that was about. I suspect Desire's brother Time, aiding Her to my benefit."

"You speak of the titanics as if they lived down the hall from you," said Mother Vajpai.

"You follow a goddess who is active in the world," I blurted. Already I was losing my place in this conversation. "You have seen miracles."

"Flower petals. Water falling from the indoor air. Words from the mouth of a woman in a trance." She sounded as if she had swallowed a lemon. "Not miracles that can move oceans."

"So much more," Ilona added.

"A difference of degree!" I exploded, shouting so loudly, the babies startled and little Federo began to squall. "Nothing you have not seen. We are being of common purpose here, by the Wheel. What has changed?"

"Not just miracles." Mother Argai finally spoke up as Ilona calmed the baby. "You fight differently now."

"I fight for my life." Petulantly, I added, "As I was taught. And besides, my babies were threatened."

"We are not a death cult," Mother Vajpai said mildly. "Lily Blades fight to win, not to kill."

She was right. How many had I slain today? A dozen? A score? More? I could not lay them out, but at the least I could light candles for them in the garden and speak to their sins and virtues. Honor their deaths, if not their lives.

That thought in turn brought me back to Counselor Lampet and his foolish head. "They attack me with everything in their power. How can I do less? At least, do less and expect to survive?"

"There is no answer." Ponce remained miserable, from his tone. "We are here for you, for the missing girls."

"Samma." I was angry now. Angry at them, angry at my enemies, angry at myself. We'd crossed an ocean to rescue both my first lover and Ilona's daughter. "Corinthia Anastasia. Those missing girls have *names*. And we are here to make them whole. *All* of us. Or should I have left you back in Copper Downs?"

He found some courage to look me in the eye though my temper was aflame. "No. But you are becoming someone else, Green."

"Someone who calls oceans to her, and rains death down upon her enemies?" I hated the screech in my voice, but I *hurt*, and I was frightened as much as I was angry.

"Yes." Ponce's voice was stark.

Mother Vajpai stood, stepped toward me on my stool, and tried to fold me into a hug. I shrugged her off, jabbing with my elbows, then wrapped my arms around myself to rock back and forth in the protecting darkness. "I must go wash out my leathers," I muttered. "And I would light some candles for the dead."

"I will find you tapers," said Ilona. "A house such as this must have them laid by. And the pond in the back has water." After a brief pause, she added, "Do you wish some help?"

"*No!*"

Gathering my bundle, I found the door leading into the pantry, and beyond that, the outside. There, at least, I would be among those who loved me. Which was right now precisely no one.

The pond was scummed, the water remarkably cool for Selistan, where everything seemed to be warm. I sat with my legs submerged up to the knees and scrubbed at the leather with a rag snipped from the edge of the furniture cover fallen down around my waist. The god-blooded short knife surely had its uses.

At least the monkeys were asleep for the night.

The grounds here gave the same impression as they had around the servants' gate—a long and overwhelming lack of maintenance. Grasses and vines sprouted from gaps in the flagstones of the patio and walkways. A dozen species of trees were grown thick and crowded, in many cases their branches dipping unpruned to the ground. Ferns and more vines and thick bushes bunched beneath. Several animals of size watched my progress, their musky odor and rattling breath obvious to my senses, but they were not aggressive enough to stalk from shelter.

Or perhaps even animals knew death when she walked among them.

The house bulked behind me. It was built in multiple wings and layers, huge pillars and airy walkways connecting different sections. No Stone Coast architect would ever have designed such a residence. Winter snows would render the place useless. I suspected in daylight and with a good cleaning, the courtyards and walkways would be stunning. Even now, moonlight and decay painted the sweeping arcs of the rooflines and the brooding bulk of the pillars in a striking contrast.

Impressed despite myself, I wondered again why this place stood empty and to whom it actually might belong.

In the shallow, scummy pool I scrubbed awhile, until I'd done almost everything I could and needed oil instead of water to finish the job. Likewise for cleaning my weapons. My feet were wrinkling in the water as well, and something had tried to nibble my toes.

My anger was gone. I felt drained, without the energy to be sad. I realized that sometime during my scrubbing, Ilona must have come and gone with candles and a small punk pot. They were not tapers, but little fat pillars meant for bedroom reading lights.

That suited me better. Quiet, empty, I counted out my dead as best I could. I was forced to slice each candle into two shorter ones to make enough for my needs, and when I was done, I sat amid a spreading mandala of waxy fat and trimmed wicks that would resemble a temple ceremony if I lit them all at once.

We were in hiding here. I could not betray us with such an offering of light. Instead, I lit them two by two, whispering of the virtues of children and the vice of soldiers in place of knowing nothing of the men I'd killed today other than their attempts to kill me first. Each pair I extinguished before lighting the next.

It was all I could do.

In the end, I sat amid an acrid cloud and felt little better. Still, I had done what was right by my dead. I had offered what could be offered in this place and moment.

The dead had the luxury of patience now. It was their greatest resource. Here in life, my children needed me, and I needed my friends, even if they were frightened of me. I padded back indoors with my damp leathers in my arms, weapons tucked within.

Everyone seemed to have gone to bed except Mother Argai. The babies must be with Ilona, which was all right with me. Here in the kitchen, my sister Blade had managed a tiny, smokeless flame from an oil lamp. She was very patiently heating water. I received a rare smile. "Soup," she said. "Eventually."

"Yes." I smiled back. It seemed easier than not smiling. At least she was willing to speak to me. "I need oil."

"Over by the fireplace. We found a bit in the pantry."

On inspection, I saw that indeed they had. A small glass bottle of some nut oil I could not quite place awaited me there. Also a stash of torn rags. And some metal polish, for my knives.

I sat in one of the wooden chairs and began the process of restoring my leathers to their expected suppleness. I was ready to have them taken in again, nearly back to my pre-pregnancy body fitness and form.

After a little while, Mother Argai sat in the other wooden chair, my stool still between us. "Many of us Blades have been surprised at what we will do."

I thought about that a little while. "You all seem more surprised than I am."

"You have always been a girl who fills more of the world than anyone can account for." For the usually laconic Mother Argai, that was close to a speech. "I am not surprised. Saddened, perhaps."

My ears perked at that comment, which so much reflected my own hard thoughts of the past hour or so. "Saddened?"

She burst into a spate of words. "Most Aspirants live their lives, girl and Blade, without being called upon for much. We fight. Sometimes we kill. But almost always within a handle. No one has remorse when she is defending her Sisters. Even the Mother whose handle it is can comfort herself with the knowledge she protected her fellow Blades. You, though, have been denied that fellowship. Almost all your greatest and worst deeds were being done alone."

I had never considered Mother Argai a deep thinker. She was showing me the lie of my own assumptions right now. "I have always been alone," I said, then blurted, "We are all alone."

"No." Mother Argai produced one of her own short knives and began stropping the edge. This was not a threat; it was something to do—I recognized the habit. "No one needs to be alone." Her eye caught mine, her weapon moving in steady strokes. "You can choose to love and be loved, to always be among friends at need."

"Where were my friends when Federo bought me from my father?" I demanded bitterly. I could only imagine such a thing happening to my children now. The darkness seemed to grow larger as I spoke. Closer, heavier. "Where were my friends when Mistress Tirelle bent me low to the Factor's will? Where were my friends when I was sent to kill the Duke? Where were my friends . . ." I stopped, sobs that I would not release building in my throat.

"Your friends have long since found you," she said mildly. "But you carry more burden than most. How could any of us stand for being a toy for the gods?"

"I do what I do." Misery flooded me. "What I must. To survive. And now, for my children."

"In your anger you slew more than a dozen men today and called up a demon in the sea. That is a great deal of *doing*." She stood, touched my shoulder, and smiled again. "Sometimes you must still be merely human."

"That's all I want to be!" I was almost crying now, despite my resolve.

"No. You are wanting to be everything." With those words, she went back to her little soup pot.

I thought awhile on Desire's offer to elevate me to the station of one of Her daughters. A goddess, like the Lily Goddess. I'd refused, appalled. But how different was I if I could dance death through crowds of armed men and call great, watery fists from the sea?

This was not who I wanted to be. If my enemies would only leave me alone, I could be someone else. More peaceful. Or perhaps less. But *me*.

My children would have those choices. Even if I had to be anyone but me to ensure that they were free of this trap in which I dwelt.

Eventually I shuffled off to my room, to sew the missing days' bells for both me and Marya, then find my way to dreamless sleep far from either the dead or the living alike.

I woke feeling more myself. As I'd slept, someone had brought me my children. A stranger's footfall would have woken me to rapid action, but everyone here was trusted by me, even in those moments when we did not love one another. As to who had done this, I rather hoped it was Ilona. The sight of my unclad form was probably more than Ponce needed right now.

Or ever, really.

Whereas I could hope for feelings that such a glimpse might stir in Ilona.

Kissing my children gently awake was a pleasure. Lately they'd begun to focus their gaze, both of them, so when Federo smiled at me, I felt a sense of genuine connection. Another outburst of that foolish love, as well.

Cuddling them awhile, I allowed my foolishness to overflow. Both my babies giggled as they swatted at me and each other, crying out with small pleasures.

In time I rose and stalked around the room by the dim light of day leaking through the shuttered windows. Some ragged robes and a sari hung inside a narrow piece of furniture. I could clothe myself without being ready for battle at all times. This was a nice change given how much I'd left behind in Copper Downs and again on *Prince Enero*. I dressed, then cleaned and dressed the babies as well. When that was done, I slid the door open and padded down the dusty hallway toward the great hall and the kitchen beyond.

A breakfast of fruit awaited me. Nothing hot, despite Mother Argai's experiments with the oil lamp. Still, I could be pleased with this.

All my companions were there as well. The four of them seemed considerably less disturbed than they had the night before.

"Good morning," I told them all in Petraean, for Ilona still had little Seliu then. Now was a time for being thoughtful.

A muttered round of greetings answered me. I saw smiles, at least on Mother Argai. Ponce brightened as well as Ilona's hand brushed his, then fell away.

That I ignored with a stirring in my heart. "What do we do today?"

"Await calm," said Mother Vajpai. "Look for my daughter," Ilona blurted at the some moment.

"And Samma," I said, afraid that no one would argue so fiercely for my flawed fellow Blade as Ilona ever would for her daughter. "I am fine with both plans." I plopped the children on the floor within the circle of chairs before the cold fireplace. "How secret must we be here?"

"I doubt anyone minds our presence," Mother Vajpai said, "but we would hate to be found out by carelessness or a nosy servant."

"Who owns this house?"

The two senior Blades exchanged a glance. With a faint nod to Mother Argai, Mother Vajpai took that question as well. "The Lily Blades do."

"Not the temple?" I asked. "The Blades, separately?" I had not known that was possible.

"We have been making plans for years."

"So I see." Curiosity stirred within. "How did we, who hold so few possessions, come to own such a place?"

Mother Argai shook her head, as if dismissing a pointless question, but Mother Vajpai took it up. "Many Aspirants come to the temple from wealth. Sometimes offerings are given to the temple; sometimes they are given directly to the order. So it is the Blades themselves hold resources and property in quiet trust. Such as this house."

That made sense to me, who had never held wealth or property of my own. All I had that was truly mine were my leathers, my blades, and my children. I wondered what it must be like to have parents who would give up a house worth a cartload of paisas for the sake of a place I'd been offered on nothing more than the strength of someone else's prophecy and my own bloodstained hand. Even more, I wondered whose parents had given this house. I found myself oddly reluctant to inquire.

I did not ask why we did not open the house if it were ours. Too many perfectly clear reasons made themselves known with barely any thought at all. Just as I had not lit all the candles the previous night. Still, a fire in the hypocaust might have been a nice thing. "This neighborhood, we are on Shalavana Avenue, are we not?"

Another one of those glances, except it went all four ways around me this time. Mother Vajpai's voice was very careful now. "Yes . . ."

"The Bittern Court's palace is a few blocks from here." I offered that as a flat statement, but the suggestion was painfully implicit.

"No," said Mother Vajpai. For the first time in quite a while, she was asserting her authority over me. "I shall chain you to one of the ornamental boulders in the garden if you act without full discussion among us."

"We must be a council," Ilona added, surprising me a bit. "You cannot do this on your own, Green." She approached, taking my hands in hers until we faced each other with our arms like a bridge between us. I thrilled at her touch, though I knew it was not intimacy Ilona sought. "Too much is at risk here. We will follow, you will lead, but we must decide together."

"Don't be alone," Mother Argai said.

I shot her a look, but all I received in return was an expression tinged with compassion. "Very well." Unfortunately, I could not disguise the reluctance in my voice.

"No one will embarrass you by asking for an oath, Green," Mother Vajpai told me, and her voice was kind as well. "But please be sensible. Careful."

"Sensible, careful," I echoed. "Those are qualities for which I am justly famed."

They laughed at that, which pleased me.

"Well . . ." I offered my most pleasant smile. "We are here, and free to talk as we will. So, what do we do today?"

What we did that day was rest quietly in the shadowed house while Mother Argai slipped out for food and rumors. I was much sore and strained from the previous two days of effort. Heartsick, too, at being cast out from the Temple of the Silver Lily.

I did give her my letters to Chowdry, tied up neatly in a packet. Several of the freight brokers down along the Street of Ships would arrange correspondence to foreign ports for a suitable fee. I had no money, and so far as I knew, neither did Mother Argai. Still, both the temple as a whole and the Blades in particular maintained accounts at various businesses—something I'd been only vaguely aware of, if at all, when last I was here. Only now did I realize our order of the Lily Blades might actually be wealthy in its own right.

The economic and social activities of the temple were far more significant to me than they had been in the past. Business, after all, was driven by money. And money had to be somewhere at the heart of Mother Srirani's betrayals of her Sisters.

"What do you believe is behind this rending between the Justiciars and the Blades?" I asked Mother Vajpai. We sat in the front parlor of the house. Tall windows were blocked by more shutters, but bars of sunlight stabbed across the room to illuminate the teak floors and rolled-up carpets. Federo and Marya cooed and giggled at one another on a nest of muslin furniture covers. They were surely quite far from words yet, but both my children had recently become enthralled with the noises that they could make with their soft little mouths.

I myself sat in finer estate. With its embroidered silk cushions and intricately carved arms and backrest, the chair I occupied would have fetched a fortune from the right buyer in Copper Downs; Mother Vajpai's was no less ornate and elaborate. Here in Kalimpura, they were just old furniture in a forgotten house.

"Power flows back and forth." Her voice mused. "As I told you before, the usual trend is between the permissive and the careful. Of this last decade or so, well . . . Let me say first I do not believe Mother Srirani to be venal, and even less do I suspect Mother Umaavani before her."

"Do you suspect someone else high in their—no, *our*—councils of taking bribes?"

"Not that." She sighed. "A temple is not a business. We do not have incomes from manufactures or goods traded or labor hired out."

"I always assumed there were offerings . . . ," I began, then stopped. How many women from outside came to services? It was mostly my Sisters in the temple. Or was all our wealth in donations such as this house?

"Gifts, more like it. We hold a special place in the lives of women in Kalimpura, from the very great who might offer us ten thousand silver paisas at the birth of a daughter, to the beggar who calls at the back alley with a handful of wilted flowers to grace a Mother's table."

Flowers were all well and good, but it cost money to maintain a roof or fix plumbing. The economies of estates were a subject well covered in my education at the Factor's house. I'd simply not been thinking of such on my last sojourn here among the Blades.

"I would assume those larger gifts are kept against future need, rather than spent in the moment."

"Well, yes. There are counting houses here in Kalimpura who will hold money over time, or notes written against property, and pay out extra portions in return. They make back the expense from lending out funds elsewhere at higher charges."

Copper Downs actually had a banking system, an innovation originally borrowed from the Hanchu if I understood the history correctly. Letters of credit were critical to a city that lived on trade. While Kalimpura was also a substantial port, much more of its economy came from the surrounding lands and more distant precincts. It did not live and die by what came through the waterfront from distant shores.

"This I understand."

"Well, if those . . . investments . . . are poorly made, or poorly guarded, money can be lost. A special form of theft."

That line of reasoning led in an obvious direction. "And a special form of thief might arrange such losses."

Mother Vajpai looked both surprised and pleased at my comment. "Well, yes. You have the right of that, Green. What some of us believe has happened is manipulations among the counting houses by the Bittern Court have forced our temple funds into loss. This would be part of a larger game."

"Sap the temple's power, and it follows that the Blades lose power. She could arrange in time to have the Death Right granted to the Street Guild."

We had long held the Death Right in part because the Lily Blades were generally seen as both honest and disinterested. Neither of those things could be said of the Street Guild, even by their most ardent admirers, should they have any. And the Street Guild served the Bittern Court.

"The game of rulership. But there is another layer to all this."

"Always there is another layer," I said ruefully, thinking of my own experiences with the no-less-lethal politics of Copper Downs.

"Surali was once an Aspirant in our temple."

That shocked me into amazed silence. I'd had no notion. "A *Blade* Aspirant?" I finally managed to choke out in little more than a whisper. Had it been *her* family who'd given this house? The irony of *that* would have beggared belief.

"Yes. We trained together awhile, until she was ordered to leave."

"Why?" There was an event that had echoed down the years. No wonder the Bittern Court woman had hated the temple. And me? How did her animosity toward me fit into this? I knew why she hated me *now*, but the origins of that despisal had never been clear.

"She killed another Aspirant." As I opened my mouth, Mother Vajpai raised a hand to halt my words. "*Not* in the training rooms, though that can happen. When it does, we do not name it a crime. Weapons are, well, weapons. No, she strangled poor Gilles in her bed."

"In the dormitories? Before the other girls?"

"I tried to stop her." Mother Vajpai's voice was decades distant in that moment. "But I had come too late. Surali denied everything before Mother Meiko and the Temple Mother. I had *seen* her, so had some of the other girls, and still she denied."

"Why?"

"Love, I think." The distance still rang in Mother Vajpai's voice. "Gilles had lain with Surali awhile, then moved on to another girl who had also let Surali go."

"We do not kill for love," I said without considering my words.

That brought her back into the moment. "How many have you killed for love of your children?"

"Not the same," I insisted, flushed with a sudden, wounded pride.

"Hmm." Mother Vajpai gave me a long, slow appraisal, one of the bars of light making a glowing spot on her cheek that caught at my own eye so that I could not match her gaze. "Surali was sent home in disgrace. She had been fostered, not given over. Her mother forced the girl to servitude in her own house. She won her way back up through sheer ruthlessness, and entered the employ of the Bittern Court in her father's footsteps. Always she has harbored a grudge against the temple and the Lily Blades.

"But to conspire against us? That took a bigger game than mere vengeance. Surali is not too proud to claim her retribution when she can, but she is not so stupid as to fight just for that."

I waited to see if Mother Vajpai had anything more to add to this remarkable story. She lapsed into silence, so I joined her there. It did not take great intelligence to guess who this other girl had been in the triangle between Surali and Gilles. Such tangled love could destroy both hearts and lives.

Still, I tried to imagine carrying a hate so hot for long enough to wait a generation's time to destroy an entire temple and everyone in it.

Unfortunately for me, I *could* imagine that. I could also, for the first time ever, summon a bit of sympathy for Surali.

In time I was to realize that it would have been better if I had simply gone on hating her.

Mother Argai returned later that day. Though she was not breathing hard, I could tell she had run. I mimed drawing a blade, meaning to ask, *Street Guild?* without alarming Ponce or Ilona.

She nodded, her face uneasy. They knew we were in the city, but I trusted Mother Argai to have shaken her pursuit before returning to this place. Still, she must have been followed awhile. My fellow Blade could not have fought them, not with the woven sack she carried. It was full of vegetables and flatbreads, along with a selection of spreads, pastes, and spices. In another time, I might have admired the cloth of the sack itself and the workmanship that had gone into it, but I was bursting for news of the city, of Samma, of Corinthia Anastasia. Even of her pursuit.

Any news at all.

We gathered in the kitchen once more to share out jicama and taro. Mother Argai chopped with one of the house's cooking knives, a twinkle in her eyes replacing her earlier veiled look of worry. She was enjoying keeping us waiting. Looking around, I realized she was enjoying keeping *me* waiting.

"I was pursued," she reported finally. "The Street Guild are being oafs and fools, and so I lost them in the Greater Beast Market hunting me among the mounds of camel dung."

I snorted at that. Ponce smiled nervously. She had found a way to warn us of the danger without causing panic.

"Indeed, you are a mighty quarry," I replied in Petraean.

No one seemed to catch the joke. Mother Argai raised an eyebrow at me, though, before going on. "I have heard nothing of our lost girls."

It would have been surprising if anyone had spoken rumors of Corinthia Anastasia—who was she here, besides another child more pale than usual?—but a Lily Blade being held captive was the sort of thing that would spark talk. "No word of Samma at all?"

Mother Argai sighed. "None." She focused a few moments on the chopping, to the point where my hands itched to step in and do it myself. "The wave did quite a bit of damage along the Street of Ships," she reported finally. "At least a dozen were crushed or drowned." The gleam was gone from her eyes now.

I felt a rush of guilt. People died because of me too often, but they were usually people who deserved it. Or at least had chosen violence. When innocents died because of me, that felt different.

And every one of those lost had been someone's baby once. I would light the candles again tonight.

"Is there talk of who raised it?" I asked.

She shook her head. "Yes and no. A dozen rumors. Each as clearly ridiculous as the last. No one is speaking of the Lily Goddess."

After a short, painful wait, I could no longer contain myself. ". . . or of me?"

"Or of you, Green."

In truth, who would? The crew of *Prince Enero* ought to have a very good idea, but I doubted they were passing rumors over the rail. Not about this. Very few of them spoke Seliu, and having been invaded during the riot, I could only imagine how much they wished to cast off and depart.

"Was our ship damaged?"

"I do not know." She took a bite of the flatbread dipped in gazpacho paste. I waited for Mother Argai to finish chewing, illogically resenting her need for food.

Finally, she spoke again. "The Bittern Court has closed down all loading and unloading along the waterfront to ensure order, or so they say. The Harbormaster has likewise ordered all vessels to remain in place."

"That won't last long," observed Mother Vajpai. "Too much money tied up in blocked slips and stalled cargo."

I quickly translated all this into Petraean for Ilona and Ponce.

Ponce glanced at Mother Argai. "The wave was right behind *Prince Enero*. Will the Bittern Court or whoever not question them?"

"The wave was at the head of Agina's Pier," said Mother Vajpai in his language. "So yes, perhaps to question them, but also to question a dozen other captains."

"I do not think the officers or crew will say anything useful, even if the Bittern Court or the Harbormaster comes calling," I added. Lalo would not let that happen.

"It is not as if they are not already looking for you, Green," Ilona said. "And really, all of us."

"No," I replied, agreement in my tone of voice despite my denial. "But some suspicions drive more passion than others. Surali's vengeance is essentially a private matter, even if it is a private matter involving scores of Street Guild goons. A dockside riot, well, this *is* Kalimpura. But calling an outside force like that wave? Threatening, then damaging the waterfront? And people being killed in so, so . . . *baroque* . . . a fashion. If more thought I had a role in that last, yes, more would be looking for me."

"Did you call the wave?" Mother Argai asked in her thickly accented Petraean.

That was the crux of the matter here. Why they'd all been so strangely tense with me the night before. That was where our trust in one another had gone.

"I know this was not some small miracle of rain and flowers," I said slowly, picking my words not so much for their sake as for mine. "Those little miracles are easy. Like frost on the window." A metaphor that would have been lost on any Selistani who had not at some point in her life spent a winter north of the Storm Sea. "But I cannot call rain and flowers any more than I can summon power from the vasty deep."

"You prayed the ocean still." Mother Vajpai was obviously picking her own words with similar care. "That is a power, or a magic, far beyond the reach of even the most blesséd among our people's holy. Rain and flowers might at most move someone's heart. To halt a storm . . ."

We were once more at odds amid mistrust, clearly. At least they were acting less emotional about the whole business. Today I did not feel so much at risk of being cast out.

"I did not halt the storm. Some other power did, yes, at my prayer. I called something great." Even admitting that was painful, for all the time we'd spent picking at such questions in the later part of our voyage aboard *Prince Enero*. "Likely a titanic, as I've said before. But this is still *me*."

With an almost vapid look at me, Ponce spoke up again. "It followed you to the harbor here. That is another kind of danger. Or you summoned it in your fit of anger."

Even his words brought a flash of red heat behind my eyes. "My children were at risk. I fought like a thing possessed, perhaps. But I did not call the ocean to my bidding."

Mother Vajpai nodded at that. "It is difficult to say which is more troublesome—that you would have the power to call such things at will, or that they would come to you unsummoned."

She certainly had a point. Time for more care with my words, though I was decidedly tiring of this topic. I saw no end to this but deeper discomfort and an increasingly large sense of threat all around. "I suspect something was come to collect a price deferred by that unnatural calm at sea."

"Something that came at the moment of your need," Mother Argai said in Seliu, then went back to eating.

I had no answer to that, and no one else seemed inclined to add to it, so we all fell to our small meal.

There is truly no end to the marvels one can work with olive oil, a few kinds of beans, and a bit of spice and flavor. I had asked for an oil stove, if such a thing could be found, that we might at least warm stock and possibly grill some of these fine fruits and vegetables without making smoke in the chimneys to betray our presence in the house. For that day, I contented myself transforming the somewhat eccentric collection of provisions brought by Mother Argai into a more delectable selection of foods.

Ponce scoured the pantries and passageways for anything still edible that might have been overlooked when the house was last closed up. I chartered him to be especially watchful for pickles, vinegary sauces, and cured meats. Bringing them to me one by one, he found occasions to brush his arm against mine, or favor me with an extra smile.

Ilona worked close beside me, grinding and chopping and mixing as I did. Though her entire cottage could have fit within this massive kitchen, there was still an element of our old times together cooking rabbits and apples. My heart was eased by her closeness, by the hold her scent had upon me. I found occasions to brush my arm against hers, or favor her with an extra smile.

It was good to feel something between us besides loss and regret, if only for a little while.

I was itching to be away after our missing hostages, but the senior Mothers were right. This was not the moment to stir further trouble in the city. Especially with the Street Guild on alert for us.

Within a day or two, the wave would be just another piece of Kalimpuri street chatter, the novelty overtaken by some festival procession or funeral or bloody murder in the marketplace. We were not a people given to obsession over events, not in our public lives. Deeper grudges might last decades or even generations, but daily life in Kalimpura was an ever-changing carnival without end.

Sometimes I'd wondered if a lack of winter season did this. Along the Stone Coast, and in the lands rising to the north, people spent months mostly or entirely indoors. Plenty of time to focus on the smallest elements in their lives, while the public square remained largely empty except for those scurrying unfortunates out in the weather.

Not literally true, of course, but close enough. Down here, though, even peasants like my father enjoyed three or four harvests every year. Farmers in the distant north saw their fields lie fallow for months between the last burning and the first plowing.

Life was so different. I wondered how Corinthia Anastasia was bearing up, what they had her doing. Was Samma with her, or were they separated?

"Do you suppose," I asked Ilona quietly, "that our missing girls are permitted to cook? Or kept in silent rooms all the day long?"

Ilona's knife suddenly chopped very hard and fast through some old, hard onions before pattering to a halt. "We are close to them, Green. I feel as if I could walk out the front gate and discover my daughter."

"You possibly could, at that," I said, my tone gentle. "Chances are very good she and Samma are being held in this part of the city. But you would not find your way back from there once you had located them. Those who hold her would take you up as well."

"You are a storm of swords. Even those terrible women we travel with have become frightened of you." Her voice was ragged. "I cannot defend my daughter as you defend your own children."

Wishing I could embrace her right then and there, I touched Ilona's arm gently, but she hid fiercely behind the shield of the cutting knife. "I defend only because I am attacked."

"You are attacked because your defenses are so vigorous as to make you seem a danger to others."

I'd never quite thought of it that way. "Like the wave? . . ."

Ilona sighed, giving me an exasperated stare as her knife finally stilled. "*Prince Enero*'s men might not talk here in Kalimpura. They have their own skins to think of. But they will sail away, and sailors will tell their tales. Tales will be retold, again and again. In a year's time, you will be known in a dozen other ports as a Selistani storm goddess. In this port, if that rumor ever crosses back over the rail, everyone will fear you. *Everyone.*"

"And what people fear, they attack."

"You must make yourself less frightening." She turned, the knife in her hand quivering in a fashion that would have been a threat from almost anyone else. "Green, I know you well and care for you deeply, but still you frighten *me*. And I've seen some dreadful things."

"I've *done* some dreadful things," I muttered, putting the rest of her words away to savor later in private.

She cares for me deeply. That I dared not answer. I wished I did not frighten her as well.

"Precisely."

For a while I ground chickpeas in a bowl. We had found paprika, of all things, and it would go well with a bit of oil there. In time, as I worked, I spoke again. "How do I become less frightening?"

"You will never seem a safe person to the rest of us." I might have bristled at her honesty, but Ilona strained to speak the truth. Her words were worthy of my respect. "Right now, though, you do not even have rules to follow. If you were bound in service to your Lily Temple once more, or to Endurance, then you'd have, well, a framework for your powers."

"Even calling down the sea all unknowing?"

She smiled ruefully. "Perhaps not that. I do have one request, though."

"Mmm?"

Ilona's eyes held mine, and I saw tears standing in her gaze. Her smile fled as if it had never been there. "Do not bind your power away until my daughter is safe with me once more."

"You'd rather have me be the storm of blades until then?"

"I am a mother," Ilona said, her voice stark. "Anything that gets me back my child."

Laying down my spoons, I took her in my arms. Ilona went willingly, bending her face down to my shoulder. I hugged her till she sobbed, then hugged her harder awhile, breathing in the scent of her and containing her shuddering grief.

In a different time and place, we might have found more ways to banish her pain, but this would have to do for now.

Late that afternoon Mother Argai was back with my oil stove and a string of harbor carp, as well as a fresh supply of rumor. Street Guild were out in unusual numbers, but they hadn't succeeded in following her back. I was irritated—the activity meant I could not yet safely leave the compound. Not with Surali's thugs on their greatest alert.

We gathered with the babies around the great chopping tables in the kitchen so I could skin and debone the fish, preparing fillets to be cooked on the little flame. Ponce I sent to brave the golden monkeys in the garden for limes or lemons or anything of that sort. I had all else I needed.

"The wave is still much discussed," Mother Argai said. "No one has blamed any of us yet."

Given my own presumptive agency in those events, I thought that was diplomatically put, but I kept to my work and figured my fellow Blade would say what she must. She had never lacked for directness.

Mother Argai did not disappoint.

"I spoke in deep confidence to some of our friends among the Blades." She glanced at Mother Vajpai. "We need to find a way for you to meet with them."

Temple politics was far more Mother Vajpai's strength than Mother Argai's. "We shall soon," the Blade Mother answered.

"Great disagreement echoes inside the temple now," Mother Argai continued.

"Good," I said, slamming my knife much harder than required into the cutting block. "Mother Srirani needs reasons to think a bit deeper. A missing Blade in the hands of our enemies might be one of them, if she had a care for her duties as Temple Mother."

Mother Vajpai's hand brushed my arm. "I will handle those reasons. Patience, please, Green. Samma has been held for months now. If we wait a few days and let this brew, our own goals may be easier to attain."

"How will that help us go over the walls into the Bittern Court?" I demanded.

Her response was acerbic, in that same arresting tone that had dominated so much of my learning years in the Temple of the Silver Lily. "Would you rather fight them alone, or with three score Blades at your back?"

Those words were solid and true. "I understand," I said more quietly. Though I did not yet realize it then, my political education was fully under way at that time. So far in my life, I had been a weapon in the politics of others, albeit a weapon with my own interests and intentions. To be an *actor* in politics was far more empowering, even if one did not wield either the blades or the votes directly in one's own hands.

Then something else was said that would become critical for all our futures. It is odd in looking back to see how some moments in time are pivots from which so much else unfolds.

"Green," said Mother Argai. "You had asked about these Saffron Tower renegades."

"Yes," I replied. "The other god-killers, whom Iso and Osi had been following."

"A Red Man passed through this city several years ago. He stayed a season or two, then went on to the Fire Lakes." She looked at me solemnly. "They say he had an apsara with him."

That would have to be Firesetter and Fantail, the Saffron Tower agents who'd found their way to Copper Downs shortly after my slaying of the Duke. Laris had told Mother Vajpai of them, back in Copper Downs, and of the encounter between the two god-killers and Marya, before the twins had finally finished the task that their predecessors had abandoned. We had much discussed the missing pair during the recent sea voyage here.

I wanted to find those two, badly. With their cooperation, I might be able to peel back some of the Saffron Tower's secrets. If they would talk to me. Assuming their abandonment of their mission was real and not some effort at misdirection, I was almost certain they were rebels against their masters' rule. That meant they might be willing to share some of their secrets. Or even aid us, holding hope against hope in this process.

Even if they were not truly renegade, I needed to know whether they still hunted the Lily Goddess. After all, it could just as well have been those two She had prophesied as being a threat to Her from my own heart. If one interpreted my heart to be Copper Downs. Prophetic language being as elliptical as it was, that wouldn't be unreasonable.

It had always irked me that gods never said, "Next Tuesday, Rajit will be struck with boils in his mouth and choke to death." What good was prophecy if you had to live through the events foretold before you could begin to understand them?

"Have they returned from their journey?" The Fire Lakes were a mountainous badland country far to the south and west of Kalimpura, where the Red Men were said to originate.

Mother Argai shrugged. "If so, no one seems to have heard of it."

A dead lead, then. A lead nonetheless. By the Wheel, a live one might be nicer still. It was all well and good for me to raise waves from the ocean, but why couldn't they bear the people I needed on their foaming shoulders?

If only water could wash Corinthia Anastasia and Samma out from whatever hole Surali had plunged them into.

We are trapped in this place. I shall not say where, lest someone else read this missive, but we are not prisoners except of our own caution. Inaction was never my way.

I know you would probably approve. No one is being pursued or assaulted or made to bend a knee beneath a blade. I also know you would counsel that there are many solutions to every problem, and most of them begin with patience.

Patience was never my way, either. I have the stomach for talk, when it is useful and especially when I hold the upper hand. But the people who oppose us here will not listen to anything we might say. I also believe that time is their friend, and our enemy.

In our small half handle, I suspect I am the only one who sees things so.

Another problem beyond the obvious worried me here in our little retreat. Of all of us, only Mother Argai could go out. Even she was often followed now, which meant risk that we could all be discovered at a moment's ill luck. Mother Vajpai and I had been marked by both the Temple of the Silver Lily and by the Street Guild. Ponce had a Selistani face, but his command of Seliu was poor, and he knew nothing of life in Kalimpura. Ilona was utterly foreign of face and skin here, and her Seliu was not even as good as Ponce's.

So, Mother Argai went out for food, for information, to scout, and I could swear, just to stretch her legs in peace away from our smoldering and bickering.

Idle, the rest of us turned toward one another. As my life had unfolded since, those days of bitter quiet have been quite a lesson for me, but at the time I did not appreciate anything beyond the tension that stretched us thin, heart and body.

Ilona was moody and withdrawn, even more than she had been back in Copper Downs or aboard *Prince Enero*. I understood why—completely—but this made her an increasingly difficult companion. My own affections for her continued in their ever-frustrated fashion, drawing from earlier times when she had been so much more than a distraught mother, but she had eyes only for my children. And for Ponce.

In turn, his devotion to me was becoming an embarrassment. He took to following me around the house, offering services large and small. Nothing crude. Not his way, to be sure. But the intimacy he craved was painfully clear to everyone. My own attachment to Ilona meant nothing to him in the face of the incontrovertible evidence that I had previously shared the love of a man.

Mother Argai fled. Mother Vajpai was simply irritated at the lot of us. She several times was quite cross, accusing Ilona, Ponce, and me of being not much better than children. I could only spend so much time sewing bells and dandling babies, so as a relief, I cleared a room and passed many hours in training. At night I went outside to hunt down and kill those pestilent golden monkeys in the garden. That was effort never wasted. The downside was that when I worked my body indoors during the day, Ponce would come and watch me move, stretch, and sweat until I began throwing my knife and let it come too close to him more than once.

I had to repeat that nasty trick several times over.

Waiting for our two lost ones, we were on a slow boil, in other words. A kettle with a sealed lid ready to explode.

It was my fervent desire for that explosion to be directed outward. There it might do some good. Otherwise, we were only furthering the cause of our enemies.

Gathered in the kitchen over a cold, simple meal of mango slices with rock salt and powdered red pepper, along with a bit of the goat milk Mother Argai bought daily against my children's need in my absence, I pressed my case.

"We have been here five days now," I grumbled.

"No one has lost track of the time, Green." Mother Vajpai's voice was unusually tart for her.

"I would go to the Bittern Court and scout for our missing hostages."

Ilona stirred from her gloomy silence. "Yes. Please, why are we not finding my daughter now?" I understood her single-minded concern, but her fears were a spiked barrier between us now as they had not been back at Copper Downs after Corinthia Anastasia had been taken.

Ponce rocked Federo and glanced at me with worry in his eyes, but did not speak up.

Turning back to the other two Blades, I locked gazes with each of them. Both women knew me quite well. Both understood how I chafed.

"I respect that you have given your word, Green," said Mother Vajpai. "And that you are keeping it. I respect even more your need to act on this. But consider that we have been months on this trail. A day or two more will not bring new harm to either Samma or the girl."

"A day, or two, or three, or eight," I said bitterly. "We sit, while the city whirls around us. Surali *knows* we are in Kalimpura. Everyone who cares to know is being aware of that." My frustration built behind my words. "We lose time, initiative."

Mother Argai "We confound her more with silence than with action."

"Following that strategy, no one would ever raise a weapon in defense."

"A few more days," Mother Vajpai said by way of answer. "The Street Guild is already settling down, as Mother Argai tells it. Rumor sweeps on past us to other fascinations. Let people forget the wave, and not connect the beggars' riot to us."

"Surali is no fool." The growl in my voice startled even me. I knew precisely when I had begun to see her as a human being instead of an enemy, and I did not appreciate that shift inside my head. Far better that the Bittern Court woman remain a monster to my way of thinking. "She will infer what we have done. The longer we wait, the more time her agents have to ferret out Little Kareen or someone else who can betray our part in the beggars' riot and the rest of the business at the waterfront. The more time there is for her to decide to use Samma or Corinthia Anastasia against us somehow. Not just a prisoner or a hostage, but to make a victim of either of them." I knew my voice was pitched with anger. I did not try to swallow it.

Mother Vajpai drummed her fingers on the table. "So what if she does? We will move against her soon enough, at a time of our choosing. Let her fear our influence."

I snorted. "Influence among the lowest of the people of the street."

"We all saw their power," said Ilona. "You stopped the waterfront, and rescued us from that ship."

"Will I storm the Bittern Court with an army of the poor?" I laid my hands flat, looked around at them. "Please, let me go look for Corinthia Anastasia, for Samma."

"I agree." Ilona nodded.

Mother Argai shook her head. "No. Too soon."

"For what do we wait?"

"For aid from the Blades," snapped Mother Vajpai. "Let us do our work, and make our path easier. We've already discussed this, Green. It is too soon."

I turned to Ponce, the tie-breaking vote in our little council. Shameless, I cast him a sorrowful, suffering look. "Please . . . What do you think?"

He shook his head. "I cannot know. None of this is my way. I . . . I will not block you, but I will not agree."

All the more frustrated, I stomped out of the kitchen toward my informal practice room. Over my shoulder, I shouted, "I will obey!"

I did not have to like it.

Mother Argai came over the back wall the next day bleeding and at a dead run. I was in the garden with Ilona and the babies, which was safer now that I had discouraged the golden monkeys from their dung-flinging depredations. I realized a man was following my Blade Sister over the top of the masonry.

"Take them," I growled to Ilona as I leapt to my feet.

She stifled a shriek, but grabbed the children to race toward the house.

Meanwhile, Mother Argai nodded to me as she raced forward, her chin thrown to one side to point over her shoulder. Though innocent of my leathers in one of the old robes from my room, I of course had my god-blooded knife strapped to my wrist.

The man was armored in light scale—Street Guild, then—and laughed when he saw my little blade. I stepped around his sword and let him impale himself upon my weapon.

Though we Lily Blades did not normally fight to kill, he could not be allowed to leave this place knowing we were here. I rocked back a pace with the shock of the impact and turned the knife to his left, cutting into his heart even as his face betrayed his surprise.

With a sigh, the man died, blood spurting out of the wound to spray me crimson and brown.

I lowered him to the ground and quickly dragged the body into the shade of the ragged trees of our garden. Mother Argai came to squat next to me, breathing hard.

"I could not afford to kill him in the road behind us," she said. "Too public and too close."

"Are you hurt?" I asked her.

She glanced down at her own leathers. "Oh. This is not my blood."

"Where are his fellows?" Street Guild almost never worked alone.

She touched the blood smearing her midsection. "I killed two several blocks away. This one lost his head and pursued alone."

I looked down at the still face. Not unhandsome, though someone had once broken his nose for him. His big brown eyes that might have wooed maidens—or men—had already dulled. I felt sadness, unusual for me at a death. Almost regret. As if he and I might have been friends meeting some other way. As if he had not come to threaten me and my children.

"This was too close," I told Mother Argai.

"Yes." Mother Vajpai had joined us. I saw Ilona peering out from the house, and gave her a wave to signal that I was all right. "Too close." It was as near as she would come to scolding her old friend.

Mother Argai nodded. "We can hide only so long."

"Now you sound like Green," Mother Vajpai said.

For once, I decided to let the argument make itself without my help. Instead, I went to find a shovel. We would need to bury this man here in the garden. Where we sat in a trap, rotting like fruit in a basket.

Later, after we'd cleaned up and everyone's panic had subsided, we met in the kitchen.

"I cannot say what possessed him." Mother Argai was sharpening her long knife and not meeting anyone's eye. Which was very unlike her.

"Our secrecy will not hold much longer," I said, pointing out the obvious. "He will be missed. They'll know from the other bodies what area of the city we are in."

"They likely know that now," said Mother Vajpai heavily. "But we can't simply march out of here with weapons drawn."

"Nor can we wait for forty of that poor bastard's fellows to come pouring over the back wall and slit my children's throats," I snapped.

I'd pulled something in my back digging the grave, and still felt oddly guilty about the killing.

"Soon," she counseled, but I could see her words seemed weak, even to her.

There was little else to say on this. We all knew the arguments already. Perhaps to distract me, Mother Argai gave me another letter. Smeared with blood I trusted was fresh, it was of course from Chowdry. Though my old pirate-priest could not be replying to me yet. My own first letter to him would still be weeks in the travel. I had not yet sent the one I was writing now. I was not sure if I would send it, in any case.

The arrival of a new missive was either pleasing or alarming, depending on the view that I chose to take. I stared awhile at the sealed packet that she had handed me. A coarse, rough paper wrapped the outside, brown and speckled and strange, wrapped with string and sealed with wax blobs in several colors. Plus a spatter of some Street Guildsman's blood.

Was the artistry an excess of creativity on Chowdry's part? Or the marks of various couriers along the way?

"How did it arrive here?" I asked Mother Argai. We were in the kitchen, sharing cups of wine. I still had dirt under my fingernails, even after washing carefully. We would have to burn or bury the robe I'd been wearing.

"Friends in the temple passed it to me."

Of course Chowdry had sent a letter for me to the Temple of the Silver Lily. Where else would he have known to send it? Our casting out was news that would not reach him for a while.

"Thank you," I said quietly. After yesterday's argument, I had been reminded all over again how difficult a line Mother Argai walked right now. *She* had not been ejected, but everyone would know she was here on Mother Vajpai's behalf. One angry Blade, one overheard conversation, and the Temple Mother could with a few words extend our order of banishment to cover Mother Argai.

Or was that lack of pressure a form of cooperation from Mother Srirani? I was coming to understand much better how someone could be trapped in a course of action they neither intended nor approved of.

The letter beckoned me. My racing thoughts did me no favors, and there was small point in postponing reading this. Chowdry was never much for words, not as I had known him. Anything he troubled to tell me from across the sea was probably something I needed to hear.

I broke the seals and unraveled the string. The rough paper fell away from a torn sheet of creamy parchment. The Temple of Endurance had peculiar donations, I knew, but fine writing supplies seemed stranger than usual. I wondered whose hand had written it out for him.

Greetings to Green, once of Copper Downs and departed now to Kalimpura, it read in Petraean. The rest was in Seliu.

> *You have not been gone three days and already there is being a new stir in the city. Someone has arrived seeking the twins who so troubled you this past season.*
>
> *A man has come to the Temple of Endurance asking after you. We have not said much, other than what is already known—that you have left. Everyone who cares to think of it can tell your destination.*
>
> *His name is "Mafic." I believe he comes from the Saffron Tower, the source of so much of your recent troubles. A tall man, and smoldering as if he carries a fire within.*
>
> *I fear for you, Green. If this Mafic sails on toward Kalimpura to challenge you, that will lead to greater troubles even than those twins you fought against. And for your goddess there as well.*
>
> *There is too much of this violence around you. If you would lay down your weapons, others would stop seeking you. I counsel on behalf of Endurance that you take up a long and peaceful life.*
>
> *It is to be wishing you well.*
>
> *Chowdry, of Endurance*

The Saffron Tower. We had heard rumor of the apostate Red Man and his apsara. My need for them was much stronger now.

This had to be bound up in the taking of Corinthia Anastasia and Samma. Certainly Iso and Osi had been part of Surali's plot before, as she worked against the Lily Goddess through Her now-slain sister goddess Marya. What I could not see was whether this Mafic was another part of Surali's schemes, or if he was seeking a separate vengeance on the part of the Saffron Tower for the fate of the twins.

Surali was acting through the Quiet Men now, it seemed, not through her erstwhile allies.

Perhaps the details did not matter. In either case, the outcome was the same to me.

"What news?" asked Ilona, having seen me lay down the sheets of the letter and stare at our empty counters and tabletops. Mother Argai watched me in shrewd silence.

"Chowdry writes of a new agent of the Saffron Tower pursuing the fate of Iso and Osi." I sighed heavily as I described the import of his letter. Then: "I had thought their threat settled. Now another seeks them and through them seeks me."

"We do not yet know the fate of the Red Man," said Mother Argai.

"He would be a valuable ally." I passed the papers to her—Ilona could not read Seliu, so there was small point in handing the letter that way. "I would give much to have an hour's honest conversation with the Red Man and his apsara."

Ilona reached into the heart of the matter. "What does this have to do with finding my daughter?"

"I cannot say," I confessed. "But the Saffron Tower was bound up in the original kidnapping through Surali's plotting. If this Mafic who pursues is cause or consequence, I cannot say. Chowdry did not know to tell me. My heart believes these things are connected."

"Chowdry writes of events in Copper Downs, weeks' sail away," she pointed out.

"Mafic could have come on the same ship as this letter," I replied. "Time and distance are not necessarily our armor here. If we knew where to find the Red Man, we might understand more of what we face in this Mafic. Through that, we would be better prepared to deal once and for all with Surali."

"Yesterday you were hot to free my daughter. Today you worry about a man who is almost certainly an ocean away." Ilona's voice was bitter. "I see nothing actually being done to rescue Corinthia Anastasia."

"Nor Samma," added Mother Argai, passing the papers along to my old friend.

I reached for Ilona's hand. She clutched my fingers tight, despite her doubts. The touch of her skin was like a balm to me, as always it had been.

"I do not yet know how to rescue them," I told her. "But I will. Mother Argai and Mother Vajpai tell us we await allies. Now we also await an enemy, hiding from others who grow closer every day. The trick of the thing will be to gauge our stroke most effectively."

"We've been gauging our stroke for months."

I pointed at the babies sitting in the sun, cooing at each other. "It was time spent for what was needful."

She began to weep. I was embarrassed for myself, and for her. And frustrated. Others were moving against us, and in doing so closing off our choices one by one.

I awoke late that night, my back still aching a bit and the scent of candles yet on me from my earlier praying over the Street Guilds-man's garden grave. The babies snored gently, each wheezing in their sleep. Checking close, their milk breath was refreshing. My children.

There was nothing about Ilona's hurt that I did not understand completely. I had already stood firm in defense of my children more than once. She had no weapon but me. She could not raise a hand against her enemies, not a tenth part so well as I could.

A Blade served all women, not just herself.

But sometimes a Blade had to serve herself in order to serve others.

Besides, I was sick of waiting. Sick of obedience. As I'd said to myself time and again, patience was never my way. Surely I could slip over the wall, learn what was needful, and slip home again with no one the wiser. Another night of enforced rest was likely to make me scream with frustration.

I gathered my sleeping children and took them into Ilona's room. We had spread out in this large house, but she had taken a maid's quarters. Whether the open spaces bothered her, or she just felt safer enclosed, I had not inquired.

She woke muzzy when I came in. I placed a child in each of her arms, so they snugged against one breast and the other. "Say noth-ing," I whispered. "I will be back before the dawn."

Ilona smiled for the first time in days, then hugged my children close. I was tempted to abandon my plan and slip into the bed with her. That would address a different frustration of mine, to be sure. Instead, I kissed her gently as a promise—unreliable though I knew that promise to be under the current circumstances—and slipped out as the three of them settled deeper into sleep.

It did not take me so long to don my leathers. My long knife went in my thigh scabbard. My god-blooded short knife was tucked into my right forearm. I had not yet replaced the left knife.

This would be simple, easy. Just a little reconnaissance. I might even be lucky enough to find what I sought. I knew nothing would go wrong, I had that much confidence in myself. Our secrecy would be preserved, and we would know more than we did.

More to the point, I would have taken action. Done something for myself, for Samma and Corinthia Anastasia.

For all of us.

Departing the house was no great trick. As I'd written to Chowdry, we were not prisoners. Not in the conventional sense. There were no locks except on the outer gates, and those keys we ourselves held.

Still I went over the wall, for practice and stealth both, and left my promises behind. Some needs were greater than others. I was finally listening to my conscience.

The Bittern Court also stood on Shalavana Avenue, near the intersection with the Gita, a ceremonial highway of ancient times long since converted to a city street. Their compound was a large complex even by the standards of wealthy property in this city. Where we had been sheltering in a great house, in the Petraean sense, the Bittern Court was quite literally a palace.

For all that Surali and the schemes of the Bittern Court had reached into my life so deeply, I had never set foot there before. I was out this night against my given word to learn something. Anything, in a sense, but most specifically the disposition of their prisoners of my conscience.

I ghosted along the little jig-jagging street that ran roughly parallel to Shalavana Avenue, serving as a sort of alley behind the great properties that lined that road. To my left loomed walls and gates and stable arches and little docks where carts could unload whatever the needs of the wealthy and powerful had caused to be delivered. To my right were rows of modest homes, all of them much smaller, that housed servants, guards, and lesser relatives, along with anyone else whose affairs required such constant closeness to their betters.

The silent walls of the wealthy bore me little threat. I was more concerned with watchful eyes from the windows of their retainers.

Still, as I had long known, there is an art to skulking. It largely consists of not seeming to skulk. I walked boldly in my leathers, whistling silently—not being a complete fool—for the air it gave me.

This would not be a case of rushing the front gate with weapons in hand. I'd done that before, most notably to Surali's rented house in Copper Downs with the Rectifier at my back. My gigantic pardine friend was not here, however. More to the point, I did not want to draw anywhere near such attention to myself. Alerting Surali's guards that I had trespassed their grounds would be more dangerous to Corinthia Anastasia and to Samma than almost anything else I could do.

My steps faltered with that thought.

Dare I?

The stillness was a torture of its own. Lying low served as a kind of defeat. Once I'd scouted, I'd be much better prepared to lead the Blade allies Mother Vajpai kept not-quite-promising me.

We would not go blind into this place. Yes, I assured myself, this was the responsible thing to do.

Over the years I have come to realize that most decisions are made in the absence of ratiocination, convenient facts being marshaled afterwards to support the deeds of the moment. That night may have been the nadir of such behavior on my part.

Still, even now, I would rather reason with forward momentum and sufficient force than lurk like a woman-spider in some web. The irony of this does not escape me, and the much younger Green in that alley would have laughed to see me now.

I approached the Bittern Court's back wall with a confident stride. This would be roof work, and windows, along with subduing both guards and servants before they could spot me. If I found myself in a stand-up fight tonight, I would already have lost before the first blood was drawn.

The wall presented no great challenge. It was not so much defense as boundary. I scrambled up a stack of broken-down crates awaiting the wood cart and slipped over the top into the thick garden beyond. I had been certain of my destination thanks to the bushy treetops gleaming in the moonlight from above the wall's height.

In this, I was not disappointed. The garden was another matter. Someone with sense had trimmed back the undergrowth so I had no cover beneath the papaya trees but night's shadow. Much of what grew before me in the open ground beyond the trees had been planted in great iron or clay pots. The ground was largely raked gravel.

At least no one was out for a midnight stroll. The guards, wherever they were, did not seem to be in evidence here with me.

I crouched back into the shadows and studied the way the garden unfolded, and the buildings beyond. They definitely were buildings in the plural, I noted with no little disappointment. I had been expecting something like the great house in which we were sheltered.

Kalimpuri architecture was more idiosyncratic, less enclosed, than the run of buildings on the Stone Coast. Much less need to shelter from the weather encouraged creativity in the placement of walls, I supposed. But this place had been built as what the Petraeans would have called a folly.

A large central building dominated the land. It was quite tall, perhaps four storeys, with a swaybacked roof peaked at each end and long, sweeping eaves, all covered in tile that glittered pale in the night. The side I could see, the *back*, was faced with enormous pillars three or four rods high. In the shadows, I thought I could spy a pair of massively tall doors.

A hall, then. A throne room, in fact.

Almost a dozen lesser structures surrounded the central building. Some were barely more than pavilions; others had the thick-walled look of kitchens, storehouses, or barracks. Roofed walkways joined them together. Certain of those had screened or paneled walls; others were wide open. A few were elevated, passing across plantings, ponds, and other walkways.

This was like the open plan of our own hideaway house taken to an extreme.

It also made my scouting prospects very difficult indeed.

A series of structures laid out like this would not have convenient servants' hallways running behind the main rooms, as so many houses in Copper Downs did. It was also quite unlikely that any system of underground passages connected them: even if Kalimpura's limited sewers ran here—and I had no idea whether they did or did not—those tunnels would at most connect in one or two places.

I would have to do this the hard way. And hope everyone was very much asleep.

At least in sliding along the wall, I could keep to the shadows. I'd marked an elevated stone patio as my destination. It came closest to the boundary of anything in my line of sight, and seemed to be a jumble of furniture and potted palms, as if someone had hosted a banquet up there and not yet gotten around to sending everything back to the storerooms.

I could work with the broken sight lines and jumbled shadows up there. At least no one had left torches or lamps burning the garden. The hall and its satellite structures were quite dark.

Once I was done with Surali, she would never sleep without lights again.

The west wall of the great hall was composed of ornately carved panels. On close inspection, I declined to climb it. Getting around the deep eaves at the top would be an ugly business. After that, well, what would I have? A roof difficult to get back down from, and a slightly better view than I already enjoyed.

Instead, I scrambled up to the top of one of the covered walkways and began to trot lightly along their length. I was interested in the second- and third-storey windows of the smaller buildings. Seeing who slept where seemed a productive pursuit. If I were lucky, I would find thick shutters barred from the outside. Then I would know where my prisoners were.

A brief fantasy of a swift, quiet escape flitted through my head. I envisioned myself sneaking Corinthia Anastasia and Samma back into our hidden retreat, simply allowing them to be discovered in the kitchen come morning, sipping tea and ready to tell of their misadventures.

That was just silly, and I knew better, even then. Girls dream of heroism and high accomplishments. Women do the job before them.

My job was to keep looking.

A creaking door caused me to halt and bend low in place. A walkway three rods to my left glowed with the bobbing of a candle. I remained still, a lumpy shadow, and watched an old woman shuffle along with a taper held close in her hand.

She walked like someone sleepy and safe in her own home. A servant or a mistress, I could not tell. I watched her pass through another doorway into a squat, three-storey building with several dozen windows. A twenty-count later, the shutters of one of the upstairs windows glowed briefly.

Sitting up with the sick? Or a servant at the long end of her day?

I crept awhile among the scents of frangipani and bougainvillea. There were windows to peer into, doors to watch. Paths to make note of.

What there lacked was any sign of a block of cells, or a heavily guarded building, or a desperate note from one of my missing lodged in a window shutter. Even mugging a servant or a guard was unlikely to be helpful here, given the complexity of the place. Besides, where would I find one right at that moment?

All too sadly quiet, in other words. Both in the back of the property and around to the front.

The Rectifier and I had braced Surali's rented mansion in Copper Downs more or less single-handedly, helped by the limited entrances and exits, and the relatively compact structure. This place was a warren. An entire army of Blades could become lost here, chasing themselves around.

How am I going to accomplish this?

With help, of course. With lots of help. Exactly as Mother Vajpai had been counseling me.

I'd needed to come look, regardless. At least now I knew.

Back to the rear gardens and over the wall, then. I wondered if I could conceal my little excursion completely from Mother Vajpai and Mother Argai. Probably not, unfortunately.

I sidled across the patio, moving irregularly among the shadows of furniture and potted palms. Once I was down among those bushy papaya trees, I would be on my way back, cover or no cover.

The first crossbow quarrel sliced the air by my ear with a noise like torn cloth. It spanged off a rock not far in front of me, implying a high angle from the bowman.

Stealth abandoned, I sprinted for the back wall. This was no place for a fight, especially not if they could identify me in the process. A pair of guards loomed up in front of me, spears forward.

I was in no mood to charge braced shafts. Instead, I swerved rightward and scrambled up the east wall. That would put me in the neighboring yard rather than out in the public street, but, well, I could always send a note of apology later.

Over the top and I was down into someone's banana trees. They crashed loudly, broad leaves ripping. Several of the shallow-rooted trunks toppled with squelching noises.

By the Wheel, that was not good. This would raise the house guards here as well. I kept running, breathing a little hard now and wondering both how to look like a mere burglar and what to do next.

Crashing through the brush near the back wall of the neighboring property, I heard shouting behind me. No other crossbow quarrels had come close yet, but I did not doubt they were being loosed as well. Torches flared, too—that I could tell by the changing shadows around me.

I pushed through a stand of tall ornamental sedge and bounced off something large. Large and warm. Two glowing spots about a foot apart loomed in front of me. Hot, meaty breath blew and I heard a slow rumble amid the unmistakable rankness of a very large cat.

My legs warmed as I wet myself. This was a tiger. Loose in someone's yard. Looking at me from less than an arm's length away.

Cover already blown, I screamed and milled my arms. The tiger took a half step back, becoming shadow in deeper shadow, then rose. No, it was on its haunches. If they hunted like housecats, this one was about to leap. I glanced down at a pale paw as big around as my face, then leapt forward myself, shoulder first, to plow into the tiger and roll across its back.

It spun. The tail whipped at me, but I was already sprinting for the wall that loomed only a rod or two away. Behind me a roar echoed, followed immediately by the distant laughter of men.

They thought they had me, the bastards.

This wall was smooth stone, close-set without convenient mortared handholds. I slid to my right, running, hearing the tiger move behind me. I didn't *want* to fight it, I didn't know *how* to fight it, and if I spent more than few seconds doing so, those crossbowmen would find me in the dark just by the noise.

Unless Surali's men have been warned not to shoot her neighbor's tiger . . .

That thought caused me to juke to the right again. I turned hard on one heel and raced directly toward my human pursuers. Grass crackled behind me as the tiger paced.

He was a cat. He would play before he killed. *Fine,* I told myself, *play with me just few seconds longer.*

I was out on the broader lawn now. Half a dozen men with torches approached, talking loudly. I knew this brag. It was how they nerved themselves to face something they were afraid of. Me, an armed shadow. The tiger, a quantity they possibly knew all too well.

Racing toward them out of the darkness, I shouted, "He's got the poor bastard!" I glanced over my shoulder to see that yes, I was still being pursued.

Crossbows came up and swords were lifted. I'd faced both of those before. Head down, god-blooded short knife out, I bowled right into them. I heard at least two sets of strings twang, followed by the bellowing roar of the tiger and a strangled yelp from someone.

Then I was gone and they were screaming.

I ran so hard, I burst into the back of this house. It seemed to be laid out more like our own a few blocks away. Taking heart from that, I raced down a wide hallway lined with small sculptures on narrow plinths, into an open room covered with rugs, and toward the tall doors to the front.

The men were shouting close behind me. My shoulders itched for the strike of another bolt from a crossbow, but then I realized that these fools were no longer chasing me. They were running from the tiger, too. Which roared again.

Bursting out the front door, I skidded down a set of marble steps with a banister carved like a naga and sprinted all the more swiftly through the formal front garden. By now, lights were flickering from various directions.

This was an utter disaster.

I hit the tripled front gate and went right over the top of the central entrance reserved for the master of the house and the most important guests. They boomed a moment later as the knot of frightened men literally ran into the wood. I heard scrabbling for the bar, followed by meaty thumps.

That business was between them and the tiger. Someone screamed from inside that house as well, loudly enough to be heard outside the walls. For my own part, I legged it hard down the Gita. I was looking for a cross-street. I could not possibly lead these men to our hideaway. Not where my children were. That would be execrably foolish.

Away. I needed to be away. More shouts behind me only told that story all the more.

Run, Green, run.

I raced through dark, unfamiliar streets. Copper Downs had gas lamps in various parts of the city. Kalimpura provided no municipal lighting, though some streets, and even a few entire districts, were studded with cressets on poles, funded by the local families and merchants.

And I did not know this city as I knew Copper Downs. We had run often as Blades, of course, but on set paths for the most part. And never in these wealthier quarters where private guards were the norm and our armed presence was unwelcome.

If I could just pull far enough away from my pursuers, I could *stop* running and attract less attention. Some of the markets were open all hours of the night and day, and the areas around the waterfront and the various gates were always busy.

I needed to be off these quiet streets.

Another side road beckoned. This part of the city was too monied for mere alleys. I slipped into the deeper darkness and pulled myself swiftly to the vestigial roof of a small gatehouse.

Half a dozen men ran by a few seconds later. They wore two different uniforms, and seemed more a mob than an organized pursuit. I could see several more passing by in the larger street. Somewhere nearby the tiger roared once more, but it did not sound as if it were at the chase as well.

Right now I was more afraid of the tiger than I was of the men. The big cat had a *nose*.

After a short while, the clattering and shouting had died down. Occasional calls still echoed, people walking the streets, but there were no longer packs on my heels. I slipped down off the gatehouse roof and walked quietly into the deeper dark.

At almost the same moment that I heard a twanging snap, a crossbow quarrel grazed my cheek without actually burying itself in me.

By the Wheel, they are trickier than I credited.

The only way to defeat a bowman was to rush him. I sprinted forward into deeper shadow with my short knife before me. To my horror, I realized I had not counted the number of weapons on the men who'd passed me heading this way.

I met the first of them by burying my short knife to the hilt in his breastbone in nearly total darkness. He gasped. Something swished near my head. I could hear the clicking of a crossbow's pawl.

The street behind me was serving a backlight, I realized. Dancing hard to the left, I crouched and swung low. Thighs, groins, butts—it did not matter. I needed to slow them down more than I needed to kill them.

One of the men began shouting for help, which was enough for me to find his throat. Knife still in, I grabbed his thrashing arm and swung us both around in a gavotte.

The clicking stopped and another quarrel buried itself in his chest, right in front of me. This time I found the bowman by dint of thrusting his friend's body forward. I could not follow up, for someone else clouted me in the head with the flat of a sword.

I could not stay enmeshed in this.

Slightly dizzy, I dropped and rolled three times, slashing ankle tendons on the way, right through leather boots. This god-blooded blade was something I could certainly get used to.

Then I scrambled to my feet, slipping on body fluids, and fled the keening of one or another of my wounded. More men entered the side street behind me, flickering torches held high. That was fine with me. Everyone's night vision but mine would be ruined.

Two or three streets later, I loped into an area where a few other people passed furtively. People who were not hunting me, more to the point. The lights of a market burned ahead. I saw the obelisk and realized it was the Munchatti Market, which supplied foodstuffs and textiles to those households wealthy enough to buy well but not large or monied enough to contract their own jobbers directly.

Fortunately, that meant more people. A lot more.

Unfortunately, that also meant guards and armed retainers. The sort of men who might not look hard at me in my Blade leathers, but would definitely respond to a shouting, bloody-handed pursuit by some of their fellow men-at-arms.

Fortunately, the Umagavanai Fountain there drained through a grate that led into such a Below as Kalimpura did possess. From there the tunnel led toward the waterfront. There it met up with two others beneath the Rice Exchange building.

If I could get down Below, I could lead my pursuers in circles or simply ambush them myself.

Either way, I was farther and farther from my children with every passing moment. *That* was what I wanted right now.

I strode firmly through the market past the stalls with the early morning eggs and the first of the fresh vegetables. Let them wonder why a Blade was walking alone—something we rarely if ever did. My leathers would not show the blood of others, much, though I could do little to stem my bleeding cheek.

They would remember me. That was too bad. Surali surely suspected, but when she heard the word from the Munchatti Market, she would *know*.

Mother Vajpai's likely observations already rang sharp in my head. *I can critique this disaster just fine all by myself, thank you,* I told my mental image of her.

The fountain was just ahead. As always, its water ran rusty and slightly brown. Unlike the folk of Copper Downs, no one was foolish enough even in this city to ascribe healing properties to what was only bad plumbing. The grate was clear, but getting down it unremarked would be a neat trick, indeed, given that there were now several dozen people within convenient earshot and eyeshot.

My problem was abruptly solved for me by a loud roar. Or more to the point, by the sudden screaming panic that erupted at the appearance of a bloody-mouthed tiger along the market's edge.

I dropped to my knees, slipped my fingers into the grate, and levered it up. Sliding in, I was pushed down by a trampling stampede that nearly smashed my fingers for me. I dropped to the floor of the conduit, which was quite small here. There I began waddling in a painful crouch toward the Rice Exchange.

Surely I had not been so much smaller the last time I passed this way?

A minute or two later, some man splashed cursing behind me in the tunnel. I *still* had not shaken them off.

At least that wretched tiger was not going to follow me down here.

My pursuer hadn't brought a torch, and neither had I. But I would put my abilities at moving in the dark up against any human being in Kalimpura. Besides that, the bastard behind me was backlit now, from the glow of the grate's shaft.

I crouched stock-still, mouth open, barely breathing. My short knife I held forward, point first. He literally walked right into it, catching the point somewhere in his face before pulling back with a yelp. I leaned forward, mindful of my enemy's blade and slid my own deeper into whatever it had caught upon.

A bubbling whimper was good enough for me. Let his comrades get by *him* in this cramped tunnel. I turned and scampered away, aching to stand taller.

Somebody was too blesséd smart for my own good tonight, and it was not me. There was a knot of men—well, people, but I rather assumed they were men—in front of me where the tunnels met under the Rice Exchange. Whoever was leading this pursuit of me had thought ahead. Not only that, but they were also smart enough not to be show-ing torches. The only reason I knew they were there is that a handful of men with weapons at the ready are not *quiet*.

Women truly are much better at this, I thought with a grim smile.

But right now . . . My choices were a bit limited.

I could go back. I could go forward. That was about the extent of my options.

At least I knew how to do both those things.

The short knife weighed heavily in my hand. I considered throwing it, but was appalled at the thought of losing the weapon here in the dark, either to sheer obscurity or to a quick-thinking enemy. If I rushed them, they would hear me coming and simply shoot me down. Even this pack of fools could pump arrows and quarrels into a narrow tun-nel. Whoever had been smart enough to put them down here would also have been smart enough to arm them correctly.

My only ally was the intense darkness. That and my superior knowledge of the layout.

I lowered myself slowly into the running water. It was cold and smelly, but it was not sewage. After a minute of listening to large men try to be silent, I began to slither forward. I was careful not to dam the flow. Surely even these fools would notice that.

My nose very nearly met a boot before I realized I was upon them. The water had dropped as well, spreading out shallowly into a larger space. I sat still, listening to them breathe and clank.

How many?

They had to be lucky only one time, and in this dark I would not see the blow coming.

Taking a long, slow, very shallow breath, I leapt to my feet in an explosion of rust-scented water, screaming at the top of my lungs. Four or five voices screamed back.

I didn't stop to fight, just slammed through them shoulder first, caromed off an arched wall, and splashed away in the darkness.

Exhausted, I rested in a pit beneath a closed-over well. Dull gray flecks above me testified to pits and cracks in the wood and the pre-dawn light behind them. I'd heard some shouting and splashing, and more than once spotted the flicker of torches, but they'd never found me.

This was below the Plaza of Seven Stars, I was almost certain. If so, I was only a handful of blocks from Street of Ships and the waterfront, should I dare to show my face. My arms shook a bit, as they did sometimes after a fight. I was cold. I was hungry. I missed my children. My breasts ached with milk.

Most of all, I was alive.

To my surprise, I began to weep.

Such a mess I'd made.

It had been stupid of me to go out like that. Without permission, without backup, without even a simple, stupid plan. And everything had gone wrong, then more wrong. Surali knew beyond a doubt that I hunted her and her prisoners—the woman was no fool, whatever else I might think of her. Mother Vajpai and Mother Argai would be confronted with my unplanned absence, at least until they asked Ilona. Or even just looked closely at her. She could hold her tongue, my sweet Ilona, but her heart traveled on her face.

And my children. They would not know, they were too young, but I would not be there to feed and hold them. I wept some more, until I slept awhile, standing up with my back against the curving wall of the old well shaft.

I startled awake, afraid. The usual racket of the city went on not far above me. It was probably the firecrackers that had ripped me from uneasy sleep.

Mother Vajpai and Mother Argai had been counseling caution, but with me gone, would they heed their own advice? That was my new worry. That others might do something even more foolish in my absence than I had done myself.

Above, someone whistled sharply. A hunting call. The noise of the street changed a bit, too. Were they *still* looking for me? Admittedly, Surali could turn out the entire Street Guild should she have a mind to do so, but at some point they had to go back to their petty thievery and shakedowns. Or simply sleep.

Those men did not share among themselves the loyalty that the Lily Blades held for one another; I was certain of it.

Little else presented itself but to wait for evening. With my scarred cheeks and nose, and notched ears, no one would mistake me in daylight. Under the cover of night's shadow, earlier in the evening when the streets were still crowded was my best bet. In time, I dozed again.

Desire came to me in my little, dim shaft. She was a whirlwind of all women everywhere, as She had once before manifested to me. I did not hear Her voice, only Her words, somewhat like how Chowdry reported Endurance's will.

Green, She said, or did not say. *Those you seek are safe for now. Every table must have its stakes. Leave them in play.*

"You are no god of gambling," I murmured. Disrespect was not intended, only truth.

The god-killers. The Red Man and his little sprite. Seek them instead. They are the keys to break open this lock. The wager that will sweep the table.

"Brooms sweep." With those words, I startled awake. My stomach was sour and sharply pained.

Had that been a true sending of Desire? Always before I had met the divine wide awake. I suspected my own thoughts of playing tricks on me.

In any case, no omens presented themselves by way of either validation or contradiction. I could not tell which it was; sending or subtle thoughts of my own. And perhaps it did not matter.

Loitering at the bottom of a well to talk to goddesses and titanics in one's sleep smacked of haruspication in any case. I was no fortune-teller to say sooth and cast the future.

In truth, what had the gods ever done but trouble me? At that thought, I mumbled a silent prayer of apology to the Lily Goddess for doubting Her. If any of them could hear me down here, it was She, whose temple was not so far away, and whose city this was. At least in part.

Above, the shouting changed tone again. I cocked my head to an odd rushing noise. High wind passing through the city, perhaps. I wondered at that. What *was* I hearing?

Screaming started again. This time I seriously doubted it was the tiger. Not in broad daylight. Screaming, then shouting about the harbor, followed by the sound of a large mass of people moving in a very determined manner in a common direction.

I did not like hiding in the sewers. Not when strange doings were afoot in the city.

The rushing noise grew louder. I realized water was pooling around my feet and pouring into the well shaft next to me. Brown and bubbling, it smelled brackish.

I stepped through the little embrasure that led into the tunnels beyond. Water was flowing over the lip there. In the tunnel, it ran calf-deep.

The wrong way.

This stream was coming *up* from the outflows at the harbor's edge. Water was entering the city from the ocean. I trailed my fingers in it, though that was hardly necessary to experience the rank, salty odor. The harbor was climbing to meet me once more.

And it was doing so in a manner sufficient to cause a panic in the streets above.

Already the water was at my knees. I could read this situation as well as any other woman who was not also a fool. Whether Desire had come to me in a dream or I'd imagined Her message for myself, the meaning was the same. No longer could I hide down here.

No longer could I hide at all.

Not that this argument was difficult for me. I rarely turned away from confrontation. I just needed a different way of facing Surali.

Water swirled around me with more force now. Coming from the harbor, it was still mucky. Bits of wood and slime and all the odd jetsam of a waterfront were carried on its dark eddies. I began pushing against the flow, trying for the few blocks to reach the harbor outflow before it rose too high for me to continue.

It swiftly became apparent that my problem would not be the depth of the water, but the force. Any fluid is heavy stuff. Pushing against the flow was like lifting a dead weight with every step. Though I held my knives in my hands, they were growing wet with the salt water. That, in turn, would endanger the blades.

Up and out. I looked for a ladder, a hatch, a grate.

Again I missed the Below of Copper Downs. That city was lousy with tunnels, undermined as any insect warren. One could go almost anywhere and emerge easily enough. Kalimpuri had never spent so much effort building down. For one thing, this place was not located atop an ancient set of mines.

This city was, however, located on a harbor front that seemed intent on finding its way to me.

After a very hard block's push, I came upon another access. A wooden ladder was bolted to the wall of a wider vault. The rising harbor water swirled there in a deeper eddy—there was enough space here for that countercurrent to move freely. A trapdoor blocked the top of the ladder. I could see by the faint light around its loose edges.

One of the ice warehouses, I thought. During the northern winters, they brought blocks of the stuff in from the Stone Coast in straw-packed holds of fast ships, then stored it in thick-walled warehouses. Something that was a dreadful nuisance in Copper Downs was a fantastic luxury in Kalimpura, commanding almost its own weight in gold.

And sometimes it needed to be dumped, when it grew too rotten or dirty to be used.

I set my shoulder against the trap and pushed up. Water climbed below me, plucking like eager hands.

The trap did not budge. Latched. Or worse. Perhaps something heavy had been set across it from above.

Balancing on the ladder, I studied the faintly illuminated edges. Light from above was my friend right now. Hinges were shadows on the sides to my right and my left. The split in the middle did not admit any glow, so there was a lath or similar overlap between the panels of the trap. One would not put a bar in the midst of a trapdoor, I did not think.

But I could not see another latch blocking light at the edges.

I pushed up at the center of the door with my long knife. Water swirled at my waist now. If I'd remained in the tunnel below, I'd be breathing either that stuff or stone. My choices might not be much better here soon either.

"I understand," I told whoever might be listening. Not prayer, exactly. "I am leaving as quickly as I can."

The long knife didn't do much. Clinging to the ladder still, I carefully switched to the short knife. I hated how much I was coming to depend on that blade. Any weapon you could not throw away at need was a weakness.

That blade went through the split in the doors as if the wood were damp paper. I leaned out and dragged the knife from one end to the other. That also had the advantage of admitting a little bit more light.

Another push with my shoulders, water above my waist now, and the doors lifted. I scrambled up into a fairly large room gasping with the panic I had not allowed myself to feel until I was free of that increasingly small space.

This was a moment I needed to allow myself—hands on knees, head bent low, breath whooping, my entire body shivering with a bitter, frightening cold.

You could not fight water. It did not care for blades or strength. Fists of the world, indeed. How did sailors stand going down to sea?

Shaking off the panic as water began to pool around me, I looked around. I had been correct about this being an icehouse. This was a cutting and weighing room, where the blocks were counted out. Several large scales waited along one wall like great brass scuttles. Chains overhead allowed the blocks to be maneuvered rather than simply shifted by brute force. The floor was littered with grit and straw and puddles of melt. A thick sliding door to my right must lead toward the cold rooms—twice my height, and even wider than it was tall, huge enough that someone could have driven a wagon through it.

And possibly they did. As I recalled, ice was heavy. How did one shift it about, even inside a warehouse?

I slid open the other door, a much thinner one that led to a loading dock as I'd expected. People milled about in the streets, a babble of activity and panic rising like steam from a griddle.

I jumped down from the dock. Fingers of water crept along the cobbles.

It was time for me to face the sea again.

That thought brought a twist of stomach-wrenching dread. There was nothing for me to do but turn toward my fear.

Sheathing my knives, for they would do me no good now, I trotted toward the Street of Ships and the harbor that clawed restive from its basin to mount the land like an eager paramour.

The quays and piers were awash. Water flowed ankle-deep on the Street of Ships itself, which ran atop the seawall that edged the waterfront district. People had taken to the roofs and loading docks of the buildings along the roadway. The ships tied up were crowded at the rails—some of the captains must have allowed the panicked dockside folk aboard. Or perhaps they had not been given much of a choice.

Seawater surged toward me as the tide would do when driven by a great storm. But there was no storm. The ocean crested here in eerie silence as if it were being drained into Kalimpura. Looking *up* at water was an unnerving experience on a ship at sea. Standing on the shore and looking up at water churned my guts to jelly.

I drew my short knife. Blackblood's ichor had cut the wind and rain before. And it gave me a prop, something with which to point. Gripping the weapon in an unsteady hand, I advanced down the Coin Pier, as that was closest to me.

"Return to sleep," I said loudly to the waters boiling cold around me. "I call on the Lily Goddess. I call upon Endurance. I call upon Desire, and Her brother Time Himself. Bend back this tide and return us to balance."

Salt water swirled around me. Sea foam danced, twisted, tormented as if by wind and wave, though the air was as flatly still as that in any wine cellar. And, for Kalimpura, as strangely cool. Still, the water piled up.

I tried to push, seeking to recapture what I had felt from the bridge walkway of *Prince Enero*. But much as when I had called the ox god into being on the street in front of the Textile Bourse, I could recall the moment without remembering how I had found my way there.

The memory of the divine is like the memory of pain—you know you have experienced it, but you cannot relive the experience. In the years since, I have come to realize this protects us all from the sharp edges with which the world is filled. Every day dawns like shattered glass, then passes to depart on bladed wings, which only the ignorant and the lucky survive unscathed.

How mightily I tried to cast off my ignorance in that moment. The water mounted around me, swirling, until I stood knee-deep at the bottom of a bowl of air, its sides defined by racing foam and the rippling dance of the skin of the sea. I smelled seaweed and iodine and fish and wet, dank death—reminded suddenly of the great, toothed monster that had reached to grasp my life when I'd first fled Federo off the deck of *Fortune's Flight* back near the beginning of my life.

The sky narrowed above me, the water closing like a fist. Words came to me unbidden, in the manner of a spell remembered without ever having been memorized. "Back into your bed, Mother Ocean!" I shouted. My voice boomed, as if I had lungs the size of houses, and the great slow breathing of forest and field. "Now is not yet the time when you can claim the land for your own."

When would that be? I thought idiotically, struck by a vision of both my countries being conquered by tall, white-haired armies of waves.

Something rippled in the round patch of sky above me. This was how the air must look to a frog at the bottom of a pond, perhaps. Everything became thick, wet, until the tip of my knife was met by the tightening wall of water closing around me like a liquid coffin.

Spray spouted where the god-blooded tip scored the dancing surface. The enclosing wave opened like a wound. The ocean crashed around me, drenching me, but somehow I stood my ground while it poured away in a rush of bubbling foam and flopping fish. Ships along the Coin Pier swayed in danger of turning turtle as the water raced back to join its source.

Around me the streets drained. This rogue arm of the ocean rushed past me bearing dead rats, bedraggled cats, bruised fruit, shoes—all the debris of the daylight city. It flowed into the harbor in a thinning waterfall over the edge of the seawall. What had taken the better part of an hour to wash into the city was gone in minutes.

I stood watching a bright silver fish flop and gasp in a stray puddle and wondered once again what I had just done. My body had the shivering, addled feeling I'd come to associate with the divine. Once more I whispered quiet gratitude to my goddesses.

Gods were a greater pain to me than men—I would have sworn to it in that moment. And many times since, for that matter. What do any of us know, after all, except what we are shown? And who can show more than a god?

Still, any time give me a decent curry and a good night's sleep by preference over a mountaintop and the kingdoms of the world.

They came for me before I'd retreated a dozen steps from the water's edge. Not the Street Guild, but rather the street itself. First it was a knot of beggars, cooing at me and crying to touch even my boots. Then a crowd of sailors and merchants of the usual dockside order. They shouted an erupting chaos of thanks and praise and effusive tears.

I tried to eel out of the line of grasping hands, to escape into streetwise anonymity, but these were having nothing of that. Some even knew my name, and soon the chant was "Green, Green, Green."

These were not people toward whom I would bare a blade, or strike with fist and foot. So I allowed them to sweep me along. What else was I to do?

We paraded down the Street of Ships to the Great Chain, then back again to the Coin Pier. I was soon riding on shoulders. People brought out poles from which dangled strings of firecrackers. Their rippling explosions reminded me painfully of the long guns used aboard *Prince Enero,* but nothing buzzed past my face; no death blossomed from this one's chest or that one's head.

Gongs, too, and bells liberated from temple precincts. A pushcart that had somehow survived the flood appeared with fire and hot nuts. Three tiny men in greasy red silk tunics and flat hats arrived with long metal skewers impaling haunches of meat dripping with fat and cracklings. The smells reached my nose even above the fug of the crowd and made me realize my hunger. I beckoned for one, reckoning the gesture futile, but one of the men grinned, showing filed teeth stained crimson. He flicked his pole so the topmost haunch slipped free and tumbled through the air.

I caught it like a thrown knife, huge as the hunk of meat was, and tore into the roasted flesh. Uncaring, I dripped fat on the people carrying me, but they grinned and waved and shouted. Soon I was being overloaded with food and flowers like some household god on a funeral palanquin.

It was a dream, a strange dream, and in this dream I was hideously vulnerable. Visible to anyone with a bow or spear, bareheaded beneath the morning sky, surrounded by a singing, shouting swirl of waterfront humanity. Music blared loudly. A cart with a coal demon statue rumbled after us.

This was truly a festival. These same people could just as easily have torn me limb from limb for bringing the killing water down upon them, but of course, *they had not seen that.* Any more than they'd known I was aboard *Prince Enero* those days ago, or had the least notion of what took place out upon the Storm Sea.

All they'd seen was me laying the water to rest. I could fight this mass of people even less than I could have fought the tide, had some god or goddess—which, I did not know—not heeded me. Ilona's warning about me becoming a Selistani storm goddess might have been more prophetic than she knew.

Still, there was nothing for it. I smiled, caught more flowers, was showered with mostly copper coins, and allowed myself to borne toward the statue of Maja's Boar on Savvatana Street.

In all this messy business, I realized I had not seen any Street Guild. These laborers and stevedores and sailors and tavern wenches and shopkeepers and beggars and brokers were all people with little cause to love the Street Guild. And they knew I had fought their enemies before.

I was safer here and now than I would be among a Blade handle on a run. In a sense, this was a restaging of the beggars' riot I'd helped put on not too many days ago.

The chanting and shouting continued. I tried to listen, but it was hard to pick out words amid the rising and falling racket. They shouted against the Bittern Court, against the Street Guild, and for the Blades. Not so much for the Lily Goddess or Her temple, not that I could hear, but for now, I was among them, being carried as theirs.

I would take this for what it was.

Eventually I was set down in Ardi Square, where bonfires were being built out of smashed market booths and overturned carts. More food appeared, and tall poles with flags, and even more of those foolish fireworks that now sounded too much like weapons to me.

Set down, I took a deep draft of a proffered bowl of what turned out to be rice wine. Offered a pair of arms, I danced. Handed a child, I dandled her. Everyone wanted to touch me. After a while, it felt as though everyone had done so. No tiger roared, no angry armored men chased after me, and though my children were still too distant for my comfort, otherwise it was not so bad a way to pass the lengthening day. Hidden, as it were, in the plainest sight.

Once the madness finally died down, I slipped away in the shadows of evening. Fortified by strong drink and rich food, I did not walk in so straight a line as I might have liked. I counted the day a success in that I had not collected that arrow in the back I'd been fearing.

Half the city had seen me, and what little protection my remaining anonymity had granted me was long lost. Still, I had done some good from the mess I'd created the night before.

How to explain all this to the Mothers and Ponce and Ilona, though . . .

I'd acquired someone's midnight blue robe and wore it now, along with several garlands of flowers. I seemed to be carrying a pair of protesting chickens. Their feet were wired together. When had I picked them up?

Well, no one looking for the renegade Lily Blade Green would see me in the staggering progress of a half-drunk poultry seller. Or poultry buyer. Or whatever I was. At least the Street Guild would not be likely to know me either.

It occurred to me somewhat belatedly that I could not simply hammer on the front gate of our hidden house. The place was not supposed to be inhabited, after all. And I wasn't sure how Mother Argai found her way in and out. *I* had gone over the wall very late at night when no one was looking.

Picking my path with some care, I found myself in the narrow street behind our back wall. This faced onto another row of great houses, unlike the back of the Bittern Court's compound. So fewer eyes, and even fewer suspicions unless I was spotted by happenstance.

I sidled up to the service entrance of our house, glanced around, then tossed the chickens over the top of the gate. After that, I stumbled a bit farther down the street, not waiting to see if anyone noticed. Looking around in a guilty manner was like hanging a sign.

Near the corner of the property, I scrambled up the wall and dropped into the neighboring lot. There I crashed into a large stand of ferns. I lay there awhile, breathing shallow, and strained to listen for any hue and cry. If someone had noticed me, they would surely raise the alarm. Preferably with the neighbors rather than to the supposedly empty house.

Five minutes went by, then five more. Nothing whatsoever happened other than some low, distressed clucking from my own yard next door. I hoped the chickens had not gotten free. The hassle of catching them would be more noise and trouble than the birds were worth.

With a hiss of breath, I startled awake. I had not realized I'd fallen asleep. Too much strong drink, too long a day. I quietly cursed my loss of time, and thanked whoever among my various gods that might be listening for a continued lack of tigers.

I lay there a few more minutes and tried to sort out how long I'd been asleep. The stars were visible now, but being for the most part fixed and unchanging in the sky, they were little help. No moon only meant it was still fairly early, as the moon currently rose about midnight.

Enough, I thought. *Up and moving before someone finds you here and proves you to be the fool you are currently acting the part of.* I rose to a crouch, quietly stretched, then sprang for the wall dividing this property from ours.

A brief search for the chickens was fruitless. The little beggars had escaped after all. A problem for another time. No one should mind that so much, I realized. They had both been hens and were thus unlikely to set to crowing with the dawn.

I slid through the shadows of the rear expanse of the property, careful not to walk too openly where there were sight lines from the neighboring houses. When I finally sidled into our kitchen, I found six pairs of eyes glittering at me.

Everyone was up waiting for me.

"Hello," I said, at a sudden loss for further words.

"Thank you for the chickens," Mother Vajpai replied solemnly. Her expression was far more grim than her words.

"I . . . I am sorry." Suddenly my feet were quite interesting, but I would not play the child. Looking up again, I said, "I have a great deal to confess."

Ilona stepped forward and handed me Federo. Ponce followed a moment later with Marya. Both of them looked at me sourly. Then the four adults drifted to our circle of chairs by the fire, where the smokeless oil stove Mother Argai had managed to secure was positioned.

I followed, balancing two squirming, gurgling babies. "It has been quite a day," I began, but Mother Vajpai raised her hand.

"Mother Argai attended a festival near the docks today," she announced.

"Ah." Once more I was at a loss for words.

"She learned much there."

Mother Argai nodded along to those statements. Ilona sighed and studied her own hands. Ponce just appeared sad, and confused. But then, he generally did of late.

"Wh-what did she learn?" I finally asked.

"Amazing things," Mother Argai said. "That you are commanding the waves. That you fight tigers. That you have slain the entire Street Guild to a man. That you plan to slay the entire Street Guild. That you are secretly being a northern goddess come to twist the heads of our children."

"Amazing, indeed," I echoed, keeping my voice careful. I rather wished the floor would open up and swallow me whole.

Mother Vajpai spoke once more. "Mostly we have learned that you are in the city again, and that you are seeking to right the wrongs done against you. Every beggar and errand boy and scullion in Kalimpura knows this by now." She leaned forward, hands on her knees.

I saw her fingers tremble. The knuckles stretched tight and white. "*What* were you thinking?"

I started to defend myself, then broke off. What was the point? I had been wrong to leave. I had been wrong to stir trouble at the palace of the Bittern Court. Though I had certainly never intended all that had taken place, everything that had happened this last day, for good or ill, rose from those two decisions.

"It does not matter," I finally said. "What is done is done. And I have learned much."

"*What?*" shouted Ilona, almost ready to explode. Her anger seared my heart.

"I have learned that we will not take Corinthia Anastasia and Samma from the Bittern Court by stealthy force. The place is too large, and complex, to sneak into as a half handle of searchers and hope to profit anything. We must apply guile, and negotiate."

A long, contemplative silence followed my statement.

"Negotiate?" Mother Argai finally said. "You are Green. You have never negotiated in your life."

"On the contrary, I do it all the time." In an eruption of self-honesty, I pointed out, "I'm doing it now. Besides, going in low and hard with one's weapons bristling is just another form of negotiation."

That drew a grunt of surprised amusement from Mother Vajpai, which she quickly covered with a glower.

I sighed. It was not that they didn't know me. It was not that they didn't have the right to be angry with me, each of my friends for their own reasons. But there was no *point*. The argument would be lengthy and without purpose, because we would wind up back where were right in that moment.

"Listen. I was wrong to leave. I knew that when I did it, and I know that now. But I understand more than I did about the problem to which we have set ourselves." I also understood I would be much happier if I avoided the waterfront for a while. And tigers. Definitely avoiding tigers. "I would rather expend our energy on sorting out our next plans for Samma and Corinthia Anastasia than on criticizing our past actions."

"*Your* past actions." Ponce spoke up in Petraean. He must have followed enough of the discussion in Seliu, then.

"Yes," I snapped. "Mine."

"And what happens when they come here for us?" Ilona asked softly in the same language. "I am no fighter. Even I know our protection in this house is secrecy. Not walls, not force. Just secrecy." Her eyes brimmed with tears. "Which you broke! My daughter is lost and perhaps never coming home. She could be dead *now*. Will you lose yours as well, for the sake of your stupid, stupid pride?"

Ilona began to cry in earnest. With my babies in my arms, I could not comfort her. Even if she would have me. Ponce leaned close to her, taking one arm fondly. I felt a stab of jealousy.

Jealous?

Me?

Of what?

Not of either of *them*, I told myself scornfully.

"Stop." Mother Vajpai's voice was cold and quiet. This was the old Blade Mother. Commanding, dangerous. Maybe coming home to Kalimpura had revived her spirit. "You are all fools," she went on. "Green is right. What is done is done, and cannot be unmade. Are we worse off for Surali knowing her enemy is close? Probably, but then Surali already knew us to be in Kalimpura. Are we worse off for Green being a hero in the streets? Probably not. For the moment, at least, we have a thousand eyes and ears.

"And it does . . . not . . . *matter*." Now her tongue lashed us like a whip. "We are in the midst of a mission. Green's mission. This is her run. She has made errors, errors that may prove fatal for some or all of us. That happens. All we can do now is choose to continue to follow where she leads, or back away and leave her to find her path alone."

That speech was greeted by another silence broken only by the gurgling of my children and the faint ticking of the oil stove's metal shell. I realized from the scent of mustard seed and saffron that they had been cooking, which in turn stirred my hunger.

After a little while, waiting to see if anyone cared to add to Mother Vajpai's outburst, I spoke once more in Seliu. "We will never find our lost ones by stealth. The grounds of the Bittern Court hold two dozen buildings. They are connected by bridges and walkways. We could search all night, and have the girls moved just ahead or behind of us all unknowing the entire time. Without our temple's backing, and the full force of the Blades, there is small purpose in even trying those walls around Surali."

"Trying those walls again," Mother Argai put in.

"Trying them again," I said, staring at her unashamed. "I was wrong in how I went about it, but I was not wrong in what I did."

"And the tiger?" asked Mother Vajpai.

"It was not my tiger," I pointed out. "You never taught me how to face one of those, but I survived anyway."

Another amused snort greeted that remark. I took this as an invitation to continue. "If we can find the Red Man and his apsara, they may be able to tell us more of what the Saffron Tower was about. They may even have been in on some early portion of Surali's schemes and know more of what she was about. But more important, they are the only string we have to pull that she *is not aware of*. The woman is no fool. She knows full well that Mother Vajpai will seek to turn the Blades away from Mother Srirani. She understands we will seek her out ourselves if need be.

"Hidden strength is the greatest power," I concluded, quoting the Stone Coast military philosopher Chard Lindsley. "And those two are our greatest hidden power." Of course, Surali had a hidden strength of her own in her contract with the Quiet Men, about whom even Mother Vajpai knew very little—when we'd talked aboard the ship, all she could say was that they were rumors, perhaps private agents to the highest houses and courts but outside even the street-level justice of the Lily Blades. Dangerous, yes, but not necessarily our enemies.

Not until now.

However I was trying to rally my half handle, not discourage them, so I said nothing of this thought. Instead, I glanced at Ponce and Ilona to see how much of that they had understood.

He did not look puzzled. Ilona cradled her face in one hand, the other twined finger-to-finger with Ponce. That sight made me feel very strange. It should have been me who comforted her. Still, to my considerable relief, she was no longer sobbing.

Both Mother Argai and Mother Vajpai appeared thoughtful.

I shifted the weight of my children. Had they somehow grown over the brief time I was gone? Such large little things they were. Two pairs of eyes—one blue gray, the other brown—stared back at me.

Each small forehead seemed to beg for a kiss, so I planted one on first my daughter, then my son. That was better than thinking about Ilona, which would only lead me to brooding and anger. Clutching the babies close, I continued in Petraean, which I reckoned Mother Argai could follow enough of. "Without the full backing of the Temple of the Silver Lily, we do not have the power to force Surali to negotiate. Picking at her secrets, unraveling her plans, even her old plans, may give us that leverage in another form."

"We are working on the problem of the temple," Mother Vajpai said almost grudgingly.

"I know. And you shall solve it quite well. But now I know my own best path will not work. I cannot be a large enough storm of blades against them. Not as we are constituted today."

"What of that cold tide?" Mother Argai asked.

That caught me short. "My pardons, what?"

"The people on the docks are calling the water swellings cold tides. Either you are summoning them, or they are following you."

"Yes," I breathed, wondering if I could possibly give her a worthwhile answer. Almost certainly not. "In any case, Surali has not been obliging enough to place herself at the waterfront. If I could somehow pull the tide to the Bittern Court's palace, it would destroy half the city."

"The ocean is in love with you," Ilona blurted.

We all stared at her. Once again, I felt that I'd missed an important turn in the discussion. "The ocean, well, it just *is*," I finally said.

"Oceanus was one of Desire's brothers. One of the titanics."

"Yes." That much was true. "But the titanics are long gone from the plate of the world."

"Not Desire."

"No . . ." Despite the best efforts of the Saffron Tower in that regard, either. Or perhaps not their best, not yet. I still had to meet this Mafic about whom Chowdry had written me in such haste. "Not Desire."

"It reaches out for you," Ilona persisted. "We both read *Goddes ande Theyre Desyres* back in our days at the Factor's house. You know the lore. Perhaps too well."

"It's lore. And old lore at that. Not law. The ocean weaves through the plate of the world, an endless braid of salt water. If Oceanus is still walking the Earth, he cannot possibly focus on me any more than he could focus on a single grain of sand along one of his beaches."

"Desire has focused on you," she persisted.

"Through the lens of the Lily Goddess, and lost Marya!" At the sound of her name in my raised voice, my dozing daughter stirred and coughed.

"Through the lens of Desire . . ." Ilona's voice trailed off. She seemed ready to drop the question.

"It does not matter," I told them. "I cannot control that power, no matter to whom it might belong. The tide is not mine to raise. The Red Man is mine to seek out, though. He is all of ours to seek."

"There was talk today," Mother Argai said into the silence that followed. "From your street festival."

"Of the Red Man?"

"Yes." She tapped her fingers together. There was no point in urging her to continue speaking. I waited to let Mother Argai frame her thoughts, as was her way. "Word has been that he is off in the high, hard country of the Fire Lakes. But today some said they had seen a Red Man drinking in a tavern near the Evenfire Gate."

"Well, that seems appropriate," I muttered.

She shrugged. "I do not know. But we can search here with some hope."

"Surely you were not thinking of haring off to the Fire Lakes yourself, Green?" asked Mother Vajpai in astonishment.

Actually, I had been thinking exactly that, but the prospect was grotesque. Besides the logistical issues, such an expedition would take me too far from Samma and Corinthia Anastasia. "No," I lied cheerfully. "We have a lead to follow here. Find them, and we have strength as well."

"I will inquire quietly around the Evenfire Gate," Mother Argai said. "One such as he should be difficult to hide."

"Good." I finally sat to ease the strain on my back from standing and pacing with both babies in my arms. They needed to be fed in any case, and I desperately needed to feed them. "Now that we have an oil stove, I will cook a chicken for dinner. Ponce, will you please go kill and dress one of the hens I brought?"

He murmured some dejected assent and left. Which nicely got him away from Ilona. Hopefully I could tempt her into helping me with dinner. Kitchens were always a place for propinquity.

Setting that thought aside, I placed the babies at my feet, opened my robe, and unlaced my leather tunic to release my breasts. It was time to feed my children. And baring myself in front of Ponce when he was touching Ilona . . . It had felt just wrong.

The chicken turned out well, for all that I could not coax much heat from the little stove. Nor from Ilona either, unfortunately. A simmer is as good as a roast, if one is patient. It felt like real cooking to work with fresh meat and the increasingly improved larder provided by both Mother Argai's rangings about town and our own continued careful searches of this house. Spices, for one, were now in relative abundance.

Working alone despite my best intentions, I shredded the meat, soaked it awhile in sesame oil with red peppers chopped in, then set all in a pan of small beer to cook slowly while I worked with fresh vegetables, fruits, rock salt, and paprika to make a medley that crossed half a dozen flavors into a tangy, blended whole. There was enough Stone Coast cooking in my blood to make me wish for bread in the absence of the rice we would have trouble preparing over the weak fire.

Still, it made for marvelous eating, albeit quite late. Afterwards, the children sleeping once more and hopefully for the rest of the night, I sat outside with Ilona. She'd recovered herself enough to be willing to hold my hand in the dark. Whatever they meant to her, Ilona's fingers twined in mine were water in the desert of my love.

"She is still alive," I whispered after a while. Nighthawks peeped overhead, and occasionally a bat would whir by in a staggering flitter of small, leathery wings.

"I cannot know." Ilona's voice hitched. "When you went there, they might have taken their s-swords to her."

"They did not trouble to carry your daughter across an entire ocean only to put her to death at the first sign of difficulty." I doubted the same could be said of Samma, given the old enmities in play here, but that did not bear speaking aloud. Not in this moment.

"You stirred their nest." Now her words were so small, they barely fit into my ears. Like catching dust motes.

"They knew I was here even before we stepped off the ship." That sounded like an excuse, though I did not mean my words as such.

"I know."

We lapsed into silence awhile, but she did not release my hand. Something larger and slower swooped overhead—perhaps one of the flying foxes that lived among the papaya trees.

"Green . . ."

"Yes, dear?"

"If she is . . . is . . . is no longer here to be rescued . . ."

"Yes?"

"I do not think I can go on. Or go back."

"Leave it be," I said, squeezing her hand. "There is so much trouble to be had here already. We have no need to borrow more."

After a while she rose, kissed me on the cheek, and drifted indoors. Wishing mightily that I could follow Ilona right into her bed, instead I stared at the night sky and the treetops. At the least, I should be grateful that this house and its surrounds were laid out such that we could find a place to sit outside that was not within sight of the neighbors. Not to mention the noisome, nosy Street Guild that clattered through the city searching for me.

I was alone now, as alone as anyone ever managed to be in a place so crowded as Kalimpura. I found I did not like this so much. So I took myself to think upon my dead awhile, clinging to that ritual of candle and prayer that released me from their ghosts.

When I tired of my thoughts, I went to sew my bells, then sleep beside my children. Ponce snored in my bed with them. I did not roust him out, for company seemed better than not. Even if he had been sniffing after Ilona. When he awoke later and embraced me, I let him. I did not even move his hands away from where they wandered, though I did not open myself to the firmness of his need.

The next day, I wanted to go over the wall with Mother Argai, but Mother Vajpai forbade that plan. "After your little street festival, your name will be on everyone's lips."

"Just as much tomorrow."

"Perhaps. But let it rest. Besides, you are still very much being chased. Allow them to spend themselves awhile in casting about as you rest to rebuild your own strength."

So I brushed out my borrowed blue robe and cleaned my leathers and tended my children and managed to feel generally useless. I tried thinking of ways to fight tigers, then tried thinking of how many houses or compounds in Kalimpura might even *have* tigers.

As soon fight the tide, which at least appeared on a twice-daily basis. Tigers were hardly unknown, but they were notably scarce within the walls of most cities. Recent experiences notwithstanding.

Marya was trying to crawl now, though Federo just watched her in amazement as she wriggled herself against the furniture and squirmed, squirmed, squirmed as she cooed. I wished mightily for an ox that she might play under, and my son also at her side. Still, I saw myself most in her ragged, unsteady persistence. A child determined to be more than she was.

"You have no grandmother to love you, or for you to bury," I told them both sternly. "And I have already sent a troop of shades to someday guard your way into the next life. So stay here awhile, and be the delights of my world."

They both burbled at me. I received a gummy smile from Federo.

That was good enough for me.

Mother Argai came back that afternoon with a sack of sweets, some new knives that had obviously been extracted from the temple armory, and another letter from Chowdry. Also addressed to me at the Temple of the Silver Lily.

I supposed I should count myself lucky that Mother Srirani had not ordered them destroyed. Likely she was unaware of the existence of the missives.

In my whole life, I had never received a letter. Now here were two in the span of a week. Not even troubling with choosing from among the new weapons yet, I took Chowdry's missive and retired to a chair to read it while others played with the babies and the knives.

Greetings to Green, from Copper Downs and now of Kalimpura.

This place will never be settled, I am swearing on it. Councilor Jeschonek has come twice asking after the day of your return. I told him to wait until the phoenix drowns.

Putting my words to paper is not so simple, and Sister Gammage advises me how to say things when the words are trapped. I am thanking you for your patiences and her for her hand in writing.

The Mafic I told you of sails for Kalimpura. He knows about you and seeks you. I did not tell him anything. He also carries mystic

weapons from the distant east that kill with a look by sending a thun-
derbolt.

I have seen this once, and am thinking it magic, but I have been
told there is an art to this thing, just like kettle ships are an art as well.

In any case, it does not matter. This Mafic seeks you, he can kill
with a look, and you must be on your guard. He also is seeking two
named Firesetter and Fantail, though I am not knowing if and how
they are bonded to you.

Stay well. Do not let yourself be taken like the drowned phoenix.
It is to be wishing you well.

Chowdry, of Endurance

I smiled a bit at the letter, then took it to Mother Vajpai to see what
she made of the news. The words of my old pirate-turned-priest
seemed clear enough. Chowdry had never been one to speak in rid-
dles. I did not count him so clever as to try a code. And why should
he bother?

Mafic was coming, and he possessed those selfsame firearms that
Lalo's men had used aboard *Prince Enero*. I'd seen them close by. They
were frightening. I wanted no part of such things here in Kalimpura.

Unfortunately, the only people with the authority to forbid the
weapons entry to our harbor, or confiscate them if they did come, were
the Bittern Court. Their control of the affairs of the portside was
close enough to complete, and well settled in the fragmented mass of
customs and half-remembered wisdom that passed for the law here
in Kalimpura. Besides, none of the other Courts would welcome the
precedent of interference in their own prerogatives.

For a long moment, I wished for *Prince Enero* back. Lalo close at
hand might have been comforting, even more than Ponce's warm,
supple body had been in the night.

Mother Argai handed me back my letter. "Firesetter," she said. "If
his name is carrying meaning, he might be easier to find."

So far as I knew, never having seen one for myself, Red Men resembled the coal demons that were paraded at so many of our Kalimpuri festivals. Usually caged statues, sometimes mummers or priests
wandering free in makeup and a mask and stilts beneath upon their
feet, they were human in shape, but terribly oversized and ridiculously
wide, their snarling faces filled with sharp teeth.

Not unlike larger versions of the tiny men passing out meat at the beginning of my festival. I tried to put those two ideas together, but could not make them fit. At least not right there in the moment.

"Did you find any evidence of him?"

She laughed softly. "Most of the merchant caravans from Shaggat, Malahar, and the westward extents are coming through the Evenfire Gate. Do you know how many little taverns lie within a few blocks of there?"

"More than one woman could visit in an afternoon, I should imagine."

"More than a dozen women could."

Among the hulking, strange creatures sometimes found guarding caravans, a Red Man might not even be so immediately remarkable as he would elsewhere in the city of Kalimpura. Such a one could not simply throw a cloak over his head and shoulders and wander the streets freely outside an area like that.

Unlike, say, me.

"I would go with you tomorrow and check these places some more." It was an effort to keep the urgency out of my voice.

Mother Argai shrugged. "I cannot stop you. You might be covering yourself more, I am thinking."

The blue robe, of course. I wished I had my old Neckbreaker mask, but if I improvised a veil, I might pass that way. Covering the face was not a Kalimpuri tradition, but there were enough women from Sind and the other provinces to the west who did so that it would not be so especially remarkable.

"I will be covered," I promised her.

The next morning we slipped over the back wall before dawn. Together we found a teahouse and sat in the morning gloom until the brilliant tropical day had taken back the streets that, in truth, always belonged to the heat.

The bitter brew steamed in tiny cups painted with flowers and birds. A plate of salted pineapple stood between us, along with balls of rice and honey. I loved the smells but ate sparingly. Though I did not expect to fight today, I wanted to be prepared.

Besides, the knot in my gut would not have let so much food past in any case. And eating through the veil would be annoying at best.

Mother Argai spent quite some time watching me. Finally, whatever had been bubbling with her came to her lips. "You are not so much the hothead anymore, Green."

I nodded, acknowledging her statement without committing myself to a reaction, or the words that tried to jump to my own lips.

"Someday you may be wise. You will always be strong." One hand gripped her tea tight, and I realized for the first time that her fingers had grown wrinkled and were even becoming gnarled. Time's arrow slew us all, no matter how lucky we might otherwise be. "Be fortunate awhile, and you will be a woman to follow."

"I don't want anyone to follow me," I said truthfully.

"It is too late for that."

At those words, we lapsed back into silence and waited for the streets to finish awakening so that we might carry on unremarked and unremarkable amid the endless crowds.

I'd managed to claim another pair of short knives from the cache Mother Argai brought back to the house the night before. Once they were in my possession, I'd spent some time throwing them in one of the unused rooms of the house. Some of the carved wooden screens would never be the same again, but I once more possessed weapons I'd actually be willing to cast aside or leave buried in an enemy's guts. Truly, the god-blooded blade was an amazing artifact, but my fear of losing it was beginning to cripple my fighting style.

So today I moved through the streets wrapped in my slightly too loose leathers beneath my robe, the mundane short knives at each wrist, and the god-blooded knife in my thigh scabbard in place of the usual long blade I kept there. The entire affair, including the robe and veil, seemed heavy and hot, but I did not wish to pass unarmed through this city. Not with so many enemies. Even if I had a thousand friends, I had hundreds more who would kill me on sight. Any member of the Street Guild, just to start.

One of the charms of the Evenfire Gate was that it stood far from the Street Guild's usual haunts. The western boundary of Kalimpura was as distant from the waterfront as any other corner of the city.

I had passed through those neighborhoods more than once, but these had never been my usual haunts, either. Walking there with Mother Argai, I had to revise my opinion of Kalimpura as a Selistani city. There were more foreigners here than down by the docks, many more. Quite a few of them were not particularly human.

Copper Downs had its pardines, and the rare, stranger folk who strayed in by ship or over the wild lands of the Stone Coast interior, but most people there were Petraeans. Even the migrants, such as the Selistani community gathered around Chowdry and the Tavernkeep's place, were still a mere smattering among a large mass of pale faces.

Likewise the Kalimpuri waterfronts, where crews from dozens of lands might meet and mix, pass between ships, or drink and fight in the waterfront taverns. Few of them remained much longer than required to work another passage. Their needs were seen to by Kalimpuri who spoke more than one language, or sometimes just the language of money.

Here, though . . . It was a bazaar of people and their practices. The Sindu, of whom I was making a pretense of being one myself, were numerous, but they seemed for the most part to be Kalimpuri with an odd taste in clothes. There were more of the very short men in red silk, passing intent on errands, a number of them with those long metal skewers that I realized could be used as a pike or other weapon, even against a man ahorse. Other hues of skin and hair and eye presented themselves, most of which I could not name by origin or country.

More different were the three women I saw with rough-studded skin, like crocodile leather but almost lavender. Their eyes were narrow and gold with barred pupils, and each wore silver chains between their left hand and their neck, though their clothes were rich as any spice merchant's.

Slaves? Divine commandment? Marriage jewelry? I would never know.

And stranger things than those women shambled through this part of the city. I found myself wishing I'd been more aware of the district around the Evenfire Gate when I was living in the temple as a Blade Aspirant. I might have passed many fascinating hours here.

Likewise of interest were the shop goods, and even the shops themselves. I trailed Mother Argai at a bit of a distance with both of us on the lookout for places where a giant of a man with pepper-red skin might be found. That meant I was looking, truly looking, at what I passed.

When one walks through a city, most of what one sees soon becomes something of a blur. This counting house here looks much like the next customs broker's office. Bakeries and tea shops blend together. Spice markets and root markets are both full of stalls, wagons, shouting merchants, and their racing boy assistants. So you tend to see things in groups. It's easy to pass over the details, except for the ones your own training and experience have focused you on.

In that sense, I am always looking for bowmen on rooftops, regardless of whether I feel threatened. Likewise the flash of a blade. Persons with their arms out from their body, as if carrying a weapon. People moving too fast. Or with too much intensity. Signs of violence, signs of danger.

I should imagine an ostler moves through the crowd noting the horses and mules. Their color and conformation would mean something to him. Likewise the height of each animal and its age, how it walks or stands, the yellowing of the teeth. To me those beasts are for the most part little more than mobile landscape, but to such a one as my imagined ostler, everything in traces or reins is a wealth of information.

So we each look with the eyes that we have been given by our lives. I for one have never been able to set that sight aside, nor do I particularly wish to. Noticing weapons has saved my life a number of times. Even to this day such practices are part of my ordinary experience.

That day, though, I was noticing people and their places. Oh, those places . . .

Some were almost familiar. A fruit stall is a fruit stall until you attend to what is being laid out for sale. In Copper Downs, I would expect to see at the least apples, pears, cherries, and plums, depending on the season, as well as a dozen varieties of berry. Here in Kalimpura, pineapples, mangoes, papayas, guavas, plantains, and bananas would be the more usual case. Furthermore, our growing seasons were nearly year-round.

But around the Evenfire Gate, I did not even have names for many of the fruits I saw. The cook in me wanted to stop and sample the waxy yellow gourdlike thing that resembled a nine-fingered hand. I wondered at the enormous fruits like giant, armored papayas covered with spiky bumps. Some I did recognize but only as rarities in my experience—pale fleshed lychees like overgrown strawberries fallen on hard times, for example. The scents were a barrage of the curious and the strange.

I could have spent a productive hour there with a small knife and a good cloth, tasting. The chutneys and sauces and cold plates that would come from such an expedition tantalized me.

The vegetable stands were just the same. Crowded walls of leafy greens I could not identify rose in bruised array as if defending the squirmy, fine-haired roots piled behind them. Long, purple stems like giant radishes reeked in so fine a fashion that I knew they must cook down to some other scent entirely. Cheerful peppers of dozens of different sizes and shapes dangled in strings or glowered in tiny baskets.

And the smells of those . . .

The fresh food had its own sharp signifiers. The cooked food being sold from carts and little trays and baskets and sometimes from outstretched hands bore the scent of more cuisines than I could name. I might have gained five pounds of weight that day if I'd allowed myself to stop and sample along the way.

The meat stalls were a bit stranger. Cages of future meals barked, mewed, hissed, clucked, and whirred. Eyes ranging from tiny compound jewels to great, slow blue plates blinked at me from behind bamboo weavings or wire meshes. Disinterested goat heads stared down from hooks, while the beaks of a dozen kinds of fowl lay silent on chopping blocks. Oh, the meats.

The wonders were found not just among the food, either. Everything was sold here that one might expect to find in a caravan marketplace. Goods I had no notion of lay in piles with their straps or buckles or woven cords. Leatherworkers bent industriously at their tasks next to stalls where a large animal might be shod or a small one collared. Painters and prayer-men and arbogasters mixed shoulders with the hungry and the hunted and the simply curious.

It was a glorious place.

I wondered how a Red Man would fit in here.

Which of the food stalls might he eat from? I had no notion of what foodstuffs could be found in the Fire Lakes where his kind were said to hail from. It sounded like a district of thorns and rocks from both the name and the reputation.

If Firesetter were here, someone sold him his dinner. No one hunted their own food in a city, and only the wealthy had gardens enough to pluck the harvest for their table.

Eels writhed in a wooden bucket as I passed a fishmonger's stall. That seemed an oddity to me this far from the waterfront, but I paused and looked behind his table to see an open-fronted shed filled with troughs and tanks.

Here was a farmer of sorts, even in the midst of the city. Did my Red Man pluck these narrow, curious fish from their enclosing water and eat them whole?

Rocks and thorns seemed more likely. That in turn spoke to me of small, hard fruits and lean game hunted over long distances. Not the rich lushness of our local ingredients here in Kalimpura. Nor the thin-sliced mixtures of Hanchu cooking, where chronic scarcity had been transformed into a sort of gustatory art.

Someone here must sell narrow strips of sliced cactus and dried snake meat and other such desert fare. Of course, though I did not know it at the time, my Red Man ate none of that. He like me had been raised among strangers far from home, and found his comforts in ways that would have seemed alien to his own kin.

In any case, I looked. And looked. And looked.

Mother Argai slowed and let me drift to her side in a shaded little nook by the city wall. The roads in this end of Kalimpura tended to indifferent paving largely consisting of mud and muck punctuated by the occasional lonely cobble. She'd found a spot slightly built up, and not currently occupied by either a beggar or a merchant. That suggested to me that we were now standing on a trash heap, but as a long-time sewer runner, I did not find this thought disturbing. Neither did I mind the smell, though other women might have quailed at it.

The wall here had lost some of its plastering. Gritty stone beneath had been exposed. Weeds and tiny flowers struggled from the cracks in the masonry, and some inept, badly spelled graffiti had been left there for public edification.

All in all, a comfortable enough spot, and safely anonymous for a few moments at least. I squatted on my heels in the shade of the wall and wished I'd brought a waterskin.

Peering up at Mother Argai, I asked, "How do you find anything here?"

"You look." She glanced along the street. "The gate itself is half a dozen rods farther up. Yesterday I passed through five taverns and never left sight of it."

I looked where she had. The structures here tended to be either large old stables and coaching inns—though surely they called them caravanserais here—that had been divided and subdivided into brawling little knots of business and residence and the Lily Goddess only knew what else; or else they were small sheds and shacks standing wall-to-wall in any patch of formerly open ground.

It was all use and reuse of the buildings of a city. The ingenuity of the poor was something I'd observed in Copper Downs. It was no less on display here.

Ingenuity or not, there was nothing in sight that I would have identified as a tavern.

"I do not mean to sound foolish," I began.

Mother Argai chuckled, waving me to silence, then pointing. "See those poles there. With the checkered awning . . ."

What looked like an entire bolt of Hanchu trade fabric sagged over a motley collection of chairs and benches that I'd taken for a used furniture broker's stock-in-trade. *Very* used furniture, at that. A handful of men stood or sat in the dubious shade provided by the cloth.

No women, but then there were not so many women visible here near the Evenfire Gate in any case.

"That is a tavern?" I said, questioning. "They usually appear somewhat . . . different."

"You drink along waterfronts, Green, and have an unhealthy affinity for sailors."

I could have argued that second point, perhaps severely, but she was certainly correct about my relationship to waterfronts. My life has ever been about coming and going. Belonging was another matter entirely.

"Yes. To me, taverns have thick walls and shuttered windows and quiet wood-floored rooms." A moment later, I added, "And perhaps upper storeys, or a stableyard out back."

"Drinking houses are illegal in this portion of Kalimpura," she said.

That was news to me. That anyone banned anything in Kalimpura was news to me, quite frankly. "How so?"

"The Agha of Sind is represented here by an amir. I have been told that ancient trade treaties keep the caravan routes open, and provide the amir with authority over the Sindu who live within a thousand paces of the Evenfire Gate."

I vaguely recalled that the Sindu religion forbade excesses of the flesh. Presumably alcohol consumption was one of them. "So how is that not a drinking house?"

"It is place where men may rent a seat by the quarter hour. For a copper paisa, you buy a place to sit so long as a little candle burns. The more paisas, the more candles, or the thicker the candles. While the candle is burning, you may be offered refreshments by the owner. Purely as a courtesy."

I filled in the rest, impressed by the legalistic cleverness. "The thicker the candle, the stronger the refreshments, presumably."

She snorted. "Your understanding of the male mind is not lacking, Green."

"We learn what we may in this life." I watched another man wander in and select a seat seemingly at random. Most of the drinkers were elaborately alone, neither facing toward nor away from one another. "And I would guess that the fabric pavilion means this is not a house, should someone at least question the drinking that goes on."

"Precisely." Another snort. "Certain establishments masquerade as restaurants, but the arrangement is somewhat the same."

"If they mostly drink out of doors here—which must be inconvenient when the monsoons come—one would think spotting a Red Man might not be so difficult."

"It is the sheer number of these places," Mother Argai grumbled. "Many of them are hidden in central courts or down tiny alleys."

I had not given that any thought at all. We'd been walking the Bounded Road, which followed the wall from one end of the Street of Ships to the other, circling Kalimpura. The parts of the city I spent most of my time in were built up, well paved, and laid out not unlike Copper Downs in distinct blocks or districts. The crowded mass of great old buildings and small flimsy shelters here was built up all at cups and crosses. I had not marked the lack of side streets.

"Anything you can get a donkey down is a street in these quarters of the city, though it might be someone's living room as well. Anything you can walk down on your own two feet is an alley."

I glanced over at Mother Argai. The disgust in her tone seemed unlike her. "You do not like the Sind?"

"The Sindu are who they are. But I do not like the way they treat their women," she said darkly. Then, after a long, slow glance at me, "Nor their children."

That stirred dark feelings in my own heart. Though I was on another mission at the moment, the question of the child trade was never too far from me, nor had it been all my life. Not since I had been sold as a girl.

And especially not now that I was a mother. My breasts ached at that thought. Brushing the sensation aside, I studied Mother Argai for a long moment. Would she be a problem here? Would I, for that matter?

"We are not here for their women," I said slowly or carefully. "Nor even for their children." I hated to hear myself say that. "We are here for the Red Man, who in turn may help us free our own missing woman and child." *Samma,* I thought, *I am so sorry.*

"I am knowing this," she said acerbically. "You are to be knowing it, too."

"Of course." I stared at the narrow spaces between the buildings and wondered at the secret lives of these people. So colorful, so brash in the street, did they turn inward to a quiet fog of kava and qat leaf and silent, shaded halls? "You say some of the taverns are within those hidden alleys?"

"Yes. But you would not do well to go there dressed as a woman of Sind."

"That I can resolve." I drew off the makeshift veil and skinned out of the robe. There were no Street Guild here to mark me. Walking as a Lily Blade, even in this part of town where we rarely ventured, would garner me a respect that a Sindu woman could never hope for. At least as I was coming to understand things.

I liked these people less and less the more I knew of them. "Is there someplace I should start?"

Mother Argai shrugged. "I have not been off this street yet. That alley is as useful as any other. Begin there, work your way back, make a note of where you have looked."

There was no point in asking what I searched *for*. She did not know any better than I did. An oversized chair at one of taverns. A doorway made taller with recent masonry. A massive footprint in the muck of a shaded alleyway.

All we knew of Firesetter was that he was enormous, and red as a pepper. Not so easy to hide out here on the street, but within the guarded walls where the sheltered Sindu kept their secrets?

In the years since, I have learned something of the walled compounds and blade-ringed gardens of our cousins to the far west. I have even learned something of the women of Sind, and how their place in the life of their country is neither so wretched as I had first believed, nor so desperate. At that age, though, I was still leading myself through life by the point, and thought any woman who turned along another path to be either a coward or a deluded fool.

So I slipped into the darkness of the alley, which without Mother Argai's advice I might have mistaken for someone's front door. A small porcelain tile set about the eye level of a tall man held several of the joined, sinuous Sindi characters by way of announcing whatever lay beyond, but that script was as closed of meaning to me as the chatter of the birds.

A battered marble block served as sort of a jamb to separate the alley from the street. Later I understood this marked a gate in the compound wall in countries where the Sindu could not build their own houses. The darkness beyond was starkly cool, especially for Kalimpura. A sliver of daylight glowed overhead, mostly blocked by inward-leaning and overhanging balconies of wood and wattle.

Narrow silks, scarcely wider than scarves, hung shivering slightly in the breeze that seemed to play through this elided space like a musician's breath within her flute. I walked along paving so irregular as to be either artwork or meaningless. Each cobble or slab had been salvaged from elsewhere. Some were inscribed, as if they had once been gravestones or plinths. The doors were set back deep within the walls, most painted bright red or orange. A few were a deep blue.

Something was signified here, but the meaning escaped me. More of those small porcelain tiles marked this entrance or that. I realized these were the true businessmen of the Sind Quarter. The street hawkers were like a floral border around a deep and ancient grove where all the real growth towered.

Smells, too, were different here. The air was redolent of spices heavier than our Kalimpuri flavors. Several I could not identify at all; otherwise coriander, rue, cardamom, a wide range of peppers. Something dark and musky as well, that teased at me. Sandalwood, from incense. Soapy water. Damp metal. Cats and children with their attendant odors. Rotted wood and fresh paint and the glue from a furniture works and a whiff of blood from some hidden abattoir.

The alley was like following a creek through the woods. It branched, turned, changed. After a few dozen paces I felt lost, though I knew I could trace my route back out in less than a minute. I pushed on, following a murmur of voices, until I found another of those strange taverns.

This one stood in a court beneath a square, niggard patch of sky. The walls around it were heavily overgrown with an orange-flowering vine I did not know the name of. Those blossoms made the air thick to the point of syrupy. The dozen men gathered there stop talking at my approach. All eyes were upon me.

Well, that was nothing new.

And I could hardly interrogate the entire quarter, tavern by tavern. I contented myself with a long, slow scan for overlarge chairs. I was looked over slowly in return. With a sharp nod, I finally moved on.

How much these Sindu obeyed their Agha and his amir was unclear. Every drinker I'd seen so far had been one of these people, as best I could tell. It made me no difference one way or the other, so I chalked the question up to the strangeness of men.

Thus it went for an hour or more. Soft voices sometimes called to me from deep doorways, but I understood that it would be a poor idea for me to enter within. I saw a woman once, bathing behind a screen that left little of her pale flesh to the imagination. I took no notice and hurried on. Stopping to look might have been fatal in this place where ambush could lurk behind every crack and join.

In the third great ramble of buildings I searched, between my sixth and seventh tavern, I found another court. This one was vacant. A stand rose at one end, great rings of iron set in its front. Little rows of benches were arrayed before it as if a congregation were to meet there.

The cages at the back told me the story, though. This was no temple. It was a slave market.

They were small cages, too. For small slaves. The bars were set close to keep little hands from reaching out.

A murderous rage welled up within me. In my earliest youth I had been taken, sold, shipped away from my own home, and sent beyond hope or rescue. Treated cruelly as well, though I was also given many luxuries. I had not ended my young life in a foundry or pushing wood into a hungry blade or crying beneath the weight of man after man who paid someone else for the use of me. No, I had grown into more.

Slavery itself was not illegal in Kalimpura, but the buying and selling of slaves was discouraged. We had no overarching law here, just the contracts and franchises that bound the Courts and Guilds together, and beneath them allowed the merchants and their companies to function and prosper. But the slave trade had never been one of our great economic miracles.

I would take it away even from the margins of money. When my other business was done, I would return for these Sindu. I swore those words quietly, and later in my life lived up to them, but that is a tale for another time. All I could do then was move on.

So I did. My memories were dark. Even when I met up with Mother Argai once more out in the daylit street, I still brooded.

More to the point, I had no sign of the Red Man. She shook her head as well, discouraged.

It was time to slip back into my robe and veil and head for our temporary home. I needed to wash the grime off myself, and I needed to see my children as they were, happy and free. Mother Argai shielded me from view as I donned the clothing; then we walked away from the district around the Evenfire Gate.

The streets filled with shops and shouting men were not nearly so charming or interesting as they had seemed before. Everything was faintly sinister now. I looked at each of the rare children I saw and wondered if someone, somewhere, held them in bondage like an ox or a tool.

Mother Argai took my arm and steered me onward awhile. We walked carefully, wary of Street Guild and other, less obvious enemies.

At home, I nursed my twins, ate a cold plate supper, sewed bells for me and my daughter, and wept a little. By that point I could not even say for certain what had me in tears. Just that the world seemed hard and unjust.

Which was not precisely news.

News, of course, was what we had none of. "I do not think this searching about will boot us much," I admitted after we'd all finished our evening meal.

Once again we were gathered in the kitchen. Though we were around the oil stove, it was far too warm to light the fire.

"The Red Man has not shown himself," Mother Vajpai said. "He would be hard to miss if he had."

"He has either gone to ground in some very deep hole," I replied. "Or found a clever way to hide in plain sight."

"How do you hide a red giant?" asked Ponce, whose Seliu had improved to the point where he could follow most of our discussions if they did not grow so heated that we spoke swift and hard.

"I do not know," I said mournfully. Something about that question nagged at me. Whatever it was would come in time.

That night I slept with Ilona. Ponce was too ardent for my comfort. She did not want me now, not as a woman wants another woman, but she did not mind lying close. Her nearness fed the fires in my heart, though I continued to be silently troubled by her growing connection with Ponce.

I took what comforts I could in the warmth of her slumbering embrace, wept a little more, then passed into a dreamless darkness.

Three days passed in fruitless searching. I was coming to know the area around the Evenfire Gate rather better than I might have wished. If there were other slave markets, I had not found them. But I did take note of a sufficiency of iron rings and chains to tell me that at some times of the day, or possibly the year, they came and went here. And often enough to make the trouble of such permanent installations seem reasonable.

Still, I watched for women and children, seeing very few of either.

Shadows and quiet spaces and suspicious, resentful men in plenty. The smiles these people turned on the sunny streets were swallowed up once one passed within their hidden hearts.

On the third day, the answer to what had been bothering me made itself apparent. We were heading away from the Evenfire Gate again in the shadows of late afternoon. Even the buildings seemed to be sweating today. All the more so us ordinary women.

Another of Kalimpura's endless street festivals approached from the other direction. This would be one of those that paraded the circuit of the city, dragging hundreds in its wake, the sponsors throwing food and little leathern sacks of beer to cheering spectators. Even here by the Evenfire Gate among the Sindu and the various strange and alien folk who dwelt beside them there would be a welcome.

And, well, if there were not, what of it? This was Kalimpura. These were Kalimpuri about their celebrations. Foreigners could go whistle for their differences.

Gongs shivered and drums rattled like hail on a rooftop. Someone shouted, a priest declaiming perhaps, but I could not make out the words and he bore nothing distinctive enough for me to know him by his god.

The crowd danced, trailing beads . . . no, strings of grain or rice. Many carried flails, which they whirled with abandon to the cost of a number of bloody noses and bruised skulls as best I could tell. I had no great desire to be caught up in this particular variety of self-flagellation.

Mother Argai did not either, it seemed, because she made no objection as we retreated into a stall where dozens of scrolls were for sale. Books, in the Hanchu style, for Kalimpuri books were traditionally folded slats of bamboo or balsa stitched together with cotton thread dyed a color to tell the reader what they might find within. In my experience, the Stone Coast style of book, being flat papers bound between leathern or boarded covers, was far more practical, but scrolls had their uses. Long lists, for one thing.

At another time I would have admired the books, or passed the time in conversation with the old scribe painfully rendering calligraphy at a little table. This afternoon, I turned my back on him and watched the procession snake by.

Banners soon appeared, and in reading them I knew what it was we saw. The Guild of Reapers, Threshers, and Rice Brokers was out to honor their masters past and present. A festival that celebrated both the ghosts and the living.

This I could approve of.

And while rice was not quite the universal staple in Selistan that it was in the Hanchu lands, I did appreciate how much these folk kept my fellow citizens alive and well fed.

Three coal demons rumbled by on carts. Statues, in chains of foil and rope to catch the eye. They were followed by three more who danced and shuffled, raising great, hairy hands to the crowd in an occasional roar.

Well, I realized, two of them danced and shuffled. The third strode long-legged and intent, with a scowl that I might have expected to see on a real demon.

With a chill, I realized I was not looking at a mummer on stilts in a tall mask with oversized gloves and paint across his skin.

This was no capering Guildsman from the Poppet Dancers. This was my Red Man. Or one of his similars. How many could there be in Kalimpura?

I elbowed Mother Argai in the ribs and pointed with my chin. "Him," I whispered, as if anyone could have heard a word that passed between us above the racketing noise of the crowd.

She followed my gaze. Her lips parted briefly in a small moue of astonishment. Then our eyes met, we nodded at each other, and dived into the festival crowd. For now, following our Red Man would not be difficult.

I was not sure what would come later.

I thought our pursuit would not be hard, but I had not figured on the slow, leaping pace of the festival crowd. The gyrations of the people around us were both contagious and dangerous. Once, I had to subdue a dancer with his own rice flails to keep him from cracking everyone else around him in the head.

And we could not walk scowling as our target did. I'd already slipped out of—and lost—my robe and veil. Even as Blades, Mother Argai and I both needed to blend with the festival crowd or be marked out, especially once we left the Evenfire Gate District and moved around toward the Landward Gate and, among other things, the more usual haunts of the Street Guild.

So we danced our way, and shouted from time to time, and grinned when we were grinned at. It was foolish and delightful at once. Like a parody of a Blade run. And much as with being at the center of the beggars' riot, I felt safe among the crowd. *Let the Street Guild try to take me here*, I thought.

I grinned for real at that.

It was, however, deeply tiring.

In time the procession circled the city and proceeded along the Street of Ships until they turned up Savvatana Street and ended at the Rice Exchange. Of course that made sense. We were deep in Street Guild territory now, and fairly close to the Blood Fountain and the Temple of the Silver Lily.

Not precisely among friends. I was beginning to regret casting away my veil. Though I'd hated the pretense of being Sindu.

Mother Argai led me aside into a shadow between the pillars of the Rice Exchange's façade. These were great, squat-bellied things painted green and red as if grasses grew before a bloody pool. I could not say so much for the taste of our accidental hosts, but we were able to lurk quietly and watch as the festival broke up in earnest.

Most people just drifted off, of course. Many of them carried the party to Prince Kittathang Park, I was certain. The banyans there were gentle shelter against the brief, intense rains that often came at evening, and no one would bother to run them out unless these folk began to set fires or otherwise significantly disturb the peace.

Laborers from the Guild of Poppet Dancers came and helped the mummers undo their masks. They loaded the demon statues onto a cart. My Red Man climbed aboard among the statues and sat quietly there until one of the laborers threw a length of sacking across his shoulders as a cloak.

Two score paces across the square, I could hear his rumbled thanks. *His Seliu has a Petraean accent.* Firesetter had come here from the Stone Coast, though I did not imagine for a moment that my quarry originally hailed from Copper Downs, any more than I did.

"Him," I whispered to Mother Argai, jabbing my finger.

With this confirmation, we were so much closer to finding Corinthia Anastasia and Samma than we had been since arriving in this city. I clasped myself with shivering joy.

I signed to her that I planned to follow the cart. She leaned close, grabbed my wrist, and tapped out the Blade code that meant she would join me.

Home, I responded. Meaning, *Go home and tell them what is afoot.* She shook her head.

Well, I understood the reluctance to let me run around by myself, given recent events. I would have felt much the same had our roles been reversed.

Still, I wanted word to go to Mother Vajpai and the others. More to the point, I did *not* want to let Firesetter out of my sight.

There was small purpose in further argument. We waited until the cart creaked into motion, along with three others belonging to—or hired by—the Poppet Dancers. Then we followed.

If there is one thing Blades have the skill to do, it is pursue our quarry through the streets of Kalimpura, our city.

My breasts ached enough that they began to leak as Mother Argai and I slipped through the dark of the evening. The wagons followed a meandering route that I soon realized was meant to minimize the number of tight turns the drivers and their teams would be forced to make.

We kept up easily. The Poppet Dancers were in no hurry. I saw the spark of flints and the glow of pipes from the buckboards of two of their wagons. These were men drawing near the end of their day. Their heaviest props were probably those statues, and everything the wagons hauled was meant to be carried by people dancing in the streets, so their unloading would not be overtaxing.

The carts passed through several areas of increasingly ramshackle warehouses and businesses. They avoided streets with large houses even when those would have shortened what I guessed was their route to the cheapest districts near the landward gate. The patient oxen seemed to know their way.

We were moving slowly enough for me to claim a pair of skewers with dripping bird thighs upon them from a wraith-thin woman wrapped in ragged gray who tended a little grill beneath a dead banyan tree. I overpaid her from the handful of paisas I'd accumulated living in our safe house—we'd found several small jars of coins tucked here and there, the caches of servants or children.

The meat was hot and almost sweet upon my tongue. She'd marinated it in honey and orange peels, which impressed me. The food was a sufficient distraction from my thoughts of my children. They were safe enough, and so was I. We were not walking into the faces of our enemies here. Whatever Firesetter might be to me, I did not fear him.

Foolish as that possibly was, when he climbed aboard the wagon, I had not seen in those great, dull eyes the kind of anger that would have made me afraid.

Mother Argai slurped at the last of her bird, then cast the wooden skewer in the gutter along with the bones she'd passed over. I dropped my bones, but kept my skewer by the simple expedient of sliding it into my hair and ignoring the grease. At the moment, it was long enough to need coiling up when I was working, and so the skewer did handy duty in place.

After a while, the carts rumbled onto Geelatti Road, which ran roughly parallel to the Bounded Road here along the northern verge of the city. As I'd expected, we were not too far from the Landward Gate. This was an area of large, decaying warehouses, left over from the days when some trade had required high roofs and large courtyards, before moving on to better markets or fancier quarters.

The Poppet Dancer carts passed through an open gate, their wheels echoing on the cobbles. The oxen were obviously eager to be home. I glanced at Mother Argai. Our eyes met, but neither of us seemed to feel too much caution here, so we simply walked in after the last cart.

The courtyard was fairly large, enough for the four wagons to pull into a semicircle. Several more were parked around the margins. A stable was open-walled in the back of the court, the familiar smell of livestock emitting from the shadows there. Otherwise we were surrounded by high wooden walls with enormous doors, one of which had been thrown open. The gate through which we'd passed had been nothing but a passage in the street-facing wall. Torches of twisted straw set into cressets illuminated the scene with dancing shadows edged orange. Everything was in need of paint, of care, of attention, of time and money that no one here had, clearly.

Already they were unloading. The laborers were mostly older men, some of them stooped or lame. I wondered if they had been mummers once, or were cheaper in their hire due to age and infirmity. Several glanced incuriously at me, but no one seemed alarmed.

The Red Man slid off the tailboard of his wagon. All he really needed do was stretch his legs and stand. His eyes met mine, and now his gaze was not nearly so dull. In fact, he almost glowed.

I met his look with a nod. We had acknowledged each other. With a brush to Mother Argai's wrist, I turned and left the mummers' men to their work. We passed out into Geelatti Road and rousted a trio of beggars from their shelter within a good-sized crate across the way. There we settled down to watch.

After a while, I was bored. I looked over at Mother Argai. She appeared to be sleeping with her eyes open.

Small harm in trying. "No Blade run is likely to pass us here, I suppose."

"No," she said shortly. "But the Street Guild might be by here sooner or later. They patrol warehouses."

"Whenever they happen to recall that they are supposed to be more than a gang," I said ungraciously. Not incorrectly, however.

Late-working merchants passed us by with the occasional nervous glance. Most of them had a stout lad or two walking alongside, many carrying a good-sized staff. Because of the Death Right, people in Kalimpura generally didn't bother with edged weapons unless they had the means to back themselves up. For the most part, that meant criminals, the larger groups of private guards, and whoever carried weapons for the Courts and Guilds.

And the Blades, of course.

We were supposed to be Kalimpura's weapons. Just of late I was learning how much of the city stood outside our view. Outside our notions of justice. The Sindu and their practices. The Quiet Men, whoever they truly were. Paths within paths, hidden in plain sight.

This was knowledge that would serve me in good stead later on, but at the time it was something like becoming aware of a toothache.

Nagging, painful, and not much subject to resolution at any command of mine.

Besides the merchants, servants passed. Laborers, too, often in little knots as they all left their employment for the night. Twice the sleeping carts that never stopped trundling about the city went by as well. Presumably the laborers were large among their custom. A few children out playing the dark. A self-important clerk in a green salwar kameez, pressed as if for an appearance before a judge even in this late evening.

I tried to amuse myself making up stories, but my imagination was consumed with Firesetter, while my body ached for my children. Wishing I had Mother Argai's knack for sleeping whenever there was opportunity, I wound up watching the gate across the road and the occasional glimpses of folk moving beyond it.

From what I could tell, the Red Man was unloading the wagons. Of course he would do so. He was large and strong and could probably shift more than any three of those men. That he bothered to help them told me much about him.

In time the wagons were drawn away from my view. Shadows deepened in the courtyard as the torches guttered out or were doused. The laborers departed, querulous and bickering as old friends will be after a day of working hard.

The last person to come out was Firesetter himself. He wore a long shapeless cloak that made him seem a gigantic scarecrow who had lurched to life. A huge dark figure was probably preferable to being a huge red figure.

A very small, draggled woman followed him out. The apsara! I struggled for her name, until it came to me: Fantail.

Firesetter walked straight for me. "You are Green," he said in a voice that rumbled into my bones.

I was shocked.

Mother Argai's eyes flashed open, and she grinned.

"Hello, Firesetter," I finally managed to reply.

We stared at each other in the dark like old friends who had never met before.

They knew of a basement two blocks down where Firesetter claimed that a quiet woman served sour beer and people rarely asked questions.

Before we left, he pulled the warehouse gates shut. A rippled length of iron as big around as my two thumbs together dangled on the bars of one side of the gate. Firesetter took it in his hands and absently twisted it to bind the two sides together.

"Better than any lock," I whispered.

"Harder to pick, too." The apsara's voice was much more pleasant than her aspect. I began to wonder if the dragglement were a guise or truly her appearance.

"Discouraging," added Mother Argai. She seemed fascinated by Firesetter, in a way I had never seen her respond to a man.

"Um, yes," I added. "Shall we go?"

We walked along the shadowed gutter, avoiding the center of the road. The basement proved almost three blocks away, down a flight of narrow, rubbish-strewn stairs to which I would never have given a second look. Beyond was a low-ceiling taproom that Firesetter very nearly had to waddle through to reach a huge chair at the back. Just as I'd expected, except I'd been looking in the wrong part of Kalimpura. He tugged a table in front of his seat, while we collected three more ordinary chairs.

I was not so keen to sit with my back to the door, but I wanted to face him.

Cheap, sour beer was forthcoming in shallow bowls at a copper paisa for every two. People came to this place to get drunk, I realized, not to sit and drink. The four or five others in the room paid us no more mind than they paid the rotten rushes on the floor.

"So you are here," I said carefully once our bowls were settled and the old woman was back to her laconic busyness behind the rough-hewn bar.

Firesetter rumbled something into his bowl—it was, like the chair, bigger than ours. "We have been for months," Fantail answered. "Living quietly among the Poppet Dancers."

"It is a brilliant disguise," I admitted. "When I finally sorted out what you had done, I was amazed. We spent much time around the Evenfire Gate trying to pick up your trail."

"Hmm," said Mother Argai, still transfixed by Firesetter. *What* had gotten into her?

"Did not like that place." The Red Man's voice echoed like rocks on more rocks.

Fantail brushed a hand against his arm. "We were safe enough." The lilt in her Seliu was far stranger even than Firesetter's accent. "But it was difficult to go in and out. The longer you live among the Sindu, the more they come to expect you to understand and follow their rules."

This time his voice was an earthquake rumble. "Enough rules."

"Indeed." I couldn't see yet how to introduce what I most desperately wanted to ask. These two were so clearly in hard luck, and so clearly tired of whatever they'd been running from. Or toward.

"Mummers are not so bad," he added. "They do not mind what I am. And no one has tried to rob the warehouse since I tore the head off that obnoxious little man."

Definitely a northern accent in his Seliu, though now that I was hearing him speak at greater length, I was not so sure if Firesetter had learned the language among Petraeans or farther east along the north margin of the Storm Sea.

"We all abide where the world brings us." I cursed myself for uttering such foolishly pious words. "I must ask, though, how did you know me?"

His rejoinder was quick and to the point. "How did you know me?"

"No one looks like you."

A great red hand reached across the width of the table to brush my scarred cheek with an astonishing gentleness. "No one looks like you, either, Green."

"Probably not," I admitted. "But how did you know of me at all?"

"People speak of you. We were fresh to Kalimpura when the Prince set sail for the north. We heard that the Bittern Court hunted you all the way across the Storm Sea."

"That alone makes you something of a hero in certain places of this city," Fantail added. "If you were to be declaring yourself, many would stand behind you."

"Declare myself for what?" I asked with disgust. "Copper Downs gave me my fill of civic politics. Enough for the rest of my life, I am quite certain of it."

Firesetter waved my words away. "The rich grow wealthier while the poor starve a little more each year."

Mother Argai finally spoke, though there was something brittle in her voice. "When I was a girl, the Guilds and Courts still hired many.

They have become more about money and less about the people of Kalimpura."

"And the Bittern Court is central to all of this, of course," I said.

"Bittern Court, yes." She sipped her bowl, as if to cover some confusion, before saying in a swift rush, "I was born in Attarapa."

I had no idea what that blurted statement meant, as I had never heard of Attarapa. I had also never heard Mother Argai speak of her past. Firesetter stared at her briefly with a bland expression. A tiny smile crossed Fantail's face, so fleeting I was not certain I had seen it.

Disappointment flooded Mother Argai's expression for a longer moment, before being replaced by resolution. "In the Stickleridge Mountains, just north of the Fire Lakes," she added.

Firesetter's face transformed from bland to predatory in the space of a breath. "You know," he said, followed by a burst of words in a language I did not recognize.

Mother Argai answered with a few fumbling, halting words of her own in that language before switching back to Seliu. "No," she continued. "You were gods to us."

"Did you ever meet any of my people?" The pain in his voice was strange to hear. Like watching a shark beg.

"Distant gods," Mother Argai amended herself. "Vanished." She stared down into her beer.

In the silence that followed, I realized I couldn't speak to whatever was between them. History, future, fascination; it was not a problem for today. Instead, I brought the conversation back to the present. "What do you want? Surely not to be lying low in a warehouse for the rest of your days."

"We have been looking," Fantail answered. "And waiting."

"For what? . . ."

"My people." Firesetter shivered, then gripped the edge of the table so hard, it splintered. The wood around his fingers smoldered.

Fantail brushed her hand lightly down his arm and murmured a few words I could not distinguish.

He nodded, chin tucked low, and hunched in on himself.

"Great spells have been set around him," she explained. "From the time he was whelped. Some questions cannot be asked without the risk of provoking him to great violence at their very words." At my expression, Fantail hastily added, "Against his will."

"The Saffron Tower did this to him?" I asked, my voice tight.

"Yes." By her tone, she seemed unsurprised that I knew of them.

"They sent you to Copper Downs."

A nod from Fantail. Firesetter still studied the wood grain of the table as if his life depended on it. Or possibly our lives.

"After you left, they sent another pair."

"Ah." Her eyes left mine briefly, then returned. "Who?"

"Twins. A pair of older Hanchu men named Iso and Osi. I was much deceived by them at first."

"We know them." Her voice was so tight, I could have cut with it. "What . . . what became of these twins?"

"They slew the goddess Marya." At my words, Fantail winced but did not speak up. I continued, memories flooding me. "They very nearly did for another god, but were brought down. They did not rise again with their lives in their hands."

She gasped. "You *slew* them?"

That brought me back into the moment. "Me, personally? No. But yes, I was responsible for their ending." If you could call it that, praying down the women who'd followed Desire's daughters, and having them touch those two strange old men to death.

Fantail touched Firesetter's arm again. He, too, was gone from this place and moment. She seemed to be calling him back.

Finally he stopped shivering and looked up. The glow in his eyes had died. The wood where his fingers rested was no longer smoldering.

"She slew the twins," the apsara told her Red Man.

"They were . . ." Words rumbled unspoken in his mouth. Then: "Difficult."

I had a sense that this man had known difficult much as I had known difficult. "We need your help," I said, an appeal from one lost child to another.

Firesetter shook his head. Fantail glanced from him to me and back. Something between desperation and hope gleamed in her eyes. Mother Argai tracked this, staring intently at the apsara.

"What do you wait here for if not change?" I was speaking to her now, more than to him.

"We spent three years in the Fire Lakes," she said quietly. "A hotter, drier, scantier hell you could not imagine even if you were a god and the land awaited molding. We never found a sign of his people."

"Legends," breathed Mother Argai. "As a girl, I was taught that his kind had passed on into time's embrace."

"Legends walk every day," I pointed out. "A legend is just a story made bold by time and distance." Uncomfortably, I was reminded of what Ilona had said about the tales *Prince Enero* would carry away from here regarding that business in the harbor. That *first* round of business in the harbor.

"We know." Her face closed. "We hunted goddesses for the Saffron Tower for almost three decades."

Hunting deities was about like hunting legends, I should have thought. I wondered how many Maryas had been struck down by them. "In my childhood, I was trained to kill a certain person. Or at least a certain kind of person." I did not speak of this often, and my own words surprised me. "The two of you must have been fostered with similar purpose."

She nodded. Firesetter's stare settled on me with the smoldering power of a forge's flame.

I continued. "I would also imagine a similar discipline. And cruelty."

"There are things I cannot even say, or think, about myself." Desperation rumbled in his voice. He began to shake as he went on. "They told me I was a made thing, that there was only a single one of me anywhere on the plate of the world. When I found out differently, in Copper Downs, we came here looking for my k-kind. I hoped they could loosen these invisible chains."

"Indivisible chains," Fantail added.

Firesetter's hands had begun to smolder again.

"Your people have passed into myth." I looked at Mother Argai again. She still seemed awestruck, or perhaps lovestruck. I could not tell. *That* disturbed me, coming from this capable, sanguine woman. "But you have not."

"Can you find them?" Fantail asked, pleading.

"I do not know." It was my turn to study my hands as the odor of scorched wood rose around us. "Any promises I make now are empty.

I hold no power but that of my arms and mind. The Fire Lakes are unknown to me, and so I can bring no understanding to this."

Meeting their gazes once more, I continued. "But once I prevail in my current business, I can turn my attention to persuading the Temple of the Silver Lily to putting its resources toward helping you. Over three hundred capable women, access to libraries and funds, and a goddess who can be an oracle." I shot Mother Argai another look. "And at least one of us who does know the Fire Lakes."

She nodded with a smile that bordered on the idiotic.

"But I need something in return," I added.

"Every bargain must have its coin." Fantail brushed her fingers down Firesetter's arm again. Calming him? Or herself. He seemed to be finding his control once more. I wondered why I had not been frightened at such an obvious and powerful anger on his part.

No, I realized, not anger. That was why I was not frightened. He was not angry at me, or perhaps at anyone at all. Firesetter was in the grips of some cruel spell or curse or prayerful binding that kept him from his own essence.

He might be dangerous—almost certainly was—but he was not ill-intended.

"My coin is this," I explained, my words coming fresh on the heels of that new insight. "I need your help in fighting the Saffron Tower." As she opened her mouth, I held up my hand. "Not directly. We do not face them in some battle in this place. But their schemes reach here. It is my hope to learn from you of their methods and purposes, that I might turn that against my own enemies who are allied with the Saffron Tower against me and mine."

If nothing else, it was a pretty little speech.

"No," rumbled Firesetter. "We will not oppose them."

"You have left their service," I said.

"That does not mean we stand against the Tower."

We were at a point of frustration. I did not know how to move them away from his objection. What I could offer was not sufficient.

"In the mountains above my village," said Mother Argai, her voice distant, "there was a place we called a temple. Building, cave, ruin. It was all three. With doors cut for people half a rod tall. Blackened troughs that had once held pools of flame. A place of your people, we were always told." She sounded almost ashamed when she concluded, "We worshipped you there."

This was more than I had ever heard of Mother Argai's life before the Blades in the entire time I'd known her.

"But we were gone," said Firesetter mournfully.

"From that place, yes. Gone, but not forgotten."

I watched the two of them, wondering if somehow this connection they shared could bind Firesetter to our cause. His Fantail, I thought, wanted to join us.

It was enough to drop this for now. She would seek to convince him. All I could do was push in a way that likely harmed my chances of securing what I wished.

"We should go home," I told Mother Argai.

She drained her wretched beer and set the wooden bowl on the table. I could not face my own drink with its skunky taste, and so left it behind as we rose.

"Good evening to you both," I said. "If your minds change, send word."

"How shall we do that?" asked Fantail.

"A letter to Mother Argai at the Temple of the Silver Lily. Though it would be best to remain discreet in anything you write."

Mother Argai nodded her agreement. "Do what she has said. I check there several times in every week."

"Farewell," said Fantail. Firesetter rumbled some vague agreement.

We turned toward the door and our faces to the world. I was disappointed, but not bitterly so. These two were not done with us, nor were we with them.

As I touched the handle, the door banged open from outside. Three big men shouldered in. The last glanced up at me, his mouth forming words when he stopped. Then: *"You!"*

They all three drew knives and had me hedged with blades in that moment. Mother Argai dropped back and pulled her own weapons, but I was trapped. Points pressed into my leathers at my gut and my chest.

"Hello," I said. "Street Guild, come for a drink after a hard day of duty?"

———

They backed me into the wall by the door. Mother Argai hovered behind them, frustrated in her attack by my helplessness. The barkeep swept up her cashbox and disappeared through a door at the back of the room. Most of the few customers followed her.

Firesetter and Fantail did not do so, I noted.

"Back away, woman," growled one of the Guildsmen to Mother Argai. "This is not being your fight."

"Any Blade is every Blade," I said pleasantly.

"But we knows you ain't no Blade," one of my other attackers said. "You been read out."

I could attack them at any moment, and they knew it, too. But with three knives pressed into me, whatever effort I made would impale me on their points. By the same token, they could not compel me to much, because once they moved me out of this position, I would be very difficult to contain.

"You have only two choices here, lads." I let my face bloom into a smile that was hopefully worrisome to them. "Let me go, or kill me where I stand."

"Killing you wouldn't be the worst thing," muttered their apparent leader. He'd obviously come to the same realization I had. There were not *enough* of them. It took three to contain me like this. If they sent one for allies, Mother Argai and I would best the other two. Or we could just all stand here until someone's bladder drove them to desperation.

"No, not the worst thing," I agreed, and marked him for special punishment. "But not the best, either. Instead, why don't you take a message back to your masters, for that bitch Surali?"

His face scrunched with thought. Neither of his fellows looked any swifter of intellect. "Walk away?"

"Walk away with my message," I said patiently. "Carry word back that you have met the fearsome monster Green, and she has a bargain to offer the Bittern Court."

"What is it?"

"Give me back the hostages, and I will grant Surali what she wants most." Even I did not know what that would be, other than my head on a spear, but I wanted to get out of this situation intact. Besides which, it would be worth the trouble if she did respond. Talking rather than fighting was always a good sign. A lesson I'd come to late, but was learning to appreciate.

"You don't—" He was interrupted by the door banging open again.

All three of them glanced to their left. Two of the knifepoints wavered, weapons following the eye as I had been drilled so thoroughly by Mother Vajpai and my other training Mothers.

Mother Argai was already in motion. Me no less. I tried to slide around the last knife rather than onto it, but the point caught my leathers and scored the side of my chest. Even as that wound bloomed pain like fire, my knee caught the silent one of the three in the groin. Mother Argai's knives took the thinker in the kidneys from behind. The third turned with a look of triumph already dying on his face and dragged his knife back across my fresh wound.

I gave him a faceful of my own knife, then slumped against the wall. Mother Argai had already turned toward the four new men who'd come in. They drew their weapons with a speed that spoke of training.

More Street Guildsmen, fellows of these three we'd just dealt with.

Pushing off from the wall, I followed Mother Argai to meet their steel with mine.

Two on four was not improbable odds, but the Street Guild had trained to fight the Blades. Some among them had studied us with care. They knew at least certain of the tricks of our fighting style.

That meant I found my first three or four thrusts blocked. Mother Argai had scored a touch, but her man was not down yet. We were fighting in an open doorway. People in the street would hear. More would come soon. And we had no maneuvering room or reserves of our own.

What I needed most was not to beat these men down, but to get away before more arrived to block my escape. Otherwise I risked capture. At this point, that might be worse than death.

"The back door!" I shouted in Petraean, slashing at one of these four. They were bunched up together as well, or they would have been more dangerous to us.

"At the count of three," she called back.

Then an enormous red fist whistled past me and simply *shattered* the skull of the man I was fighting closest. He collapsed with his face in a pulp.

A knife tip scored my forearm through my leathers as I turned to the next Street Guildsman. Firesetter reached in and grabbed that fellow's weapon hand with the blade still in it. His much larger fingers closed over with crushing strength, judging by the man's screaming. The Red Man yanked and my opponent stumbled forward to fall full length on the floor.

The other two retreated hastily up the stairs. Already I could hear shouting outside. "Let's go," I snapped, still in Petraean.

Mother Argai led us out the rear door, deeper into these cellars but farther away from the street entrance and the panicked violence surely building outside. Firesetter and Fantail followed.

A few minutes later we sheltered in the loft of another stable. I would rather have taken my rest in the Poppet Dancers' ox-house, amid the memory of Endurance and perhaps some of the god's favor, but our swiftest path had not led that way. Or perhaps Firesetter meant to protect his own. Six or seven shivering mules huddled below in the farthest corner from us. They were too frightened even to bray, and besides Fantail had silenced them with a touch and whisper as we'd arrived in this shelter.

Firesetter was shivering, too. I worried for the straw in which we all crouched. Shouts in the street continued. I was very glad that Kalimpura did not have a city watch. The Street Guild would come in more force, and soon, but this was not the part of the city where their sway was strongest. They would have trouble sweeping freely from house to house and building to building as they might have done down along the waterfront.

Not for the first time, I wished this city had a decent Below. We could have made our escape good long since.

"Why were those fools coming here to drink?" I wondered aloud, though my voice was still a whisper.

"Surely avoiding their serjeant," said Mother Argai.

Well, that made sense. To a point. As we had gone there because the place was cheap and anonymous. Those qualities were attractive to many people besides us.

Still, I wondered if more was afoot. "I wish I knew if that Mafic had arrived in port yet," I muttered.

"Mafic?" asked Fantail over Firesetter's rising rumble.

I smelled smoke for real now. That was serious business around stables and straw. "Make him stop!" I hissed. "Or we'll be burned out of here."

She touched the Red Man. "Mafic," he said. It was like listening to a building speak.

Now was definitely not the time for this, but I had to understand more. "You know him?"

The words came from very far away. "He was my fa— trainer."

"He is here, or will be soon," I said. "Pursuing me in the matter of the death of the Saffron Tower's twins." And possibly them as well, though they did not need to hear that from me. These two understood who and what they were far better than anything I might say to them.

"You . . . fight . . . Mafic. . . ." The burning smell was distinct. One of the mules finally brayed even through whatever glamour Firesetter had placed upon them.

"Yes. And I'm about to fight a fire if you don't stop this!"

As if called by me, open flames began to dance around him, lighting the straw dust in his hair and rendering Firesetter's face into that of a true coal demon. "Mafic!" he roared.

The mules screamed and bolted. Fire erupted all about the Red Man. I cursed and jumped down out of the loft. Landing hard on the wooden floor below, I realized a moment later that no one had jumped after me.

That was alarming.

I looked back up. Sparks already flew in the air, straw crackling as it burned. Fires were vile things to be inside a building with, and I knew full well what could happen to blaze in a stable or a granary.

"Get down here!" I shouted.

Mother Argai peered over the edge of the loft. "We cannot move him."

The obvious did not occur to me. We all nearly died because I did not stop to think. All I could encompass right then was to wonder whether Firesetter had no sense of self-preservation.

Scrambling back up the ladder, I found myself in choking smoke. Outside, someone was already ringing a bell and shouting frantically. There would be buckets of water and tense, angry men here very soon. If we were thought to have set the fire, it wouldn't matter what the Street Guild wanted with me. The local residents would beat us to death.

Firesetter lay on the loft floor, curled in a protective ball. A gigantic protective ball, but the position was so similar to one my babies sometimes adopted that my heart surged. Mother Argai crouched beside him. Her eyes flickered with desperation. Fantail had her hands on his arms, and seemed to be pouring water onto him from nowhere at all. Out of the air? *How?*

Much more to the focus of my attention, flames raced through the straw and licked at the posts supporting the stable's ceiling.

"We go now," I growled.

He rolled over and blinked at me. Those eyes seemed as bright a red as if the flames had originated from within. "No." Firesetter's voice was a collapsing wall.

Fantail looked up at me, and oddly, she seemed more exasperated than desperate. I was surprised. "You need to leave," she said.

The hissing and cracking of the flame were becoming louder. Outside, someone shouted again. How had they known so soon?

The mules, I recalled. Someone must have seen them bolt and spotted the glow within.

I grabbed Mother Argai's arm and wrenched her toward the edge. She did not want to come with me, still held by that strange fascination she'd evidenced with the Red Man.

"It won't matter for us if we wait another minute longer!" I shouted in her ear. "Nothing will. These two can take care of themselves."

She didn't believe that, and neither did I, but we *did* share a sense of self-preservation, and so we jumped. This time the floorboards cracked beneath us, raising a cloud of dust. The sparks drifting down had set piled hay and straw to smoldering.

My instinct was to descend to whatever level lay beneath the floor—storage, I presumed—but I feared being trapped there. So I sprinted out of the shadows and into the courtyard beyond.

At least the stable had not faced the outside. Instead of a whole street's-worth of people, there were only a dozen men gathered, already organizing into a bucket brigade. And none of them were Street Guild.

"You bastards!" shouted one of the men. He charged me, swinging his bucket for a bludgeon. I ducked the heavy wood and caught at his arm to pull him around. I did not need to fight these men.

"The fire!" I screamed back at him. "We're here to help you, by the Wheel."

He paused, confused even in his rage. I grabbed the bucket out of his hand and raced for the well pump that was already being furiously operated by one of his fellows. Mother Argai followed, pushed the man aside with a nod, and continued working the handle.

Whatever rough justice was intended for us was postponed in the face of fighting the fire. The stable was not inside the buildings of this court, unlike the Poppet Dancers' stable, but was rather a separate structure backing against the rear wall of the enclosing buildings. The roof already smoldered, well out of our reach.

Racing back toward the fire with my own bucket, I realized the men weren't trying to dampen the flames already burning. Rather, they were throwing water on the face of the surrounding structure, where the stable met the building wall.

That made sense. I had an idea, and grabbed at the leader. "Do you have a team of oxen?"

"Here?"

"Anywhere! We can pull the stable down into the court, away from the buildings."

He nodded, realization dawning on his face.

There had been all sorts of tack and equipment inside. I'd raced past it without looking. Mule harnesses were not normally an interest of mine. But if rope or chains hung there . . .

I handed my bucket off to a new volunteer and headed back into the stable. Smoke was settling from above, oozing out the top of the doorway.

Inside, I saw no sign of Firesetter or Fantail, but the glow from the loft was much worse. The little fires down below had caught and were trying to combine. The air was acrid, thick, foul. I found it hard to see or even think.

Still, my purposes were simple.

And both chains and rope were present.

I wrapped chains around the two wooden pillars that rose beneath the leading edge of the loft. They were the central support of this part of the roof. Taking a rope thicker than my thumb, I bound the chains together. Another, longer rope, I tied off in a T to the cross-line, then paid out toward the door.

"The building will fall down," I called, or tried to, but the effort of speaking loudly in the thickening smoke made me cough so hard, I started to cry.

I stumbled out with the rope in hand to drop it, then began retching. It was as if I'd been poisoned. I was miserable, too. We were going to lose both Firesetter and Fantail to something so pointless as this. They would be dead. My best path to our missing hostages would be closed off.

It made me want to scream with frustration, but my throat was too raw.

Mother Argai knelt beside me. "Are you going to be well?"

Unable to speak, I nodded furiously.

"This would be a good time to pray up the tide, if you can."

That made me laugh, which was painful. This far from the waterfront? I could only imagine what the ocean would do to the city if I somehow called its finger down upon myself once more so distant from Street of Ships.

Finally I managed to stand. Someone was hup-hupping at a team of four very reluctant oxen. *They* weren't going near the fire. My rope had been joined by a longer chain, which meant another brave soul had run at least briefly into the stable. Two boys were flipping the paired rope and chain over and over, spinning a simple braid for strength, while another man signaled the ox-driver to get his team into position.

This time it was not Oceanus or Time or whichever titanic had sent the waters to me that I needed to address in prayer now. Endurance, my ox god, would surely see this as a sacrament of his power.

Still the Red Man and his apsara had not appeared. The stable was going to be a total loss, flames now reaching up out of the poorly shingled roof. The building behind was already being singed. And the stench was overwhelming.

If it spread, I realized, the whole block could burn.

Something rumbled, like Firesetter's voice but much bigger and deeper. I looked up above the top of the burning stable to see clouds swirling.

Not my doing.

But I could do something now, while my body shivered and my lungs ached and my throat was too raw. I closed my eyes to focus.

Endurance, I thought, for there was small purpose in praying aloud and my ragged throat would not have tolerated it well in any case. *You are far away from this place, but this is the country of our birth. Yours and mine. Give strength to these your mute brothers, and courage, too, as they work to save what should not have been destroyed in the first place. Help us help ourselves remedy this wrong. And if you can, spare a blessing for Firesetter and Fantail lost this day.*

When I opened my eyes, the team was hooked up. The oxen faced the gate to the street and needed no encouragement to walk away from the fire. The twisted rope and chain tightened, then lifted.

If my knots broke, or the chains I had set on the wooden posts within slipped, this would all be in vain. It was fortunate that I'd spent enough time aboard ships to have learned something of the art of securing a line.

This would be my test. The collapsing embers would be the memorial for my two new friends and allies, already lost to me. I began to cry for them, then as swiftly fought back the tears.

The men of the bucket brigade—and, I noted, several women now—backed well away from the stable, toward the forward wall of the court. The rope-and-chain line tightened further, creaking so loudly, it could be heard above the crackle of the fire. The swirling clouds overhead thundered again. The acrid reek of burning threatened to deaden all our senses.

Something inside the building cracked with a noise like a large firework. The towline twitched as one of the oxen stumbled. Wood groaned, fire hissed, and the front of the stable began to lean forward, toward the middle of the courtyard. Boards popped free from the upper part of the wall, above the door. More smoke poured out of them in black arms that swiftly blended with the cloud-dark night sky above.

The groan intensified to a noise like a hinge the size of the city. The building began to slump just as the clouds overhead dropped pattering, sizzling rain upon us. With a mighty crash, the stables died, disintegrating from a building to a high-piled jumble of burning wood being soaked by sudden, heavy rain so that steam hissed and billowed all around.

Without the shooting flames, the courtyard was much darker.

So much for the funeral pyre of Firesetter and Fantail.

I lurched to my feet, intent on finding escape before we were rounded up either as arsonists or for whatever reward the Street Guild might be offering for us. My eyes were still light-blinded and filled with tears, and I could not spot Mother Argai.

A man loomed out of the darkness—the bucketeer who'd first attacked me. "Next time you run into the fire, cover your mouth and nose with a wet cloth," he said.

It was such an oddly prosaic comment for such a difficult moment. All I could think to do was thank him.

He grabbed my arm. "*Did* you set it?"

"N-no," I gasped, finally finding my voice, raw as it was. It was hard to talk loudly enough over the pounding rain that now soaked us both. "We were hiding f-from the Street Guild."

"*Those* bastards tried to burn you out?"

Now there was a convenient lie, and it had not even passed my own lips. I nodded furiously. "We lost two of our fellows inside, to the fire." Then I added, "You know the Street Guild." Neither of which statements were actually untrue.

So far as it went, everybody knew the Street Guild. Maybe if I inspired sufficient anger in these people, they would send some Street Guild dead off to guard Firesetter wherever the souls of dead Red Men went.

The man who'd addressed me turned back to his crowd of helpers, who were drifting together in a knot. "We need to—," he began, but was interrupted when the woodpile screeched and set up a shower of sparks visible even in the dark and rain. Every head turned that way in horrified fascination as the top of the ruined mound unfolded like a charred, steaming flower.

"Oh, by the gods and their Wheel," someone nearby muttered.

That was when I learned something I should have seen for myself all along. The Red Man pushed his way out of the pile of ash and char and smoldering lumber to stand atop it. He was visible even through the rain in the light of the glowering coals exposed by his exit from the collapsed mess. Firesetter surveyed us as if he were the victor on a field of battle. Victory at cost, as it always was, for he held a small body in his arms as a mother might carry a lost child.

No, I thought. I could not decide if it was worse that he had survived or that she had not.

Greeted by absolute, frozen silence, he climbed down off the mess that had been the stable. By the time he reached the foot of the mound, Firesetter was little more than a large, dark shadow moving through the courtyard. I fell in behind him as he walked out the gate. Mother Argai joined me. She kept one hand on my elbow as if to steer me forward.

Was I that badly taken by the smoke?

The rain was less powerful in the street beyond. Many more folk stood there, watching the spectacle. Firesetter picked his path among them, walking with his back straight and his head high into the deeper night. We continued to follow him while the sky above wept for Fantail.

Of course a Red Man of the Fire Lakes would come through a holocaust unscathed. But an apsara . . . ? She was no creature of fire, after all. Not like him.

I wept some, too, and walked with the tense shoulders of a woman who expects a Street Guild arrow in the back. No one shouted, no one shot, no one followed, and so we stalked away from the scene of our crimes.

Lives in the Face of Fire and Blood

THE NEXT MORNING they let me sleep long. I needed it, the Lily Goddess knew. Someone had taken my babies before their fussing woke me, though it was the aching in my breasts to feed them that finally did bring me back to consciousness.

Light filtered in through the shuttered windows of my room. My hair and body stank of fire and blood, and my wounds stung. At least they were not deep enough to ache. I lay in the soft, warm sheets and stared awhile at the painted ceiling. I did not know all the gods and legends of Kalimpura as I did of Copper Downs, for my education here had been of a more practical nature, but I realized this morning that what I'd always taken for a mural of a coal demon amid a setting of battle was in fact a Red Man. Was he trying to slay the Kalimpuri heroes who faced him in their bright, silk-wrapped armor, or was he trying to succor them?

Memories of the previous evening were both bruise-tender and cut-sharp. They were all too clear to me in the moment. Finding and losing my hoped-for ally, then finding him again. Following him a while through the streets until Mother Argai had plucked at his arm and set a course for our home. Exhausted past the point of wariness, we had not bothered with secrecy or slipping over the wall here, but simply used the servants' gate again. I wondered if she had bothered to reset the seals.

The last time I'd seen Firesetter, he was in the kitchen with Fantail, who had been laid out on one of the long work blocks there. I'd stumbled off to feed my children and collapse. The memory of his stricken face would stay with me the rest of my life.

She had been so still. And, very strangely for someone who'd been through both a fire and the collapse of a building, unmarked.

There was much I did not understand. I would not understand it, either, unless I found my feet and rejoined my little circle of friends. Selfishly, I was glad that we might still have Firesetter's advice and experience. Even so, I did not imagine for a moment that he, or any of the rest of us, considered that worth the price.

My feet were where I had left them at the end of my legs. Somewhat unsteadily I rose, wrapped myself in the old furniture cover I'd been using for a robe, and stumbled coughing for the kitchen.

I fed the babies, a contented moment against my larger distresses. My leathers needed cleaning and repair, my wounds needed seeing to, and I should make some accounting for the latest of my dead, but I was not yet ready for those tasks. Mother Argai sat before the empty fireplace looking glum. She was certainly the most phlegmatic of us all, and so I did not find this an encouraging development.

No one else was about. Fantail's body was gone from the long table. I could not decide if that was alarming or relieving.

"Is there kava?" I muttered, shifting Marya to a better position. The habit had become more appealing of late.

A shrug. She looked at me, her face set. "Last night was not so well done."

"I know." We sat in silence until the children were finished and my breasts felt not so swollen. Setting the babies on a borrowed rug laid here for that purpose, I puttered, finding some cold tea in a pot. How we had become accustomed to our little oil stove. "We have found our allies, and lost one. By now everyone in the city knows of it."

"You were craving secrecy." She sighed before lapsing into a deeper silence.

I could only agree with her regrets. Nothing we had done yesterday was worth Fantail's life. And what must Firesetter think of us? We would be fortunate if he only confined himself to a sullen hatred.

Bedeviled by dark thoughts, I drank the cold tea, ate a bit of roast pigeon that was just as cold, then left Marya and Federo with Mother Argai while I padded out into the sheltered area of the garden where we'd permitted ourselves exercise and sunlight outside the house.

The Red Man knelt by the scummed-over ornamental pond. He might as well have been one of the Poppet Dancers' statues. Mother Vajpai sat in the shadows closer to the house, watching him with a thoughtful expression on her face. The burning smell was stronger out here—not on me, then, after all. And definitely from a building aflame. The pungent scents of tar and paint and other things mixed with the honest tang of burnt wood.

I wondered if the fire from last night had somehow spread despite the rain.

"What is he doing?" I asked Mother Vajpai in a quiet voice. My nose itched, and the smell reminded me that my breathing still ached.

"I do not know." She nodded, indicating that I might step forward and look.

With a glance around to see if anyone was staring over our garden walls, I walked up next to Firesetter.

Fantail lay within the pond before him. The murky waters obscured her face, so she seemed almost a ghost staring up from the overgrown shallows.

This cannot be a funeral rite of the Fire Lakes, I thought wildly. Did the Saffron Tower bury their dead in water? So to speak . . .

I brushed my fingers across his shoulder. He was solid to the touch, and colder than I expected.

He spoke, which surprised me. "There is a burning." Though Firesetter's lips parted to grudgingly release the words, the rest of him remained stock-still.

Once more I sniffed. "I'd thought it to be smoke on me."

"Not my fire."

Of course not. He would know. I stared down at Fantail again. A few bubbles marked the surface of the pond. The next question welled up inside me and carelessly escaped my lips. "Whose fire is it?"

"Not mine."

He lapsed into a silence far more stolid than even Mother Argai's had been. I retreated to Mother Vajpai's side. Already I had been exposed to view too long. "What burns?" I asked her.

"Did you not set the fire?"

"He says it is not his." I glanced back at the immobile Red Man. "If anyone should know, it is him."

Mother Vajpai grunted, then pointed at the sky. "Even the sun is hazy."

I had not looked up at all on coming out of doors, but she was right. Whatever had burned was substantial. My heart froze in my chest. The target of any vengeance arson seemed obvious to me, given Surali's nature and the fundamental lawlessness of the Street Guild. "Not the Temple of the Silver Lily—"

Our eyes met in a brief flare of mutual panic. Mother Vajpai shook her head slowly. "Would you not have known in your heart if our goddess had lost Her altar?"

"Yes." *Maybe.* "But now I must go see, to be certain."

"Take Mother Argai with you."

I nodded, not truly listening, and stepped swiftly back inside to don my damaged leathers and take up my weapons. My other duties would have to wait.

Mother Argai and I did leave the compound together, Ilona watching over the babes in my stead. We went our separate ways out on the street. I wore another shapeless servant's robe and a Sindu veil in hopes that the thin disguise would do me some good. She ran as a Blade, being able to still walk openly in Kalimpura.

At least, I hoped she could still walk openly after yesterday's misadventures. For my own part, both my breath and body protested.

As I walked, I found that the business of the streets continued unabated. Of course, if the plate of the world should crack and all the waters of Creation come rushing in, the people of this city would still be buying and selling until the darkness had closed around them for the last time. Even so, there was a current of unquiet nervousness.

I listened as I pushed through the increasing crowds closer to the docks. I wanted to see the Temple of the Silver Lily for myself, but so long as we'd troubled to go out, I wanted to see the rest of that part of the city, too.

Arguments raged, far louder and uglier than the usual aggressive street-corner posturing and vicious bargaining. Fisticuffs as well. And twice outright street battles between the retainers of this Court and that Guild.

Everyone was on edge. Decidedly including me.

Their words were on edge as well.

". . . the Prince of the City taken. Those damnable Street Guild thugs . . ."

". . . doesn't matter anyway. What do the likes of us care for who . . ."

". . . Bittern Court. Issuing orders and everything. Why, my cousin said . . ."

". . . not from the Starling Court. They sent two patrols out . . ."

". . . fighting all along the monied streets. Been a long time since I was grateful to be poor . . ."

Words, words, and more words, building the sort of picture that rumor so often can create. Fragments of fear and confusion and misunderstanding spread around me like wood chips on the rising tide. Not panic, not that—to most of these people, the contests for power that ranged among the wealthy were at best a sport viewed from a distance. Everyone needed to eat; everyone needed water carried and roofs repaired and the business of the city to go on.

Still, when the great came to trading blows, it was almost always the small who took the wounds.

That was precisely what worried me the most. If the tensions here had escalated to open fighting, how would that bitch Surali view the hostage value of Corinthia Anastasia and Samma? I was not certain she would see any further point in negotiating when everything was teetering on the risk of bare blades and flowing blood.

Surely anyone as high in the courts as she was must be too canny a player to throw aside an advantage. Keeping our two missing alive was cheap enough, and not nearly so irreversible as killing them. That thought was small comfort. Likewise the realization that Surali was far more likely to kill them in front of me, and thus was probably maintaining both of my lost ones with that goal in mind.

The Blades had never played the game of hostages or kidnapping. When we took on a Death Right killing, it was straight to the target. Surali's way of fighting soiled everyone.

Increasingly irritated by my own thinking, I stalked through the plaza that stretched before the temple, past the Beast Market and the

Blood Fountain. To my immense relief, the Temple of the Silver Lily stood intact. Wherever the flames were, they were not here. The goddess' house seemed closed in, drawn down upon itself, but I realized that sense must come as much from my own feelings about being cast out as from any aspect of the building that was home to so many of my former Sisters.

Future Sisters, as well, though in that moment I could not have known what was to come. Even now, I would not change that if I could. But then, had I known, I might have refused my destiny.

Satisfied that the temple was not afire, I followed rumor and smoke to the Street of Feathers. There a number of the Courts and Guilds had their chief houses. Much like the Bittern Court's palace along Shalavana Avenue, these were enormous compounds. Some enclosed massive structures, others a wider scattering of buildings and housing.

One of them billowed black smoke into the sky. Here the complex stench was palpable. My lungs burned anew. The road was full of servants and guards trying to bring water up in buckets and carts, trying to keep the fire from spreading, trying to hold off the curious, the inimical and—probably—the looters.

I did not need to get caught up in the mass of people. The Hawk Court was burning; that was enough for me to mark for further thought as I hurried away.

Why them? They controlled the granaries and riceries of the city, managed the Rice Exchange, taxed what came in the gates. Without the Hawk Court's work among the farmers and brokers for thirty or forty leagues around the city, Kalimpura would starve. So why burn them out?

Not vengeance, as I had suspected at the first thought that the fire might be at my temple. Control, of course. Surali was not normally this crude. Her plotting tended more to the baroque, and any fire-setting at the Temple of the Silver Lily would have been paying back like for like, but I thought I could still see her hand in this. The fire might even have been an accident, an intended threat grown out of control.

No, I corrected myself. The Bittern Court's threats were very real. Nothing "intended" about them.

Wondering why anyone would *want* to control Kalimpura, I headed back for our safe house. Safe for not much longer, to be sure. I knew I must tend to myself, my gear, and my dead. And more to the point, it was time to sort through what we must do next. Secrecy was no longer much of a cloak for me and mine.

At the house, I found my children sleeping in my room. Grateful for the peace, I slid free of my leathers and spent time tending both their wounds and mine. Candles for the dead would come later, I knew.

After an hour or so, my children awoke, but they'd given me time to clean and sew and oil. I felt like I might be ready for whatever came next. I gathered the fussing babies up and set out from my room.

Ilona and Ponce were talking in the hallway, fingers entwined as their faces almost touched. Both appeared vaguely guilty when I emerged. If my nose were not still so loaded with fire reek and ashy grit, I could have smelled the lust upon them.

So *that* was the way of it? As if I had not seen this coming. I found myself flashing into anger again, though I could not say toward whom or why. Ponce was never mine, I had not wanted him even as he made his interests clear. To whatever degree Ilona had been mine, her heart was long lost to me along with her stolen daughter.

Feeling surly, I wordlessly handed Marya to Ilona, then opened my robe to feed Federo. Let them both glimpse my breast and think on what it was they desired. Once my son had settled his too-painful mouth grip on me, I favored the two of them with a tight smile. "We must all talk."

Ilona blushed, visibly restraining herself from glancing at Ponce. "Wh-what is happening in the city?"

"A burning," I said, quoting Firesetter.

We muddled into the kitchen. I sent Ponce out to fetch Mother Vajpai. There was no point in bothering Firesetter. I'd glimpsed him in the garden, still locked in his mourning. He was not yet one of us. After his losing Fantail, I seriously doubted he would become so.

"There is a fire at the Hawk Court," I said without preamble. "The compound is ablaze."

"Why?" asked Ponce. "Who is the Hawk Court?"

"They provide rice and grain to the city," Mother Vajpai replied shortly. "And profit much thereby. Someone else is seeking to take over both that monopoly and that revenue."

"The Bittern Court's argument is obvious enough," I replied, having considered this on my way home. It was good to talk of something that didn't remind me of Ponce and Ilona with their heads bent close together. "They control the docks now, including the handling of what the fishing fleet brings in. A selfless offer to assist in the management of the Hawk Court's responsibilities would be sensible enough. Food flowing into the city is a longtime stock-in-trade of theirs."

"The Bittern Court is burning out their rivals. . . ." Ilona looked thoughtful. She had Marya now, who was fussing, perhaps at the tension in our words. "They are moving ahead." She clutched my daughter so tightly that Marya squeaked. "What will become of Corinthia Anastasia?"

"I have much the same fear for Samma," I confessed, damning my own honesty as Ilona's face crumpled. "We will act soon. As soon as we can manage to do so."

"It will never be soon enough," she whispered. "Far too late for that already."

"What do you propose, Green?" asked Mother Vajpai tartly. I knew she was trying to divert the despair toward which this conversation was driving.

"Now is the time to call up whatever allies we can. Mother Argai's work among the Blades will either bear fruit or it will not. But we must move against Surali. Our time for patience is at an end."

Ilona made as if to rise from her chair, but I raised a hand, shifting Federo's weight in my other arm. "Not yet," I added. "Like I said, let us seek out our friends. If I need to, I will do this alone. But far better not to."

How I would do this alone was beyond me.

"Mother Argai is still on the streets," Mother Vajpai pointed out.

"Then I will go to the temple. I can enter through the kitchens. They will not betray me."

"No." Her voice was flat, final.

"No?" I looked Mother Vajpai over carefully, trying to sort out if that had been an order or advice, or something else. Her deference to me seemed highly variable.

"I shall go. If things are awry within the temple, better that they fall on me than on you, Green. Should you be taken up or held against your will, I cannot myself carry the fight to the Bittern Court." Her smile was crooked as one hand waved at her maimed feet. "Besides, if there is a discussion to be had, the senior Mothers will listen to me far more closely than they will heed you. They have known me longer, and I do not have your erratic history."

The desire to argue with her was almost overwhelming, but her logic was correct. If our last, desperate hope was a small raid on the Bittern Court, I would be the one to take such action. Preferably with Mother Argai at my side, but alone if need be. Mother Vajpai's grasp of temple politics and personalities was decades better honed than mine. She could call on old trusts, forgotten favors, and all the complexities of a long life among women I had known only a few years.

And in the end, I was still a foreigner to them.

"Go, then," I said gracelessly. "Find what you will. If you are not back tonight, we will decide what must be done next."

"Mother Argai will aid you." Mother Vajpai's voice was uncomfortable. I wondered, as she obviously did, if Mother Argai was now a target as well.

"I would escort you," I told her, my voice soft in one last try.

"No, Green. Stay here and think on what to do."

What to do if she came back, or what to do if she did not come back, Mother Vajpai had not said. I bowed my head to her and watched my second-greatest teacher limp from our little council of war.

Then it was time to switch the babies and breasts, and do what was needful for them awhile. Being a mother did not stop even for the possible fall of a city.

After a time, I went back out to see what Firesetter was about. He still knelt in exactly the same position as I had last found him. A coal demon statue indeed, though he was not so threatening as they. Not like this, a giant man drawn into himself on a rack of grief and mourning.

"That was not your fire on the morning air," I told him. To the Smagadine hells with the neighbors. If they saw me, I would slay them, too.

My only answer was a rumbling noise. At least he'd heard.

Or so I thought.

I tried again. "The Bittern Court is killing this city in pieces. They will remake it as their own."

Gravel slid along his throat. "What is this to me?"

A rough response, but it was a response. Firesetter could hardly be anything but awkward right now, mourning the death of Fantail, whoever she had been to him.

"This is nothing to you, most likely." I saw no point in being anything but honest with him. "Kalimpura is not your city, is it?"

More silence awhile. Then: "I have no cities. I am a Red Man of Selistan. Our cities are long gone to glittering dust."

Where are your people? I thought, but did not say, for it seemed cruel. Firesetter was like me, raised far away from those who should have known and loved him best. It was a strange kinship, but I understood his loss deep down in my bones. "This is the principal metropolis of Selistan. You have a claim on this place. This place has a claim on you." The same was certainly true of me.

"Once there was a great city of brass and iron amid the Fire Lakes. . . ." His voice trailed off, chasing his thoughts into some private oblivion.

I gave his introspection some time, for I did neither of us a service in pressing him. After a while I picked up where Firesetter had left off. "Your city of brass is lost now, like so much. We cannot walk backwards through our lives."

Still he was awkward in conversation. "I would walk backwards through the past day."

Both of us glanced down at Fantail, resting peacefully in the bottom of the pond. Firesetter's movements were strangely precise, as if he'd become mechanically jointed. As his words had been.

"There is much I would take back and do over," I told him. "My woes are thick and my enemies legion. All I can do is take arms against them and swim onward through this sea of strife."

His response to that was both cryptic and encouraging. "Mafic . . ."

Wisps of steam rose off the pond. That was not so much encouraging, given what had happened the last time we had discussed Firesetter's old teacher. Trainer. Slavemaster. Whatever Mafic had been.

I stated the obvious by way of encouragement. "That man is the source of much of your trouble."

"Trouble is as we allow it." The steam stopped rising. "They . . . hurt . . . me."

"You were beaten as a child?" This hurt I could certainly grasp from my own experience.

Firesetter slowly turned his head to stare at his arm as if he'd never seen it before. "With this skin? It would have done them no good." Then his long, sloping face rotated toward me and our gazes met. I realized that this Red Man was quite handsome in his strange way. "It takes much to harm me."

A strange vision occurred to me, of Firesetter and the Rectifier sparring. There was a match I might have given a great deal to witness, in happier times. These were not happy times. Not now. "The hurts were in your heart." This, too, I understood.

"Mmm . . ." Another of those graveled rumbles. "Your mind seems to be your own. Not ensnared by others."

"Well, perhaps." I'd always thought so, at least; whatever others might have done to twist and train my thoughts, they were still *my* thoughts. Still, was this ever truly the case? Federo-the-man and the Factor had certainly ensnared my mind in the years of my upbringing under their care.

"My mind is not my own. Not so much. Some things when brought to my notice hurt me. Some things hurt me until I leave them off, for fear they will shatter me."

Yet he claimed to be difficult to harm. The greatest weapons were the ones that worked from within. A blade's edge could only stop a heart; it could not break one. "Ah." I had no idea what else to say. I could not assuage the wounds upon his soul. The only one who could do so lay in the bottom of the pond before us. A strange funeral rite, but no stranger than the sky burials of the Bhopuri people in the land of my birth. There are, after all, only four elements. Each of us must each go back to one or another of them in our time.

Still, a response seemed called for. "To speak of Mafic raises this hurt, then?"

He nodded too precisely. More steam wisped on the pond. At least we were unlikely to set a fire out here. It seemed worth my time to map the edges of his pain, for they might tell me something of the Saffron Tower, or at least its methods. And Firesetter was cooperating, in his strange, sullen way.

"Also it hurts you to speak on how you were raised."

Another nod. More steam. Firesetter looked sidelong at me again, only his head moving as before so that he seemed as a statue swiveling only one of its parts. "And to think on where my kind had come from. They told me I was a made thing. Belonging to the Tower. Having no others in the world but *me*."

Now he was wreathed in hot clouds of water. The surface of the pond was beginning to churn.

"Let it go if you can." I touched his arm again. His skin was warmer, too, still slick and solid as stone. "You are beyond their reach."

"No one is beyond their reach." His voice was what passed for a mumble in such a giant of a man.

"I do not believe that. The plate of the world is infinitely longer than a man can walk in a lifetime." I thought back on something the Dancing Mistress had told me quite some time ago, and felt a stab of heart's pain for my troubles. "Somewhere there are purple seas, where people converse in a language of flowers. Somewhere on this earth there is anything you can imagine. The writ of the Saffron Tower cannot run everywhere."

"Everywhere I might go," he amended grudgingly. The pond was calm again.

"Iso and Osi told me much," I said, angling into the subject from a new direction. "About the fall of the titanics, and theogenic dispersion, and the Saffron Tower's purpose in correcting what they see as an ancient wrong between men and women." That was putting the matter far more kindly that it actually deserved, but I did not intend to argue either theology or gender with Firesetter.

"I am no monk." He sighed with a noise like the great kettle boiling at the heart of one of those iron ships from the Sunward Sea. "Fantail knew more of this. They always sent their orders through her."

That piqued my curiosity. "How?"

"Messenger, mostly."

Well, *that* was mundane.

He continued: "Sometimes through wind and wave."

Wind and wave? My heart fluttered. I'd had more than enough of wind and wave lately, sufficient to frighten the experienced crew of *Prince Enero* as well as half the waterfront population of Kalimpura. "Why that method?"

He seemed surprised, and that emotion drew a more genuine, open expression onto his face than what the withdrawal of grief had left there. "Fantail is—was—a water sprite. She can hear the right call across an ocean's distance."

"Ah." I had not yet met Fantail when the storm at sea was calmed. It could not have been her doing, I realized. Nor did she likely have so much power. Those were the acts of a god. Or a titanic. "Thank you."

"Mmm." His body settled, muscles shifting for the first time I'd seen that day. As if the statue were waking up.

I took that for encouragement and tried to drive the conversation further forward. "So you did not worry much about the purpose of your work."

"What I did is what I did. Who has purpose, really?"

"Slaying goddesses? That is not just employment. Or adventure, even. That is a mission. A . . . a *quest*."

"Life is a quest, Mistress Green. Most pursue it no further than their doorstep, but it is still a quest."

Well, he certainly had the right of that. "Your quest is finding the wellspring of your people," I said softly.

That was met with another of those steam-kettle sighs. The pond bubbled a bit more.

The idea that had been glimmering in my head burst into light. Before I could think too hard on my own words, I blurted, "If I could find a way to free your mind from Mafic's chains, would you aid me?" Could it be so much harder than calming a storm at sea?

"I will help you in any case," he replied. "All my own purposes are spent. I might as well pursue yours." He smiled without humor. It was like watching a forge grin. "You propose to stand against Mafic. That cannot be so wrong."

Though it burned my hand, I touched his cheek. "Your purposes are not so dead as you think, Red Man." I would have pitied him then, but he was beyond pity and into another place where I could not follow.

We sat in silence awhile until the steam had cooled again. The sun climbed past its zenith and began the long, slow slide toward the western horizon. I might have taken his hand, but it seemed disrespectful to Fantail and besides, not likely what the Red Man needed in that moment.

Eventually we spoke further, talking for quite a while. I fenced with exquisite care around the borders of the spell that lay across his mind. In return, I learned more of the Saffron Tower and its methods. The men—and it was exclusively men who made decisions and took actions there, Fantail notwithstanding—who sat in their high platforms staring out across the Riven Strait and thinking on the state of the world were more scholars than monks. The Saffron Tower celebrated a number of rites that coexisted more or less in harmony, as they all served the larger end.

Firesetter could not tell me if it was divine energy or a more human sort of magic that drove their miraculous powers. At that time in my life, I had yet to meet a wizard, and indeed barely knew rumors of their existence, and so was far more inclined to ascribe miracles and wonders to the touch of a god. Such had been my experience, after all. To a carpenter with a hammer, everything is a nail and the world is made of wood.

What troubled me was that the Saffron Tower seemed to have no god as such. At most, what Firesetter described was a species of dedication to the masculine principle. They tore down the Daughters of Desire not to replace those goddesses with anything else, but to reduce the power and protection of women until the only shelter left to the wives and daughters of this world was the strong arms of their husbands and fathers.

That wasn't a theology; that was just simple control.

We talked about the hunters they sent out. We discussed how the art of god-killing was honed and pursued. We went over in great detail the training they had received in everything from roundhouse punches to rhetoric, so those warrior-monks and their agents could persuade as well as pursue.

When I finally went back into the kitchen to seek some clean water and to feed my children at my breast once more, I was left with the impression that Mafic would be dangerous, possibly extremely dangerous, but that he would be just one man. A nearly fatal mistake that proved to be, but not due to any faithlessness on Firesetter's part.

My dear Chowdry;

I have found that I miss your company. Neither of us is perhaps blessed with wisdom, but you are not afraid of me, nor do you see a child when you look into my face. No one else treats me as I am, not quite the way you do.

This city stands on the brink of ruin. I am quite tired of politics. Though, in truth, I suppose the struggle here can be seen as the same struggle back there in Copper Downs. Why anyone longs for such power is past my understanding. It comes only with the need to defend ever more.

This I know from my own experience, and my power does not even exist.

I have learned more of the man Mafic, of whom you warned me. There is one here he once trained, who was turned down another path. I know that I would not fight Mafic if I had the choice. There are further methods of opposition, but they are being closed off one by one through circumstance or the plotting of others.

All I want now is for the affairs of Kalimpura to settle sufficiently for my children to be safe here. I may have to settle these affairs myself.

Be well, build your temple, and pray this trouble does not come back to you.

Though Mother Argai returned at dusk, Mother Vajpai did not. The Red Man continued to rest in stony silence by the pond, now that our earlier interview had ended. He showed no signs of stirring. The rest of us sat vigil in the kitchen. I sewed that day's bell onto my silk and Marya's both, and inspected the knots on my older work.

"The fire at the Hawk Court is still being at smolder," Mother Argai said in her slightly odd Petraean. She seemed tired, and occasionally glanced toward the door leading to the back garden and Firesetter.

I continued to wonder about that fascination, but the news of the moment was far more important. "Nothing else caught in the blaze, I trust?"

"Not from that fire, no." She rubbed at her eyes. "There are being least six other burnings about the city."

"Is that normal?" asked Ilona. Ponce stirred, Federo sleeping in his arms, but said nothing.

What a strange question, I thought. "Are building fires ever normal?"

"No, that is not what I meant. Does this city burn much on its own, or are these fires entirely part of the street fighting?"

I glanced at Mother Argai. She'd lived here all her adult life, unlike me. "It rains enough here," she said, "that we are not for the most part fearing a great burning."

"More attacks from the Street Guild and the Bittern Court, then," I said.

"Perhaps. Many old grudges were being contested this day."

She had the right of that. The Saffron Tower's grudge was the oldest of all, if their stories were to be believed. And that certainly was being contested to this day.

"What else?" I asked her.

She slipped into Seliu, a more comfortable tongue for her. "Rumors and more rumors. No one has seen the Prince of the City. His guards are gone from their posts. Most foreign captains have fled the port. Cargo sits idled on the docks. The fishing fleet is thinning as those boats head up the coast to hide in smaller, quieter places." She gave me a long, hard glare. "The recent rising of the waters is as big a factor there as any violence in the streets."

I ignored the implied reprimand and answered in Petraean so Ilona and Ponce could follow better. "With the burning of the Hawk Court and the thinning of the fishing fleet, people will soon start to be hungry here in the city. It will not take too long for that to become a wider issue than Surali can manage."

"Or anyone else," said Ponce finally. "I know little of this city, but in Copper Downs my father is the master of the Green Market. I do know something of how many cartloads of food it takes to keep a city eating for a day. Everyone from the wealthiest to the beggars depends on what comes through the gates and off the docks. If you do not fix that problem quickly, it may become unfixable."

"I am not in a position to raise the Hawk Court from its ashes," I said, stung. "I did not do this to Kalimpura."

"Be telling that to the captains of the fishing fleet," snapped Mother Argai.

Opening my mouth for further hot words, I closed it instead of replying in kind. She certainly had the right of this situation.

I did not know how I had raised the sea. How could I possibly not-raise the sea well enough to assure everyone on the waterfront of their safety? As soon prove it would never rain again. Or always.

"In a word," Ilona said, her own voice leaden, "despair. Your city despairs."

"Not yet," answered Mother Argai, "but that is coming."

Closing the circle of the argument, I added, "And Mother Vajpai is not."

Everyone fell into thoughtful silence for a few moments. I settled Marya against my shoulder and let her sleep. Soon I would trade off with Ponce and have Federo at my breast awhile.

The quiet was finally interrupted by the hitch of a sob from Ilona. "We are no closer to my daughter." Her voice trembled.

"I will go and fetch both her and Samma from the Bittern Court," I promised, striving for loyalty to our other lost hostage. "Before dawn, if Mother Vajpai does not come back with some other, better news in the meantime."

"No," said Mother Argai as Ilona began to say something in response.

Ilona's face darkened. "No?"

"We need to do this properly. Or it will not be done at all. I think one of us should seek after Mother Vajpai. The value of the Blades in this would be incalculable."

"You don't have—" Ilona stopped herself. She and Mother Argai shared a long, slow look suffused with shame and grief on both their parts. Samma was daughter to none of us, but clearly had been a lover of Mother Argai's after my departure. And she was a Blade Sister to me.

"Everyone's heart is in this," I said slowly and carefully. "The question is not whether we act, but how. And we are all agreed that waiting is no longer the best strategy. Yes . . . ?"

That question elicited a series of nods.

"Fair enough, then. Here is my proposal: I favor going straight into the Bittern Court before Surali has an opportunity to further deepen our troubles." I nodded at Mother Argai.

She understood what I was doing well enough. "Green and I cannot be succeeding on such an effort without help. We know this because she was being at the Bittern Court before, and that was a price too high to be paying for nothing. We need the Blades too badly to not try to seek them one more time."

"And if we lose you or her as we have lost Mother Vajpai?" asked Ilona. "Then what? Ponce and I can hardly go knocking at Surali's front gate."

"Mother Vajpai is not lost," I said. "Merely misplaced." Looking around, I gathered them all in by eye. "I will go to the Temple of the Silver Lily if it is your will. To seek her, and to try to raise the Blades myself."

"Better I should be going, Green," said Mother Argai quietly.

"No." I was afraid she might have her own agenda, secret orders or some agreement with Mother Vajpai to which I was not privy. But I could hardly say that aloud. "I will go. You know how the Blades see me. If I appear now, it will be as a call to action."

"Some of them hate you," she offered. "And many of the Mothers of the other orders are not so fond of you."

"And some of them love me. You yourself told how they have begged for my return."

"No one is neutral toward you, Green," said Ponce unexpectedly. "I know nothing of the Blades, but I do know you. And you are, well . . . inspirational."

Mother Argai nodded reluctant agreement to that last. "People are following Green even when they are knowing better."

"Especially you," I said with a smile.

"Especially me."

"Then I will go," I announced. "Before dawn. You must care for the children, and help Mother Argai make ready to move swiftly when the need arises." I glanced at the doors leading outside. "It might be well to try to speak with Firesetter again. He was willing to talk with me this afternoon."

Mother Argai looked interested in this development. "I will sit with him awhile."

I still could not sort out whether her interest in the Red Man was lust, or worship, or possibly both. But she was not mine to command. Even if Mother Argai had been so, I could not determine what would be best to do in this case.

She slipped out the door, a jug of water in her hand. After she went, I turned to Ilona and Ponce. "As for you two . . ."

"As for us two what?" Ilona asked. Her voice was soft again. "You are not here to tend our hearts or our bodies. You go over the walls in darkness, and return wrapped in moody silence, and sometimes barely remember your children. We are here, and will continue to do what is needful, but do not recount us our wrongs."

Ponce winced at this speech, but did not look away or contradict her.

"I had not planned to call you wrong on anything," I lied. "Just to ask you what you might be able to do with the children while I was gone."

"Same as we ever do," Ponce said with a strange look on his face, somewhere between frustration and anger.

At that, I gave up. Instead, I took my daughter from him—in this we could still cooperate peaceably—and went to lie down awhile in the sleepless dark with both my babies. Their gurgling breath in time with each other reminded me all too sharply how every one of us was someone's child. Even Surali.

How could I kill, knowing what effort had gone into making each life that stood before me?

Rage, replied a voice deeper inside me. *Anger will always power your arm when a blade is needed.*

I am ashamed to say that even to this day that is still true, though wisdom and age have done much to temper me. Even words can strike a man down, when spoken to the right person, and this I have had to learn as well, to my further shame.

An hour before dawn, I was in the kitchen ready to leave. I had slept poorly, and my wounds itched abominably. Fear of Mother Vajpai's fate had crept into my mind during the night like the tide rising. For her sake, I left my children behind once more in the care of others. The goat milk we had been procuring would continue to serve to keep them fed until my return.

My leathers were cleaned, mended, and finally fitted me to their proper snugness, My blades were honed—even the god-blooded short knife required attention from time to time. I had pulled a shapeless gray robe over me. No pretense of being Sindu this morning. Those women did not work as servants in the quarters of the city much beyond their own. I planned to approach the Temple of the Silver Lily as I had last left it, in the guise of a kitchen drab. A large, crude basket under my arm gave me the excuse I needed. Ponce had picked fruit from the yard under the cover of darkness to fill it and so grant me plausibility.

"I do not know how long I will be gone," I told them. "But I hope to be back in a few hours." Glancing at Mother Argai, I added, "What of Firesetter?" If I failed, he might be her only ally in entering the Bittern Court by force.

"He steams the pond with his tears for his consort," she said with an odd formality.

I kissed Ilona, then Ponce, and hugged Mother Argai close. "Tend to him," I whispered, in hopes it would heal them both.

Going out the back way, I paused beside the Red Man. Though he had settled some, he still held the same position in which had been kneeling for over a day now. Any human would have long since collapsed from joint pain. "You have been a friend to me already," I told him.

He turned his head to look at me. In the predawn darkness, his eyes smoldered like glowing coals. "You have paid too much to fail."

With that benediction in my ears, I slipped out the postern gate in the rear. We'd given up pretense of secrecy, as there seemed small purpose in it now. All I needed do was walk away quietly.

At the hour of dawn, the cats go to the tops of their walls and the curbs that bound their small, vicious domains to welcome in the new day. I have sometimes thought of them as being present to carry away the shadows of night on their fog-soft feet, but they are most likely keeping an eye on one another. Those who hunt are ever suspicious and resentful not of their prey, but of their rivals.

Walking past these small, poised sentries, I wondered on my friend the tiger. Had he gone back to his garden? Or was he slain by one set of panicked guards or another? It was hard to imagine him stalking the streets of Kalimpura, but perhaps he had found a nest among the banyans of Prince Kittathang Park and sat even now to watch the dawn like the thousand thousand of his small similars that dotted the city.

Today it was just me, the cats, and the bakers' boys out with their morning flatbreads. The odor of burning still hung low over the city, but it more resembled an old rot now, not the open wound of yesterday. Whatever fighting there had been seemed not to have spilled through the darkness. I had seen enough of that in Copper Downs, with torchlight hunts and drunken gangs of guards or soldiers rampaging through the city,

Was it that here in Kalimpura even enemies agreed to sleep? Or were we simply too tired to carry the fight through all the watches of the night?

The fatalistic mood carried me all the way to the Beast Market and the square around the Blood Fountain. Already the cages squeaked and groaned as they were brought from their warehouses and quiet courtyards. Two dozen sorts of animals muttered and groaned and squawked, each complaining in the manner of its kind.

The fountain flowed, too. The red stone that lent its color to the name still looked black in this dim light. The temple was quiet. I noted the steps still seemed far more clear than normal. The usual assortment of beggars, petty merchants, and the simply homeless were largely absent. At least this morning their places had not been taken by masses of the Street Guild as on my last visit.

Those bastards, too, were doubtless sleeping their way toward another day of thuggery. At that time in my life, I had already understood no one is a villain in their own story, but I did wonder what tales the men who did the fighting, and the bullying, and the swaggering, told themselves of the rightness of their cause. Did the poorest deserve to have their fingers stepped upon so they would give up their last copper half paisa to buy a fighting man's evening ale?

At least my acts had purpose.

Or so went the tale I told myself.

Without purpose, I was no better than they.

I drifted away from the plaza, down Juggaratta Street to where I could corner to my left and find the alley that led to the various back entrances and exits of the Temple of the Silver Lily. As with any great house or public building, the façade of power at the front was supported by a warren of the small and functional at the back. We even had our own smith, though she and her apprentices forged blades rather than horseshoes and wheel straps.

Several cart teams idled in the alley, their drivers each waiting his turn to unload. Fish for the day's stew, bags of rice that the head steward must already be regretting the rising price of, and a load of small, promising barrels all lingered for induction into the maw of the kitchen.

I walked swiftly past the quiet argument at the loading dock and up the steps that led into the kitchen's vestibule and mudroom. Beyond the crowded space of cloaks and boots—some of the undercooks and scullions had walked through ash and muck to reach their work this morning—was a familiar space of clanging pans, roiling steam, and smoky odors.

Home, the thought came unbidden. Home, where they were having poached eggs and spinach for breakfast, from the smell. And rice stew, of course. Always rice stew, for those who did not have time or privileges to sit in the refectory.

I slipped in with my basket and headed for the cool room to deposit the fruit. It was a prop, but that was no reason to waste what I had brought. Fondly I imagined taking a turn at the stew pot. Some of the papayas I'd brought could be cut into it to render a meal more suited for daybreak, but that was not my purpose here. I'd practically been living in a kitchen for the past weeks, but except for our tiny oil stove, we'd made no decent use of it at all.

No one met my eye, which seemed odd. I'd never been in a large kitchen where a stranger was not instantly visible. These people worked arm in arm every day from dawn till dusk, and overnight as well for some of them. I glanced around and realized that no one was looking at me at all.

If one had looked down from the gallery, one would have seen me passing through the kitchen in a little pool of invisibility and silence.

They were ignoring me with an elaboration that spoke volumes.

I slipped into the cold room, which was empty at that moment, and set the papayas on a higher shelf. They'd keep well enough not to need the space closest to the precious troughs of straw-covered ice below the shelves.

My basket I left there as well, and my gray cloak. Here inside the temple, I would be a Blade, by the Wheel. Woe to anyone who challenged me on that. I checked my weapons, then stepped back out into the kitchen. Silence followed me past the chopping tables and the baking ovens, right until I reached the podium where Mother Tonjaree surveyed her domain.

She stood there now, one of Sister Shatta's fresh sweet rolls in her hand, and smiled down at me. I slowed my stride and smiled back. The sweet roll descended and I took it from her without stopping. We exchanged a final nod; then I passed out of the kitchen like cook-smoke, up the back stairs that would take me to halls running behind and between the dormitories. There I might find a quiet, friendly ear and learn more.

I knew from what Mother Argai had told us that there was much sympathy for me and Mother Vajpai among the Blades. In our banishment, their honor and pride had also been reduced. Mother Srirani had trod too heavily on everyone's oaths of obedience.

Besides which, we were sworn to the Temple of the Silver Lily and to the Lily Goddess Herself. Not to the Temple Mother. She was, after all, merely the chief among servants.

This in turn meant that if I managed to avoid the Justiciary Mothers as I moved about the temple, I was far less likely to be called out or turned in. I would not fight my own Sisters here, but neither would I allow myself simply to be quashed.

Nor would I skulk. Here, architecture was my friend. The sweeping, curved lines of the temple, which some wags both in and out of our Sisterhood had likened to a woman's sweetpocket, meant that there were very few interior walls that ran straight and true. Rather, everything curved or angled. This in turn meant short sight lines, multiple turnings, and a number of odd little spaces that were often used for art, storage, or other miscellaneous purposes. When I had been an Aspirant, we'd played hide-and-find among these halls with chalk-tipped sticks to mark our "kills."

Today I would be no one's kill.

Instead, I slipped up a curving staircase into the second-storey back corridor. The central space of the sanctuary was behind the wall to my right. A layer of rooms wrapped around it on the outside of the building. The sanctuary narrowed more rapidly than the exterior lines of the building, which meant the layers of rooms grew wider and more complex level by level.

The second storey was mostly offices and portions of our temple library. I highly approved of quiet little rooms stocked with books.

For one thing, I might find a senior Blade Aspirant on her sixth or seventh petal in here studying against the chance of some quiz from a teaching Mother.

Assuming, of course, that Mother Srirani had not halted the Blades' training progress along with her banning of their runs.

Insanity, I thought. Who would hold the Death Right if we did not? Only an arrant fool would give that power to the Street Guild.

A servant trotted down the corridor in the other direction behind an armload of linen. I stepped aside to let her pass—not an ordinary courtesy in caste- and class-conscious Kalimpura, but something we practiced among women here within our walls. There were no male servants, or men resident of any kind. Only a few visitors on sufferance for needed errands or important business.

"Thank you," she muttered, then glimpsed my face and stumbled to a halt.

I am distinctive. Deeply so. In Copper Downs, it was as much for the color of my skin as for anything else. Here in Kalimpura, the scars slashing my cheeks were like a banner advertising my identity. Not to mention the healed wounds in my nose, courtesy of the late, unlamented Councilor Lampet. There might be a thousand young women in this city with my build, but there was only one with my face.

"Hello," I said quietly, reaching for this one's name and utterly failing. Touching a finger to my lips, I added, "This is a quiet visit."

She nodded vigorously, a gleam in her eye. That encouraged me. To ask silence for a little while was one thing. To request conspiracy was another. Still, I had to start somewhere.

"Have you seen or heard word of Mother Vajpai?"

"No, Mother Gr— No, Mother, I have not."

"Thank you." With an answering nod, I moved on.

Three book rooms and an empty office later, I was at another stair. I'd never known its official name, or even if the stair had such a name, but when I was an Aspirant we'd called this one the Pink Stairs, for the rather unfortunately suggestive color of the marble used to line the walls.

Up toward the dormitories on the third storey? Or around to the next swath of offices? If memory served, there was one more book repository, then several small chambers often used to meet with officials from other temples, Guilds, or Courts. The Justiciary Mothers had their formal hearing rooms on the floor below me, but they some-times came up here as well.

None of *them* would hesitate to cry me out. Not with one of their own standing at the altar as Temple Mother. I knew they were wrong, but it was reasonably possible that they themselves did not under-stand the situation fully.

Up the stairs it was.

I drifted into the spiraling rise, listening for voices or the squeak of footsteps. Nothing. The Pink Stairs leaned inward as they ascended, so to speak—that is, the shaft had the same curve as the outer shell of the temple. This meant that there were odd angles of view both up and down, but they were not consistent.

So long as no one lurked for me above I was safe.

At the third storey, I stopped just within the opening to the corri-dor beyond. There was no door, just a doorway. I let myself be flat against the wall as voices passed close by. I did not recognize either of them, which meant they were probably not Blade Mothers.

". . . we'll have to wait for word."

"Yes, but will *she*?"

The first woman, the back of her head now visible to me, grunted in apparent dissatisfaction. They proceeded along the corridor and out of sight. Justiciary Mothers, from their layered white robes.

To my left was an Aspirants' dormitory—or at least it had been the last time I lived inside the temple. Past that, a bathing room and a privy. Then a larger sleeping room shared by some of the junior Blade Mothers. I would head there.

My luck broke badly as another Justiciary Mother stepped out of the privy just as I passed by the entrance. She was adjusting the fall of her overgarment, and so did not see me immediately. I ducked my head to step past as she looked up smiling and said, "Oh, please . . ."

I had been recognized.

Throwing my silent self-promises to the winds, I shouldered her back into the privy, knocking the wind from her shout in the same movement. The two of us were crowded into the small closet with its raised wooden seat. I jammed the door closed behind me, then grabbed her by the hair to tug her head far back, exposing the throat.

"Either you believe Mother Srirani, and I am a dangerous apostate," I growled. "Or you do not, and I am being slandered." My breath was hot in her ear, I knew, and I watched the whites of her eyes widen. "Which do you choose to believe?"

"I do not know," she squeaked.

"Well, at least you're honest. Unlike too many of the rest of your Sisters in the Justiciary." I slammed her down onto the seat of ease, then sliced away several strips from her hem. It was a terrible thing to do to good silk, but time was not on my side here.

"Stay quiet for an hour," I warned her. "Half a candle, if you count that way. I'll be gone by then." Or captured. There was small purpose in confessing that fear of mine to this one. I backed out, slipping the latch from the outside—that was a childish trick that all the Blade Aspirants knew, and therefore so did all the Blade Mothers.

The Justiciary Aspirants were too prissy to play such games, or so I'd always thought. With this one, I'd be lucky if she remained shut up and quiet for twenty minutes. If nothing else, someone would eventually force her way in here after banging on the door and hearing no reply.

I knew I wouldn't be here long, no matter what. Swiftly I darted into the first of the dormitories.

Three young women—no, girls—whom I did not know leapt to their feet. They saw my leathers and bowed briefly, as Aspirants are trained to do on meeting a Mother for the first time in a day. Several smaller children hid behind them. All the Aspirants were wearing the knee-length gray dresses and undertrousers we'd favored when not actually at our training. The room was achingly familiar with its up-swept walls, narrow windows admitted daylight through frosted glass, and the double row of beds each with its small chest for personal belongings.

"Do you know me?" I asked, perhaps more fiercely than I meant to.

Two of them exchanged a glance. The third spoke up, her eyes bright with excitement. "You are Mother Green."

"Well, yes." The not-quite-fully-earned honorific still bothered me, even though it was literally correct. "Do you know why I am here?"

The girl who'd spoken up now looked to her fellow Aspirants for support. Her voice dropped to a whisper, as if Mother Srirani were in the far corner of this room. "They said you would come for Mother Vajpai."

Ah . . . "They who?" This was an important question.

"Th-the other Mothers." She was unsure of herself now.

I grinned. "They are right. Uh . . . and just where *is* Mother Vajpai?"

"Down in the practice rooms," said the spokesgirl.

That would be the temple's basement, which unlike the upper levels was quite rectilinear. Also, three levels below me. Getting there would involve some fast moving. Still, there was nothing too surprising about the location. The practice rooms tended to have padded doors that could be barred against interruption or stray weapons in either direction.

If one wanted to keep a prisoner under guard here in the Temple of the Silver Lily, those basement chambers were some of the better places. Also, it was sufficiently out of the way to cut down the passing of too many women who might ask questions of the guard.

We among the Temple of the Silver Lily might be sworn to obedience, but we weren't very good at it.

I touched my finger to my lips again. "Silence, then, along with my thanks. And, well, I was never here." I winked before slipping back out into the corridor.

The Pink Stairs would take me down to the first storey, just above the kitchen. From there I'd have to either go back through the kitchen or make my way around to the Little Stairs to get into the basement level where the practice rooms lay. We had more storage down there, including both the root cellar and the fruit cellar, along with the curing room and some of the other, slower annexes of the kitchen.

No time like the moment. Even as I planned my route, I slipped back into the Pink Stairs and softly padded downward. Voices echoed above me, a burst of laughter, as several Mothers passed in from one of the floors farther up. I paused, then matched my descent to theirs, so I would never pass into the sight line. I thought I recognized the voices, Mother Shesturi's, at least, whose handle I used to run in. After our experience at the docks with Mother Surekha, I was not willing to risk myself to another's goodwill just yet. Not without need.

They seemed to be coming all the way down to at least the first storey. I was reluctant to slip through the kitchen again—I did not want to risk the Mother Tonjaree's safety by making her seem my accomplice.

I stepped out instead and headed for the Little Stairs. That would take me past one of the side entrances to the sanctuary. Not one used for services, generally, but rather to carry in votive supplies, altar greens, and other requirements of the Temple Mother and her services.

The handy part was that the several other doors in that area opened into storage. I would not risk much here. That thought in mind, I trotted around the curve of the corridor for the Little Stairs. They lay almost at the great juncture of the front corridor, this back corridor and the anteroom to the sanctuary, where we often gathered when a group needed to meet that was too large for the classrooms, but not full enough for the refectory or the sanctuary.

A buzz of voices began to lift just as I reached my target. I saw the backs and shoulders of several dozen women, a mix of our temple's orders. Ducking my head, I walked quickly down the steps. From behind, I was just another Blade Mother on an errand.

Down in the basement, things were quieter. Corridors spoked away in three directions from the bottom of the Little Stairs. A Justiciary Mother sat before a doorway about five rods from me along the rightmost corridor.

I'd been disgraced here before.

Thinking quickly, I ran toward her. "Upstairs!" I shouted. "Mother Srirani, she needs you." It was no trouble at all to put a realistic gasp in my voice.

She jumped up, tipping over her wooden chair. "You're not— Where's Mother Akkarli?"

"With Mother Srirani," I said, glancing up then right back at my feet again. This would have been more convincing if I'd been dressed as an Aspirant. "Hurry," I added. "I'll wait right here for Mother Akkarli."

The Justiciary Mother took a step toward the stairs, then paused to stare at me. "You," she began.

By way of rejoinder, I smacked her in the side of the head with my fist, then eased her to the floor. There was no point in hurting the woman further.

I threw aside the bar that had been so obviously installed in haste on the outside, then pushed the door open.

"Mother Vajpai?"

"Green." Her voice was tense, and she looked tired, but not as if someone had been trying to hurt her. She squatted against the far wall. Waiting. For me? The sputtering lamp by the door lit her face so oddly, I could not make out her expression.

"Come on," I told her. "We've only got a minute or two. I came to find you and see whether we could raise the Blades or not. Our time is running out for Corinthia Anastasia and Samma."

"It will not work." The fatigue in her voice worried me.

"Fine. Then *you* come with me, at least, and we can deny Surali one more of her prizes."

She rose and stumbled toward. "Your feet—?" I asked in horror.

"Just that it is damp down here, and I was not permitted a blanket."

I tugged open the door to face three big Street Guildsmen with crossbows in the corridor beyond. Behind them was a gaggle of Mothers—very few Blades in this crowd, I noted with a dispassionate sense of observation somewhere deep inside me.

Mother Srirani stepped close, but still behind her crossbowmen. "You will surrender your weapons, Green."

"I am Mother Green," I said quietly, so quietly that the others had to lean closer to hear. Technically not true, given that I'd never taken final vows, but my point stood. "Could you not find a Lily Blade to stand guard within our own temple, Mother?"

"You are banished, and no longer a Mother," she said, but I caught the quaver in her voice.

"I will not fight you," I announced. The knot of women behind her seemed to sigh. The smile on the faces of the crossbowmen was far less comforting. "But I will not surrender my weapons except to another Blade."

After brief confusion, Mother Surekha stepped forward.

"So how are your runs now?" I asked her.

She looked as if she might cry, but held out her hand for my weapons.

Very slowly and carefully, I unsheathed my long knife and handed it to her, hilt first. Then the ordinary short knife. I was very reluctant to pass over the god-blooded knife, but she would know I had it. Instead, I stopped before that one and waited to see what Mother Surekha would say. Mother Srirani would be less likely to know what was I was supposed to be carrying.

Mother Surekha's mouth opened and shut twice, but whatever words she had for me failed. She turned away and nodded at the Temple Mother.

"Lock them in," announced Mother Srirani. "We will deal with this sordid affair as soon as possible."

As soon as possible sounds good, I thought as the practice room door swung shut. I turned back to Mother Vajpai, who squatted once more against the far wall. "I could not rush them all," I said. "And would not do so to my own Sisters, in any event."

"You cannot rush history, Green. We have lost this struggle."

I stomped around the room, kicking at the wood chips and straw that were all that remained of whatever target dummies and weapon mounts had been in here before.

We had not been left with so much as a bench. "Did they feed you, at least?"

"No."

"Not since yesterday!" I was outraged.

"Green. Please. Sit down."

After a little while, I did that thing.

"So, what happened to you?" I finally asked, at the end of a period of sullen silence.

"Exactly as I feared." She sighed, long and slow. "I came openly to the temple and began consulting with my Blade Sisters. Mother Srirani arrived and made a show of arresting me."

"With Street Guild?" There was another outrage, armed men—our longtime enemies, at that—within the temple walls, and the Blades enjoined from action.

"No. She had Mother Surekha and Mother Padmatti with her."

Mother Surekha I already knew about. She was not so much older than I. Padmatti had still been an Aspirant when I left the temple several years ago. "So none of the senior Blade Mothers will stand against you?"

A small smile of satisfaction quirked Mother Vajpai's face, though it was nearly an illusion in this flickering light. "None of them would accept appointment in my place as Blade Mother. Mother Srirani is furious about that, or so I'm told."

"Good." My anger began to cool a little. "Has she simply sold us for high bid?"

"Nothing so venal, I'm afraid." Now Mother Vajpai was frowning. "Mother Srirani cooperates with Surali. Not for anything so cheap as profit."

"*Why?* The woman is a killer and a cheat and a plotter against the very existence of the Lily Goddess."

"Green. Who knows this for certain besides you and I? Think on how much effort Mother Srirani has put into undermining the worth of our word. She cannot back down now without admitting she has been wrong all along. That would be difficult for her . . . continued leadership, let us say."

"Surali cut off your *toes*. This is not so difficult to prove."

"Only to those who wish to hear the message. Most of the Justiciary Mothers and many from the other orders are caught up with the idea of making peace with the Bittern Court and the Street Guild. They tire of the struggle."

"I would struggle myself, between calling them traitors or branding them cowards." If I contrived to escape again, there would be many among my Sisters here who would swiftly come to regret their foolishness.

She sighed, again my teacher, with me once more the obstreperous student. "You are a Lily Blade. You face down the consequences of violence every day. So we have trained you. Who among the Justiciary Mothers must do that? Or the Mothers Intercessory? Or any of the other orders? Of course they are tired and frightened. Mother Srirani offers a solution that eases the threat of force and disruption."

"Only by selling us to the very people who first came calling at sword's point." I jumped up and resumed my stomping around the empty room.

"And what of it?" asked Mother Vajpai softly.

"And what of Surali's dealings with the Saffron Tower? Where is our precious peace if those lunatics succeed in slaying the Lily Goddess out of hand as they did with Marya back in Copper Downs? Then we will be nothing but a gaggle of women in a gilded barn of a building, under no protection at all. We must stop her!"

"Who, Green? Surali? Mother Srirani? She is the Temple Mother: she speaks for the Lily Goddess."

"And she is wrong. No one is infallible here. Not even the goddess Herself."

Mother Vajpai laughed, swinging somewhere between bitterness and astonishment. "Nor you, nor I. Something it might do you good to recall."

"If we were infallible," I admitted, "we would not be stuck here."

"I didn't have to be, you know."

"Have to be what?"

"Have to be stuck here, in our little not-a-dungeon." Mother Vajpai grimaced. "When she found me, Mother Srirani offered to release me from my temple punishment if I knelt to her and acknowledged the new role of the Blades."

"The much-reduced role of the Blades," I said.

"Well, yes." She spread her hands wide. "As you might have gathered, I did not kneel."

"So who is in the wrong now?" Despite myself, I started to giggle. "Are we two the only ones in the entire temple who are in the right?"

She giggled with me. We sat like two madwomen in the damp straw, our shadows leaping in the guttering light of the lamp. Everyone's fate was out of my hands, for now.

Especially my own.

We were fed, finally, and our lamp replaced before it burned out completely. No one was foolish enough to linger in here refilling the oil on our old lamp. No one wanted to make of themselves so much a target.

A fresh bucket was left behind as well, which was helpful for the inevitable.

After a time, my milk began to ache. I had to express some more. It seemed a waste to put the fluid in the bucket with our piss, but what else was I to do? My children would be safe enough where they were. Mother Argai and Firesetter were formidable. Ilona and Ponce would care for the twins, keep them fed on goat milk and pabulum.

As for Corinthia Anastasia and Samma, I set them aside in my mind and heart. I could do nothing for them until I could get out of this place.

So we waited amid flickering shadows. After all the time we'd spent together, we knew each other's stories. Such as they were in my case. Though I would have much resented being called this at the time, I was still too young to have enough to say. And a great deal of what I could say could not be said. Even then, I understood that much.

Finally I convinced Mother Vajpai to work out with me. She could not spar so well with her feet maimed, but there were still many moves we could practice. Plus the activity warmed her up.

Throwing each other and wrestling, it occurred to me that I had not seen her work so in a long time. Aboard *Prince Enero*, Mother Argai had been my sparring partner. Since then, well, there had not been so much sparring for any of us.

Mother Vajpai was out of shape and off balance, but still far more canny than I. This woman had not so long ago been the deadliest person in Kalimpura. In maiming her, Surali had made a statement far more powerful than a simple killing would have.

My Blade Mother had been *depressed,* I realized suddenly.

I drove her hard, then, goading her with both words and actions until her eyes lit up with a fury. She knew well enough what I was doing. She followed me anyway. We worked for hours, until we were slicked with sweat, bloodied in more than a few places, and had both nearly broken bones in our falls without any of the room's usual pads and straw bales.

Finally, we slept close together, as if we might have been lovers once, though we never were that.

The next morning they came for us again. At least, I thought it was morning.

I knew we were both grimed, Mother Vajpai and I, and grubby from our fighting the day before. Still, we grinned like loons when the door banged open. Half a dozen crossbowmen this time, all Street Guild, and another squad with drawn swords out in the corridor.

Mother Srirani was taking no chances with us. Least of all having us guarded by our Sister Blades. *Let her send these men for us in the heart of the temple,* I thought. *It will only make her weakness more apparent to my Sisters of all the orders. Even some of the Justiciary Mothers must be feeling a pause at letting such masculine force loose among our own.*

Mother Vajpai walked more straight than I'd seen in a while, though she still limped. Her spirit was restored, at the least. That might be all we had left—spirit—but I was proud of her. As for me, I retained my god-blooded blade up my right sleeve. Thus far no one had been fool enough to search me directly. I promised myself that I would not bare steel in the sanctuary of the Lily Goddess, but it might yet serve a useful purpose.

I did not expect this day to be dull. Not in the slightest.

They shoved us roughly through a side door of the sanctuary, so we stumbled into the nave under the view of most of the Mothers, Sisters, and Aspirants of the Temple of the Silver Lily. They filled the rising galleries above us with a hubbub of chattering rumor. Malice, too, I was certain of it, but far more just curiosity. The swordsmen lining up behind us were certainly a subject of comment.

The Temple Mother awaited us before the altar, which itself was like her dressed for a high service. With her was a smiling man of gentle aspect, his skin ocean-tanned so that he might be of almost any paler race, head shaved smooth as glass. He wore the same saffron robes in the Hanchu style that I'd once seen on Iso and Osi.

This was Mafic, then. Our enemy. Firesetter's old slavemaster. The man Chowdry had warned me about, with his magic weapons and his ancient hatred toward all things female. How must it feel to him to be here amid a temple filled with women serving one of the Daughters of Desire that he and all of his were sworn to hunt down and exterminate. He would be here to somehow claim me and take me away; I was sure of it.

Good luck and bad cess to him, then. I smiled sweetly and let him see the full beauty of my hatred.

Mother Srirani raised her hands to call down silence. She then began to invoke the Lily Goddess' blessing on this day, this service before the temple assembled. From the stares and mutterings above I guessed that it had been some time since She had manifested. Given who was here now, and whom Mother Srirani had been cooperating with, I could hardly blame our goddess. She knew what these people were, even if Her servants, my Sisters, pretended not to.

"How long has it been since the Lily Goddess has appeared or spoken?" I whispered to Mother Vajpai.

"Months before we left for Copper Downs," she answered. The satisfaction in her voice was unmistakable. So was the slap to my head by the studded leather glove of the Street Guildsman behind me.

I could have snapped his neck for his troubles, or slit his throat right there, but I knew it was far more important that I hold both my temper and my fists for now. Instead, I consoled myself with a backward glance, murder in my eye that even the most boorish pig of a guard could not mistake.

That smirk would be the first thing I would slice from his face.

Mother Srirani continued her invocation. She sounded tired. Even I could call upon the Lily Goddess with more success than this. Had She turned Her face away from Her temple here? The Blades certainly seemed to have been abandoned, bereft of the cloak of Her regard.

If She was gone, perhaps I could call upon Mother Iron, or even Desire Herself, so that we were not, as I had predicted, just a swarm of women in a building too large for us.

More to the point, if She were watching over us but ignoring the Temple Mother's call, perhaps I could put paid to that.

In time, the prayers ran down. The gallery sighed as one woman. They had been hoping against hope—sparked by my return, perhaps? I had performed a memorable summoning once before in this very place, while on trial before the altar under the stern eye of Mother Umaavani, the previous Temple Mother.

In any case, Mother Srirani was done with the invocation. "Sisters," she called. Her voice was clearer, more strong, now that she was firmly back on political ground instead of the treacherous terrain of the spiritual. If only we had been a Court or a Guild, this woman might even have led us well. "Green is before us once more. She is here in violation of the terms of her banishment. Rather than subject her to temple punishment that she will not heed or serve the terms of, time has come for us to hand her over to the proper authorities.

"The Bittern Court has graciously agreed to try Green for her crimes both here in Kalimpura and in foreign places across the oceans, where she has also wronged them."

That incited a buzz of mixed anger and confusion. Mother Srirani raised her hands for silence once more, waiting for the last whisper to die away before she continued. "As many of you know, I have worked diligently to end this pointless feud with the Bittern Court and the Street Guild."

Behind me, one of the guards snorted. A small smile chased itself across Mafic's face. It occurred to me that from their current position, the guards had the Temple Mother under threat of their blades just as much as they had me.

"Setting Green before their justice will do much to right the wrongs of the past. I have also been asked by the Prince of the City to help stem our temple's provocations against the peace."

What? Still I kept my mouth shut, though it was becoming torture not to leap up and shout against her lies. The shocked silence from the gallery confirmed that I was not alone in my reaction.

"The Lily Blades have already suspended their runs at my request, to reduce pressure during these troubled times. By agreement of the senior Mothers of all the orders, our Blade Sisters will be standing down permanently from their duties outside the temple walls. Most of them are in contemplative retreat now."

"She has overreached," I hissed with glee, just under my breath so only Mother Vajpai could hear me. Besides which, I was certain no senior Blade Mother had agreed to such terms. It was simply not possible.

The rage that had been flooding me passed away as swiftly as a summer wind. I found myself in a place of calm, thinking furiously. Above me, angry shouts and arguments were breaking out all around the gallery. Let them argue. It bought me time to consider.

This city had even less governance than Copper Downs, though more by design than by the accident I'd inflicted upon the Duke across the sea. And let them try me for that! But what governance there was here was all in the balance between many different forces. The Bittern Court was upsetting those old balances, in the service of their own hunger for power. In the process, the Lily Goddess would be reduced or eliminated.

Nothing about this situation served Her interests, or those of the temple and the women of this city. Mother Srirani was no traitor, I believe that even now, but it was clear that she had been played for a fool and more than a fool by Surali. Great wrongs were only being made greater through her acts.

One did not bargain away one's own strength for the sake of peace with a stronger enemy. Sooner open the doors to their soldiers directly. As, indeed, Mother Srirani had also done.

What did she think she was doing? Did this emerge from some notion of fairness? Surely not all the Justiciars were such fools as this.

The Temple Mother still had her hands up for silence, but she was being ignored. Some of the senior Mothers of the orders might have been behind these maneuvers, but their own constituents had not been informed; that much was obvious. The temple was hardly a democracy. Even so, forcing the power of high office was never a way to accomplish anything of consequence among my Sisters.

Mafic just smiled, silent and intense. I could see where Firesetter had gotten the habit of sitting statue-still.

What was he doing here? What was the man waiting for?

For that matter, what was I waiting for?

I stepped forward, out of the shadows where the witness bench at the base of the well stood, and into the light of the altar. Every woman in the gallery could see me.

That silenced them, as the Temple Mother had been unable to do. I shared my sweetest smile with her as well. It was just a brief glance, but one I knew she would read.

"Sisters." I did not call loudly, for their attention was already upon me. The shape of the gallery was intended to concentrate the voice so that listeners even in the highest benches could hear what transpired at the altar.

Besides, a quiet tone commanded far better than a loud one.

Two hundred pairs of eyes glittered down at me.

"I am returned." Beside me, Mother Srirani stirred, making a signal to the Street Guild guards. It was a calculated gamble that she would not simply have me slain in front of the congregation. "Despite the efforts to silence me." I pointed at my guards, half a dozen hard-faced men with their hands on their sword hilts. "Would you have these men, our enemies, dictate who might speak among us?"

That raised another buzz, mutters of denial and anger. I passed over the question of whether I had a right to speak at the altar. As a Blade Mother of this temple, whatever rights I did have certainly trumped the force of the Street Guild and their masters in the Bittern Court.

"I will now call upon the Lily Goddess to bless us with Her presence."

Surely Mother Srirani had seen me make this same play before the altar with Mother Umaavani. She leaned close to threaten in some wise or another, but Mother Vajpai called the same bluff I had and stepped into the circle to grasp Mother Srirani's arm.

"Not now, Rani," she said quietly. That carried, too. A smattering of applause was her response from the gallery.

I might be well regarded in some circles of this temple, but Mother Vajpai was held in the utmost respect by virtually everyone. And she *was* the Blade Mother.

Bowing my head, I began to pray. Not a braying invocation to demonstrate my piety or authority, as the Temple Mother had done, but a personal conversation with the Lily Goddess, as I had experienced perhaps too often before.

That the gods would use someone who had before opened herself to them was an incontrovertible proposition to me. I'd fenced around that idea with Iso and Osi, with the Rectifier, with Chowdry. Certainly I had already touched and been touched by more gods than most people encountered in a lifetime of contemplative prayer. Like a tree on a hilltop draws lightning strokes from the heavens, I seemed to attract them. Often with just as much fire and pain.

Goddess, I prayed. *I know You hear me. You always have, even when I have not meant to call upon You. Your affection for me in this world is ever a mystery, but I welcome Your attentions.*

A breeze began to stir. It smelled of rain.

Your house is in great disorder. Your enemies have overtaken the wits of Your servants here. The city that shelters us all comes under greater threat by the day. It is possible the very walls here will be pulled down around us, and we will lose everything that has been built up in Your name over the generations of women who have served You here.

I felt a familiar curdling in the air around me.

If this is Your will, so be it. If Your will is that we should prosper, I beg You to favor us now with Your presence, the light of Your wisdom, Your love and support and guidance. My Sisters' hunger for Your face that has been turned away from them by our misguided leaders and their wrongful acts.

Come, please. We await You.

I looked up again to see flower petals drifting above me. The congregation was silent, holding in their breath as one woman. The thickened air reminded me of so many of these moments.

Then I caught sight of Mafic. He was grinning. The expression was clearly aimed at me.

This was what the old bastard had been waiting for, I realized with dawning horror. Not to take me away as I'd first thought, but for me to call the Lily Goddess. Or perhaps both. He must certainly be that clever.

Now that I had invoked my goddess, I did not know how to stop Her coming. I did not even know if that was either possible or desirable for me to do so. I wished mightily that things had gone better with Firesetter, that his prodigious strength might be here at my back. Or even better, that the Rectifier had come across the Storm Sea with me. His power and experience at fighting priests would have served well in this terrible moment.

There was another I could call on. I looked steadily back at Mafic. If Mistress Tirelle had taught me anything during my years in the Pomegranate Court, it was to keep my thoughts and feelings from my face. So with my expression stilled, I began to pray again. Surely not even this one could take on two divine powers at the same time.

Desire, I said soundlessly, forming the words and releasing them where they might be heard. Like the Lily Goddess, the titanic listened to me. Whatever Her reasons might be. *Your enemies have come to the house of one of Your daughters. Stand forth now that we might stop them here. I offer You the chance to redress the wrongs of the long centuries, and keep another from being struck down as so many have before.*

But I had not reckoned on the depths of Mafic's intrigue, nor of Mother Srirani's foolishness. Or perhaps it was Surali's treachery I had failed to understand. I have long since realized there was no difference, that the Temple Mother and the Bittern Court woman had become two ends of the same stick.

That day, all I knew was more Street Guild were shouldering their way into the temple from one of the gallery entrances. My prayer to Desire trailed off at the sight of their weapons above me. Wood and metal stocks without the bow attached. Guns, just as Lalo's men had used aboard *Prince Enero.* The mystic weapons Chowdry had written to warn me of.

"No!" I screamed at the same time as the Temple Mother spun backwards as if kicked in the chest. The first gun barked, somehow *after* she'd been struck. She dropped to the floor to wind up leaning against the altar. Blood soaked the front of her robes. Her eyes were wide with surprise. Mother Vajpai knelt to Mother Srirani's side, heedless of the buzzing thunder chipping the marble floor around us.

Turning this way and that, I saw everything as if in one, great glance. There are moments in combat, in lovemaking, in parenting, when time slows to a nothingness and a great well of experience can fill very, very quickly. Blue black smoke drifted from the long guns. Even the men holding them seemed surprised at their effect. In the gallery, women were screaming, leaping to their feet, turning to one another. There were far too few Blades up there. Detained, perhaps, or forbidden from attending this convocation. I saw no weapons on those of my Blade Sisters who were present—had they all been disarmed at Mother Srirani's order?

It wouldn't have mattered if they were present, no one could outrun thunder. Not even a Lily Blade.

We would all be dead, or fallen, very soon.

Not knowing what else to do, I leapt atop the altar amid the confused swirl of mist and flower petals.

"You will *not*," I said, my voice low once more. I drew upon the power of every god who'd ever touched me, upon every tingle of magic or miracle that had passed through my hands thus far in my short life. Filled with a rage as great as any I had ever known in my life, I took the god-blooded short knife in my hand and pointed it at one of the gun-men.

I burned like fire. My hands twisted and popped. The long gun at which I had aimed my will exploded in a burst of fire and noise and shredded fingers.

The great, carved double doors that were the formal entrance to the sanctuary burst open in a rush of foaming water. The ocean had come for me a third time, its boundless fists battering down the swordsmen who had menaced me and sweeping them in a violent boil across the floor of the sanctuary. Mafic stood thigh-deep in the water wrestling with a whirlwind—no, *two* whirlwinds. Desire had manifested as well.

They battled in a small, fierce storm touched to ground. A waterspout, raging, crackling, hissing like some great cat in pain, spitting sparks and fire and flecks of glittering death through the air.

No matter how powerful Mafic was, he was not a god. Let alone a titanic. His trap had been laid for one, not two. The Saffron Tower could never have meant to attack Desire face-to-face under such uncontrolled circumstances. I prayed that Mafic would choke on his success in finding his quarry.

In any event, he seemed overwhelmed just as I had hoped. His gun-men, safely above the flood that lapped at the altar top now, were not. They had turned instead and were firing their weapons into the mass of my Sisters. Those women were trying to flee, being driven out.

Where are the Blades? Disarmed, and possibly confined, going by what Mother Srirani had said.

I pointed my god-blooded knife at another long gun and willed it to destruction as the first one had. The firearm erupted in a satisfying gout of flame and smoke. Its wielder dropped away handless and screaming.

That gave pause to the other Street Guildsmen up in the gallery. Wishing that I could throw the blade in my hand, but not daring to discard it, I turned toward Mafic.

Fantail caught my eye. Not dead, not at all. She had ridden the flood like a horse and even now raised long fist-headed snakes of the ocean water to strike at the other Street Guild and their terrible weapons. I jumped off the altar back into the swirling tide and fought my way waist-deep toward Mafic, who mouthed the words of some Saffron Tower ritual as he stood straight against the twinned whirlwinds of his would-be victims. Lightnings crackled around him. He was drawing a whirlwind of his own, the water dark with spume. Around their battle steam rose and smoked, as if Firesetter were here standing against his old master.

He was a human problem. I was a human solution. Soaked to the bone with salt water, burnt by the heat of it so close to this fight, I jumped onto Mafic's back and jabbed the god-blooded knife into his shoulder, just above the clavicle.

Whether a woman's touch was painful anathema to him as it had been to Iso and Osi, I did not know. But a blade sunk deep into flesh should be sufficient to interrupt any man's efforts. He twisted as I grappled around his head, digging the fingers of my free hand for his eyes even as I turned the blade in its wound.

Above me the long guns barked again. Mafic staggered as if he had been punched. His dark whirlwind collapsed, and with it the forms of the Lily Goddess and Desire. I dropped from his back to get a proper swing at him with my short knife, but the tide was already retreating. He rolled away from me with the salt water.

Fearing the firearms more in that moment, I turned my attention upward again. A handful of Blades had converged on the Street Guild in the gallery and were casting them over the rail to fall to the sanctuary floor. *Without* their weapons, I noted.

Mafic, then. He could not be permitted to get away. I whirled back toward him to see him tumbling out through the broken doors. The water was departing, much of it draining through the floor into the refectory and kitchen below, the rest retreating as it had come. A hand plucked at me to stop me from racing after him.

"Not alone, Green," said Mother Vajpai. She was as sodden with blood and salt water as I. "Not even you."

Firesetter stood amid the broken doors, glowering. Wisps of smoke danced across his massive red chest, the leather trews, the rough-spun vest.

I stood panting as quiet descended upon our temple once more. A single lily petal spun out of the air to land upon my knife blade and stick there as if it had grown from that place.

The damage to the sanctuary was considerable. Both Desire and the Lily Goddess had vanished. This did not alarm me. More to the point, we had lost many. That was a source of greater concern.

A quick count found the Temple Mother dead, though whether of her wounds or of drowning, I could not say. Six of the Street Guild were dead as well, and nine other Mothers and Sisters of the temple. Most of the slain women had been struck by the long guns. The men seemed to have perished variously of broken necks, drowning, or being beaten. And exploding firearms, I was pleased to note.

An Intercessory Aspirant raced in through the front doors, breathless. "The tide," she gasped. "It came up out of the sewers . . . and broke open . . . the Blood Fountain." She dropped to her knees. "You saved us . . . Mother Green."

Not me, I thought. Fantail. At most, I'd summoned her. From where had the Red Man's apsara come, and to where did she go? "She was alive," I said to him, ignoring the Aspirant.

"And still is," he growled. "Even now, my Fantail herds the ocean back to its bed, to keep your city dry."

"Bless you."

His smile was crooked and pained. "Perhaps you already have."

The Mothers and Sisters of the Temple of the Silver Lily were gathering close around me now. Hands reached out to brush my leathers or pluck at my sopping, sticky hair. Awed murmurs rose.

"We must go," I said, trying to shrug them off. "Mafic is loose. The game is blown wide open. Surali holds one of our own hostage, and another beside her. These two need rescue before she grows so desperate as to do worse than hold them in place. And we must smash the Street Guild and the Bittern Court while the power to do so remains in our hands."

"No," said one of the older Justiciary Mothers. Her name was Atawani, I thought. "Not yet."

"You have prayed down the Lily Goddess," another called out.

"You are the next Temple Mother!" shouted a third.

"No! Absolutely not!" That was insane on the face of things. I would no more be the next Temple Mother than I would be the next Prince of the City. "You will find a Mother in the usual way"—through meetings among the heads of the orders and a vote of the senior Mothers—"but for now, we must release and rearm the Blades. Every Mother and senior Aspirant, so that we might strike while disarray is still upon our enemies."

Some of them were willing to argue more, especially the Justiciary Mothers, but the rest moved off quickly enough to obey me. I shoved the last of my would-be advisors aside and strode about the sanctuary collecting the surviving long guns. They stank of sulfur and blood. Mother Vajpai walked with me, her former strength of spirit fully restored here in the temple.

"Here," I said, putting one of the infernal things into her hands. "Please figure what you can of their operation. Whether we wish to use these or not, we need to begin an understanding of how to fight against them."

Mother Vajpai sat down in a salty puddle on one of the flights leading up into the gallery and began examining the weapon closely. I noticed she was careful not to point the tip at me or anyone else. Herself most definitely included.

I turned and approached Firesetter. He sat smoldering on one of the benches where I had waited my turn at trial earlier. I swore to myself those benches would be taken out of here if I ever had anything to say about it.

"Where are the others from the safe house?"

"Here," he said. "I could not leave them behind."

"My children? . . ."

He turned and stepped out the doors. A moment later, Ilona and Ponce crowded in, each carrying one of my babies. Mother Argai followed close behind, looking rather more pleased with herself than usual.

I kissed my two caregivers and gathered my children in my arms. It was not unheard of for Blades to bear children, but we rarely bothered with such things. That I had two so small here in the temple would have been a curiosity on a normal day.

Today, with the sanctuary and galleries refilling, it was a wonder. I looked around to see Blades, Justiciars, Intercessors, Domiciliars—every order of the temple was filing in. Following the noise, following the news.

Mother Srirani had been laid across the flower altar itself. The babies cooing and babbling in my arms, I knelt before her and the goddess she had served in so misguided a fashion.

"These are my children," I told the Lily Goddess and all Her followers crowding in around and above me. "I beg of You that they will be safe here, kept so by Your divine regard and my strong hands."

Turning, I looked over the gathering storm of women. They had purpose now, reminding me of nothing so much as the mob outside Blackblood's temple back in Copper Downs, the night I'd caused Iso and Osi to be struck down.

Fantail was back, too, standing with her arm raised around Firesetter's waist, though he was three times her height. Ponce, Ilona, and Mother Argai watched me carefully. I knew what they wanted. Likewise Mother Vajpai gave me a lengthy, approving stare, one of the long guns across her lap. In point of fact, most of the temple now watched me and waited for my words—Mother Surekha and Mother Shesturi, Mother Tonjaree, and so many others known to me.

"I ask my friends from across the sea to stay here and watch over my children one more time." They came and took my babies from me. Little Federo fussed at this; Marya just stared so intently that I wondered not for the first time who it was that looked out from those wide brown eyes. "I ask Mother Argai to stay to protect them here in the safety of the temple. As to who should stand here before the altar, we will answer that question. But not *yet*. Now it is time to rescue one of our own, that Mother Srirani allowed to languish in the clutches of the Bittern Court. Now is the time to rescue the daughter of one very dear to me.

"Now is the time to *act*." I raised my god-blooded knife high. "I pursue Mafic and Surali to the Bittern Court. There we will free their hostages and end this feud once and for all, as Mother Srirani spoke of. Not on their terms, but on ours."

With those words, I strode toward the broken doors. Thankfully, Firesetter and Fantail both followed me. Behind them came dozens of Blades, almost our entire force. Sisters and Mothers of all the orders poured out onto the front steps to watch us march forth from the watery chaos of the Blood Fountain's plaza. Beggars crying out half-drowned, Beast Market merchants chasing down their wares, carters struggling to rehitch their calming teams—they all paused in their efforts. Hundreds more Selistani faces turned to me in a shared, silent amazement.

The women of the Temple of the Silver Lily had all obeyed me without argument, I realized, once the first impulse to look to authority had been settled. I would give back my borrowed power like a cloak once this was done. For now, even the notoriously proud Justiciary Mothers had not raised a significant protest.

Even Mother Vajpai, the Blade Mother herself, had followed my bidding. She stood on the steps with one of the long guns cradled in her arms. Others bobbed in the hands of some of the senior Blade Mothers. The look on Mother Vajpai's face I could only describe as delighted pride.

I was both horrified and thrilled. Most of all, the sheer lack of argument from this fractious bunch of women pleased me.

"We go to free their prisoners and put their leaders to the sword!" I shouted. "I claim Death Right against the entire Bittern Court!"

With that, I began to run. Behind me, the largest Blade handle in my lifetime ran with me. One way or another, this would be over soon.

We raced up Shalavana Avenue. Everyone had gotten out of our way. Even the armed guards we met. Even the Street Guild we met. I did not waste energy or violence on those small patrols. Such fighting would only have broken our momentum.

More than fifty Blades was a force fit not just to be reckoned with, but to terrify. We were all armored with rage at the violation of our temple and its sanctuary. That the Red Man loped gracefully in our midst, an escaped coal demon bearing his own flame, only made us all the more a terror to those we passed along the way.

Massed fighting was not the usual way of things in Kalimpura. Even the worst of the street wars between Guilds and Courts were affairs of pinpoint struggles, targeted killings, and quiet work in the dark. Or politics. Or all of that together. The Street Guild's increasing boldness had raised uneasy scandal.

We were settling that unease.

I did not even need to direct my assault. My Blades stormed the Bittern Court's postern gate and went over the walls in a tide of leather and steel that rolled up the opposition before us. Whatever Mafic might have done with more of those firearms, the outside guards did not have them.

Firesetter did not bother with the postern or the wall. Instead he simply struck down the great carriage gates facing onto Shalavana Avenue with his fists and stormed into their front garden. I knew a mob of regular folk would follow swiftly as their own boldness dared—to loot, to stare, to bear witness to the fall of a power.

The power that fell had better be the Bittern Court. I cast aside the possibility that the Blades might break upon this rock, and through us the Temple of the Silver Lily fail.

"Find if there are more of those weapons!" I shouted to Mother Vajpai. "We cannot have them used against us."

"Do you want us to use them at all?" she asked.

I glanced at the Bittern Court's great hall, where knots of fighting were visible. Women in black swarmed through the gardens, kicked open doors, subdued servants, and battled guards. "Not unless they do so first. Let us make this no worse than it already must be."

"We only found five," she said, and was off.

Five what? I wondered, but the thought was lost as a crossbow quarrel nearly gutted me. I charged the man who had hidden in a thorn tree before he could fire again, and lost track of what would later become a fatally important question—where all the long guns had gotten to.

Fantail beat me to my assailant, and drowned him where he sat in the branches by filling his lungs with water. I cut the string of his dropped bow so that some desperate fellow could not use it behind me. "Where is Firesetter?"

She pointed to where smoke already rose from one of the garden follies—a little six-sided gazebo overlooking a mound of reeds that hinted at a pond.

"Get him and come with me. We must find Surali, and we must rescue our prisoners." I had hopes of finding their account books as well, for later when reason might once more prevail and we would be set to untangling very many messes.

She gathered Firesetter as I trotted toward a two-storey building that showed more signs of being a stronghouse than a bathing house. My hostages would not be somewhere ornate. They would be somewhere easily guarded.

The Red Man touched the door and it burst into flaming flinders. The two guards within ran screaming without stopping to fight us off. We entered, racing through rooms in search of our missing before they became our dead.

The curse I had called down on Surali back in Copper Downs was coming to fruition. I had promised to follow her across the ocean, and burn down the Bittern Court, to sift the ashes for her bones and break them all one by one, then dance on the shards. I had sworn before the gods to cut all their throats and feed them to the pigs.

Though I was already sickening at our slaughter, I could not then have said I was sorrowing. Not yet.

Emerging from the cellars of the third building we'd searched, I realized the grounds were flooding with even more who were not my people. Guards in the uniforms of some of the other Guilds and Courts marched in small formations, swords and bows at the ready. Laborers, servants, and beggars rushed by in an echo of the beggars' riot we'd launched down at the dockside just a few days past. Their participation was the result of the swaggering Surali and hers had done these past months.

This was how Kalimpura restored the balance among its powers. Not through the small forces of the wealthy, but through the pressure of the streets. Officers of the Bittern Court were being dragged out, stripped, and beaten by people I did not know. Sometimes bloody knives flashed.

Too bad for all of them.

We had raced for another set of stairs leading down below the building that housed the kitchens, my ears pricked for news, when I saw Ilona running from the gates.

"I will follow!" I shouted to Firesetter and the two Blades who had joined us, then whirled to meet my erstwhile lover. *"What are you do-ing here?"* I shouted. "You could be killed."

"Corinthia Anastasia," she panted. Then, in Petraean, "I claim the right to find my daughter. *You* would do no less."

That I could not argue with. "Fair enough," I groused. "But stay close to me, and stay safe."

She kissed me then, tasting of salt water and fear, and whispered into my ear, "No one close to you is ever safe, dear Green."

Those words stung my eyes with tears. The kiss stung my heart even more. I blinked away the emotion along with my irritation at Ilona for putting herself into harm's way, then followed swiftly after my little party where they'd gone down among the root cellars and cold rooms that had fed this place.

Thunder echoed as I clattered down the flight of stairs. By the Wheel, I was late and someone would be hurt. I burst into a lower hall and tripped over the body of a Blade—Mother Fastanjana, I thought. She'd died with one of the long guns in her hand. Another had left her chest a sickening mess.

Vile weapons. They had no honesty behind them. If I lived through this day, I would have to think hard on what to do.

Before me, Firesetter used a dead guard's body to club two other Street Guild. The hall was filled with the dark, acrid smoke of the accursed firearms. Our enemies collapsed with one final cry. The Red Man threw down his corpse-weapon to grab at his own arm.

Fantail leapt to Firesetter's side. I saw that he had been hit there as well by one of the long guns. Not torn wide open, as Mother Fastanjana had, but a furrow shredded through muscle and skin where copper brown blood fizzed as it oozed from him.

"Something important is here," I said. "They would not be guarding taro roots with those weapons." Where had the other Blade Mothers gotten to? I wasn't even certain who'd joined us in the rush outside.

Wood splintered above my head as thunder barked again. I realized there was still an ambush in progress. A table overturned two rods down the hall sheltered more defenders.

Firearms or not, there was nothing for it but to rush them. Screaming red rage and bloody murder, I did so. Another crack came so close I swear I felt it. Then I was over the table and among three of them, swinging wildly with my single, god-blooded knife. Why had I not stopped to find other weapons?

It did not matter. That unholy edge sliced through even the iron length of the long gun, and took one man's face halfway off. Another tried to jab at me with his weapon, for he had not yet finished replenishing the thunder within. I took his hands off at the wrist. Then I kicked him in the fork that he might sit down and bleed to death out of my way.

The third man's head exploded with another echoing bark so loud my ears rang. I whirled to see Ilona standing on the other side of the table, long gun shivering in her hand. Tears coursed down her face.

"Well done," I growled. If she wanted to come play Blade, she damned well could play the full part. I would no more let her fall into crying now than I would have permitted any of my Sisters to do so.

Someone screamed close by, through one of the storeroom doors. I yanked it open—the bar was on the outside, of course—to find sacks of flour threatening nobody.

By the Wheel, I will not fail now.

The next door yielded barrels, but no prisoners or Street Guild or Surali.

The third door opened onto the bark of another firearm. Wood exploded in my face, giving me half a hundred bloody splinters. My eyes stung, too, which could not be good.

Samma!

My heart raced. She was here, bound and gagged upon the floor. Corinthia Anastasia had been gagged as well, but it had slipped or she had worked it off, for it was she who shrieked. The Street Guilds-man who'd just fired at me tossed his useless weapon away and pulled a knife to cut the girl's throat. Behind me, Ilona shouted. I wasted a precious second turning to see her being rushed by another Street Guildsman. *Where is Firesetter?*

There was no more time.

My heart pounded, counting out the precious moments of which I had too few. After all these months, I had no time to act, to save them both.

If I could.

Spinning, I threw the god-blooded knife into the eye of the man drawing steel even now across Corinthia Anastasia's throat, and spun again to leap into the hall.

Too late, by all the Smagadine hells.

Ilona was already collapsing with a blade stuck into her chest. I broke her assailant's neck with a high blow, then caught at my friend and lover. We both sank to our knees. A glance showed me Corinthia Anastasia wriggling out from under the dropped body of her last guard. Her mouth was open, but nothing came out.

I cradled Ilona's head, praying wordlessly even as she began to vomit a sticky, scarlet mass of blood and bile. This woman I had loved in one form or another down the years since we'd first met. Now I'd chosen wrongly.

There had been no right choice.

It was either Ilona or her daughter. One would have died while I saved the other.

Corinthia Anastasia pushed out of the storeroom with my god-blooded knife in her hand. Her throat showed a thin line of red, but the knife had not opened her fully. Thank the Lily Goddess for that.

"You killed her," she shrieked, then dropped to hug her mother's bloody chest. "Get away, get away, get *away*."

My rage burst its banks as never before, even as measured by the violence that made up my life. It did not matter that I had let her mother die to save the child. It did not matter that Samma lived, waiting only to be freed now. Boiling, I cut her bonds.

"Green," she gasped. The look she gave me was somewhere be-tween wretched gratitude and naked fear.

Behind me, Corinthia Anastasia wailed her grief. I tried to say something, to welcome Samma back, to tell her to be glad she still lived. Something.

The words would not come. Only a great shivering of my body and heat in my blood like I had never known.

Ilona.

Turning away from Samma, I took up my weapon and stalked back down the hall, grabbing a hanging lantern as I went. Outside, I spread fire and sword and death until even the very sky was sickened of it.

No one of the Bittern Court was safe from my rage. Not the wounded, not the slow, not the elderly, not even those who had already laid down their weapons and sat on the ground with terror in their eyes at my coming.

In the light of the blazing great hall, Mother Vajpai and Firesetter finally managed to pull me from my slaughters. I fell to my knees crying, glad at least that Ilona had such a burning to see her soul onto the Wheel and wherever it might go from there.

After a while, I vomited, and cast the god-blooded knife into the roaring flames.

I sat on a hitching stone along Shalavana Avenue and watched the oily black smoke from a dozen burning buildings fill the sky. My eyes had dried, though I still hiccoughed my griefs. No one would come to me. Not even my closest, though Mother Vajpai and Fantail both stood nearby. Whether to protect me or to protect everyone else, I could not say.

Finally, Mother Adhiti, the oxlike woman who'd once aided me in Mother Shesturi's handle, approached, shrugging past my guardians. She stared down at me awhile before saying, "They are broken."

As are we all, I thought, but I did not make that into an answer.

Mother Adhiti went on doggedly. "We did not find Surali. Or Mafic. Many of the Street Guild were either not here or have escaped."

"They are powerless without the Bittern Court behind them," I muttered. "Just thugs with the same clothes." In that moment, I cared nothing of Surali or Mafic. Foolish though it was, I felt like a guttering candle, my fire dying out, even for my worst enemies. My thirst for vengeance had been slaked to the point of bursting.

So much death. So much destruction. At my hands and by my word. How could anyone lead Blades, or worse, an army, and survive within their own soul? There were not enough candles in the world to light the paths of the souls I'd struck down today.

I wanted to go back to my own children, but was afraid to bring the stench of death with me.

Mother Vajpai finally approached, reinforcing the stubborn Mother Adhiti. "Though it will be some time before we sort the corpses, we think Surali died in the fire of their great hall. Mafic as well."

"That was Ilona's pyre," I grumbled.

"We know." She knelt gently before me. "It is done now. We will carry out their dead and ours, and figure the costs. But you have broken them. The Lily Goddess will stand proud. Our lost ones are returned."

"Do you not know . . . ?"

"Know what?" she asked, alert for some new disaster.

"Ilona died beneath the kitchens as we rescued the hostages."

"Ah." Mother Vajpai's eyes closed briefly. "Did her child see?"

"Yes." I stared up at her. "I had to ch-choose. Between Corinthia Anastasia and Ilona. There was no t-time to th-think."

"You know better, Green. Ilona chose when she came here with us." Mother Vajpai's voice was hard. "You saved the child, who had made no choice in the matter, did you not?"

"She was my friend. And almost my lover." My chest felt hollow; my head ached. I could not face what might come next.

"Would she have chosen any differently?"

Mother Vajpai had the right of it, but that did not make me think any better of myself. Nor, did I imagine, would it improve Corinthia Anastasia's feelings.

"Where is the girl now?" I asked sullenly. "And Samma?" I was ashamed that in my rage I had left her behind in the storeroom where her life had been held hostage.

"Stay with her," Mother Vajpai ordered Mother Adhiti, then walked away, stumbling only slightly.

Mother Adhiti sat down beside me. She did not try to offer any comfort, which would have meant nothing to me, in any case. Her company was enough, perhaps, to keep me from falling on my knife.

That, and the fact that I had no knife.

Mother Vajpai returned trailing both Samma and Corinthia Anasta-sia. Ilona's daughter clung to my long-lost Blade Sister as if she were the last line between life and death. Samma's face was bleak and she limped. Perhaps Surali had hurt her here, or perhaps the wounds she'd taken from me back in Copper Downs still troubled her. Corin-thia Anastasia would not turn her face to me at all.

I stared at them and found no comfort there. Samma shook her head slowly, then glanced at Mother Vajpai.

"They were with Mother Melia," our Blade Mother supplied. She rested one hand on Samma's shoulder. Reclaiming her, in a sense. "Waiting for word of what to do."

There was no response to that, so I shrugged.

"I will send a handle to escort you back to the temple," Mother Vajpai told Samma. "This is not a good day to be about the streets. You deserve to be welcomed home."

Corinthia Anastasia whimpered at those words. She continued to keep her face hidden from me. Though she was still quite young, I knew she was no girl anymore.

My mind seized on the needs of the moment. An escort was a good idea. Certainly there were some Bittern Court survivors out there, and the scattered Street Guild. I did not have the heart to go fire their hall as well.

A little while later, the girls walked away from me hand in hand. Neither looked back. I could do nothing for them now. Or possibly ever again. At least the six women with them would keep the pair safer than I had managed to do.

I supposed I should head to the temple as well. My children were there. It was unlikely I would simply topple off this stone and conve-niently die, so finding them again seemed the best thing to do. Knees creaking, I rose to my feet.

"Home again?" asked Mother Vajpai.

I gave her a long look. "Home is where my heart lies. With my heart in ashes . . ."

She walked back to the temple with me anyway. No one else would come near me, even now. And word must have gone around the city. I passed in an unaccustomed bubble of silence and empty cobbles, strange for Kalimpura. I was poison, frightening to any sane and reasonable person. What else was there but to flee the madwoman?

Mother Vajpai remained blessedly silent, so I spoke in a quiet voice to the Lily Goddess, to Mother Iron, to Desire. I don't suppose it mattered if they heard me or not. I just had to spit out the bile in my heart before it drowned me.

"You have given me too much," I said to the uncaring air. "And taken too much with Your other hand."

No one answered. Whatever thoughts Mother Vajpai had, she wisely kept to herself.

"I would not have paid that price. Nor the other. How was I to *know*? You might as well have asked me to choose between one of my children and the other. Your cruelty is legend."

We walked a bit farther in our bubble of silence. An ox lowed nearby, harnessed to a reeking honey wagon, but if that was a message from Endurance, I was too dense to understand. The cobbles beneath my feet were slick with crushed fruits and vegetables. The sweet rotted reek filled my nostrils. So there was a market here.

Who cared?

"I am done with You. With each of You. With all of You. I will take my children and sail until the seas are purple and there are no more horizons, and no one has ever heard of any of You." I spat. "There. You may have that from me. That is the last service You will ever get."

More steps in silence. The smell of spiced chicken roasting in a clay oven, which despite my blank despair, made my traitorous mouth water. Someone began to speak, and was shushed with a thump and a squeal. I was barely seeing my own feet now, let alone anything around me, but the city feared me.

That day, I likely could have struck anyone down, and the rest of them would only have stepped away in frightened silence. My thirst for violence was gone. I could not imagine feeling rage ever again. Where my soul had been was only a livid, burnt bruise.

"Go," I told my goddesses. "Bedevil some other poor fool. We are shut. Everyone who can be safe is safe, and the rest of us walk in chains of memory. I am done."

In time, Mother Vajpai touched my elbow. My feet had known the path back to the temple, whether or not the rest of me had been paying attention. The plaza of the Blood Fountain was a bit less of a mess. In fact, it was oddly clean. The front steps of the Temple of the Silver Lily were completely bare that day. I don't know what I would have done if there had been swaggering Street Guild awaiting me—fall on *their* swords, perhaps—but it seemed unjust that even the beggars and petty vendors could not take their ease.

I stared up at the sweeping, silvered teardrop of this, my supposed home. It truly did resemble a woman's sweetpocket, I realized, at least the upper portions. The lower levels spread in squat wings ornamented only by swooping pillars and curiously shaped windows. The Temple of the Silver Lily had not been the source of my troubles, but in a real sense, it had been the focus of them. I was reluctant to set foot within.

Mother Vajpai lightly touched my arm once more. "Your children need you."

Unspoken but clear were the words, *We need you.*

If not for my children, I might have found a place to sleep and not bothered waking up. My aching breasts reminded me of what my babies required, though, and of my own body's needs as well.

"I will go in," I said quietly. Bleak, glum, defeated. The ashes of the Bittern Court's burning were still strong upon my tongue. This was hardly victory in any sense.

"Come. I will have someone send you up some kava and a northern-style sweet roll. Sit with your children awhile, perhaps wash the battle-stink from you."

"They should be upstairs."

We walked up the unusually clean steps of the Temple of the Silver Lily and into the vestibule where I had first encountered Mother Vajpai five years earlier. At my current place in life, I realize how ridiculous this seems, but at the time it felt as if half a life had gone by between that first meeting and this moment. I am convinced that our age changes the way we see time more than anything else can possibly do.

She went around to the Kitchen Stairs; I trudged up the Pink Stairs to the Blade dormitories on the third storey. The temple was quiet, with so many of our number still at the Bittern Court or out on the streets of Kalimpura.

I wasn't sure where they would have gone, exactly. I guessed at Mother Vajpai's suite first. Whatever Mother Srirani's machinations, none of the other Blades would have dared occupy the Blade Mother's rooms unless and until they themselves had been named to the post in her stead. And more to the point, accepted that nomination.

Winding through the deserted hall, past a dozen doors, I found and heard no one. It was eerie. The place was as empty as if my vision of a temple full of women without a goddess had actually come to pass. Though at the moment, it would be more accurate to say that this was a goddess without a temple full of women.

Mother Vajpai's door was ajar. I pushed it open, curiosity sparked despite my dullness of mind. The children were starting to crawl, and could pull themselves alongside furniture or a wall, but surely they had not yet come to the point of opening doors?

It bumped against something. I slipped inside to find Mother Argai slumped on the floor in the darkened room. No lamps lit here, of course. Why would there be?

My heart hammered in my chest as everything seemed to grow cold and dark. Ilona was dead, Mother Argai here. *Where are Ponce and my children?*

Swallowing a screech of rage and grief that threatened to bubble up inside me despite my sense of deadness, I dropped to my knees beside her.

Her lips were swollen almost beyond recognition. Her breath choked. I knew from her eyes that she was dying.

"They're here," I said.

Mother Argai gave me a jerky half nod, then wheezed for a smidge of breath through what was left of her swollen mouth and throat. Some poison I'd rather not have known about. We always favored blades here for good reason.

Mafic or Surali, it did not matter. This murder was not done by one of us.

Had no one swept the temple for them as we'd all raced off to the Bittern Court? Idiocy? A late, traitorous partisan of Mother Srirani? Or concealment through Mafic's own spiritual powers?

It did not matter. Mistake or deception, the killers were loose in the house of my goddess. Where my children were.

I kissed Mother Argai with that thought, though my lips stung as well, and stroked her hair. Her hand spasmed. She was trying to direct me toward the inner chamber, I realized. This was Mother Vajpai's office, though it was unusually neat—she had not occupied the place for months, after all. Dust layered over the clean, idle surface of her desk, her leather chair, the two smaller wooden chairs for unlucky visitors.

Beyond would be a sleeping room. I'd been in there two or three times on errands, but could not recall much besides a narrow window, a narrow bed, and some chests.

Now, my children and whoever threatened them. As if I did not know my own reward.

Dead in the great hall fire, indeed. I would not truly believe that of Mafic even if I had seen the body. Surali, too, was likely to have some last fatal trick behind her fan. I wondered which of them it was. Or perhaps the Quiet Men, come for me at last through the doors of my heart.

Shouldering my resolve, I stood weaponless from Mother Argai's death agonies and did as she told me, pushing open the inner door.

My children were on the floor huddled next to Ponce. He clutched them tightly. Both Marya and Federo had their fists crammed into their mouths, faces purpled with silent screams. Ponce was wide-eyed and silent, his face bruised.

Mafic sat drawn up on the bed. He was pale and shaking, though the long gun pointed at me was held steady enough.

Most important, Surali stood behind Ponce and my babies, my other god-blooded knife in her hands. The one I'd cast aside back in Copper Downs. Mafic must have carried it across the sea.

"You have forgotten something, have you not?" Her voice was a sneer.

"It is over." I was too tired to fight even them. All I wanted was for these two, my greatest enemies, to see the pointlessness of this last gesture, and just walk away. Still, even below that dull feeling, I could feel the iron bar of my rage returning. Surali had found the one key to overcome my disgust at myself and reignite that fatal fire within.

As for Mafic, there was no purpose in fighting him. Even less in killing him. The Saffron Tower would simply send another assassin in his place, just as he had followed Iso and Osi. Though I might have shredded his flesh and danced on his corpse if I could, vengeance against him was not my luxury.

Not here. Otherwise, all that had passed this day would be wasted, and have to be fought over again at an even greater loss.

Besides, I was sick of the taste of violence.

"Just leave this place," I added, answering their silence. "Go. I will not pursue you."

Mafic shook his head, sweat pouring down his face. I saw the blood staining his yellow robes and recalled that I had stabbed him. Then he had been struck by the thunder of one of his long guns back in the sanctuary. As I'd just come to realize, he had never even left the temple. I knew only some of that art of passing through wards and guards, whatever portion Iso and Osi had been willing to teach me. Mafic must be a master at such techniques.

"You do not need to pursue me," Surali said, leering at me. She shot Mafic a quick glance. "We still have the strength to defeat you."

We?

I looked at Mafic again. He did not appear strong. In fact, he appeared as if he were dying. "Go home," I told him gently. "Find some other quarry. Your tool Surali has failed you. The power of women stands on its own here. The plate of the world is vast. You and your brothers can turn your energies elsewhere." I flexed my hands, wishing for my own knife back. "Otherwise, you and all of yours will die as Iso and Osi did. One by one. At the hands of women. Degraded. Unmourned." I lowered my voice to almost a hiss. *"Unclean."*

"You will never understand," he croaked, trying unsuccessfully to smile through his pain.

"No. I understand far too well."

Surali opened her mouth, seeking the upper hand, but Mafic's crooked, pain-filled smile broadened. I jumped aside, though not quickly enough. The thunderbolt from his long gun slammed me back against the wall like the hammer of a goddess. My right side dissolved into a hot well of pain. That arm flopped useless and beyond my control.

At this, the children began to wail. Ponce clutched them closer as Surali leaned down to grab his hair and expose his neck.

Firesetter burst into the room—drawn by the noise, I thought, through my red haze—bellowing in some eldritch language. Mafic fumbled with his long gun as he tried to insert another thunderbolt.

The Red Man fell swiftly upon Mafic, the rushing attack making the firearm useless. He grappled closely with his old master as if to crush the man. The bed began to smolder.

"Do not kill him!" I croaked.

"Too late," Surali answered. Ponce slumped, blood pouring down his chest. She had grabbed up little Federo and awaited only my attention before slaying my son.

Groaning, I pulled myself to my feet. I could barely stand. Her smile grew increasingly feral as she drank in my pain. "That's right," Surali whispered over the crackling of flames from the bed. "Come a little closer."

My baby shrieked and wiggled as I staggered toward them. Ponce rose to his feet behind her, skin now pale as a Selistani can ever be, blood sheeting down his neck and chest. With a puzzled look on his face, he drew the hem of his robe over Surali's head. I lurched forward and jabbed a clumsy left arm handstrike into her throat. My baby fell and I could not catch him with my useless right hand. Surali and Ponce both collapsed. I tried to pick up my wailing child, but could not, so once more I broke the fingers of both of Surali's hands with my boot heel as she lay choking in her own blood.

At least she would die in pain. It was all I could do for my children. I collapsed next to them as they squirmed away from the blood and tried to gather both of them in my good left arm.

Behind me, Mafic's screaming finally trailed off.

Firesetter sat next to the monk, a crackling orange aura fading from the two of them. Mafic was slumped, oddly boneless. The bedclothes smoldered; the flames were gone. At least the room was not afire.

Clutching my children as best I could, I croaked a question. "Will he live?"

The Red Man shrugged. "I have broken him on the wheel of his own power." Great satisfaction echoed in that huge, deep voice.

"H-hold my children," I told him. "There is something I must do."

Giant red hands reached down gentle as spring rain and scooped the babies up, Federo in his right, Marya in his left. They whimpered, but something in his touch seemed to ease them. It was more than I could offer them at that moment.

One-armed, I dragged myself to the bed and began to slit Mafic's robes open with the knife that had just killed Ponce. I was not so careful about whether I cut the skin below or not. When I reached his groin, I exposed his penis. It was shriveled from pain and stress.

I had been willing to let him go, but that was before he'd shot me with the thunderbolt, before his pawn Surali had tried to claim the life of my son. Forgiveness was lost now.

Still, it was not enough to simply kill him.

"You," I whispered, "will never be a man again." I gelded him then, made him as much a woman as a man can be. As with the killing of Iso and Osi at the hand of Marya's women, this was the greatest pain I knew to cause him, given the peculiar, misogynistic beliefs he followed. He needed to suffer in both body and spirit.

I took my time, drawing the knife slowly so Mafic would feel every moment of the pain. Stealing his manhood should foil the male magics of the Saffron Tower. A cross I cut in his tip for him to remember me by. He bled a great deal, so I dragged some of the smoldering bedclothes across the wound and pressed hard enough to make the monk gasp in renewed pain.

There I waited, my increasingly blurred vision focused on my children, until more of the Blades burst into the room. *Minutes too late, a lifetime too slow*, I thought in my own agony.

Consequences

MEMORY IS BOTH a blessing and a curse. Without it, we would not know who we were and what we stood for in this life. With it, we know all too well what we have done to betray those ideals.

Does anyone live long enough to meet their own standards? That is a question I have never been able to answer. The best I can settle for is the knowledge that no matter how miserably one has failed, one can only keep trying.

I slept over a day, I learned later. When they tried to rouse me with a tincture of choraka, I refused wakefulness, until the Caring Mothers despaired of my condition and sent for Mother Vajpai and some of the Mothers Intercessory.

My old teacher was one of the wisest women I have ever known. *She* sent for both of our belled silks and for my children. It was their cries that finally drew me from twisted dreams of fire and water, earth and air.

Awake was no better. My body had understood what my mind did not want to confess, even to itself. Ilona, whom I had loved, was dead by my poor choices. Ponce, who had loved me, was dead by my mischance. Mafic was not dead, when I should have simply killed him for mercy's sake. Surali's death did not bother me at all, but that very uncaring in turn bothered me. *Her* I would never light the candles for.

But they had all been someone's children once. Every single one of them. As were the others I'd slain in our sacking of the Bittern Court after Ilona's death.

Not an honor guard for the soul of my sweet friend, but ranks of shame.

Clutching my children close, I realized I was sick of death. I could not leave them here alone. What had happened to me as a small child was lesson enough. And though she hated me with good reason, I would not leave Corinthia Anastasia, either. I owed Samma much, as well, for all that she suffered through my deeds and misdeeds.

So I sat up and allowed the Mothers to give me pigeon broth, and change the dressings on my chest, and pray over me with hot water and stinging herbs. The poppy salve that the Caring Mothers kept putting on me was said to stem the pain, but you could not have told that by me.

Pain of the body, I could handle.

Pain of the heart . . . Was this what it meant to grow older? I had too many ghosts following me to count, my own handle of the dead peering over my shoulder. Judges, should I ever be found in the scales of life. I wondered if a Quiet Man would come to the temple some hour of the night and speed me on to that fate.

For a time there, I would have welcomed such.

So I ate, and wept, and tended my children. My milk was gone, shocked from my body by my injuries, but they brought me goat's milk and a sop to feed my babies. Their eyes focused so well now. Their little voices cooed and babbled. I kept listening for some wisdom from them. The first words of a child must mean something, after all.

A week later, I could walk a bit. The pain of the gun wound had lessened to a sort of ache that in fact never went away completely and bedevils me to this day. For the most part, I stayed in my bed with the window shaded and slept when my children slept. I refused visitors, I refused news of the world, I refused everything but food and healing care until Mother Vajpai came back to see me.

"I have two presents for you," she said.

Turning my face to the wall, I ignored her.

Fingers brushed my shoulder. "You must come back sometime, Green. Now is as good as any other day."

I shrugged her off, but she did not go away. Rather, the woman just sat in a chair next to my bed, waiting quietly. Soon enough, the children began to fuss awake. I could not simply hide in pretended fatigue.

Mother Vajpai leaned forth and helped me with the two, for managing twins with one arm is very nearly impossible. The Caring Mothers were apparently avoiding me for however long my visitor was here.

Once they'd been fed and put down to crawl a bit, I finally looked Mother Vajpai full in the face. She was drawn, tired, but her eye twinkled a bit.

"What is there to be happy about?" I demanded.

"Life goes on. And I have presents. As well as a request."

"You do not ask much, do you?"

"No, Green." Her smile echoed my sadness. "I ask too much. But then, is that not always the way?"

I snorted at that. She of all people understood. Perhaps only the Dancing Mistress, now lost to me, knew even better than Mother Vajpai. "I'm sorry about Mother Argai," I said.

"We lost more Blades that day than in any day in our temple's history."

"Well, the Lily Blades were never intended to be an army. I should not have used them as one."

She touched my hand, and I took her fingers in mine until we held each other's grip tight. "You did what needed to be done. Kalimpura's troubles are already receding, though plenty of new ones swiftly spring to life in their wake. Of the more ordinary sort, thankfully. Mother Srirani had been worrying more about the temple monies than about our spiritual place in the world. Foolish, perhaps, but she was no thief. Though our treasury has been impoverished, much as we'd suspected it might be. Amazingly, the Bittern Court's account books have been salvaged, which has already shed further light on some of those machinations.

"Moreover, without Surali and the Saffron Tower conspiring, I believe things will go more easily in Copper Downs as well. That our bodies and blood should be spent, it is best we be spent well. On matters of the spirit rather than matters of coin. Green, you spent us well."

"Too many died." I was thinking of not only my friends, but also all the people I'd slain in the Bittern Court. None of this was worth the price we paid.

"We had to burn your leathers," she told me. "The gore was too much."

"Is that your idea of a gift? Such news?" I wanted to roll and turn my face toward the wall again.

"No, this is." Mother Vajpai reached into her robes and pulled out a silver chain. A dull lump of metal depended from the end in a twisted silver mount.

I did not recognize it at all. "What is this?"

"The bolt from the thunder-bow that Mafic shot you with. The Caring Mothers removed it from your body."

"Ah." I took the token of my death from her with my free hand and awkwardly tugged the chain over my neck. It sat heavy between my shrinking breasts and cold upon my skin. "My thanks. I suppose."

"It seemed fitting."

"You mentioned another gift."

Mother Vajpai rose, stepped carefully over my children, who were patting their pudgy little hands together, and opened the door to my small room to wave someone in.

It was Ponce. His neck was swathed in a bandage. I pulled myself from my bed and stood to hug him. "You live," I said in Petraean.

He nodded and pointed at his throat. His breath rasped, but no words came out.

"Mute?" I asked in horrified realization.

Another nod, and tears spilled from his eyes.

"Yet you serve a mute god," I said quietly. "I cannot help but think there is some design here."

A final nod, and Ponce clutched me close. I let him hold me a bit too long, then sent them both away.

Chowdry—

I am afraid I have done a great wrong to your acolyte. He still lives where others do not, but his throat was badly hurt and he will never speak again. He communicates by writing and making signs with his hands. He indicates that he does not wish to go home to Copper Downs. Not as he is. I cannot be keeping him in the Temple of the

Silver Lily. This is a house of women. I think Ponce plans to build a shrine to Endurance here in Kalimpura.

Ilona died bravely but stupidly. I am coming to believe that most brave deaths are stupid. Better to live courageously than to die courageously. Her blood was not spilled by my own hand, but it might as well have been.

We have put paid to Surali and the Bittern Court, at least. These losses bought something of worth, though their cost was too high.

Mafic is still a problem, but in the care of women and still alive, he is a block of sorts against our enemies. When we send him back, it is in the not-unreasonable hopes of encouraging them to turn their attentions elsewhere. That pains me as well, as I should work to stop the meddling of the Saffron Tower altogether. Sadly, I have neither means nor power to do more than divert them from the goddess I serve and the two cities I call home.

The twins prosper. They will be talking soon. I am afraid of what they will say.

Ilona's daughter is a more difficult problem. I am fostering her into the Blades where she may make use of that difficulty. Mother Vajpai did well enough with me, another angry little girl from across the sea. Samma also is hurt in both body and spirit, but I expect she will recover in time.

The Mothers of the temple have made an impossible request of me here. By the time you read this, my response will be given, and all of us will have passed along to other concerns. The question is whether I am willing to make those concerns my own. Now I can see far more of your cares there at the Temple of Endurance.

With this letter I send a knife that bears the blood of a god upon its steel. I cast one into the flames, but its twin came back to me. Please have this delivered to Blackblood's temple. For my part, I believe that it should be a tool of their rites, though that must be between the god and his priests. I tire of a blade than can slice holes in the ocean and split the very wind. It makes me both too dangerous and too lazy.

I would be me, and not this weapon. I would be me, and not this goddess. I would be me, and not these children.

Someday I will be me.

———

At sixteen, I was the youngest ever to undergo this ceremony. The sanctuary was clean, the doors repaired, the gallery filled. For the induction, even the kitchen fires were banked, and the very sickest brought down from the healing rooms. Corinthia Anastasia had refused to attend. Samma watched me sadly from a bench above.

I wore my best pale robes, with my belled silk pulled around me. My grandmother would be here in spirit, at least, standing in for the generations who had come before me. Mother Adhiti and Ponce held my squirming children, the generations to come after. Ponce was robed in green now, with a crude pendant in the form of an ox head around his neck. The ropy scars there were painfully visible. I believed he was coming to take pride in them. I knew from some of our private times together that running my finger along the ridges of skin gave him a frisson that bordered between pleasure and agony.

Mother Vajpai and the other senior Mothers of each order stood before me. Water trickled down from above. Flower petals lofted on the wind. The Lily Goddess had opened Her hand over us this day.

Prayers were being said, but all I could think of was the future.

My children could not be safer than here within the Temple of the Silver Lily. As Temple Mother, if I were wise and temperate, I would be able to guarantee that safety until they were old enough for their own risks. From here, I could extend my protection to the other children of Kalimpura and wider Selistan, sheltering them and their mothers. From here, I could deal with the mystery and danger of the Quiet Men, who still waited me for in the shadows of the future.

From here, I could serve the Lily Goddess and in turn set Her to serving those in the greatest need.

There was so very much to be done. That would be true even should I live a hundred years in health, wealth, and power.

I bowed my head and said those words that needed saying, making of myself a servant to all who looked down upon me that day.

Years Passing Like Flower Petals on the Wind

I STAND WRAPPED in my belled silk, which has grown quite a bit heavier with the passing seasons of my life, and watch my daughter Marya take her vows as a Blade Mother. This moment gives a strange kind of pride. In a way, these past fifteen years have almost forced her to our life here in the Temple of the Silver Lily. In another way, she has chosen to meet me on my own ground. I could be no more proud than this, until she someday bests me.

My daughter and four other young women kiss their blades and swear obedience upon the altar in the sanctuary. It amuses me that I had never actually taken those vows myself, though anyone who knew has wisely kept that secret to themselves.

Which was almost everyone in the temple.

Still, we prosper well enough under my hand. In ways very different and far richer than poor, deluded Mother Srirani ever envisioned.

Marya's brother Federo is here, too, largely by coincidence. Some coincidences can be arranged, however. His apprenticeship as a cadet-officer under Captain Lalo aboard the kettle ship *Textile Bourse* is barely a year old. That they should be in port here for the first time since taking my boy-child aboard is good fortune, indeed.

That the ship is owned by the Temple of Endurance and flagged out of Copper Downs is also good fortune, of course.

My daughter's voice rises, strong. "And to the Temple Mother's commands I shall hew . . ."

As if, I think. She is too much like me.

Desire is here on occasion. She watches us, and sometimes we watch Her. Time, both the titanic and the passage of years, has been a great healer. Oceanus, brother of Time and Desire, will turn His watery gaze upon my son as wind and wave permit, much as He did for me for a time, in the first days of my return to Kalimpura. Or so His secret priestess Fantail tells me. That is sufficient.

As for Corinthia Anastasia, she is long lost to me. Ponce and Mother Vajpai sent her home after a few years. Chowdry writes that she lives, but I know no more than that. She will not allow him to speak of her to me. Some struggles are lost before they begin. Samma has done better for herself, becoming a teacher among the Mothers Domiciliary after it was clear that her wounds would keep her from serving as a Blade. She seemed the happier for it, though we have never again been close since her rescue.

". . . in service now and evermore to the Lily Goddess, may Her blessing rain down upon us all."

Smiling, I speak my part in this. As I always have.

Much later, in my own rooms, I toy with a pen. It is one of those brass-quilled things from the cities of the Sunward Sea, with a gorgeous cobalt blue ink bottle blown by the craftsmen of Alizar, and the ink itself from a Hanchu stone. I will write, I think, in Petraean here in my chamber in Kalimpura. And so the world goes back and forth, growing ever larger. There are troubles aplenty—there are always troubles aplenty—but nothing so personally terrible as what has gone before.

It is time to tell my children how they came to be who they are today. In order to do that, I know I must begin at my own beginning. Some stories are easier to start than they are to finish.

The bells on my silk ringing lightly as I moved, I put pen to paper, scratching away in a manner of which Mistress Danae, my old teacher who ended her life feral and mind-shattered in the High Hills of the Stone Coast, would have approved.

In the end, so is the beginning. In the beginning, so is the end.

The first thing I can remember in this life is my father driving his white ox, Endurance, to the sky burial platforms. His back was before me as we walked along a dusty road. All things were dusty in the country of my birth, unless they were flooded. A ditch yawned at each side to beckon me toward play. The fields beyond were drained of water and filled with stubble, though I could not now say which of the harvest seasons it was.

Though I would come to change the fate of cities and of gods, then I was merely a small, grubby child in a small, grubby corner of the world.